THE LOVE AND DEATH
OF CATERINA

Also by Andrew Nicoll

The Good Mayor

THE LOVE AND DEATH OF CATERINA

Andrew Nicoll

Quercus

First published in Great Britain in 2011 by

Quercus
21 Bloomsbury Square
London
WC1A 2NS

A CIP catalogue record for this book is available
from the British Library

ISBN 978 1 84916 471 9

10 9 8 7 6 5 4 3 2 1

Typeset by Ellipsis Books Limited, Glasgow

Printed and bound in Great Britain by Clays Ltd, St Ives plc

For Kenny, Margaret and Angus

ONLY A FEW weeks after it happened, Luciano Hernando Valdez was almost unable to believe that he had ever been a murderer. It was an act he had often contemplated in his novels, of course, but those had not been murders, not truly murders. Men died, women too sometimes, but because they deserved to die. Invariably it was an affair of honour over a wronged wife, a sister ruined, a husband betrayed, or because death at the point of a knife or kneeling, blindfold, in some stinking shack in the *barriada* was the inescapable last act in an opera of tragedy and lust and revenge and redemption. Reading the novels of Mr Valdez, one felt the bloodied victims he left oozing life on the floor of a forgotten tango hall or dumped in a public fountain at midnight would have been disgraced for ever if he had imagined some less brutal end for them or, worse yet, if he had allowed them to live out their days in solitude as shopkeepers or cinema projectionists or provincial priests. Much better for a fictional character to make his exit in a bloody flourish with his head full of holes but his honour intact.

Real people are different, as Mr Valdez discovered.

But let's go back a little, to before he had made that discovery.

Mr Valdez was sitting on his usual bench beside the steps that lead down from the square to the river. The Merino was looking particularly sluggish that day as it flowed, green as sap and every bit as sticky, towards the distant sea. It seemed to Mr Valdez that, just under the surface, it still carried with it the dark shadows of the interior, as if, somewhere upriver, the little people of the jungle had gazed into its pools with their black eyes and the blackness stuck.

Mr Valdez had a book open beside him on the bench and a notepad of yellow, lined paper open on his knee. There was nothing written in it, which was hardly surprising, since Mr Valdez was holding his pen between his teeth like a literary pirate preparing to board the defenceless page.

He sat staring across the river at a floating tree which had remained in exactly the same place, like an anchored liner, for over half an hour.

'It must be stuck,' said Mr Valdez to himself. But then a pelican, which had sat with its wings folded on a branch overhanging the river, flapped gracelessly into the air and the whole tree sank at one end, rebalanced itself, bobbed and sent out a single, greasy ripple across the surface of the water.

'Remarkable,' said Mr Valdez, inwardly, since the pen in his mouth made speech impossible.

Far away a steam whistle blew three sharp whoops and Mr Valdez turned his head a little to the left. Halfway across the river, it seemed almost on the horizon, almost at the edge of the world, he knew they must be changing flags, running down the three bars of white and gold and red and replacing them with three stripes of white and red and gold. It hardly mattered. Either flag would do. Each would hang just as flat and limp as the other, all the way across the river and all the way back.

'Remarkable,' thought Mr Valdez, although he had seen it happen a thousand times before on a thousand other sunny mornings.

Only a little further along the shore, two giant cranes stood ready to begin the day's work. Shoulders hunched, legs firmly planted, their huge derricks dipped right down to the quayside, they looked like a pair of vast iron golfers ready to drive a ball across the river and into enemy territory. They gave a cough. Machinery began turning. The cranes began to lift.

Little by little the golfers turned into donkeys and then, tottering across the square, came Señor Doctor Joaquin Cochrane, the learned Dr Cochrane whose Scottish name could not disguise the flat nose, the shovel teeth, the plum-black, flat-iron-smooth hair of his Indian ancestors.

'Mr Valdez! Mr Valdez!' His cane slipped a little on the mosaic pavement as he hurried forward. 'Mr Valdez. Oh, I feared you had not seen me.'

Smiling weakly, Mr Valdez took the pen from between his teeth and folded it shut between the blank pages of his yellow notebook. 'Señor Dr Cochrane,' he said. That was all.

'May I sit down?' said the doctor, sitting down on the bench just as Mr Valdez snatched his book away. 'How inspiring it is to see you here, pen in hand, drawing inspiration of your own from the mighty Merino.' The doctor pointed his cane from horizon to horizon in case anybody had failed to notice the river in front of them. 'The mighty Merino – should I not say "our" Merino – the scene of so many triumphs by my courageous ancestor, the great Admiral Cochrane, in his struggle for the liberty of our people.'

Silent, as if he still held his pen between his teeth, Mr Valdez thought: 'Your ancestors sailed the Merino sitting on a log with the piranhas nibbling at their toes,' but he smiled and nodded and said: 'Are you well, Dr Cochrane?'

'Thank you, yes, I am well. And your latest novel, it progresses?'

'Yes, it progresses.' Mr Valdez folded his hands over the notebook on his knees and locked his fingers together.

'I cannot tell you enough that which you already know but which cannot be adequately expressed, I cannot say often enough what an ornament you are to the faculty of our poor university, how the presence of such a great author as yourself, the eminent Luciano Hernando Valdez, enhances its reputation as a seat of learning and,' Dr Cochrane seemed to have forgotten his plans for the end of that sentence so he smiled and made another slow sweep of the river with his cane and smiled again.

'Yes,' he said. 'And the novel progresses?'

'Yes,' said Mr Valdez. 'Yes, it goes well.'

'Good. Yes. It progresses. I am delighted. And you are here, every morning, with your notebooks, creating in ink people, lives, cities that will last longer than the pyramids. It is an immortal achievement.'

'Well, I . . .'

'Forgive me. I have embarrassed you. I behave like a school-girl but how could I pretend that I am not an aficionado? Only last night, when I was reading again for the tenth time – as if for the first time – your heroic *Mad Dog of San Clemente*, I realized an amazing thing.' Without waiting for encouragement, he said: 'I realized that, when the landlord, Carlos, is murdered in front of the whole town and the people line the streets to watch and do nothing and he is stabbed two times at the fish stall and runs away to the hat shop where he is stabbed two times more and then he crawls to the steps of the Post Office where three more blows finish him off, then I saw.'

Mr Valdez said nothing. In spite of himself he may have cocked an eyebrow or the brim of his hat may have overemphasized a tiny movement of his head, but it was enough for the doctor.

'Yes, I know. I see you are testing me, but I know. Seven stab wounds ending in death. They represent the seven deadly sins, do they not? I am right?'

He said it questioningly so Mr Valdez had no choice but to say: 'You are a very perceptive reader.'

Dr Cochrane gave a little bow. 'And as a reward for my devotion, may I, would it be too much to ask, might I hear a few words from your current work?'

'Oh, no! I don't think. That is. I.'

'I understand. You need say no more. Would you, could you, say even a word about the theme?'

'Forgive me if I say only . . .'

'I understand. But the title. Even to know that, it would be a flavour to hold in the mouth.'

'I am superstitious, like a mother waiting to bring forth. Forgive me. I cannot. Truly.'

Dr Cochrane looked down at the tip of his cane where it rested on the dusty pavement and sighed.

'But perhaps, you would permit me to buy you coffee, to make it up to you? Breakfast? Have you eaten?'

'That would be delightful. And we could talk more about your books.'

'Yes,' said Valdez, 'but let's stick to those already on your shelves.' He stood up easily and waited, hands crossed in front of him over the large yellow notebook, like a footballer waiting to deflect a free kick. He was a slim man, tall and fit, but Dr Cochrane made a less graceful picture, planting two hands on the silver top of his cane and hauling himself off the bench with a groan.

Mr Valdez cupped a steadying hand round the doctor's elbow and they walked off together towards Café Phoenix, the shadowy cavern of mirrors and moulded wood panelling where the university set liked to take its coffee.

At the corner of the square, an early workman had leaned his ladder against the green cross flashing from the wall of the chemist's shop.

He had already unscrewed the iron sign that said: 'Square of May 15' and another, stamped 'Square of the September Revolution', was waiting at the bottom of the ladder. There, on the wall, pale where it had been protected from the grime of the city, the two men saw 'Square of the Black Horse' cut into the stone in a sharply chiselled Roman script.

Dr Cochrane tutted and shook his head. 'May 15. September Revolution. Black Horse. Who cares? For me this will be always the Square of January 18. The old Colonel, I liked him a lot. I knew him, did I tell you?'

'Yes,' said Valdez, 'you told me.'

'Well, I think he deserves a bit of loyalty, that's all. Don't you think? Anyway, that's what I think.'

'I think everybody knows what you think. I think everybody knows that you knew the old Colonel and liked him a lot. Maybe, if nobody knew, the Chair of Mathematics might have been yours by now.'

'That is a remark unworthy of the man who wrote *The Killings at the Bridge of San Miguel*.' Dr Cochrane looked wounded as he shifted his cane to his left hand and leaned on the door of the Phoenix. 'And, anyway, mathematics is above mere politics.'

'Not in this sad little country of ours,' said Valdez. 'Here, each new revolution changes everything. They start with pi and move on from there.'

IT WAS AT the Phoenix that Mr L.H. Valdez, acclaimed literary figure, teacher, polo enthusiast, dandy, lover, cynic, author of over a dozen novels that were not only best-sellers but also 'important' works of fiction, first met the young woman he would murder just a short time later.

Coming in from the street, his eyes took a little time to become accustomed to the cool shadow of the café. He hesitated, but Dr Cochrane, in spite of his cane, forged ahead between the tables. 'Jungle eyes,' thought Valdez. 'Undoubtedly the eyes of an Indian.' They made their way to the back of the room where Costa from Classics and De Silva, who taught law, were hunched over a tiny chessboard with Gonzalez the Jesuit, uncomfortably close to their elbows, snooping like a poker cheat.

'Good morning, colleagues and friends,' said Dr Cochrane. 'Move up now, make a little room. Valdez has offered me breakfast and – yet more nourishing – his conversation.'

The little group shuffled along the brown benches on polished trousers.

'Now you have to move your bishop. You have to!' said De Silva.

'I don't "have to" do anything of the sort.'

'Costa, you touched it. You have to.'

'I did not touch it.'

'Don't be stupid, you touched it.'

'Stupid? Nice. That's nice. A nice game of chess and now it's "stupid" is it? I moved the board so that Cochrane could sit down, that's all.'

'And are you denying that you touched the bishop?'

'Don't talk to me as if you're addressing a class on contract law.'

'Costa, you touched the bishop!'

'By accident!'

'The rules are simple and clear; clear so anyone can understand them, simple for the avoidance of doubt.'

On a normal day, Valdez would have enjoyed that little quarrel. He would have watched it carefully, observed the jabs of fingers, traced the trajectories of tiny bullets of rainbow spit, made lengthy mental notes of every silly, angry word just in case, please God, there might come a day when he could write them down again in a story. Even now, when hope was almost dead, when he struggled day after day with a clean page and left it, sometimes hours later, with no mark on the paper, like an impotent lover, limp and embarrassed, he might still have paid attention. But there was the girl.

She was a waitress, but the only thing that gave her away was a pad of flimsy paper with a slip of carbon under the top leaf. No crisp white shirt, no smart black skirt, nothing to mark her out from the bunch of laughing students – the sons and daughters of dentists and accountants and colonels, all trying to look like Che – she was serving at a table in the opposite corner. She wore jeans.

Mr Valdez disapproved of jeans, but all the students wore them and she wore hers indecently low so a tempting blush of shadow or curve or imagination, hinting at something wonderful, appeared, briefly, at the waistband.

'On a plumber, that would be disgusting,' thought Mr Valdez as he traced the shape of her with his eyes, faded blue cotton taut over the curve of her arse and a line of pale flesh that slid in an elegant parabola to an improbably tiny waist and a narrow back.

'She's a child,' Valdez told himself. 'An infant.' But then she turned round and, in spite of himself, Mr Valdez gasped for, although she was slim and dainty, the girl had amazing, beautiful, impossible breasts – the sort of breasts he had imagined existed only in the pages of those magazines he purchased at that little shop behind the church on his monthly visits to Punto del Rey, astounding, miraculous breasts, like peaked cannonballs hung in bags of ivory silk.

'The face of an angel and the body of Lilith!' Mr Valdez looked quickly at the floor, at his shoes, over at the angry chess game. He discovered a sudden fascination with the polished head of Dr Cochrane's cane and fixed his gaze on that as if his head had been held in a vice and he looked and he looked and he looked at that until she stood at his shoulder. And then she said: 'May I take your order?'

At the other end of the table the squabbling stopped and the priest let the air blow out between his teeth like a man who sees the gates of Heaven across an uncrossable gap. Mr Valdez did not look up. He dared not look up. He could not. He was afraid to move his gaze from Dr Cochrane's cane.

'Coffee,' said Costa.

'Coffee,' said De Silva.

'Black,' said the priest.

'Yes, yes,' Dr Cochrane said enthusiastically.

'Three coffees for my friends and another for me and some rolls – soft rolls – and ham and two boiled eggs.'

And then there was a moment of silence, a drip or two of

embarrassment before she said: 'And anything for you, Mr Valdez?'

She said his name. She said his name and that meant she knew his name, she knew who he was and she said his name because she wanted him to know that she knew.

'Coffee,' he said and looked up. 'Coffee.'

The girl repeated the order, made a tick on the notepad and smiled and walked away.

'Just tell me again. Just try to explain. Tell me what it's like,' said the priest.

De Silva gave his hand a friendly pat and said: 'Best not to think about it. They ask too much of you, those clerical bastards with their stupid rules. Better just to cut your balls off than make you wear them and never use them. Best not to think of it.'

Around the table they looked at one another like men discovered in something shameful and they looked again and studied the backs of their hands, except for Dr Cochrane, who was too old or too weak or too stupid to feel the electricity of her passing.

'Pretty girl,' he said. 'The waitress. Did you notice her? Quite pretty.'

They looked at him as if he were an idiot.

'Caterina. That's her name. One of my best students. I'm surprised to see her here but I suppose she's hard up, needs a little money, like the rest of us.'

All of them, except Dr Cochrane himself and, perhaps, the priest, heard those words, 'hard up, needs a little money', and, for a moment, thought exactly the same thing. Valdez was the first to drive the notion from his head. Anything that could be bought with coin could never truly be his, and he had already decided that he must possess this Caterina completely.

'She seems to know you, Valdez,' said the doctor.

'Yes. I can't think how.' From the far end of the table the others looked at him enviously.

'Like me, she is an aficionada, I'm afraid. Whenever she comes into class there's always one of your novels piled on the top of her textbooks. This week it's *The Fisherman Chavez*, I think.'

Mr Valdez held his empty notebook a little more tightly, until he felt the yellow paper start to squeak under his fingers. 'Really?' That was all he managed to say before Father Gonzalez made a face like a simpleton again.

'Oh, God,' he said, 'she's coming back.'

The others stiffened, afraid to follow his gaze. They sat, facing inwards across the table at Dr Cochrane, who smiled a welcome to her. Even when she put the cups down on the table – 'Coffee, coffee, coffee and your rolls, Dr Cochrane. Ham. The eggs. Coffee for you, Mr Valdez' – even then they sat rigid in their places, terrified to move when she passed so close in case (Oh, please God, let it happen – no, don't) some part of her might brush some part of them.

'Let me know if there's anything else,' she said, and left.

They all turned to watch her go and De Silva made a hungry growl. 'Let me know if there's anything else? Dear God, I can think of a few things. You know, I've seen shows where they charge money to watch and I'm telling you it's nothing – nothing! – compared with her just walking across the room.' He seemed to realize he had said too much and shrugged apologetically. 'Of course, that was when I was in the Navy,' he said.

'Of course, that was when we had a navy,' said Costa.

'We've still got a navy.'

'So all we need now is a coast.'

'We'll get it back. Those bastards can't hang on to it for ever. Next time they start something, we'll get it back. Señor Colonel the President isn't going to take any crap from that bunch of sheep-shaggers. I'm telling you. Five years – at the most – and we'll get the coast back and then you'll be glad we kept the Navy.'

Costa said nothing.

'You will! I'm telling you.'

Costa was trying not to laugh.

De Silva glanced down at the chessboard, coiled his finger against his thumb and flicked his king over. 'Aww, shut up and drink your coffee,' he said.

'Our friend is right,' said Dr Cochrane, shovelling eggs eagerly. 'The survival of our Navy is essential to the survival of our national pride. Ours is a nation with seawater in its veins. The waves of our stolen coast truly lap at the edges of our most distant jungle clearings and wash even the heights of our snowy mountains.'

'Are you getting this down?' De Silva asked from the corner but, before anybody could reply, Dr Cochrane had begun again, talking proudly of 'my glorious ancestor, the Admiral', and the national destiny.

'I'm sorry, I can't stay,' said Valdez. 'Enjoy your coffee, gentlemen. My treat,' and, nodding to Father Gonzalez because his mother had engrained in him a proper respect for the clergy, he stood up and turned towards the door.

The coffee he hurried to finish had scalded his mouth and he was painfully aware that a single, dark brown spot stained his shirt front just above the pocket, but he had noticed Caterina sitting at the cash desk and decided.

She did not look up as he approached and that suited him. Mr Valdez was uncertain how he would have responded if she had turned those eyes upon him.

Even when he put his yellow notebook down on the counter and reached for his wallet, she still ignored him, flicking her pencil over some quick arithmetic on her order pad. That suited

him too. He had some time to breathe her in, taste the glory of
her.

Mr Valdez felt five seconds pass, or maybe just two, and in
that time he suffered a revelation. He saw — and he knew for
certain he was the first man who had ever seen this — a halo of
pearl that glowed around the girl's body. It was a thing of quite
extraordinary loveliness, a thing he had seen only once before in
his life, and then only in a picture. It mimicked exactly the almost
invisible, shimmering aura that Velazquez had painted around the
invitational arse of his Venus as she flaunted herself on a couch
of silken drapes. It meant 'sex', the holiness of it, the sacrament
of pleasure and lust and heat. Mr Valdez had imagined it was a
beautiful conceit but, no, it had been real all along, perhaps visible
only to a fellow artist but undeniable, nonetheless. And, though
it glowed only from the delicious, welcoming, bounce-some backside of the goddess, it whipped and curled around every portion
of Caterina. He saw it and, in that — one and two, breathe in and
out — moment, Mr Valdez knew that he must bathe himself in
that glow, that it would make him a man again, complete him
and, finally, break the dam that was holding back his words.

Caterina finished her sums and put down her pad.

'I'd like to pay now,' said Valdez.

She pulled a piece of thick, pulpy paper from a clip at the side
of the cash drawer, ran her finger down it and said: 'I think that's
right,' as she handed it to him.

Valdez was almost afraid to touch it, as if, having touched her,
it might spark fire from his skin. He didn't bother to read it but
simply folded it up inside a large note.

'Keep the change,' he said, 'Caterina.'

She was shocked. 'It's too much. Half of that would be too
much.'

'No, no. Please permit it. Dr Cochrane told us you are one of his best students and working to pay your bills. That is to be encouraged.'

'You're kind. Thank you.'

'Thank you,' he said. His mind was tumbling over itself. Had he done enough to make an impression? Would a moment longer be too much? But she already knew of him. She was an aficionada, Cochrane said. She knew his name. So, was she disappointed to meet him face to face? Had he made himself ridiculous? How long could he keep looking at that beautiful face without kissing it or worse yet, letting his eyes wander to there, or there or, NO!

'Well, I must be going,' he said.

She only smiled a little and nodded weakly and said: 'Yes,' and 'Thank you,' again.

Mr Valdez picked up his notebook, with the front cover firmly closed. 'The university. Work. You know. Perhaps I'll see you there.'

She nodded and Valdez stepped out the door and into the little calle. He had gone only a few steps into the street and his eyes were still adjusting to the sunshine when he heard the door of the Phoenix bang and the girl appeared at his side.

She was holding out a piece of paper, like a relay runner, ready to pass it on, fast, with no touching. 'Mr Valdez, your receipt! You left your receipt!' She pressed it into his hand and, before he could say anything, she fled back to the café.

Valdez looked down at the paper in his hand. It was blank except for two words in pencil: 'I write.'

MR L.H. VALDEZ, the celebrated author, the pole star around which the rest of the faculty rotated, who had already willed his desk to the national museum, whose portrait – wearing a snow-white Panama hat of distinctive style – appeared in the windows of no fewer than fourteen bookshops in the capital, was due to lecture on Shakespeare. The Sonnets. That morning he would explain, not poetry, of which he knew almost nothing, but obsessive love, of which he knew even less outside the pages of his novels. That mattered little. Like all teachers, he need be only one lesson ahead of his pupils and he was smug behind a carapace of reputation.

The lecture bored him. He had delivered it so many times before that he knew it by heart, spotted the signposts that indicated this wise observation, that witty insight or pointed the way to a long avenue of brilliant wordsmithing and on to his heartbreakingly beautiful conclusion.

He recited without incident and stood before the students like a confident tennis pro, facing the children of the beginners' class, forcing them to squint into the sun and effortlessly batting away expected, predictable questions. And nothing that he said, nothing that he quoted, nothing that he read aloud was half so important as those two words, scrawled down with a blunt, grey pencil on a scrap of damp paper.

I write.

He could feel that tiny sentence burning its way through the leather of his wallet, through his shirt, through his flesh until it burrowed between his bones and into his heart.

I write.

'I write,' he thought. 'I write too.' But that was not quite true. 'I wrote.' That would be more accurate. 'I wrote this and this and this and I will write. I will write again.'

While he stood, regurgitating the old lie that Shakespeare was by no means unnatural in his appetites, that the experience of intense male friendship can be found everywhere in literature from the *Iliad* to *The Adventures of Sherlock Holmes*, Mr L.H. Valdez decided to turn his critical eye fully on Caterina's note.

'I write.'

Not the shortest sentence it was possible to create but pretty near. Impersonal, in spite of the aggressive personal pronoun, something René Magritte might have inscribed on the side of a pencil: 'I write' or 'This is not a writer', either would do. A bald statement of fact, then?

No, not that. The author of this piece did not intend to convey simply that she makes marks on a page. One could not infer 'shopping lists' as the next phrase in the sentence. No, a confession of that magnitude could be followed only by a word of great moment: 'stories' or 'poetry'.

And yet – he wanted to stop wasting his words on Shakespeare and direct the class instead to study the epic that was glowing inside his wallet – she had chosen not to say more.

In the lecture inside his head, the lecture not given, Mr Valdez pointed out that the sensitive critic can reveal as much from what is not said as from what is. In this case the author had said: 'I write.' She had not said: 'too.'

This was a message addressed to the foremost author of his

generation. How could she have written 'too'? That would be to put herself on a level with him. Impossible. Unthinkable. But it was still a message semaphored from the foothills to the mountaintops, a flag waved, a rocket sent up to say: 'See me. Notice me, please.'

She was so far below as to be almost out of sight and she had no idea that, up on the summit, he had already begun to slide down the far side, clutching at rocks as he fell, tearing his hands open, kicking up pebbles, scrabbling.

I write. She meant it as a plea for attention. For a man clinging on over an empty chasm, it sounded like a promise of rescue.

WHEN HE LEFT the lecture hall at a little after noon, Mr Valdez walked across the courtyard that separates the Faculty of Arts from Modern Languages. The long, narrow lawns of coarse grass, imitations of something someone had once seen in a mezzotint of a Cambridge college, were always kept green and damp. Water trickled off between their brick edges and soaked into the yellow gravel paths where laburnum trees – another affectation – cast a feathery shade on the park benches that lined the way. Mr Valdez hated those benches. Their brass plaques offended him. He thought them tasteless. He thought them pointless. He thought them silly and, above all, tedious.

'In Memory of Professor So-and-So' or 'An Affectionate Tribute to Dr Such-and-Such'. Ghastly. Better no monument at all than a park bench left outside for pigeons to shit on while cigarette butts piled up around the legs. Mr Valdez shuddered at the thought.

He looked at those benches as the natives of the interior looked at cameras, as if they somehow held the power to capture a man's soul, as if the nobodies they commemorated were denied even the oblivion of erasure and, instead, faced their eternity disturbed by an intermittent chorus of questioning 'Who?'s.

Mr Valdez sprang up the three stone steps at the end of the path, little dusty bits of gravel crunching under the thin soles of his expensive shoes, and pushed open the double doors that lead into Modern Languages. He stood for a moment in the empty corridor, listening.

When he heard voices in the staffroom he walked on through the brown corridor and out of the matching doors at the other end into the sunshine of the street. He wanted coffee, not conversation, so he crossed the road and sat down at a table in front of Bar America where the waiters were quick and efficient, which he liked, and where they never asked about his books, which he liked even better.

They brought him a double espresso and, without his asking, a glass of water that stood sweating blue beads on a saucer of its own. It was a quality establishment. The water would be safe to drink. After a polite nod, the waiter retreated indoors to the shade and Mr Valdez heard the electric gabble of a sports broadcast murmuring faintly behind.

He put his hand on his yellow notebook and considered opening the cover. He lifted his hand again and reached inside his jacket for a pen, took off the cap, gripped the pen between his teeth just as he had done that morning and opened the notebook. He sat there like that for quite some time, writing nothing.

Not a word.

For a long time.

Mr Valdez was very angry with himself. He knew that his failure to write was nothing more than a failure of will, a moral failure, a deliberate act of laziness and cowardice and stupidity, and it could be overcome by the simple act of writing something. He looked out into the street and he saw a yellow cat, belly down, slinky, hurrying out from the shade of a parked car.

'The yellow cat crossed the road,' he wrote. Six words. He examined them. They were not enough. They said nothing. Why did the yellow cat cross the road? Whose cat was it? Where was it going? How could a cat crossing the road become a novel? The whole idea was madness. Six words of rubbish. He looked again and made a little arrow, upwards, through the line between 'The' and 'yellow'.

Then he added 'tawny' and looked again, like an artist stepping back from his canvas. 'The tawny yellow cat crossed the road.' It was coming on.

He clamped the pen between his teeth and pondered and then, in a fit of inspiration, he wrote 'scrawny'.

The scrawny, tawny, yellow cat crossed the road.

He decided on a hyphen. 'Scrawny-tawny.' He liked that. Then he hated it. Dismal, pathetic, affected, purple nonsense. Mr Valdez scratched his pen angrily through 'tawny'.

The scrawny yellow cat crossed the road.

He began to wonder if he had meant to say that, if he might not have scratched out the wrong word. Scrawny. Tawny. Scrawny? Tawny?

Mr Valdez took a sip of coffee. He leaned over his notebook with his head propped on his elbow, fighting down the rage and panic and frustration that were already boiling in his chest. He was close to tears with fury.

Mr Valdez leaned back in his chair and drew his hands down his face with a tired sigh. When he took them away again and opened his eyes, a woman was standing just on the other side of his table.

'Hello, Chano,' she said.

'Good afternoon, Maria. You look well.' She did.

Kitten heels, a simple, scoop-necked dress of burnt-orange linen that set off her tanned arms and picked up the colours of her necklace. It was perhaps a bit tight over the swell of her hips. Mr Valdez realized a little sadly that, in a year or two, maybe three, Maria would be past her best. But, for now, she smouldered. She always wore clothes of brown or, more truly, clothes of browns. Crocus yellow and amber, cream and ivory – which are all, whatever you might think, brown – right through to the black of liquorice which is still, if you look closely enough, brown. She had a long, narrow silk scarf, all in pleats of alternate coffee and cream and fringed with tassels of wild pearls, and she wore jewellery that was designed to scandalize – stuff that looked as if it came from a school workshop in the Indian missions; polished shells and seeds strung on leather cords. If she had arrived for coffee with a shrunken head on a necklace, no one would have turned a hair and all the women would have hurried home and screamed until their husbands got them a shrunken head too.

She wore those things, that rubbish, all the time, even in bed, even when she was naked. And when she was clothed they made her look naked, like the priestess of some jungle cult, waiting to receive her worshippers, ready to bathe in the gore of a blood sacrifice.

'Aren't you going to invite me to sit down?' she said. There was a hint of a pout on her full lips.

'Of course,' Mr Valdez stood up and offered a chair. 'You must let me get you something. What would you like?'

'Just hot water and lemon. I must watch my figure.'

Mr Valdez signalled to the waiter with a two-fingered gesture like a Papal blessing.

Maria looked put out. 'That was your chance to say something gallant, Chano. I say "I must watch my figure" and you say how lovely it is or how every man in the city is doing that for me or "Oh, no. Let me". Honestly, darling, it's no use if I have to invent my own compliments.'

'I'm sorry,' he said. 'I was distracted.'

'The book, I suppose. How's it coming along?' Her dress gaped prettily as she leaned over the table to look at his notebook – which he casually flipped shut.

'It's going very well. Very well indeed. You know, I feel I've made a real breakthrough. The words are just pouring out of my pen.'

'So you're almost finished?'

'Sometimes I think I am, yes. Almost finished.' Mr Valdez said nothing for a moment and then made a dismissive wave over his notebook and added: 'But then there's the editing. Cut and cut and cut. That's the only way. Perhaps I will run a pencil through every single word I've written today.'

'What a waste.'

The waiter appeared and took their order and left again.

'It's not a waste. Not at all. The pieces the diamond cutter throws away aren't wasted.'

'Can I see?' she asked and pawed at the notebook. 'Just a little peek.' She had her head tilted towards the table so she could look up at him through heavy lashes. It was an obvious gesture, unsubtle but stirring.

Mr Valdez snatched the notebook away playfully. 'No, you can't. You'll have to wait like everybody else. And I can't stay, I'm afraid. I have an appointment at the bank.'

'The bank? I like banks. I like anything to do with money.'

He stood up and dropped a few notes on the table.

'Yes,' he said, 'I know you do.'

Mr Valdez waited until the traffic cleared, then he stepped off the pavement, crossed the road back to the university and walked three streets south towards the river and into the bank.

It annoyed him that the directors had decided to employ a professional greeter, a uniformed flunkey whose only job was to approach customers and ask them their business. That was a wage that could have been paid out in interest or to share-holders, and both of those would have suited Mr Valdez very well.

'I am here to see Mr Ernesto Marrom,' he said. 'I have an appointment.'

'What name, sir?'

'Valdez.'

The man walked off, past the fat security guard leaning on the counter at the back of the banking hall with his belly hanging over his gun belt, and through a gorgeously carved door at the rear.

The Merino and National Banking Company was nothing if not opulent, with lots of heavy carving on the walls and deep plaster work on the roof: allegorical figures of agriculture and industry, an overflowing cornucopia spilling fruit in every corner of the ceiling, and fat putti toiling under the weight of sacks bulging with coins. Mr Valdez stood for a few moments, tracing their laboured flight around the ceiling until he was summoned for his interview.

The flunkey led him through a brief corridor, no more than the gap between two doors, into the manager's office where Ernesto Marrom was already rising from behind his desk with his hand extended.

'Nice to see you, Valdez. You are well, I trust?'

'Very well, thanks. You?'

'Oh, you know, busy.'

'And Mrs Marrom?'

'Fine thanks. Fine. Now, what can I do for you?'

Mr Valdez reached inside his jacket and took out his wallet. 'A couple of royalty cheques,' he said. When he tugged them free, Caterina's note came loose with them and fluttered down onto the desk.

Marrom picked it up and handed it back. 'I write,' he said. 'A reminder, Valdez, in case you get lost?'

Lost. Yes, it was something very like that. The sort of thing old men put in their wallets with their names and addresses in case they should be found dead at a bus station or, worse yet, find themselves far from home with no idea where they came from or how they got there.

Valdez hated him for daring to touch that little bit of paper. He hated him for mocking it. A character in a novel by L.H. Valdez would have found an excuse for murder in that harmless action, but L.H. Valdez himself said only: 'Yes, that's the idea,' and took back the note carefully between two fingers.

'You could simply have paid these cheques in over the counter, you know,' the bank manager said.

'Yes, I know. I hate to bother you with this but I want that money to go into the special overseas account.'

'They will have to clear through your ordinary account here first.'

'Will they? Is that absolutely necessary? So much paperwork.'

'And not to mention the tax.'

'No,' said Mr Valdez. 'Let's not mention the tax.'

'I'll see to it.'

'I hate to be a bother, but can it be done today?'

'Today?' Mr Marrom gave a good-natured sigh. 'Oh, I suppose so. Things are a bit busy, but I'll work through lunch. I had wanted to get home early but . . . Oh, well. Don't think I'd do this for everybody.'

'I am very appreciative,' said Mr Valdez. 'Really, very appreciative.' He stood up and shook hands. 'I'll find my own way out.'

Out in the sunshine of the street again, Mr Valdez walked three blocks north and found Maria still at the same table, legs elegantly crossed, one expensive shoe swinging provocatively from her toes.

'Still here, Mrs Marrom? I'm astonished.'

'You're not the slightest bit astonished, you bad man.'

'I've just been speaking to Ernesto.'

Maria looked down the street as if nothing could interest her less.

'He says . . .'

'Oh, what does he say?'

'He says he must work through lunch and won't be home until the usual time tonight.'

Maria brightened visibly.

'So I was wondering.'

'Yes?'

'So, I was wondering if you would like to come to bed with me, Mrs Marrom.'

'Chano, darling, what a lovely idea!' She slipped her toes neatly back into her shoe, took his arm and hurried to the taxi rank.

THE MERINO IS the pendulum that drives the town. When snow melts in the mountains or thunderclouds, fat as udders, burst over the jungle then, a week or two later, the Merino notices. Water hurries by the wharfs, there are waves in the river and a breeze that stirs the flag on the ferry, and naval officers on half pay with no ships will turn like weather vanes and gaze towards the far-off stolen coast.

Then the town hurries. Then the town bustles. People go from house to house and shop to shop, looking at the sky as they walk, waiting for the first fat drops of rain to stain the pavements like blood. Then they keep their shutters flung wide so the air runs clear through their houses and their curtains bag and billow like sails. Then the people sit in cafés bright with chatter. They take a citron or a brandy. They stay late and go home to laugh a little more and sleep in crisp beds. Those are the days when the dogs trot the streets with their tails up and their noses high – and so do the women. The women sit on park benches and chat to their neighbours or parade themselves, walking slowly, lazy-hipped as Holsteins, in the gardens of the Carmelites. Men smile.

But when the Merino is still and thick as paint, when the pelicans crowd on the piers like watching vultures, when the cormorants spread their wings and stand, gasping from yellow beaks, and the flies are too tired to move, and the air is thick and damp and the drains breathe fish-stink into the streets, then the nights are sleepless. Then every street has a baby mewling hour after hour or cats fighting on top of clattering bins.

And in the daytime the women leave the gardens of the Carmelites and walk in the heat, thin dresses damp with sweat, along the other side of the park, slowly, so slowly, under the windows of the prison, and they listen to the howls as they pass and they smile.

It was that sort of afternoon when Mr Valdez sat down in the brown corridor of the maths department and waited. He had already completed his patrol of the building, found the room where Dr Cochrane was teaching, chosen a bench in the corridor that Caterina must pass on her way out from the lecture.

He had studied and perfected his look of surprise, carefully polished the casualness of his invitation to 'coffee?' and his self-deprecating little joke about how, this time, he would be delighted to serve her. And then the conversation would turn to writing and he would show a generosity of spirit beyond her wildest imaginings, a more than polite interest, a warm and tender encouragement and slowly, gradually, she would fall in love with him.

Mr Valdez had decided the whole thing could be done in a week. And it would be beautiful. Mr Valdez had decided that. He would be magnificent and she would be beautiful and young and amazed and impressed and the thing inside him that had been broken would be healed and he would write and the first thing he wrote would be about Caterina. It would be his thanks to her. It would make her immortal, a lasting monument that would endure far longer than any plaque on any park bench. She would be his Beatrice, his Laura, his Dark Lady – none of them required a park bench – and they would part with tears and without bitterness, remembering the affair as a time of loveliness.

Beauty mattered to Mr Valdez. He liked order and neatness but he craved beauty and feared the ugly.

Sitting there on that brown bench in a brown corridor, waiting, he scuffed his feet on the brown linoleum without even noticing that they moved in time to the sound of a distant tango, playing on the wireless in the janitor's office.

The tango was everywhere. That last afternoon, when he was done with Maria Marrom, there had been an accordion playing tango, very slow. It dripped into his flat from the open door of the bar in the next street and he danced, alone, naked, gliding across the tiles of his kitchen floor.

Mr Valdez held an imaginary woman in his arms. He was unsure who she was. He had not bothered to imagine a face for her but he knew she was not Caterina. Tango takes years and experience and pain. Children cannot dance tango. Whores dance it very well.

Mr Valdez danced back into his bedroom and stopped. Maria. Mrs Maria Marrom, face down in a tangle of wet sheets, her face in the pillow, breathing in long sighs. The bed.

A mess. A glass broken on the tiles and a wine bottle on its side. He let his arms fall, let the woman pressed against his body melt away. So much more convenient than a Maria, he thought, so much easier. Mr Valdez cursed himself. If only they had gone back to the banker's house. He could have waited for a decent interval, the kind of politely appreciative moment that the girls of Madame Ottavio's house did not demand, and left with no fuss. She might even have hurried him out with kisses, tremulous, fearful lest he should delay too long and provoke a scene. But now she was there, in his bed, sticky-skinned and tousled and replete, dozing like an aunt at Christmas, immovable and embarrassing.

Mr Valdez opened the door into his bathroom and turned the shower on.

He made as much noise as he could short of singing and emerged, a few minutes later, with a fresh white towel wrapped almost twice round his waist. He slid open a drawer, took out a white shirt and bashed the drawer shut again.

'Chano, you're not getting dressed?'

'Of course.' He jangled coat-hangers in his wardrobe and took out a pair of black Chinese trousers, loose and baggy.

'Chano, you can't get dressed.'

'The afternoon is almost gone.'

'Chano.' She was soft and wheedling.

'Poor Ernesto will be home from the bank soon. Have you no shame?'

'None at all. Not a drop.' She looked at him with that same under-the-lashes look she had used in the café. An hour ago, when she was on her knees in front of him, he had found it exciting and conspiratorial. Now it was played out.

Maria pushed the hair back from her face. 'Chano?'

He said nothing.

'Chano?'

'What?'

'Do it again.'

'What?'

'Do it again.'

'Do what again?'

'Chano, you know.'

'No.'

'Yes, you do. That thing you do.'

'No.'

'Please, Chano, do it again.' She was lying on her back now, peeling back the damp sheets, making herself naked again and writhing on the mattress like a long brown cat in the sunshine.

'Chano . . .'

'No.'

Now she was touching herself, brushing the tips of her fingers over her body.

'No.'

'I'll do it myself then.'

'Look at the time. Stop that. Think of Ernesto. He'll be suspicious.'

'He knows.' Now her hands were moving in wide swoops across her body, stroking, pinching.

'He knows?'

'I'm almost sure.' Maria's eyes were closed, her tongue peeked from the corner of her mouth. She raised her knees. 'Are you watching, Chano? You are. I can feel your eyes on me.' Her head tilted back.

'He knows?'

'Shh, darling. Any man would be proud to have L.H. Valdez as his wife's lover. It's an,' she gave a little hiccuping gasp of pleasure, 'an honour.'

'He doesn't know.'

Maria said nothing.

He heard her breathing, a little rasp in the back of her throat, some bit of thick spittle clinging in her windpipe.

'Stop that. It's disgusting.'

'It's. Not. It's. Lovely. Come and. Help. Me.' She was squirming on the bed now, dancing her own tango, displaying herself like fruit from some luscious still life, hands fluttering like birds in a cage when a cat passes.

'Ernesto knows nothing,' said Mr Valdez. 'In fact he probably has a mistress of his own. He does. A mistress. I've seen them.'

On the bed Maria was biting her lip and moaning softly.

'I've seen them. Ernesto and a young girl. A beautiful young girl from the university. A goddess. Made for just one thing. Made for a man to have. I've seen them.'

Maria's eyes flickered. Her body tensed.

'I've seen them touching. I've watched them. I've seen it all. When he does vile things to her, things you couldn't pay for, she takes it all and begs for more because she wants it. Everything. She wants it all.'

Maria's back arched. She roared. She growled. The breath rushed from her body and she collapsed with a sob and curled her body in a ball, purring. 'Oh, Chano! Chano! What a storyteller you are.'

Disgusting. Waiting there in the brown corridor, he felt the sting of Maria's disbelief still and the irony of her dismissal clung in his throat. But Mr Valdez felt more puzzled than ashamed. He could not explain why he had invented a mistress for the banker Marrom and, still less, why he had made her Caterina. The ugliness of the notion turned his stomach, as much as it had to stand there watching Maria, drinking her in, wallowing in her pleasure, urging her on. As much as he disgusted himself knowing that, one day soon, on some lonely afternoon of boredom, he would find her again or he would come downstairs to unlock the brass letterbox in the lobby of his building and find there a postcard with nothing on it but '2.30?' and he would go. What a story-teller you are. No, not now. He had been, but not now. Now he was merely a nervous man waiting in a corridor for a beautiful girl.

There was a big paper bag beside him on the bench, folded over at the top and sealed with a strip of tape. He opened it and took out a large notebook of pale blue paper. Mr Valdez had decided it was time for a change of stationery. It was obvious, really. Nobody could be expected to write about a yellow cat on yellow paper.

THE LOVE AND DEATH OF CATERINA · 32

Mr Valdez reached inside his jacket, took out his pen and began to write.

The scrawny yellow cat crossed the road.

It looked very well there on the pale blue paper, in his coal-black, broad-nibbed, swirling hand. He waited for a moment, looking at the wall on the other side of the corridor, thinking. He looked again. The ink had dried. It had lost its gloss. It looked dusty now and the words seemed cramped against the top of the page. Mr Valdez decided that a novel, a great novel, well, any novel, should begin halfway down the page. It left room for a shoulder-heaving intake of breath, like the overture of an opera. He tore out the page, and halfway down the next he wrote: 'The scrawny yellow cat crossed the road.' He looked again at the wall and sighed and then an electric bell clanged just above his head and he started and then doors flung them-selves back all along the corridor and students carrying bags and books and dressed like guerrillas began jostling towards the fresh air.

Mr Valdez stood up, the backs of his knees pressed awkwardly against the bench by the crowd. He looked up and down the corridor. He could not see Caterina. And then he spotted her walking away from him, against the tide of the traffic. He began to follow, just as she ducked down a side passage at the end of the corridor.

'Excuse me. Excuse me. Excuse me,' he said. They ignored him. He dodged and elbowed his way upstream through the crowd and then, as quickly as they had arrived, the students were gone.

Mr Valdez turned left into the passage. There were two doors at the other end, each of them glazed with ground glass, a light shining from each room behind and, clearly marked in thick black paint: 'Ladies' and 'Gents'.

He was unsure how to proceed. If he returned to his seat in

the corridor she might pass the wrong way and he would be left to call after her, pursue her. No. That would lack the beauty of an accidental meeting. If he waited in the passage, she would come out of the lavatory and find him lurking. There could be no poetry in loitering outside a ladies' toilet. He decided to hide, wait and ambush her.

Mr Valdez hurried into the gents and closed the door quietly, careful to turn the doorknob and, slowly, fit the latch back in place. He stepped backwards into the centre of the room so there would be no sign of his shadow falling on the ground glass of the door. A dripping tap had left a brass-green streak in one of the sinks and the faulty washer fizzed above it, but apart from that it was quiet in there and cool. Mr Valdez held his breath and listened. There was nothing. And then the scrape and squeak of heels on the hard floor in the room next door, the sound of water flushing, another moment of silence, the bang of a door, another set of hard, metallic clicks, a tap running, squealing, complaining pipes. Mr Valdez watched her as if through a glass wall, washing her hands, stopping now for a moment to look in the mirror above the sink, curling back her lip, wiping away something that clung to a tooth, a final finger-flick of the hair.

He breathed out. The click of heels again. She was walking across the room. The door opened. She was in the passage. He let her go two paces before he flung open the door and went out.

'Oh! Caterina.' He was trying too hard to sound bright and casual. 'Nice to see you.'

She stopped and looked back at him over her shoulder with that automatic smile, so beautiful, so open, so young, so beautiful, so beautiful. And then she recognized him and she changed. Her eyes flicked to the floor for a second and, when she looked up again, she was respectful and deferential.

'Hello, Mr Valdez,' she said.

'Hello.' He had no idea what to say next so he said again: 'Nice to see you.'

She didn't reply.

'I got your note.'

'I put it in your hand.'

'Yes.' He stopped, remembering the moment. 'Yes. So, what do you write?'

'Oh, stories. Silly stuff, really.'

'If it matters to you, it's not silly.' What a lie. He rebuked himself for it. What a storyteller you are, Chano. How much rubbish had he read in his time, bits of nonsense pressed into his hand by hopeless, helpless, driven, desperate amateurs? And he'd thrown all of it into the bucket and told them to stop wasting ink and killing trees for the sake of that drivel. 'I'd be delighted to talk about your work. Maybe you'd let me buy you a cup of coffee – and this time I'll be the one serving you.' He had practised that little joke over and over and it was only now, saying it to her, that he realized how feeble it sounded.

She looked at him with something like pity. That was all right. Pity was good – well, not good but it would do if it gave him a foot in the door.

She seemed to be deciding and then she said: 'Coffee? Yes, coffee would be nice. But wouldn't you rather have sex?'

'THE SCRAWNY YELLOW cat crossed the road.'

'The scrawny yellow cat crossed the road.'

'The scrawny yellow cat crossed the road.'

Mr Valdez sat at his desk in front of his open window and wrote until the light finally faded and the street lamps came to life.

He filled pages but he wrote just one line, those same seven words, over and over, writing, stopping, thinking, imagining that damned cat, where it would go, who owned it, what it would do, who it might see, scoring out, thinking and starting again with 'The scrawny yellow cat crossed the road' until he had filled sheets and sheets of beautiful blue paper, page after page of written migraine.

At last, like a blanket drawn respectfully over the face of a corpse, shadows began to creep across his desk and all the dark, angry lines written in his notebook merged with one another, merged with the evening, quietened and disappeared. Mr Valdez was relieved. He might easily have reached across his desk and switched on his table lamp, but instead he leaned back in his chair with a sigh. He had done enough. If he measured his work for the day not in words, but in hours, he had done enough. With a gentle pull he removed the cap of his fountain pen, screwed it back into place and tucked it into the pocket of his jacket as it hung on the chair behind him.

Mr Valdez closed the cover of his notebook, twined his fingers as if in prayer and rested his hands on his desk. He sighed again.

Even with the notebook closed, that same sentence kept forming itself in his head, writing itself across the inside of his eyelids over and over, gradually unveiling itself, disappearing in a scrawl of scoring out and starting again. Those same seven words rattled between his ears like the carriage of a typewriter, like a silly tune heard on the wireless at breakfast which lingers in the brain all day long, like the throb of a toothache, like the empty, heavy, aching, itching need for a woman.

Mr Valdez looked at his watch. It was not yet 9 o'clock – still rather too early for a visit to Madame Ottavio's, although on the other hand the girls would be fresh. He could have his pick. No need to wait. No need for all the obvious, unpleasant corollaries that the wait brought with it, the slightly shudder-some, warm-toilet-seat sensations which could be banished only by a matter-of-factness that an artist like Mr Valdez could never quite muster.

But Mr Valdez felt uncertain of himself. He was uneasy. Disturbed. The feeling – was it fear? – had stayed with him all day since the corridor outside the lavatories when he stepped past Caterina and hurried away without a word.

'Wouldn't you rather have sex?'

It thrummed in his head as much as that damned cat.

When she said that, when she said: 'Wouldn't you rather have sex?' like that, the way she had, Mr Valdez felt cheated. He had been about to bestow a great treasure on her but, before he could, she had turned and snatched it out of his hands. It was as if she had bared her teeth at him, as if he had carefully tracked some beautiful deer into the forest and then, in a jungle clearing, he had found himself face to face with a snarling jaguar. He had become the hunted. He had become the prey.

It was an unbeautiful moment played out to the music of flushing urinals. It was not what he had planned.

'Wouldn't you rather have sex?'

What on earth could that mean? Was she mocking him? Was she saying: 'I know exactly what you're after and you're not getting it'?

Or was it something worse? Was she simply issuing an invitation as direct as one of Maria's anonymous postcards? That would be worse. That would be so much worse. That would make her well, what, exactly? An enthusiast?

Mr Valdez could hardly complain about that. He was an enthusiast too, an enthusiast for the act itself, for women in general, and for the moment an enthusiast for Caterina in particular. He should be pleased that she shared that enthusiasm.

Instead, it gnawed at him. Those young boys at the university with their greasy docker's jackets and their unforgivable haircuts – how many of them had shared her enthusiasm? And they were so young – she was so young! There might be comparisons. She might make comparisons. She was, after all, so very young, perhaps too young to understand, as Maria Marrom did, what an honour it was to have the novelist L.H. Valdez in her bed and he wanted her to realize that. He very much wanted her to realize that, but not to seek it too eagerly – certainly not quite as eagerly as she had.

Mr Valdez drew the flat of his hand across his barred and shuttered notebook and listened hard for the sound of words trying to escape. Of course, there was none. If there was a story dammed up in there, he knew the only way to release it was by pouring it out into the body of Caterina. The girls at Madame Ottavio's could not draw that out of him. They had in the past, but this time the only cure was to bathe himself in the pearl glow of her beauty. It was a need. It was a matter of urgency, like a medical prescription. And then the fear came back. If he could no longer write, then maybe the other thing would fade too. Perhaps he would end like Dr Cochrane, sipping a brandy in the courtyard of the Ottavio House, walking arm in arm with the girls, telling stories he hoped they would laugh at but never, ever, going upstairs.

Mr Valdez stood up and put on his jacket. As he turned the key in the lock, he was smiling. It no longer mattered to him whether Caterina was an enthusiast or not. He had seen that in her which could heal him. It was undamaged. No one else had seen it or touched it. It was still his to take. If Mr Valdez had met any of his neighbours as he walked down the stairs and into the street, he would have looked perfectly sane – not that Mr Valdez would have spoken to any of his neighbours about his sanity or anything else.

He knew no more about them than the nameplates on the letter boxes in the lobby, and that was all he wished to know – although the daughter of that dentist, Dr Nero, on the second floor had suddenly begun to blossom in unexpected ways. Perhaps later, in a year or two, when he felt better, after he finished the book, he might take her under his wing.

He pushed open the heavy glass and bronze doors of the lobby and walked out into empty Cristobal Avenue, practising his polo swing as he walked. And, as he walked, swinging his imaginary mallet, thwacking an invisible ball between two oncoming ponies, dodging them, jinking round them with a shift of his weight in the saddle, a barely perceptible tug on the reins, heading for the goal, curving across the pavement and quoting Omar Khayyam at every stride, tango music drifted from a streetful of different radios, from a kitchen window, from a bar where a dozen unfortunates were waiting for the lottery draw, from a sick room where an old man, as thin as the Host and as brittle, fed soup to his dying wife of thirty years and remembered again dancing alone with Rosita, the girl he should have married.

The whole street was packed with stories and the scrawny yellow cat of Mr Valdez might have led him to any one of them, except he had forgotten to listen to any story but his own, to dance to any music but his own, and that music was drawing him on towards the beautiful young girl he would shortly murder.

The Ottavio House stood in a quiet square just off the avenue. There was a little garden in front with a few trees – Mr Valdez had never bothered to identify them – which gave cool shade in the daytime. Now, in the evening, they rustled and whispered so there was at least the illusion of a breeze.

Mr Valdez liked that garden. It was neat and ordered and he appreciated neatness and order. He liked the pattern of square flower beds that bloomed in succession throughout the season. He liked the railings of wrought iron which mimicked exactly the screens on the windows of the houses in the square. He liked the fine gravel path and the way it was constantly dampened to keep down the dust. Mr Valdez could walk through that little garden, always careful to swing the gate shut behind him and close it with its iron latch to keep the dogs out, and he could be sure, when he reached the gate at the other side, there would be no speck of dust spoiling the mirror shine of his shoes.

It was a lovely spot, cool and calm and restful. Mr Valdez liked to imagine Madame Ottavio's girls rising late and leaving the house together, walking two by two like nuns, with broad straw hats to keep the sun off their faces and thick canvas gloves protecting hands that must be kept soft for other employment. He liked to think of them together, spending a quiet afternoon tending to the roses and sweeping the paths, laughing together in healthy outdoor recreation before it was time to take off their hats and smocks and start work for the evening.

Of course that never happened. The little garden was not a labour of love but was kept up by a subscription from every house in the square and the girls from Madame Ottavio's never worked there. The garden was tended by a beautiful young man who went hatless and shirtless in the heat of the day and clumped round in huge boots and tiny shorts. The girls at Madame Ottavio's hung from their windows and licked their lips and howled. They whispered to him, called aloud, inviting him in – no charge – just to see if he tasted as good as he looked, but he never came. The young man had a friend, a waiter in the Hotel Imperial. On hot nights they would sit together in the park and touch and kiss.

Like all the other houses in the square, the Ottavio House was built of soft red bricks and painted over with a thick layer of stucco and painted again according to the tastes of the owners so that, little by little, over the years, the architect's vision of a single, unified whole had collapsed into a cacophony of clashing shades.

In the past, Mr Valdez might have found a rich seam of metaphor there, the painted house sheltering the painted whores, each of them pretending to be something else; a solidly built mansion of stone, a devoted mistress. He might have been able to draw the whole history of the country in the history of the square and watch, on his page, the passage of time as the trees of the jungle river bank were swept away, as the ground was levelled and paved, as the little square was regimented into a gavotte of pillared house-fronts and then, bit by bit, how everything fell apart, how the door hinges sagged and the windows warped and everybody chose a different colour of paint or some abandoned paint completely.

Madame Ottavio did her best to keep up appearances but the last rains had overflowed the gutters on her house and left a damp stain down the front of the building and a cancerous bubbling in the stucco beside the open door.

The wide entrance hall was empty and, beyond it, the doors stood open to the courtyard where lanterns were hung among the trees and shadowed figures wandered. On warm evenings Madame Ottavio saw to it that the table against the back wall of the garden was loaded with bottles and buckets of ice. There was never any charge for the drinks but they were not free. Everybody understood that the price of everything, from a bottle of champagne to the smallest citron, was added to the bill. Only a very foolish customer would spoil his welcome by visiting too often for a drink without paying for something rather more substantial as well.

A dry leaf from the tree overhead had fluttered down to lie on the tablecloth. Mr Valdez picked it off, crumbled it to dust and brushed it from his hands onto the gravel of the garden path. He looked at his palms and, when he was sure they were clean, he took the metal tongs from their place in the bucket and helped himself to a good deal of ice. The broken clumps clunked in the heavy glass, melted for a moment, fused again and spun together in the tumbler. Mr Valdez did not know – because he had never stopped to ask – that the strange bottles of English lime juice which Madame Ottavio never failed to supply were furnished solely for him. Nobody else ever touched them. None of the other customers would ever have considered it. None would have dared. And, in just the same way as Marrom the banker should have overcome his squeamishness and his righteous anger to glory in the knowledge that L.H. Valdez was his wife's lover, so Madame Ottavio was honoured to indulge him with a little foreign lime juice.

Mr Valdez tipped almost half the bottle over the ice rattling in his glass and followed it with a generous measure of gin. It was a silly affectation but one he had enjoyed since university days when he had found the gimlet shining like another green fairy in the pages of Raymond Chandler. Like all green fairies, he found, it had opened the doors of creativity. Perhaps it would again. He hoped it would again.

Sitting on a plush bench under the back window of the house, Mr Valdez watched cold beads of moisture sweating on the glass and hoped.

'The scrawny yellow cat crossed the road and crept into the whorehouse.'

He was pleased. He had almost doubled his word count and he knew where the cat was going. He patted his pockets, looking for a piece of paper, hunting for his pen, and he was still patting his pockets when the hard wooden chair on the other side of the table moved backwards with a scrape.

'Good evening, Mr Valdez. Do you mind if I sit down?'

Mr Valdez minded very much. There were plenty of other tables in the garden, plenty of other rooms in the house, but the Chief of Police, with his stained and crumpled suit that had once been white, bagged at the knees, bulging at the armpit, was not a man to be refused.

'Please, Commandante Camillo, sit down.' That was all he said. Short and to the point. No more than politeness deserved. No invitation to indulge in chit-chat.

The policeman sat with his legs flung out in front of him so his large feet stuck out into the gravel path. He was not exactly a hazard to navigation for the couples who strolled quietly through the shaded garden. They could pass him easily and safely enough. Camillo was simply making a statement about his presence, the way a dog does with a lamp-post.

Mr Valdez saw it and read it as the gesture of a bully, perhaps not even deliberate but the sort of thing a policeman like Camillo would do simply because, for years and years, he has been a policeman like Camillo in a country where policemen like

Camillo are permitted to exist. Valdez could almost sympathize with him: never knowing if he had a friend, never knowing if he was loved, never knowing if he were welcome to sit down at a table or simply too terrifying to be turned away, like a customer in a whorehouse who could never leave the whorehouse.

'I haven't seen you here before,' said Camillo.

'Oh, I think you probably have,' said Mr Valdez. 'In fact, I think you probably have a very accurate idea of when I was last here.'

'Well, I don't keep records, you know.'

'Someone does.'

'Yes,' said Camillo, 'I am almost sure someone does.'

'Are there many such files?'

'Must we talk shop?' Camillo gave a bored sigh and shifted in his seat so the butt of a pistol in its brown leather holster showed at his belt. 'I suppose we have a few. A few, you know. There are hardly any notables like yourself, Mr Valdez. A few trade unionists, the odd student radical – of course, colleagues in the capital like to keep an eye on them just in case somebody stops talking about making trouble long enough to make trouble. It's purely precautionary. If we know what people are doing, we can advise. It allows us to nip things in the bud and, you must understand, what's good for the hive is good for the bee. But you are not like them. You are not under suspicion. If we are concerned with you, it is only from a fatherly interest. We cherish you. You are a national treasure, Valdez.'

The 'Mr' had disappeared. He noticed that, tasted it in his mouth for a moment, wondered what it meant, if it was an attempt at friendship or another bullying slap like the unaccidental glimpse of that second pistol.

Camillo raised his glass so quietly that the ice made no sound. 'How is your dear mother?' he asked.

'I don't think this is really the place.'

'No, of course.' Camillo took another long swig and nodded across the garden into the shadows. 'Now that one – the tall one – she came here just two weeks ago, no, three weeks ago. Straight off the farm. Way up country. If you haven't tried her yet, I would. I'd recommend her. But you didn't tell me; how is your mother?'

'How do you know my mother?'

'Did I say I knew her?'

'But you knew my father.'

Camillo put down his glass as carefully as he had picked it up. 'What makes you say that?'

'He disappeared.'

'Fathers do that. They have secrets. They just,' he tiptoed a little two-fingered mannikin along the edge of the table, 'they just walk off. They just disappear.'

'Forgive me,' said Valdez, 'my experience is so limited. I had only one father and yet, as you say, so many of them seem to disappear. Fathers, sons, uncles, daughters. All of them here one day and vanished the next but, as you say, they all have secrets. I imagine there must be an entire city of vanished fathers, living happily with their mistresses, perhaps just across the Merino.'

The policeman hooked an ice cube from his glass with two fingers and crunched it. 'You should make that place the setting for your next novel,' he said. 'After you finish this one, of course. I hear it progresses well.'

'It progresses,' said Valdez with a nod. 'Will you be spending the rest of the evening here?'

'I think so, yes,' said Camillo. 'I think that tall one deserves another lesson. You?'

'I'm afraid I must be going.'

Camillo made no attempt to rise. 'Be sure to remember me to your mother,' he said.

'Remember me to your mother too – since you're staying,' said Mr Valdez, but he waited until he was back in the square before he said it.

He was very, very angry. He wanted a woman and he had been chased away by the Commandante like a naughty schoolboy, seen off, charged down by the big bull because he refused to rise to the challenge and lock horns, because he declined to see which of them might – might what? Was Camillo expecting the girls of the Ottavio House to give marks out of ten?

Mr Valdez stopped under a street lamp at the corner where the square met Cristobal Avenue. He scratched a long match off the rough stucco of the house front and lit a cigar, inhaled deeply.

He looked west, back towards his home just around the corner. He looked east, far away towards where Cristobal Avenue ran out in the Square of the September Revolution. Tonight was not the night for Madame Ottavio's. Not tonight, just in case. He would take a stroll, find something to eat, talk books in that nice bar by the university and, perhaps, drink a brandy in the Phoenix before bed.

IS IT NOT astonishing that, in a world full of icebergs, none of us ever sees the one looming towards his own ship? Far away to the north, after creeping millennia of travel, crawling its way over the pole, the ice finally reaches the sea, finally breaks free, and floats away. There are still perhaps thousands of miles of open ocean between us and it, thousands of miles of random winds and waves and invisible currents. If that iceberg broke off ten minutes later, if we left port ten minutes earlier, nothing would happen, but instead, always, unerringly, unfailingly, we on our fragile ship and the frozen, dripping, disappearing iceberg meet in the one place where we can destroy one another. That was how it was with Mr L.H. Valdez, literato, amorato, celebrato, and with Caterina. Who can say which of them was the ship and which the iceberg? It hardly matters. Each of them was destroyed, both were wrecked, and it could so easily have been otherwise.

Poor Caterina. Almost like a character from a novel by L.H. Valdez, she found she had a gift for sobbing. But, unlike Mr Valdez, Caterina was more and more convinced that she was going insane. There could be no other explanation. She had felt it creeping up on her for days – since Mr Valdez presented himself at the till in the Phoenix and she had made such an effort to be pleasant and polite but no more than that because he was so amazing and so wonderful and so terrifying and he frightened her so much. And then there was that stupid business with the note, that stupid 'I write' nonsense – as if he would care!

Mad, all of it pure madness, but then, that morning, in the corridor, the maddest madness of all. Pure distilled lunacy. Caterina slumped backwards in her chair, thumping her temples with the heels of her hands. What had she been thinking? How? Why? Every boy in class had wanted to get into her bed at one time or another. They had tried everything short of simply handing over their wallets.

'And I know why!' she said.

None of it worked. She didn't want to. She wasn't going to. Not with them. But then he'd been there, in the corridor, in his suit, smart and older and clever and she just felt it. She just turned round and saw him and felt it. And then she said it. Said that. What had possessed her?

And what if he told the Dean? Or Dr Cochrane? He'd be within his rights. He could have her flung off the course and, even if he didn't, he'd talk. Word would get out about that little tart on the maths course. Everybody would know. They'd speak of nothing else over coffee in the Phoenix.

'Oh, Jesus, Mary and Joseph. The Phoenix! I'll lose my job.'

She was done for. Without that job and the little bit of money it brought she would have to leave the university and go home to the farm. And her brother would hate her for wasting her chance, hate her for coming home to eat, hate her for being alive, and then she would have to get a job shelling beans or slaughtering chickens until she found a bean sheller or a chicken killer to marry. 'And they'll come,' she said. 'Just for a chance to get their hands on these.' She hugged herself and rocked on the chair.

Men. Stupid shallow bastards. Show them a nice pair of tits and they'll say anything, do anything, promise anything for a chance to crawl back into the cradle and play with them.

'But not L.H. Valdez.'

Caterina knew he could have any woman he wanted. Sophisticated society salonistes, dancers, movie stars, journalists, critics, professors – the wives of professors. He could have any of them and when some young girl, barely out of her teens, offered to lie down and part her thighs, right there in the corridor outside the toilets, he didn't even notice. That's how wonderful he was. He just walked right by as if he'd never heard. That was the kind of man he was. The boys from class would have grabbed her and done it right there on the floor, just so they could tell their mates, but not Mr L.H. Valdez. He had tried to save her blushes and pretend that he never even noticed she was there, so good and kind was he.

'God damn you, L.H. Valdez!' she screamed and she folded her arms across her wonderful breasts again and rocked in her chair and sobbed, her hair hiding her face, she rocked and sobbed and cried until with a child's grace, the rhythms of all three converged and she fell sleep.

If Caterina had stayed there, hunched in that chair, sleeping crick-necked until morning, all might have been well. But instead, when Erica from across the landing knocked on her door and announced that it was time to go out, she once more damned the name of L.H. Valdez and washed her face and painted her lips and went.

And, if Mr Valdez had chosen to ignore the threatening whisper of failure – for that was what it was – if, instead of leaving Madame Ottavio's (where six of the eight girls who worked there were only then arriving for the evening), he had stayed and made at least one of those girls very, very happy, how much different might life have been?

WHEN MR VALDEZ had walked the entire length of Cristobal Avenue, tugging on his cigar until its rich demerara smoke had soothed and calmed him and made him, once more, invincible, he found the newly named Square of the September Revolution empty and abandoned. It was a 'between time'. People who had gone out for the evening had already gone and now they were comfortable and happy in this bar or that café. Maybe, in an hour or two, when it was time to go home, when it was time to stroll with a lover or brawl with a rival or walk home, alone and rejected for another night, then the square would be busy again, but for now it was silent except for the click of his heels on the chessboard tiles alongside the river and the three toots of the flag-changing party on the evening ferry.

The green cross was flashing slowly above the chemist's shop on the corner, as if there were never quite enough current in the wires to sustain its glow. It fizzed and buzzed as Mr Valdez passed beneath it and into the shadows of the little calle that hid the doors of the Phoenix. And they were, truly, almost hidden. There were so many little, hidden places like this all over town, little bars, perfectly respectable cafés, even tiny chapels with secret, jewel-box interiors where the Consecrated Host, the actual physical presence of God, was exposed and old ladies prayed behind secret doors, camouflaged and made invisible by dreariness. Only an expert could find them, only a native who knew the city as well as the blue-haired Indians knew their way from tree to tree through the jungle.

So much was hidden and yet Madame Ottavio's stood brazenly in its square, unabashed, concealing nothing, as naked as the girls inside. Mr Valdez looked at his watch. He considered walking back there. It was still early. There was no reason why not. By the time he got there Camillo would probably have left.

But he might still be there. Or he might be leaving just as Valdez arrived. They might meet.

Mr Valdez pushed on the door of the Phoenix, swung it open and went down the stairs.

'Wouldn't you rather have sex?' he asked himself.

'I would,' he said. Yes, he thought he probably would. Asked to choose between a coffee in the Phoenix or sex, he would almost certainly choose sex but, asked to choose between an evening in the Phoenix or admitting that he had run away from Camillo, well, his mind was already made up. He would rather have coffee.

They called his name the moment he set foot in the room – that same bunch from the university, still sitting round, goading one another.

'Valdez, Valdez! Over here. Come on – settle an argument. You're an expert.'

He sat down. 'What?'

'The *Odyssey* or *Don Quixote*?'

'What?'

'Which is better?'

'What?'

'Well, it's a simple enough question. Which is better?'

'I say it's *Don Quixote*,' said De Silva, 'and Father Gonzalez agrees with me but Costa says . . .'

'I can speak for myself.'

'Costa – who's been in a boat once – says that long, weary Ancient Greek tour guide is better literature.'

'We'll stick by your decision,' said Costa. 'Whatever you say.'

'I don't care,' he said.

They looked at him.

'I don't care. Who cares? How could you care? Is this the best you've got to do on a Saturday night? Is it? Just to sit here picking away at things? It doesn't matter. None of you is ever going to write the *Odyssey* and none of you is ever going to write *Don Quixote*.'

'Well, we're all very sorry we're not in your league.'

'Oh, shut up, Costa. That's not the point. I'm never going to write *Don Quixote* either. That's not the point.'

'So what's the point? Come on, tell us.'

'Well, it's not this. Not this pointless jabber. Look, wouldn't you rather have . . .' and then he couldn't say it. He almost said it but, before he could say it, he stopped for half a breath and his courage failed him, the moment passed.

'You seem upset,' said Father Gonzalez. 'Everything all right, Chano?'

'I'm fine,' he said but it sounded snappy and ill-natured when it was a chance to sound frail and tired and winning. Mr Valdez knew he had broken the rules of the group and failed to play the role they had given him too long ago to remember. There was a hierarchy. They wanted to defer to him. They wanted to confect these stupid, candy-floss arguments about damn all and hold them up for his approval like little boys coming home from school, carrying something ghastly and gaudy for their mothers to swoon over. And he'd let them down. Instead of taking their pointless argument and holding it up to the light and saying how pretty it was, he had crumpled it up and dropped it in the bin.

'Look, wouldn't you rather have a brandy?' he said. 'I'll stand us all a brandy,' and he made that gesture again, raising his hand high in blessing, like a Pope, like a matador in the ring, and he called out to the waiter: 'Brandies here. Four brandies and coffee. And make them large ones.'

So that was how he made things right, by pouring brandy into them and pontificating mightily on Homer and Cervantes.

Years later when they talked about that night – and they often talked about that night – De Silva would point to that table in the corner and say: 'That's where we were sitting, all of us, the old gang, drinking brandy at that very table. Me, Costa there, Father Gonzalez there and L.H. Valdez sitting next to him right there – in that very chair.' He said it as if he were one of Father Gonzalez's brother Jesuits, attesting the authenticity of a holy relic, as if that worn old chair could be bound round with red string and sealed under wax, stamped with a bishop's insignum and venerated for ever by students of literature while they, his friends, basked in the glow of having known him.

'That was where we were sitting, just talking about nothing in particular, when the girl came in.'

They were on their third glass of brandy by that time although, when Costa and De Silva bought a round, they did not buy doubles. They were on their third glass of brandy and laughing again, their awkward little quarrel all forgotten, when the door opened and Erica came into the room. Nobody noticed. Nothing happened. And then, just a pace behind, came Caterina and the whole place changed.

A bunch of kids at a big table over by the kitchen doors started shouting and screaming and waving and Erica smiled and started to squeeze her way between the chairs to join them, although she must have known they were not screaming for her. She must have known because, even after she sat down, they kept shouting and howling for Caterina to come and join the party, but Caterina had stopped by the door. The moment she arrived she had spotted Valdez. She saw him and hesitated – nearly fled – but that would have been even worse so, instead, she pretended not to have noticed him and looked away at some far corner of the room and went to join her friends.

'We all saw her,' De Silva said. 'She was the sort of girl you looked at. She came into a room and people noticed. Of course we had no idea. Not then. In fact, I think she went up to that other table and kissed a boy. She did.'

De Silva remembered that and added it to the story. It was there the next time and, whenever he told it again, he remembered to include it as a perfect little eyewitness detail – the sort of thing that would make his Gospel believed, the sort of thing that was written down and added to magazine interviews and dissertations, the sort of thing that got him a lot of free drinks when he was an old man.

Caterina kissed a boy and she kissed him for longer than friend-liness demanded and then she looked across to the other corner of the room, just to make sure that everybody had noticed. They noticed. They looked at her with angry, envious eyes and wished. She saw it and smiled, took the boy's glass from his hand, just as he was about to drink, and finished his wine.

'Get me some more,' she said and he obeyed her meekly. While he was gone she gabbled with Erica and the others, looking back over her shoulder, watching them watching her.

They turned away, the others. They were dazzled by the glow of her. But not Valdez. He lifted his brandy glass to his nose and looked at her across it, letting the fumes fill him and counting, silently, inwardly. One, two, measuring his breathing, three, four. She dropped his gaze after 'five'. When he reached 'eight' she glanced back and found him still fixed on her. After two more heartbeats she looked away again.

'I have her,' he thought.

Mr Valdez took out his wallet and removed a card. Behind him Gonzalez and De Silva and Costa were laughing. He looked over his shoulder at them. They were trying so hard not to look at the girl that they did not dare look in his direction. Mr Valdez took out his pen and he wrote on the card.

WHEN COSTA REACHED across his desk, pushed aside the pile of papers and answered the telephone that was ringing under them, he said: 'Classics, hello.'

There was no reply.

When he said it again, and when there was still no reply, he hung up. 'I've served my country,' he said. 'You can't tell me about patriotism. Don't talk to me about loyalty. I won't do this.' But, like Valdez walking out of the whorehouse, he waited until he had replaced the pile of papers before he said it.

When the telephone rang a few seconds later in an office on the other side of the building, Father Gonzalez answered it and said: 'Department of History,' and when nobody answered he knew who was there.

'What do you want?' he said.

There was an electric muttering in his ear.

'But you said . . .'

'No.'

'I have no idea. Please believe me.'

'You said the last time.'

'He was with that girl.'

'Yes, that girl. Yes.'

'Dr Cochrane's class, yes.'

'No.'

'I'm sorry. I don't know. How would I know?'

'He doesn't take me into his confidence in these matters. He has rather more taste.'

'No, not even in the confessional. Mr Valdez has never made his confession to me and not even you could make me repeat it if he had. Not even you.'

Dear God, he prayed, give me the strength to make that true.

'All I know is what I saw. The place was packed. I'm not telling you anything that dozens of other people couldn't tell you.'

Father Gonzalez found himself wondering how many of those dozens of others had received a call like this today, how many might, how many would find the courage not to answer.

'He bought us a brandy – me a brandy.'

'No, I meant "me".'

'No, there was nobody else with us.'

'Nobody, just Valdez and me.'

'I'm not lying.'

'Yes, all right. Yes, Costa and De Silva, yes.'

'Yes, both at the university.'

I am not alone, thought Father Gonzalez, not the only one, perhaps not the weakest. Who else? De Silva, Costa, a waiter? Perhaps one of those boys at the other table? All of them, any of them. The child herself?

'I have no idea.'

'I'm not. I'm trying to be helpful. Please believe me.'

'Thank you.'

'I don't know. All I know is he sat with us for a while and then he went and joined her.'

'No, there was no falling out. Well, perhaps a little. But that was all forgotten by then. We were all getting on and then he just left.'

'I didn't say he left the café, did I? Did I say that? You're trying to trip me up.'

'No. He left our table. Yes, our table. Me and Costa and De Silva. He just got up with no word and went to the girl's table. He didn't say "goodbye" or "good evening" or "excuse me". He simply left.'

'Nothing. We just watched.'

'Yes. Pretty much, they welcomed him.'

Of course they welcomed him. It was a mark of triumph to be noticed by L.H. Valdez. Everybody at the university knows L.H. Valdez. People who wouldn't recognize the captain of the national football team know who L.H. Valdez is. People who don't know the stars of the telenovelas have heard of L.H. Valdez and, worse still, people who know the telenovelas inside out know him too. There are janitors who swill out the lavatories every day who walk around with cheap copies of his novels folded into the back pockets of their jeans, just in case they catch him having a piss, so they can wait and ask for his autograph. Good God, even the Engineering students have heard of him.

'There was a boy. He was talking to the girl.'

'Yes, that girl.'

'Nothing. Valdez just went and sat on the very end of the bench they were sitting on and he was just sort of perched there, almost falling off the edge. There really wasn't room for him. He had his leg stuck out to keep himself in place and he put his arm along the back of the bench as if to hold on and he was ignoring the boy, leaning right in front of him and across him to talk to the girl.'

'I didn't see that.'

'I am telling you the truth. I didn't see that.'

'No, no card, no message.'

'Fine. If that's what people tell you, then maybe he did. I have no idea. I didn't see it.'

'Look, I didn't spend every moment staring at him. I was with some friends and we were talking of other things. You know these things. You know. I'm trying to help you but our entire conversation is not taken up with a moment-by-moment commentary on what Mr L.H. Valdez is up to.'

He remembered De Silva leaning in close, talking in what passes for a whisper for people who have had several brandies. 'Shh. Say nothing. Don't look. He's hitting on the girl with the tits. For God's sake! I told you not to look. Didn't I? Didn't I say that? Costa, you take a look now. What's he doing, the lucky, lucky bastard?'

And then the girl had leaned across to speak to him.

'It went on like that for a bit and then there was another girl who joined in the conversation and a couple of young men at the far end of the table. Then the boy in the middle got fed up of being talked round and went away.'

'Just the other end of the table.'

'No, he didn't look pleased.'

'Nothing happened. Valdez and the girl talked. Other people talked with them. Then the other people talked less and less and they talked more and more.'

'I mean they just went away, turned round and spoke to somebody else, got on with other things. It's as I said; not everybody is quite as obsessed with L.H. Valdez as you appear to be.'

'Are you insane? In the Phoenix? L.H. Valdez? No, he did not.'

'And I'm telling you he did not kiss her. Not when we were there.'

'I have no idea.'

'They may have done, but I don't know whether they did or not. They were still sitting together on that same bench when we left.'

'De Silva and Costa and me. We all left together. We arrived together and we left together.'

'Home, I suppose.'

'I told you, they were still there.'

'Yes, there were a few. A couple anyway. I don't know their names. I don't! They're not in my classes. Maths, I suppose. Dr Cochrane.'

'I don't know. Before midnight anyway.'

'No.'

There was a heavy click and the line went dead.

The sun was coming in at the window. Father Gonzalez found that he had spent the entire conversation gazing at that portrait of St Max Kolbe which hung on the far wall, gazing into those sad eyes behind their round, steel-rimmed glasses, and he knew in his soul that he could have done what Max Kolbe did. If someone had asked him would he take their place in the death cell he could do it and do it gladly. He would wait there, singing and praying, starving to death, dying of thirst, until they came to inject him with carbolic acid. He could do that. He could face the ugliest death. But nobody threatened him with death. They threatened to tell.

Father Gonzalez put down the phone and went back to his marking.

OF COURSE, FATHER Gonzalez had given a truthful account of what had happened that night in the Phoenix. He tried not to, he tried to dissemble about who was there and what they did, but it was pointless. So many people had been there. They saw him, they saw Valdez, they saw the girl. Poor Father Gonzalez could not know which of them was a Judas, he only knew that he was. But, as much as he had struggled to limit himself to a strictly accurate account of events, it could not be a full one. Only the girl and L.H. Valdez knew what L.H. Valdez had said to the girl.

Mr Valdez remembered it vividly – every word – as he lay in bed at the grey of dawn and mournful tango whispered from the radio by his ear. He remembered how he had made that great leap across the chasm that separated his chair from her bench. She smiled. It was a nervous smile. The boy smiled. He moved up to make room. Mr Valdez had clung to that bench for exactly thirteen minutes before he succeeded in driving the boy away and he counted each one of them off on his elegant, silver watch as he sat, left arm outstretched along the back of the bench, holding on.

And, when the boy left and there was that gap, that narrow puddle of shiny, trouser-polished wood which she slid across, then his arm stayed there, along the back of the bench, around her. What could be more natural?

'I have something for you.' Mr Valdez remembered saying it as he kicked back the sheets and let the music drift into his head. Was there music in the Phoenix? He couldn't recall. There should have been. He painted it into his memory in careful dabs.

'I have something for you,' he said, when the others had noticed there was no place for them in this particular conversation and respectfully, dutifully, withdrawn to the other end of the table.

'I have something for you,' he said. When she looked at him, smiling, wondering, a little afraid, he knew. He reached into his jacket and took from the pocket of his perfect pink shirt, uncreased, not even slightly damp, the cuffs unfrayed, pristine, the links so, so right, a calling card and placed it in her hand.

Caterina looked at it. She looked at him.

He reached gently into her cupped palms and turned it over. He had written: 'I write.'

'I felt I should return the compliment,' he said.

She was thrilled. She was smiling. L.H. Valdez concentrated on looking at her lovely smile.

She said: 'Mr Valdez!'

'Please.' He took the card from her in careful fingers and, with his pen, his beautiful, thick, heavy fountain pen, that pen with its broad, gold nib, the very pen that wrote *The Old Man of San Tomé*, the same pen with which he had written 'the scrawny yellow cat crossed the road,' over and over, he scored once through 'L.H. Valdez' and, instead, he wrote 'Chano'.

She was delighted.

Mr Valdez found himself thinking of Faust. He had beguiled the woman of his dreams with a casket of jewels dredged up from the pits of Hell. Mr Valdez managed it with a scrap of cardboard – and not a very special scrap of cardboard either. There were dozens – it must be dozens – just like that one all over town and strewn across the country from here to the capital, all of them carefully marked with that same, unique, spontaneous signature, a deep, black score and 'Chano' repeated uniquely, spontaneously, again and again and again. Sometimes Mr Valdez wondered what had happened to all those little cards. Some, he felt sure, had finished in confetti when the women who once treasured them noticed that the warm and happy 'Chano' had suddenly ended in a dark and final full stop. He could imagine those – the ones a little too close to home, the ones with nothing to lose, no husband, no position, no reputation. Even worse, the ones who were willing to sacrifice all those things, the ones who ignored the rules of that very special game and expected him to do the same. Those were the ones who had to be pulled up short. 'It's been wonderful, darling,' he would tell them, 'and I'll remember this time always, but it would be better if we ended it now and quickly. Don't call this number again.' Theirs were the calling cards that had been torn to shreds.

But there were others, he liked to think, which were treasured like holy relics, like pressed flowers that still carried the faint scent of a warm, brief summer and delicious afternoons in shady gardens. They were precious souvenirs, taken out of secret places from time to time, touched and kissed by women reverent as nuns who found those little scraps of card stirred memories of times when they had been lewd as harlots. And that was no bad thing, thought Mr Valdez.

He congratulated himself on the number of dull marriages he had saved, the anguished suicides he had prevented just by a few shared afternoons of love – or something very like it. There were husbands in every bleak little town the length of the Merino who would have woken up one day to find their throats cut but for the kind attentions of Mr L.H. Valdez and they would bless his name for it if they only knew.

'Yes,' she said, 'You write. I know. And now I'm supposed to say "So what do you write?" and you say . . .' She stopped. She was remembering their conversation outside the toilets, daring him. She had taken a little too much wine. It made her brave. She could not hear the distant cannon crack of the ice sheet shearing off and tumbling into the sea, the iceberg setting off towards her.

Lying in his bed, reliving last night's adventures, Mr Valdez gloried in the thrill of it. She was so bold, this Caterina – his Caterina – for now, in that moment, he was more certain than ever that he would have her. She was challenging him, she was inviting him to join the dance.

'Then I say. Then I say . . .' He was smiling.

'Yes? What do you say?' She could not bring herself to look at him. All the breath seemed to have left her body and she concentrated instead on watching her fingertip as it trailed damply round the edge of her wine glass, 'Chano?'

'Then I say: "Wouldn't you rather have sex?".'

She dared to look at him again. 'Should I be polite now and pretend not to have heard?'

'I wasn't being polite. You frightened me.'

'I can hardly believe that. You must have had stupid girls fling themselves at you before now.'

'Not as often as you might imagine.' What a lie. What a story-teller you are, Chano.

They both laughed at that.

'Anyway,' she said, 'I decline to answer your improper and impertinent question.'

'And I decline to answer yours.' No, I don't, he thought. I'll answer it. You'll find out soon enough. I'll show you.

Oh, but not yet. Mr Valdez could hardly believe how strong he had been, how clever he was, how much he was enjoying not having her. How could there be any pleasure more intense than waiting for this pleasure? He gloried in it: that glass of wine, the next glass of wine, the coffee, a final, large brandy, paying the bill – he had especially enjoyed paying the bill. No counting up of who had what. No dividing it all up. He wasn't a student. He could afford it and he didn't have to make a show. Just a glance at the bill, a quick fold of notes and they left together, laughing their way up the stairs and out into the dark warmth of the street. And she was beside him, arm in arm, all the way down Cristobal Avenue, yes, even past the big glass doors of his apartment block, where he was so intent on watching his own reflection that he failed to notice the man in the tight suit walking a little behind, watching, all the way to her little flat where she said it again: 'Wouldn't you rather . . . ?' standing against him with her face turned up to his and her whole body pressed to him.

'I must go,' he said.

'No. Stay. Wouldn't you rather stay?'

'I must go. Soon. I promise. Soon.'

And then he kissed his own finger and laid it against her warm lips.

'Soon,' he said.

Mr Valdez walked quickly back up the avenue to his home, and when he arrived Mrs Marrom was waiting in the marble lobby, swinging her sandal from her toe and flicking angrily through a month-old magazine, pouting.

'Chano, you are so late! Ernesto has been called away to head office and I'm lonely.'

'That's lucky,' he said. 'So am I.'

Out on the avenue, the man in the tight suit wrote a line or two in his notebook and looked at his watch. There were still four hours of his shift to go and that union organizer from the chicken factory down in Cell 7 wasn't going to knock his own teeth out. He turned and walked back up the street. His feet hurt.

NOBODY ASKED DR Cochrane to bear witness to that night in the Phoenix. The telephone did not ring on the desk of Dr Cochrane. If it had, it would have jangled there alone, ringing and ringing pointlessly until the gardeners watering the laburnum trees down in the gardens below tilted their hats and looked up with annoyed frowns, while millions and millions of specks of dust, some of them stirred up from the crumbling textbooks that lined the walls, most of them – as anybody in the Medical Faculty would testify – the jettisoned skin particles of long-forgotten students, danced in the sunbeams streaming through his window.

Dr Cochrane was not in his office. Dr Cochrane was not at home. He was not in the Phoenix and he was not strolling, pointlessly, in the gardens of the Ottavio House. Dr Cochrane had awarded himself a holiday.

He had no lectures to give and there was a large envelope pinned to his door with a note, announcing that he would not be available that day, inviting his students to leave any messages for his later attention. Nobody left any messages.

When the Dean of the Faculty of Mathematics – a man who never expressed any admiration for the late Colonel Presidente, nor made any comment on the present Colonel Presidente – saw the note and tutted his disapproval about 9.30 that morning, Dr Cochrane was already far away.

A couple of hours earlier, Dr Cochrane had joined a throng of travellers at the quayside where he was jostled and bumped along the broad gangway of the Merino ferry and up onto the waiting ship. Dr Cochrane knew the old ferry well.

It delighted him that, just below the stern rail, where lovers liked to lean and watch the churn of the propellers and gaze at the arrow wake streaming away from home, where years of paint had been layered on, as thick as wedding-cake icing, he could still read the words 'Hippocampo' and 'Glasgow'. It was a Scottish ship, as Scottish as his ancestor the Admiral and perhaps only a little more Scottish than Dr Cochrane himself.

He often stood at the river's edge to watch her tie up, waiting for the moment when one more lorry would roll down the clanging iron gangway and shift enough weight onto dry land to let the painted Plimsoll line appear from beneath the green-greasy river water. It showed the captain had faith in his old ship. He knew her. He knew what she could take. He knew she would not let him down. Dr Cochrane approved of that buccaneering defiance of the rules, just as the old Admiral would have done. But he found it easier to approve when he was safe on shore and not slipping across the oily deck with a host of other passengers, hurrying to claim a place close to the lifebelts. After all, the Merino was very wide.

Dr Cochrane drove such thoughts from his mind as he tucked his cane under his arm and gripped the handrail which was still, more or less, recognizable under layer upon layer of leprous paint and climbed up the worn metal stairway to the First Class deck.

A strange thing happened to Dr Cochrane as he climbed those steep stairs.

He seemed to unfold a little when he reached the top deck and, miraculously, he no longer needed his cane. He held it in his fist like a sword, the way the Admiral might have gripped a cutlass as he came storming down an enemy deck. He felt young.

The First Class accommodation was directly under the bridge deck. Lifeboats hung in reassuring garlands around the rails, strung together with tarry ropes and looped with automatic lamps which, the signs claimed, would light on contact with the water. Dr Cochrane could hear the captain up above, just out of sight, giving his commands in a quiet, confident voice as electric bells clanged and radio speakers squawked their replies.

From far below, through the soles of his shoes, Dr Cochrane felt the powerful stir of something awakening. At the back of the ship, the water gathered itself into a knot like clotted emeralds, swelled and boiled over, creamed and foamed. Nothing happened. And then, so slowly that at first he doubted his own senses, the ship began to move. Dr Cochrane watched a yellow beer can trapped in the narrow strip of water between the dockside and the ship. The gap was opening, widening towards the prow, and the suck of water from behind made the can rush towards the back of the boat, spinning through the narrowing gap, turning and tilting, into the shadow of the stern and then, suddenly, plucked down under the water. If he had been a poet, Dr Cochrane would have found inspiration for a sonnet in that, but he was a mathematician and he followed the can downwards in a turmoil of parabolic equations, measuring the rush and swirl of it as it went. And then the gap at the back of the ship opened. Little by little the concrete columns along the dockside began to appear from the stern shadows, the tops of them hung with old tyres, huge iron bolts holding the pillars in place, lazy green water surging around them as, at last, the ship lost its grip on the land.

Dr Cochrane could deceive himself no longer. The ship was moving. He felt sick. He spread his legs and braced himself against the rail and felt his stomach heave. In the bar of the First Class saloon the glasses on the shelf stood without so much as a tremor, the beer in the necks of the bottles was dead level. Dr Cochrane suffered a surge of shame and promised himself that, for the Admiral's sake, he would not vomit.

He concentrated. He turned his face into the wind and fixed his eyes on the horizon. It was flat. It was constant. Far ahead there was a squadron of pelicans flying along the river in an undulating line. Somehow they managed to match their movements to the very opposite of whatever the river was doing. If it rolled like olive oil in a bottle, they dipped to meet it. If it dropped away, they climbed a little with an easy flick of prehistoric wings. He felt the boat rise and fall under him as if it were ploughing through breakers.

His agony went on. He gripped the rail. His palms were slick with sweat, his mouth thick with spit. He was looking ahead to the end of the harbour wall and the little lighthouse stuck on the very tip of it like an icing-sugar castle. They would be in the river after that. There would be wind. It would strike the side of the ship. There would be waves in the river and the waves and the wind would act on the motion of the ship. He was ready. But then a sudden swirl of smoke, greasy with the smell of diesel, whipped down from the funnel and Dr Cochrane tasted bile at the back of his throat.

He stood there like that, a clammy sweat leaking from beneath his hat band, for almost two hours until it was time for the flag-changing ceremony that marked midstream.

For those few moments when he stood bareheaded, waiting for the whistle toots which would signal that the flag, out of view behind the bridge, had been properly dipped, properly hoisted, like a widow changing her loyalties with a new wedding ring, Dr Cochrane was convinced he would vomit at any second.

The heat of the sun beat down on his bare head while the

breezes of the river mopped his sweating brow with cool kisses. It was agony. He looked about for some place he could throw up discreetly. Not over the rail. The First Class deck was sharply stepped over Standard Class and, even in his distress, Dr Cochrane took pity on the family below, sitting in the sunshine with their picnic. He thought of fleeing through the First Class saloon to the toilets but he knew he could never make it without disgracing himself so he did the only thing he could do. At the very moment of the third and last blast on the whistle, just as the ferry lurched forward again over the imagined border, Dr Cochrane puked in his hat. Retching at the sight of it, he carried it like a sick-room basin and quietly, trying not to attract attention, he placed it under one of the wooden benches that lined the deck and returned to the rail, where he slumped in an agony of nausea and humiliation.

'Here, wash your mouth out.' There was a hand on his shoulder and a glass of water held in front of his half-closed eyes.

'Just spit it on the deck. In this heat it'll be gone soon. You'll feel better for it.'

Dr Cochrane did as he was told. 'Thank you,' he said.

'No, no. Thank you for coming. I know what it costs you.'

'I feared you were not aboard.'

'I waited until we were back across the line. I hid. I'm good at hiding. They can't touch me here.'

'Old friend, they could reach you anywhere if they knew where you were.'

'You worry too much. I'm small fry.'

'They don't forgive, they don't forget.'

'Here. Take a little of this brandy. Just a drop. It'll settle your stomach.'

If the captain of the ferry had chosen that very moment to fill his pipe, if he had turned to the mate and said: 'You have the wheel, Pedro,' and walked out on to the wings of his bridge, as sometimes he had to do when getting into dock was proving particularly troublesome, he could have looked down and seen two friends, one of them foolishly hatless, shoulder to shoulder, sharing a flask. Nothing odd about that. Nothing to attract attention.

But if the captain had known his patriotic duty, he would have turned his ship around and radioed ahead to have Camillo and half the battalion of police waiting for his return.

'I feel a little better now,' said Dr Cochrane. He handed back the silver flask. 'Thank you.'

'Good. Why don't we sit down on one of these benches in the shade?'

'Yes. But not that one. Let's move round a little.'

Dr Cochrane collapsed onto the bench, its wooden slats pressing uncomfortably into his backside, the hot, painted metal of the First Class saloon pressing against his back.

'I do feel better,' he said. 'A little better.'

'Good. And how are things?'

'Much the same, you know. Nothing much changes. We go along just as always. The faces change but only at the top of the tree. The truth is one colonel's uniform is much like another.'

'It's the same across the river. Everything changes and it always stays the same. Living over the Merino is like looking back from inside a mirror.'

'It's hard to believe we could have cared so much,' said Dr Cochrane.

'No. No, not really. Hope is a powerful narcotic.'

They were quiet for a while and then, as old men will do sometimes, they found themselves holding hands.

'Anyway, how is the boy?'

'Good. Very good,' said Dr Cochrane. 'But he's not a boy any longer, you know.'

'I know, I know. It's just. Well, you understand.'

'Yes. Of course.'

'Did you bring a book?'

'There is no book this year, I'm afraid. He's working on something – I saw him only the other day, sitting at the side of the river and scribbling away madly in his notebook, filling it with page after page of wonderful things. It's coming along. Perhaps next year. I'm sure it will be ready for your next birthday.'

'I am so proud of him, old friend.'

'And well you should be. He's a national treasure. Nobody understands us like Chano. We read his books and it's as if he's right there, talking to us of ourselves.'

'Do you think that? I'm glad. I like to think that. Those books are the only way I have to know him and it's good to think that he really is that man. Is he happy?'

'Is he happy?' Dr Cochrane was amazed. 'Are you? Am I? How can I tell you that? Ask me about the weather or the next month's Lottery numbers. Ask me something easy.'

'But he is well?'

'He is well and admired and honoured and wealthy and – more – he is safe.'

'That's all I wanted. All I ever wanted.'

'I know.'

'And still no wife.'

'No. He is very busy. Too busy for a wife.'

'But . . . ?'

'Oh, no! Oh, put your mind at ease about that. Your Chano is very much a ladies' man. Rather too much for his own good.'

Dr Cochrane decided not to mention anything about the Ottavio House. A man who was content to see his colleagues in such a place might, all the same, be uncomfortable to have his father hear of it.

'That's good. That's good. Not that there is anything wrong with. Well, with that kind of thing.'

'I am not offended,' said Dr Cochrane. 'My own father would not have been delighted to have a mariquita for his heir.'

There was a moment's awkwardness. 'And his mother? How is Sophia?'

'Just the same. Still sad. She never,' Dr Cochrane's sentence lost its way, as Dr Cochrane's sentences often did, 'well, she never, really.'

'No. She never did. She couldn't. I'm sorry.'

'It was for the best.'

'Was it, Cochrane? Nearly forty years and for what? Nothing's changed. And, you know, in all that time, I don't think they tried to kill me even once.'

'But if you had stayed, they would have. They would have killed you and they would have done worse. They'd have made you talk and they'd have used the boy to do it. The boy and Sophia. They are alive now because they think you are dead – them and God knows how many others. Me. You saved my life!'

They looked straight ahead, so as not to look at each other, to where the bow of the ferry was nudging through the syrupy waters of the Merino towards the opposite shore.

After a time, Dr Cochrane said: 'Have you any more of that brandy?'

'Of course. And I brought sandwiches. And birthday cake.'

'I don't think I could. My stomach, you know. But you go ahead. I will toast your anniversary in your own excellent brandy.'

'This is what we've come to, eh, Cochrane? Two firebrand revolutionaries, two comrades, two dangerous enemies of the state, eating birthday cake on a filthy old ferry.'

'One of us is eating birthday cake. I'm too busy throwing up in my hat.'

'Yes, I wondered about your hat.'

'I can get another one,' said Dr Cochrane.

'Yes, and for the record, I am officially not laughing.'

All the way across they sat together in the sunshine talking for hours of their lives, how they lived, what they hoped for in the days when they still had hope and, eventually, because all journeys eventually end, they reached the other side of the river.

'So that's it for another year,' said Dr Cochrane.

'I suppose so. I should go. Thank you again for coming. Thank you for watching over them. You are a good friend.'

'I am happy to do it,' said Dr Cochrane.

'You know, I've noticed, you never ask what I do, where I live, how I make my living. You never even ask my name.'

'If I don't ask, you won't tell me. If you don't tell me, I won't know and, if I don't know, they can't make me tell.'

'We worry too much. Sometimes I think, I'm almost sure, I could come back. I could cross over. But I'm afraid to go.'

'I'm crossing over right now and already I'm afraid. I'll be sick all the way. Stay here, Valdez. Stay here.'

THERE IS SOMETHING indescribably indulgent about a coffee tower. As cakes go, a coffee tower, properly made and well presented, is the closest thing there is to a logical proof for the existence of God. On the one hand, the atheists argue, given an infinite supply of flour and butter and endless batteries of eggs and millions of copper pans of boiling water all jostled together in an eternal kitchen from the day the stars were born until now, it is possible that choux pastry could simply have happened. More complicated things have simply happened, after all – bedbugs and bacteria and blue whales, for example. But then they would also have to believe that an infinity of bakers had dolloped the new-born choux out onto immemorial parchments and, over endless, uncountable millennia, baked them into buns and pierced them to let the steam escape and cooled them and filled them with the thickest, most perfectly coffee-scented cream, rich and soft and brown as the thighs of that new girl who has just started work at the Ottavio House.

A Florentine biscuit, with its almonds and its glacé cherries all cemented together in a circle of bitter chocolate, is wonderful enough but there is something gravelly and random about a Florentine and there are bits that can stick in the teeth, nuts that unerringly pierce the suspect filling.

A coffee tower will never do that. A coffee tower never disappoints. It sits, shivering on its tiny paper doily, fresh and bright and chill, cowering like a captured cloud and crowned with a little chocolate disc, waiting to be devoured like a virgin bride.

Father Gonzalez, if he was wise, would put aside all his theology and his dogma and his encyclicals, he would take the Catechism and the Spiritual Exercises and throw them out the window and, instead, in front of every doubting unbeliever, he would place a clean white saucer with a coffee tower in the middle of it and simply say: 'Here is proof. See you at church on Sunday.'

Mrs Sophia Antonia de la Santísima Trinidad y Torre Blanco Valdez was sitting now in front of just such a coffee tower, at a table in the Members' Dining Room of the Merino Polo Club, looking out across a tray of cakes and through the French windows to the terrace.

The terrace was England, or what she imagined England to be; old stone and small, modest flowers in becoming, ladylike hues. Nothing extravagant. Nothing ostentatious. Everything a calm dignity.

A few people stood there, looking down at the polo field with its faraway noises of horses and hoof beats, its grunts and cries, the thwack of the mallets, the polite applause. She had spent most of the afternoon down there already, sheltering from the sun under an enormous and beautiful hat, sitting in a deckchair on the edge of the field, knees together, legs locked and tilted a little to one side in that graceful, uncomfortable slant she had learned as a girl when her ankles were slim and in a perfect, one to one-and-two-thirds ratio to her calves. After so long it should be easier, less achingly painful. Life was unfair. Mrs Sophia Antonia de la Santísima Trinidad y Torre Blanco Valdez had learned that lesson long ago too.

Polo was so noisy and distressing, she found. Everything about it was a fuss and a bother; those nasty hard balls, all that impolite barging about, jangling, creaking harness, sweat and lather and long, ugly strands of drool arcing and flicking from the bridles of the ponies. No, she was almost sorry she had ever permitted Chano to get involved, but his father, his father . . .

Still, she had done her duty. Nobody could ever accuse her of failing in her duty. She had sat there for hours in the heat, bored to the point of actual distress. She had struggled, all ungainly, out of that ridiculous deckchair, forced at last to accept a helpful arm from a nice young man, and made her way to the ladies' room and then, as if to prove her devotion, she had returned to watch the end of the game and see Chano lift the cup. She had done her duty.

And now this was to be her reward. A proper table, with a proper cloth and nice, heavy cutlery and thin cups, nice thin cups with gold rims and painted roses. She deserved it. Just a little more waiting, just a little, until Chano was showered and changed and fit to be seen with his mother and all this would be hers. Mrs Valdez fiddled pointlessly with the silver spoon in her saucer. It chimed cheerfully against her cup. She admired the sugar lumps in the bowl. Real sugar lumps, random, irregular sugar lumps broken from real loaf sugar. The real thing.

'Coffee, Mrs Valdez?'

A waiter. A real waiter. Not a boy making a little extra money to get himself through university but a proper waiter with a little silver in his nicely oiled hair, trousers nicely pressed, clean nails, somebody who took a little trouble, somebody who deserved a tip.

'Coffee, Mrs Valdez?'

And there, behind him, sitting alone at a table for two, a man chewing his fingernails, a man wearing brown shoes with a black suit, a man who looked away quickly when he saw that she had noticed him, a man who looked down at the table where there was no coffee, no cakes, no cutlery, a man ignored by every waiter in the room.

'Coffee, Mrs Valdez?'

She raised just a finger in refusal. 'No. No thank you. I will wait.'

The waiter withdrew with a bow. She was so happy. He had called her by her name, not 'Madam' but 'Mrs Valdez'. He knew who she was. How wonderful. She went back to looking out the French windows with a smile.

And that was how Chano found her when he came upstairs from the locker room. She was facing away from the door, every perfect hair in place, her back cut in half by the rail of her chair, a fine gold chain glinting on her neck.

Walking towards her across the dining room, Mr Valdez had a sudden moment of recollection; seeing his mother again like that, her hair piled up and her shoulders appearing from the bench seat in the front of his father's car, his father sitting beside her at the wheel, the soft, rhythmic 'schlubbbb' of lamp-posts passing the open window. In those days, Mr Valdez remembered, he could control traffic lights with the power of his mind, making them flick from red to green all the way along Cristobal Avenue to their house on the hill. There were frightened, whispered discussions in that car – never in the house, always in the car, all of them bundled in together at any time of the day or night, driving without arriving, never going anywhere but home. Looking back now, Mr Valdez understood how his parents had tried to make things seem ordinary, but their fear seeped into the back seat and under the blanket where he lay sleeping. He knew somehow – he could not think how – that his father was in danger. He was afraid. There was the scent of warm plastic in his nose, the upholstery of the seat he lay on. It was dusty red and stamped with a pattern like woven rattan and he prayed there, offering God his power over traffic lights in exchange for his father's life.

His father had vanished, but Mr Valdez lost his ability to control the traffic lights. Every time he got in a car, he remembered why he did not believe in God.

'Hello, mother,' he said.

She held her face up to receive a kiss. 'Hello, darling. Well done. I thought you played so well. You were wonderful.'

He had been wonderful. He was wonderful. Mr Valdez was well aware of just how wonderful he was, with his perfect blazer and his perfect hair and his perfectly polished shoes.

'Oh, you smell good.'

And his perfect sandalwood cologne. But he would have preferred to have his wonderfulness acknowledged by someone rather more discriminating than his mother. For her, everything he did was 'wonderful'. It had always been 'wonderful'. Every glue-dabbed, paint-blotched creation he had carried home from school was 'wonderful', just like his novels. Exactly like his novels, in fact. Not more wonderful in any way. A paper calendar, a cardboard cat, a novel that made grown men weep, they were all equally valuable because he had made them and she treasured them all.

Mrs Valdez had an entire shelf of his novels in her flat. He made sure that she always got a copy of everything he wrote. She made sure that they were always on display, in view but out of the sunlight, always dusted. Mrs Valdez showed them to everyone who came to visit. She pointed them out to her friends but she never lent them. She conversed knowledgeably about them; plot, character, those particularly vivid passages of description. Perhaps even Señor Dr Cochrane would have regarded her with honour as another aficionada, but she knew nothing more of her son's books than what appeared in the review columns of the Sunday papers. She never read them. Mr L.H. Valdez knew all of this. When he lovingly autographed his third novel with a personal dedication, he delivered it to her flat with a 5,000-corona note slipped between the pages halfway through the book. It was still there when he checked three weeks later. Six months after that, on another visit to his mother's house, Mr Valdez took the money away again and tucked it back in his wallet.

He spent it at Madame Ottavio's that evening and he had never enjoyed a visit more. The thought that it was, somehow, Mama's little treat made every moment that much sweeter.

In spite of that, Mr Valdez still gave her the first copy of all his books, but the fourth novel and all the other novels sat on her shelves, not with money between their pages, but with some very unusual pictures, clipped from the pages of gentleman's magazines. She never found them – he hoped she never would – but it made him happy to know they were there.

Mrs Valdez poured the coffee. 'Are you taking sugar these days, darling?' She hovered the tongs above the cup. 'I don't, but they've taken so much trouble here and it's nice to see. Not those silly paper packets.'

'No.'

She laid her hand down on his and Mr Valdez saw his skin move and ruche under the weight of her touch, loose over his flesh like the skin on a chicken. She had skin like that – old woman's skin – and now she had given it to him. He adjusted his spoon in his saucer. It gave him an excuse to move his hand away.

'Thank you for coming,' he said. 'Were you very bored?'

'Nonsense. It was thrilling. And you were wonderful, darling. So many goals.'

'I think I scored twice in the whole tournament.'

'Well, those others were very selfish. They kept you out of the game.'

'Mama, I play at Number 3. It's not my job to score goals.'

'Well, you were obviously – cake, darling? – the best one in the whole team and you had the nicest horses.'

'Ponies, Mama.'

'Ponies are smaller, darling. Those are definitely horses.'

'Yes, Mama.'

'Anyway, yours were by far the nicest and anybody could see you were best at riding and best with that hitting thing – the stick.'

'Mallet.'

'Yes, the mallet, so they might at least have put you in charge.'

'They did, Mama, that's why I'm Number 3.'

'Then, they should have let you have more of the ball. But you were terrific, in spite of them, wonderful! Have a cake, darling.'

With a magician's grace she slid a modest pastry off the silver-plated cake stand and on to a plate.

'I think I'll have the coffee tower – you don't mind, do you, darling? I've had my eye on it and I do like a coffee tower although I shouldn't really. You could have it, Chano, darling. It wouldn't add a feather to your weight, not with all that running about that you do. You have it, darling.'

She lifted her pastry fork and gave the cake a little, half-hearted, sacrificial nudge towards him.

'Don't be silly. You must have it.'

'Well, if you're absolutely sure, darling.' She had done her duty. She had thought first of others. She was satisfied. 'I do like a coffee tower. I always think, it's silly I know, they are like a promise of better things to come.' She sank the edge of her fork into the choux and a tiny puff of air farted demurely through the cream like a bishop passing wind at a First Communion. 'Will there be better things to come for me, Chano?'

'Always, Mama. Rainbows and butterflies always.'

'And grandchildren?'

'And coffee towers, endless coffee towers, and you will never be one day older.'

'And grandchildren?'

'Mama, how can you always be young if you are a grand-mother? You'd hate it.'

'Don't I deserve grandchildren?' Mrs Valdez held a soft and delicious piece of coffee tower in her mouth and savoured it. The moment or two it took to swallow meant that she did not have to say: 'After all I have done.' That would have been unforgiv-able. Duty did not count the cost. Duty did not demand a reward. 'People say that you should marry, Chano.'

'Sadly, nobody I know thinks I should marry them, Mama.'

'You'd only have to ask. You're in the prime of life, successful, respected, wealthy. I'm sure I could help you find any number of nice, clever girls to choose from.'

'Mama, stop that. That's indecent.' And then he remembered the other night and the Ottavio House and all those other girls to choose from.

'How do you know Camillo, the Commandante of Police?' he asked.

'I don't.' But there was a chilliness in the way she set about stirring her coffee – coffee that contained no sugar – which made him disbelieve her. 'I know *of* him of course. Everybody knows who he is, but I don't know him.'

'You never met?'

'Didn't I just say that?'

'Only he asked me to pass on his regards.'

Mrs Valdez put down her pastry fork and wiped carefully at the corners of her mouth, so carefully that, though her napkin came away with tiny dabs of octoroon-coloured cream on it, there was no trace of lipstick.

'What did he say? Exactly. Tell me exactly what he said.'

'I don't know, Mama. Just something about asking to be remembered to you. It was only a politeness, I'm sure.'

'That man is incapable of politeness.'

'You said you didn't know him.'

'I don't know him. But he was horrible. He is horrible. He was horrible forty years ago and he is horrible now. He stood outside our house every day for weeks. He never spoke a word. Never said "Good morning" or "Good evening", he just stood there, looking, the way a cat sits looking at a garden pond, watching the goldfish going round and round. Papa knew there was no way out, just like the goldfish know. Stay away from that man, Chano. He is the Devil.'

Mrs Valdez was tearful and upset. Mrs Valdez was never tearful and upset. He pretended not to notice.

'That man killed your Papa, Chano.'

On the other side of the room the man with the brown shoes was looking at her again.

'Now, you can't know that,' said Mr Valdez, although he believed it to be true.

'I know it and if you don't think I deserve grandchildren, then ask yourself if your poor Papa does. Ask yourself that. God alone knows what that poor man suffered. Do you want his name to disappear with him?'

Mr Valdez found himself thinking of Caterina. She was young enough. She could bear him a son – perhaps many sons – and pretty daughters too. But she was not the sort of woman to take home to Mama. Not the sort of woman who could sit here, in the Merino Club, and eat cakes and drink coffee with Mama. Who was she? Who were her people? What did they do? Who did they know? Who were their relatives? How could she be the mother of his child, she who was herself a mere child? No, she was just a child. And he did not love her. He wanted her but he did not love her. He had always imagined that he would love his wife, at least for a little. But wives were so untrustworthy, and who knew that better than L.H. Valdez? What if he loved a wife and she turned out to be like Maria Marrom? What if she turned out to be like his mother? He did not want a wife.

And yet, knowing all that, fearing all that, when Mama demanded a grandchild, as she had so often done before, his mind flew to Caterina. Nothing like that had ever happened before.

'Could I be falling in love?' Mr Valdez wondered. He was aghast. He was afraid. He put his hand out, flat on the table, inviting his mother to take it, pretending it was so he might comfort her.

'Why did you never marry again, Mama?'

He tried to imagine her, for forty years, in an empty bed, without a man's heat. For forty years!

'Oh, Chano,' she said. 'I am already married.'

WHEN MR L.H. Valdez got out of bed the next morning he felt a little stiff and sore. There was an ache in his shoulders and a creaking in the long muscles of his thighs where he had gripped the saddle the day before. It surprised him. It made him think. Sometimes now he ached all over after a polo match, every joint complaining and quietly screaming. Sometimes a night of brandy would leave him with a head like angry cotton wool. Sometimes, at Madame Ottavio's, once was enough. Perhaps Mama had been right. Perhaps time was running out, even for him.

He stepped out of the shower, towelled himself, chose a soft shirt in dusty sky blue and put on a clean, caramel-coloured suit with the faintest, finest dog-tooth pattern just barely discernible in the silky weave.

His big blue notebook was still lying where he left it, dumped on his desk like a corpse in an alley. He picked it up and opened it. The first five pages were ruined. He ripped them out, folded them, tore them in half and dropped them in the rattan basket that sat beside his chair. There was a clean page in front of him. Mr Valdez smoothed it down with the edge of his hand – not that it was rough or crumpled but he simply wanted to stretch the paper, line it up, make it straight and smart and neat like a parade ground where his words could stand in proud rows, ready for inspection.

Mr Valdez took the top off his pen and, halfway down the

page, he wrote: 'The scrawny yellow cat crossed the road and crept into the whorehouse.'

It looked very fine. It was a good start.

Mr Valdez picked up his notebook, patted his pockets for the reassuring jingle of his keys and left the flat. The lift was slow and clanking. On the way down it stopped at the second floor, where Mrs Nero, the wife of the dentist, and her daughter got in. They nodded politely but that was all. Mr Valdez was surprised by the girl – what was her name? Was it Rosa? Was that really Rosa. Did she have a baby sister? He was nearly sure it was Rosa, but she had changed. She was obviously a little girl when, just a few days before, she had been on the verge of blossoming into woman- hood and Mr Valdez had been planning wonderful things for her in only a year or two. A year or two? No, more like eight or ten, surely. She would be twenty and he would be, well, older. Much older. The wrong side of fifty. Much the wrong side of fifty and sliding downhill towards sixty. Mr Valdez was disgusted with himself. It was out of the question. And in ten years' time, would he still be drinking gimlets in the gardens of the Ottavio House like Camillo? Or spending his afternoons with Maria Marrom? No, that was impossible. She would be an old woman. Maria had two or three summers left. He couldn't possibly. Not with an old woman – a woman in her sixties, a woman like Mama!

Perhaps with a woman he loved. Perhaps with a wife – a wife of his own. Perhaps with a much younger wife who adored him it might be possible still.

The lift came to a halt with a shudder at the ground floor and Rosalita and her mother got out. Mr Valdez pressed the button again and went on, down to the basement where it was dusty and greasy, where it smelled of hot oil and rubber and petrol fumes, where his car was waiting.

Mr Valdez drove an extravagant, imported, American automobile. In a life lived with quiet good taste where nothing was designed to attract attention, where everything was understated, where a peacock-blue handkerchief was his greatest flamboyance, the car stood out.

It was a classic, just as much as *Don Quixote* or the *Odyssey*. It came from a time when cars were heroic, when they offered promissory notes to a world of adventure. It was designed for commuting in the way that the galley of Odysseus was designed for commuting and it spoke with a whisky-flavoured tickle in its throat, like a beautiful nightclub singer who has known better days, like a leopard, content to gambol on a chain held by a beautiful woman but always ready to turn and devour her. It had vanes, swooping and arcing like fish tails, like the coachwork of Neptune's chariot, like the spread of an eagle's wing. Its tyres were white, its seats were leather and it gleamed in metallic Agua de la Nilo green.

Mr Valdez knew exactly how quickly he could drive up the ramp from the garage and out on to Cristobal Avenue, fast enough to make the tyres squeal impressively on that last turn but not quite fast enough to make the twin exhausts scrape as he crossed the pavement and slipped out into the traffic. Normally Mr Valdez liked to walk to work. He liked the city. He liked being seen but, on that particular day, he had an errand well beyond the university on the other side of town and he could not walk there and back and still arrive in time for his first lecture of the day.

He drove through town with the top down, slowly, very slowly, creeping along Cristobal Avenue in a long line of traffic, enjoying the sunshine until he arrived almost at the junction of University Avenue, where it curves down to meet the Merino. Ahead of him there were four cars, two trucks and a bus and he knew the lights would change before he reached them. A few moments later, the car in front of his slipped across the junction as the lights flashed to red, just as he knew they would.

Mr Valdez looked at the little black clock ticking on the dash-board. It was a shortly after nine and safe to turn on the radio with no fear of one of those dreadful news broadcasts and their hourly updates on the thoughts and deeds of the Colonel Presidente. How he loved that moment: gripping the ivorene knob with its brass cap and those deep ridges, once black with forgotten dirt but which he had lovingly cleaned with spirit and a cocktail stick, the pressure, the resistance, the solid, dependable 'click' that spoke of quality and craftsmanship like the cover shutting securely on his grandfather's watch.

The radio played. It played tango, always tango, and Mr Valdez found himself softly mouthing the words of 'La Soledad', so simple, so heartbreaking, so perfect.

> You came to me, as poetry arrives in song,
> You showed to me
> A world to which I don't belong,
> A world of love
> Without condition – right or wrong.

The lights changed. Mr Valdez slipped the car into gear and dropped the clutch.

> I was a fool. I hid my heart.
> And now I can't believe you're gone.
> Afraid to love, my heart was eaten up by fear.
> You came to me
> But I was scared to love you, dear.
> The sun has gone
> And, darling, how I want you near.
> The night has come and we're apart,
> My song of loneliness is here.

Mr Valdez turned right, into the broad highway along the bank of the Merino, changed gear and accelerated away. Before he reached the big bend in the road, the bomb went off on the steps of the university, but the engine roar was so loud that he didn't even notice.

COMMANDANTE CAMILLO KNEW a great deal about asking questions. He knew there were times when it was important not to ask a question unless he already knew the answer. He knew there were times when it was important not to ask a question unless he really, really wanted to know the answer. He knew there were times to ask questions when no answer mattered, when the point was not to ask a question but just to have an excuse to hurt somebody – whatever answer they gave. He knew there were times when any answer would do because all he wanted was that moment of defeat and concession and admission and not the information it contained. But Commandante Camillo also knew that, if he wanted to find something out, then the best questions to ask were the shortest ones.

Before he went down to the university, Commandante Camillo closed the door of his office, sat down at his desk and placed a call to the capital. It took a long time to make the connection and, while he waited, ambulances and fire engines tore past his window in a storm of sirens.

Then the line gave a click and Commandante Camillo asked for an extension. Far away, on another desk in another police station, another telephone rang. The man who answered did not give his name, so the Commandante said: 'This is Camillo. We've had an explosion. Yes, it's a bomb. So what I want to know is; is it one of ours? Yes, I'll wait.'

Commandante Camillo heard the man put the faraway telephone down. He was not certain that he heard the sound of footsteps walking away but he was sure of a heavy metal file drawer opening. A few seconds later he said: 'Absolutely nothing to do with us? Right.'

He put on his jacket. This would make life a little more difficult. If the government had planted the bomb, there would have to be an investigation to prove that they had not planted it, to prove that the nation and its leaders, the guardians of the citizens' hard-won liberty, were under attack. Such proof would be necessary to justify, however reluctantly, however unwillingly, another assault on the liberties of the citizens. Arrest without charge, perhaps for weeks at a time. Unpleasant but necessary. The times demanded it. Restrictions on assembly. A ban on the right to strike. All bitter pills which must be swallowed for the greater good, for the nation, for the economy, for the security of the whole community. There would have to be arrests, interrogations and severe punishments.

But, if the government had not planted the bomb, that made things harder. Commandante Camillo would still have to make arrests. There would still be beatings and interrogations and somebody would have to pay, only this way he would have to try to limit that to the people who were actually to blame. That would mean evidence. That would mean detective work – days and nights of it and raids and arrests and everything that went with that. Commandante Camillo was feeling his age and there were still two years left before he could retire.

The glass in the door rattled as it banged behind him. From the smoke of the Detectives' Hall he walked out into the arched grandeur of the Palace of Justice with its gilded columns standing in groups of four and its meaningless mosaic frieze; women in nightgowns looking far away as they handed pieces of paper to grateful, cowering peasants all at arm's length, at full stretch like relay runners. From the very first day he entered the building, Commandante Camillo had looked at those pictures and raged. He saw those grateful peasants and he wanted to shout: 'Get off your knees!' He wanted to take out his pistol and fire into the ceiling and order them: 'Take it. Whatever it is that she's got, if you want it, take it. You are strong. You have worked all day in the fields. You have sickles, you have mattocks and she is weak and soft. Take it!'

But nobody, not even a man like Commandante Camillo, can stay angry for four decades and now, coming to work or going out, he forgot that the pictures were even there.

It was sunny in Plaza Universidad and the smell of blood, mixed with traffic fumes, drifted across the gardens as he walked, slowly, to the bombing. Halfway there, the Commandante spotted a hand which had ploughed down a row of orange marigolds and come to rest in one of the formal flower beds. There were screams coming from the far side of the square.

Commandante Camillo noticed that everything had a shadow, the park benches, the rubbish bins, and as he got closer to the university entrance the shadows deepened. On one side, the side closest to the bomb, things were darker and behind them, behind the slim, cast-iron legs of the benches, behind the ice-cream stand, behind the lamp-posts, in the shadow, it was lighter. One side dry and clean, one side dark and damp, misted with a spray of blood and tissue, hair, clothing, rucksack, denim, the little copper studs from a pair of jeans, coins, a wallet, a plastic comb, it was all there, somewhere, shredded and minced and sieved as fine as dust and blasted out across the square in a shrieking, angry drizzle.

Crossing the square, the mist thickened into soup until, at the foot of the broad stone staircase that led up to the university entrance, it had clogged into ragout. And, as Commandante Camillo walked across the square the screams grew louder. Ambulances were jammed in at all angles. They choked the street. They were contaminating the crime scene. Some of them had already left for the hospital. There were tyre tracks in the blood.

Camillo saw one of his detectives slamming the door on an ambulance and waving it out of the square. He raised a hand and beckoned him over.

'Boss.'

'You hurt?'

'No, boss.'

'You're covered in blood.'

'Not mine.'

'How many dead?'

'I have no idea. We won't know until we start matching up the bits but I think there's about twenty on the way to the hospital and they won't all live.'

Camillo was only pretending to listen. He had no need to know how many people were dead. It made no difference to the inquiry and, anyway, it made no difference. It simply made no difference. He took out a big white handkerchief and folded it into a wad and then, with a lover's tenderness, he wiped it gently across the policeman's face.

'Stand still.'

Over his eyes, across his broad cheekbones, down the long eagle-curve of his Indian's nose, his mouth, the nub of his chin.

'Here,' Camillo folded the handkerchief in on itself to find some unbloodied cloth, 'wipe your hands.'

The man obeyed like a child.

'Noticed anybody unusual?'

'I've been busy, boss.'

'Anybody watching?'

'Dozens of them. They stand and watch. They don't come and help. They don't rush off to the hospital to give blood. They just stand around here and watch.'

'Any freaks? Anybody laughing? Anybody standing with his hand down his pants?'

'Not that I noticed, boss. I was busy. Like I said, I was busy.'

The last of the ambulances was reversing out of the square. When it reached the junction with University Avenue, the sirens came on and it sped away.

'OK, son. Go back to the Hall. Get some coffee. Have a smoke.' Camillo patted him on the shoulder and sent him on his way with a gentle shove. He walked on, across the sticky, clotting cement, to where a fat inspector in a crisp uniform was standing, arms more or less outstretched, pretending to hold back the crowd. Camillo approached him stealthily, leaned close to his ear and said: 'What are you doing?'

The man jumped. 'Crowd control, boss.'

'Well, you can stop now. Do you see over there?' Camillo pointed to where the blood was thickest, where there was a black star burnt into the concrete like the eye of a poppy, with petals of blood sprayed out from it in every direction, up the steps, across the square, washing the flower beds. 'That's where the bomb went off. I want tapes in a square, fifteen metres on each side. I want you to find a photographer and tell him from me that I want every picture he's got with faces from the crowd in it. Tell him to take lots more of them until the last rubber-necking bastard has gone home. Don't point into the crowd, don't let them see he's doing it, just make sure we get lots of happy snaps of happy citizens having a nice day out at the bombing. Got that?'

The man nodded. His jowls trembled a little and his eyes were watery.

'Good. Hurry it up and then, when you have done that, I want you to go to the,' Camillo pointed, ticking things off in the air, 'go to the one, two, three, fourth flower bed along. You will find a hand in it. Pick it up and bring it back here to where the real policemen are working.'

The inspector threw a salute and waddled away.

'Run, man! Hurry.'

The inspector waddled faster.

Commandante Camillo went back to the bottom of the steps where a man in a suit was walking carefully backwards and forwards, head bent to the ground, stopping now and then to pick something up with tweezers and drop it in a plastic bag. These bags he numbered and placed in a knapsack and, for every numbered bag, he took out a piece of folded white card, like a name card on a dinner table, and placed it carefully on the ground.

Camillo stood respectfully a little way off, careful where he put his feet. 'Got anything?' he said.

'There's not much to get. Bits and pieces, but I don't know yet what came from the bomb and what was here before. I need to take it back to the lab and wash the blood off it.'

'Is there nothing you can tell me?'

'I'm pretty sure it was an own-goal. It went off before it was meant to, while he was carrying it into the university – amateur stuff.'

'And you're sure he was headed for the university?'

'Look at the shape of it. You can see where he was standing. The bomb was in his rucksack, on his back. He was right in front of it. The blast radiated out from there, he soaked it up in that direction. That's mostly him on the steps. Out like a light.'

'Time runs more slowly in the dentist's chair,' said Camillo. He lit up a cigar. 'Got any ID?'

'Be serious. You want to know who he was, go and ask who didn't turn up for class today.'

From across the square, four flower beds further back, the police inspector came shambling up. He trotted along with his hands held in front of him, cupped together. He was pale and sweating. His uniform was stained under the arms and creased across the chest.

He was cradling the severed hand, clipped clean off at the wrist, bled white and without so much as a broken fingernail, holding it flat in the basket formed by his knotted fingers and running with it, the way a child might run with an injured bird, to bring it home, to make it better.

But, when he arrived, he realized that he had no idea what to do. He stretched out his arms a little, offering the hand like a gift to Camillo.

The inspector said: 'Sir?' and Camillo turned to the man with the tweezers and said: 'Oh, for God's sake, give him one of your bags.'

The inspector bent down and pulled his fingers apart so the hand fell, gently, to the ground. Then he took the bag, opened it carefully and threw up in it.

CATERINA WAS NOT at class that morning. When the bomb exploded in Plaza Universidad and Mr Valdez was hurrying along the Merino with the wind in his hair and tango blaring from the radio, Caterina was still in bed.

By a strange coincidence Dr Cochrane was not in class either. He had lingered too long over coffee and an old, dog-eared copy of *The Mad Dog of San Clemente* in the Phoenix. Down there in the warm, coffee-flavoured dark, nobody noticed the explosion or the sirens or the screams. When he climbed the stairs up to the street at a little before ten, the city was almost back to normal again.

Costa, De Silva and Father Gonzalez were at their desks when the bomb went off. It all showed up in the records later along with the name of one boy who could not be traced anywhere: not at the hospital, not at the morgue. Oscar Miralles, another of Dr Cochrane's students, the boy who sat next to Caterina in class, the boy who sat next to her in the Phoenix, the boy Mr L.H. Valdez chased away. Nobody knew where he was.

He was spread in a thin film of flesh up the steps from the square. They found his address. The man with the tweezers found most of his upper jaw wedged between a wall and an iron handrail. After the cops matched it up with dental records they sent it home to his parents in a coffin with three loose arms, two right feet, some shoes and a couple of sandbags for the weight.

Oscar Miralles kept a diary. The cops kicked the door down on his flat and picked it clean and, when they were finished, the diary was the most interesting thing they had. Caterina filled pages of that diary, and towards the end there was quite a lot about Mr L.H. Valdez too. Most of it was a mad, acidic scrawl, the white noise of concentrated loneliness, but with enough stupid, idealistic politics and clichéd sermons on human rights and land reform to let Camillo write a report to the capital. Still, he was interested in the other stuff. He took notes.

Sitting on the edge of a desk in the Detectives' Hall he told his men: 'This Miralles, he didn't do it on his own. He must have friends. Find them. Squeeze his parents. Get his cousins in here. I want them all questioned. Get them in and grip them by the balls – and that includes his grandmother! He must have contacts and associates. Trace them all.'

Commandante Camillo found the sergeant from the bombing and took him aside. He pointed quietly to three names in the diary. 'Not her and not him and not him. Leave them alone. For now.'

There were questionings and beatings.

But all of that was still to come. That morning Caterina was lying in bed. Lying on her belly, her hair foamed around her head, covering her face. She had kicked off the sheets in the night and now she lay there like a distant landscape of pale, rounded hills.

While she was doing that, firemen with hoses were scouring Plaza Universidad, washing the blood away, jets of water painting it into strange blossoms that melted and melded and whispered down the drains.

And while they were doing that, just a few miles away Mr L.H. Valdez was standing at the counter of his favourite florist, where the blooms were like bloody explosions in his arms.

Mr Valdez liked to buy flowers. He always had them in his home. He felt they completed the place and they could make no dent in his masculinity but he was unused to buying them for his women − not now, not before the event. For Mr Valdez, flowers were a reward, not an inducement. He never wooed.

For Mr Valdez, life was tango, and in tango the man leads, the man initiates. There is a way to walk, as a man walks, and there is the *cabeceo*, the almost invisible signals across the shadowed dance floor, a glance held, an eyebrow raised, a subtle smile, a nod, a meeting on the dance floor. It is a contract but it is invisible to all but the man and his chosen woman, subtle and indecipherable as the signals the mantis semaphores to his mate. There is room for rejection, yes, but it is an unseen rejection, one without humiliation. Everybody knows the rules. Maria Marrom understood those things instinctively. She let it be known that she was bored, receptive, available. She held his glance, she acknowledged the flick of his eyebrow, she smiled and the dance began.

But Caterina was different. She was too young, too fresh. She had not suffered enough to dance tango, she did not understand the *cabeceo*. She was so innocent that she had simply offered herself to him − not more than Maria did but clumsily. Caterina was like a new pony, too eager to join the game. He would have to teach her, slow her down. A good pony could read the game. A good pony felt the shifting weight in the saddle, moved to the press of a thigh, the slightest twitch of the reins. If Caterina were to become a wife, she would need training, and Mr Valdez was prepared to make the investment in time and in roses.

Mr Valdez dumped an armful of blood-red blooms on the counter. 'I want these,' he said.

The shopkeeper was looking out the window after a police car and two ambulances which had just gone past. 'There's something up,' she said. 'Some poor souls in trouble.'

Mr Valdez made no reply. For an artist – and he was a very great artist – Mr Valdez was a remarkably pragmatic man. He had come to buy flowers. He had come to buy flowers because they were the best way he could see to getting the woman he wanted, the way he wanted to get her, and while he was not unsympathetic to the plight of 'poor souls in trouble' they were far away and beyond any help he could offer. The police would help them. The ambulance staff would help them. Gazing out the window would not help them.

'I want these,' he said again.

'Yes. Sorry.' She was suddenly amazed. 'All of them?'

'Yes, have you any more?'

'There might be some out the back.'

'I'll take them – so long as they're fresh. Have them made up by the dozens. And strelitzia too. I want a lot of those. Have you any Lily of the Incas? I want those and keep them apart from the roses and the strelitzia. They do not go together. She won't have vases. Do you have vases?'

'Well, we have some. But they are for display.'

'Then charge me for buckets. You have buckets, don't you? This is a florist?'

'We have buckets.'

Mr Valdez grabbed a pad from the counter and scribbled on it. 'Deliver them here.'

'All of them?'

'Of course, "all of them". And I'm not finished yet.'

In a corner of the shop there was a vase of freesia, as bright and simple as a candle. Mr Valdez stood quietly, catching his breath, contemplating that sweet, beautiful thing.

'I'll take these too,' he said. 'Do you have black tissue paper?'

'We have red and we have white.'

'Then red. The white would bleed them out. Wrap them,

please.' Mr Valdez stood at the counter with his wallet in his hand. Another ambulance went by outside the window, its tyres making a noise like rain on the asphalt as it passed.

The florist was wagging the end of her pencil at bucket after bucket of blooms, counting them, adding them together, noting them down on a pad beside her. 'You really want all of these?' she asked.

'Of course.'

'And the buckets?'

She made a few more additions for buckets and some imaginary flowers which might, or might not, be in the back shop but which would certainly never be delivered. She drew a line, scribbled a number and stabbed a final full stop as emphatic as her blunt pencil would allow. 'He'll never pay it,' she thought, pushing the pad across the glass counter.

Mr Valdez flipped open his wallet and counted out a pile of notes. 'How soon can you deliver?'

'Not before noon.'

'I can pay extra. I've bought the shop – who else can need the van?'

'If you paid double I couldn't do it. I don't have a driver.'

Mr Valdez wanted the flowers delivered at once. He was in a hurry to begin the long slow business of wooing. He wanted the instant gratification of not rushing at this. He wanted her overwhelmed with delight so he could bask in it and dismiss it as nothing.

'Do what you can,' he said. He took the bunch of freesias with him as he left the shop and laid them carefully on the ribbed leather banquette of his car. It gave him a prideful delight, that upholstery; so bright, so taut, so rigid it might almost have been inflated, like the rubber tubes of a child's paddling pool. The flowers lay across it beside him, touching only on the infinite peaks of those little leather hummocks. He gunned the engine, because he could.

When he left the little side street and turned towards the concrete slip road that led back onto the highway along the Merino, Mr Valdez hit traffic. Looking ahead he saw a line of cars stretching into the distance, none of them as beautiful as his. There was still time to escape. He could reverse just a few metres and get back on to the side streets. He checked his mirror, dropped into reverse and, just then, he saw a dirty red lorry, loaded with crates, stop right against his back bumper.

Mr Valdez took the car out of gear again. Suddenly the heat became unbearable. Sitting still, surrounded by other cars, there was no wind rushing by to cool him.

The smell of burning petrol was sickening and, instantly, he felt the sweat begin to roll down his back, soaking into his shirt where it pressed against the raised upholstery, trickling in the tunnels where it did not, tickling as it rolled and then, unmistakably, arriving at the crack between his buttocks and soaking into his underpants. It was vile. Mr Valdez was disgusted at the thought of delivering his lecture drenched in his own stagnant sweat.

He took out a handkerchief and rubbed it over his eyes, looked at it, noted the exhaust smuts already spotting the white cloth and folded it away again. He wondered about putting the roof up for the shade. He decided against it. The traffic might clear at any moment and he would be left, wrestling with the mechanism and blocking the road, glared at, honked at. Anyway, it would make no difference if he grilled or baked. Mr Valdez turned the knob on the radio. There was tango. No matter how hot it was, there would always be tango.

But there was no tango. Just words, the endless electric news gabble of people talking about something shocking and important, something that they knew had happened, something that they knew almost nothing about but that they felt they must tell to others. A bomb. A bomb in Plaza Universidad. A bomb in Plaza Universidad that had killed people. A bomb in Plaza Universidad that had killed people and hurt other people. Some people. Possibly many people.

Mr Valdez slumped across the steering wheel with a sigh. He could see the university just up ahead on the other side of the highway. He could walk to it in less than a quarter of an hour. He could see the flag on the flagpole but he could see the sun in the sky too and it was as far away.

Then an extraordinary thing happened.

While Mr Valdez was looking at the roof of the university and laughing at himself because what he took to be the jagged prongs of a lightning conductor pointing at the threatening sky suddenly folded its wings and flapped clumsily towards the Merino, he found himself wondering if one of those people in the square might be Caterina. It suddenly occurred to him that she might be dead. She might be maimed. She could be suffering and he was afraid for her. Such a thing had never happened before. It was as if the gland that supplies empathy had suddenly switched itself on for the first time in his life.

Mr Valdez was alarmed. He had never before cared for anyone – not even for Mama. Not since his father. When he realized how easily the people that he loved could disappear from his life, Mr Valdez had amputated that part of himself. From time to time, he touched the white scar over the stump and found it cold and numb and that satisfied him. Nothing could grow there. It felt nothing and that suited him because the other way was too dangerous. It was too much. It was too painful.

Everything he wrote about in his books, all the jealousy and the pain and the sacrifice, it all came from love or some misguided notion of what it meant to love, and Mr Valdez had imagined all of it. He had imagined whole towns and filled them with hundreds of people and none of them had ever existed but he made them breathe on the page because he imagined them so completely. And, more than that, he imagined how they felt. He imagined it utterly. Mr Valdez might not have met the characters in his books, he might not be on close personal terms with dentists or bar girls or landlords, but he knew and understood that such people existed. He knew that, somewhere, there was a dentist and a bar girl and a landlord. But he had no idea of how they felt and yet he had created those feelings, dragged them up from his imagination and written them down so that other dentists and bar girls and landlords could read his books and say: 'Yes, that is how it is.'

It was a remarkable secret. It was as if the guides in the Sistine Chapel had turned to the latest tour party and revealed: 'When Michelangelo di Lodovico Buonarroti Simoni painted this, he was stone blind.'

But now, sitting in his lovely car, amidst the stink of petrol fumes and the unbearable heat, Mr Valdez looked down at the imagined scar that marked the place where he had cut himself off from humanity and saw that it had grown pink and tender. He felt the blood pounding in it and it hurt. Mama was to blame for that, with her talk of grandchildren and marriage. She had sparked something. But she had spoken of those things before and he had never paid her any attention. Nothing had changed, except Caterina.

He imagined her now, naked on a hospital trolley before he had seen her naked, shrapnel piercing her before he had pierced her, and he was afraid again. He was afraid that this might be love and he understood what that meant: the jealousy, the longing to possess and the dreadful vulnerability that went with it, the pain of another's pain against which there could be no defence.

The car in front gave a little jolt and began to move. A gap opened up. Mr Valdez put his car into gear and moved off behind it, up the ramp and on to the highway. Soon the traffic was moving, not quickly but smoothly. He reached the junction that leads off to Plaza Universidad but it was blocked, a row of plastic signs across it and flashing lights and three policemen standing beside their motorcycles making churning scooping movements with their arms as if to push the traffic further on.

The radio said that the university would be shut all day and perhaps again tomorrow. The students would have to wait a little longer for his Romeo and Juliet. That didn't matter. It wouldn't go bad. And now, with the day off, he could write.

He followed the broad curve of the next junction and it brought him out at the other side of the university where, by some miracle, there was a parking space waiting for him, right outside the Bar America, and there, sitting at a table in the sunshine with a tiny cup of coffee, was Mrs Maria Marrom dangling a pretty blue shoe from her toe.

She pushed her sunglasses down to the tip of her nose and looked at him behind the wheel of his gorgeous, green car. 'Hello, Chano,' she said. 'I'm glad to see you're all right. What a terrible thing.'

'Terrible. Just terrible.' And it was terrible. For the first time in his life, Mr Valdez began to understand how terrible it was and the thought of it chilled him. Between the florist's and the traffic jam he had learned to care for 'poor souls in trouble'. He wanted a cure for that and perhaps Mrs Marrom was the cure.

'People died, Chano.'

'I know, darling. It's awful.'

'Why would anybody do such a horrible thing?'

'Oh, all sorts of lunatics get all sorts of mad ideas all the time.'

'But it could have been us. You might have been killed. I might have been killed.'

'Or Ernesto.'

Maria pushed her sunglasses back up her nose and agreed. 'Yes, even Ernesto.'

'But don't you think,' said Mr Valdez, 'that the best way to fight these madmen is not to give in to them? Don't you think that, as much as they revel in death, we should,' he pretended to struggle for the right word, 'we should celebrate life?'

Mrs Marrom did not say anything. She raised her tiny cup to her mouth and took a careful sip that left no trace of lipstick on the porcelain.

'Certainly, that's what I think, Maria. That's the only human response after such a dreadful thing. We ought to offer one another a little comfort.'

This was the moment. This was the *cabeceo*. The glances had been exchanged but behind her black sunglasses it was impossible to guess what Maria Marrom might be thinking.

There was a handbag on the table in front of her, too tiny to be of any practical use and more expensive than could ever be justified. She reached for it and took out a few coins, stood up and smoothed her dress down over her knees.

Mr Valdez picked up the freesias from the front seat, wrapped his jacket gently round them and placed them carefully in the back. By the time he reached the passenger door, Mrs Marrom was waiting there, bobbing her tiny handbag from the end of a finger like a pendulum measuring his lateness.

She sat down elegantly and swung her legs into the car just as she had been taught to do, just as her mother had been taught to do, the only way that a lady could possibly get into a car. He closed the door quietly, with two hands, and it made the sort of heavy, resonant click that comes only with real quality.

She said: 'I think you're right, Chano. You are absolutely right. We should comfort one another. We should comfort one another all day and as hard as we possibly can.'

At the traffic lights, he turned to look at her and saw the front doors of the Merino and National Banking Company reflected in her dark glasses. Ernesto would be working there right now, the stupid man. Maria sat like a statue, gazing fixedly at something else.

All the way down Cristobal Avenue they said nothing, not when he turned the car down the ramp into the car park, not when they rode up in the lift together, not even when they went to the kitchen to find a bottle of wine.

Mr Valdez laid his jacket on the table, unfolded it, took out the freesias and put them flat on the top shelf of the fridge.

'Not for me, Chano?' Maria had an amazing knack of putting a moue into her voice.

'Silly girl. How could I give you flowers? You're a married woman. What would Ernesto say?'

She turned round and piled her hair on her head, exposing her neck and the collar of her dress. Mr Valdez found the zip and it came down in a single, effortless glide so the dress fell in a pool at her feet and she stepped out of it naked, or nearly naked.

'Anyway,' he said, 'I have something much nicer to give you.'

AFTERWARDS SHE SAID: 'I know you have someone else, Chano.'

'Maria, what a thing to say.'

'It's true. The flowers.'

'I always have flowers in the flat.'

'Chano, don't lie to me. If they were for you, why would you put them in the fridge? You are keeping them fresh for someone else.'

'My darling, why be jealous? It's not very fair. You have someone else.'

'No, I don't.'

'Ernesto?'

'Oh, Ernesto. Yes, there is always Ernesto. I didn't count him.'

She was quiet for as long as it would have taken to smoke half a cigarette, if she had been the sort of woman who smokes cigarettes on an afternoon like that. Then she said: 'You should settle down, Chano.'

'Everybody seems to be telling me that these days.'

'Well, it's true. You should settle down. I should settle down. None of us is getting any younger.'

He gave a hurt little snort and she pinched him under the sheets. 'Oh, don't worry, you've lost none of your youthful vigour. There are boys of twenty who would look at you with envy, you big, strong, lovely man. But it's different for women. I'll be an old lady soon. It's different for an old lady. It's not dignified.'

She was being kind and that irritated Mr Valdez. The day was turning out to be full of new experiences for him: he had found himself feeling sympathy for strangers, he had realized that he might be falling in love, and now, it seemed, Maria was dumping him. Nobody had ever dumped L.H. Valdez before. It was scandalous. It was an outrage. Maria was simply saying the things he had already decided for himself – admitting that she was past her best and there was no point in dragging this thing on – but that was beside the point. It was his place to make kind and self-deprecating comments. It was for him to be gentle and sensible and soothing and she was so bad at it. Really bad. He was not soothed. He could not see the sense of this.

Mr Valdez wondered if all the women who heard him make these little speeches had felt as he was feeling now. This loss, this humiliation, this abandonment and anger, this sudden wave of chilly loneliness. Had they felt this too?

'Ernesto is a good man,' he said.

'There are worse husbands. Yes. He is a good man. Not the man you are. Not a tenth the man you are. But we have to be sensible. Time to tidy away the toys and go in for supper.'

Lying in his bed there beside Maria Marrom, Mr Valdez knew he had no cause for complaint. He did not love her, in fact she had become tiresome to him. She was a bore and, now that there was Caterina, he had no need of her. But that wasn't the point. That was not the point. Maria had let him down. He wanted to go back to this morning, back to a time before he felt things. Maria was supposed to cure that and she had let him down. That was it. That was the point. She had let him down.

Mr Valdez lay staring at the ceiling and marvelled at the strange sensation of tears rolling into his ears.

Maria kissed him lightly. 'Shh, darling. No crying. It's only wounded pride. Soon it will barely even sting.' When he did not respond she kissed him again, threw back the sheet and found her shoes at the side of the bed.

Mr Valdez closed his eyes. He heard her heels squeak on the tiled floor and the rustle of her dress as she struggled with that awkward zipper. She said: 'Well, goodbye then, my darling.' He did not open his eyes again until he heard the door close behind her.

Lying there, like a cold corpse, the sheet flung over his face, Mr Valdez realized that Maria Marrom had left his flat without showering. She had never done that before. She was meticulous in her routine: washing without soap, drying herself on a fresh, unused towel, restoring her make-up to perfection, refreshing her perfume with perhaps an extra tiny squirt brushed through her hair so she smelled of nothing and nobody but herself, and then a final sweep of the room to make sure nothing had been left behind. And now, when at last she had decided to slip back into the role of the dutiful wife, she was leaving with his stink on her. Was that a last gift to him? Was she clinging to the last fading souvenirs of something, like wedding flowers pressed in the back of a missal? Was it recklessness? Was she defying Ernesto or telling him: 'I was his. I was'?

It was embarrassment, Mr Valdez decided. Simply a rush to escape the awkwardness of his girlish tears, that was all. No more than that.

There was a poison in his system that he could not vomit up and he wanted to cry it out.

There was mourning still to do, even if he had no idea what he was mourning. The end of Maria? No more afternoons like this? He knew there must be more, but not with Maria, and finally, one afternoon, it would be the last afternoon. This was just one from a dwindling stock. But he could not know how many were left. Nobody did. That was the terrifying part.

He stood up. His feet whispered like sandpaper on the tiled floor as he walked to the shower. It was an old man's noise, the sound of a defeated shuffle. Mr Valdez wanted the tears to come again and this time with water running down his face so he could hide them even from himself. But there was nothing. He was empty, except for the pain and the fear.

He turned on the tap and let hot water hammer down on his head like jungle rain. Mr Valdez turned his face up into the stream.

WHEN THE FLOWERS Mr Valdez had ordered were loaded in the van, Caterina was still lying in bed. She lay as she had before, on a pile of pillows, one leg pulled up and bent at the knee as if in the shape of a number 4, like a ballerina frozen in mid-pirouette. She was asleep. She lay with one hand spread open on a big yellow notebook, exactly like the big yellow notebook Mr Valdez had used except that his was empty and hers was crammed with words.

Caterina was sleeping because she had been writing almost until dawn. Every night she wrote until she fell asleep and, if she woke up in the night, her face pressed against the wire spine of her notebook, she would start again.

She loved stories. From the time she was too small to know what a word was, she would lie in the crook of her father's arm and look up into his face with eyes like a surprised kitten, watching his mouth, following the movement of his lips and the miracle of the noises that came from them. And then, when she was only a little older, the words took on a meaning and exploded inside her head, like fiesta fireworks against the black velvet sky, shooting pictures across her brain.

When he came in from the fields, stooped and exhausted, she would run to him and hold his hand although it was covered with mud and walk with him into the house and wait quietly until he had eaten his soup before she asked for another story.

She loved stories. She saw them everywhere. She took the stories they told her in church and spun them out, adding more events, more happenings, extra characters. Mama told her that was a blasphemy and she must not do it, but she walked home from church with Pappi and he laughed and asked for more. She read stories in the faces of the people in the village. She made it her business to imagine happy stories for the people who were sad and misfortunes for the people who were cruel.

At school she discovered that numbers had stories to tell as much as words. Number 6 and Number 4 were lovers who longed to make ten, like 7 and 3, like 8 and 2 but 9 and 7 disliked each other.

She remembered the day she had learned about pi, a magical, secret number that nobody knew, that just went on and on for ever, never changing, just rolling out, not repeating but wandering on down smaller and smaller paths without any end. And Fibonacci: 1 plus 2 makes 3, 2 plus 3 makes 5, 3 plus 5 makes 8, up and up and up, great towers of number, every third one an even number, every sixth one a multiple of the sixth, every eighth one a multiple of the eighth, every seventh one a multiple of the seventh and every single one of them in a perfect ratio: each one of them 1.6 times larger than the one before. She remembered the day Señora Arnaz had told them that and then solemnly marched every child to the front of the class to prove that the distance from the floor to their belly buttons, and the distance from the floor to the top of their heads was a perfect, beautiful, magic, mystic, sacramental Fibonacci number.

And then, one day when she was still quite a little girl, Pappi did not come home from the field. It grew dark. Mama lit the lamp and he still did not come home so they put on their coats and went out looking. He was in the field when they found him, lying on his face as if he had suddenly fallen asleep because he was just too tired to keep working for even one more day. His hand was clawed into the ground and, when they picked him up to take him home, a lump of earth from the field came home with him, gripped tight in his fist so the shape of his fingers and the lines of his palm were squashed into it.

Caterina made up a story about that. She wondered if he scrabbled at the dirt in pain or if he held the earth in his hand because it was his and he loved it and there was nobody else to love and be there with him when he died. She did not tell anybody else about that story. The lump of earth from his hand dried out, cracked and whispered away to dust. She brushed it outside and she did not bother with stories any more. She stuck to numbers and the numbers brought her to university and at university she was so lonely and so afraid that she began to tell herself stories again. She wrote.

When the flowers Mr Valdez had ordered at last arrived at Caterina's flat it was lunchtime. She was up and out of bed but she was not dressed and she hurried to the door, wrapping a chenille robe around herself as she went. It did not fit. It was indecently short and, in spite of the belt, Caterina instinctively held it shut with one hand gripping the lapels. A moment or two earlier she had been naked, the way the cat in the yard was naked, the way the pigeons on the window ledge were naked, natural and innocent. Now, wrapped in a worn pink dressing gown with coffee stains down the front, with everything hidden that the artists and the pornographers would want on show, now she suddenly crackled with heat.

There was another knock. 'I'm coming. I'm coming,' she said but, when she got to the door and turned the key in the lock, there was nobody there.

A voice from the stairs said: 'There's more on the way,' and Caterina saw at her feet three buckets of blooms crowding the doorstep.

For a moment she was too astonished to say anything, and when she said: 'Hang on!' the door to the street had already banged shut.

She knew it was a mistake. Nobody would send her flowers. Certainly nobody would send so many flowers.

She ran back into the flat and, in the time it took to pull on a T-shirt and jump into a pair of jeans, the delivery man had returned.

He was red in the face and wheezing after climbing the stairs with his arms full of buckets. Buckets are heavy. But he was still a man, like Costa and De Silva, like L.H. Valdez and Father Gonzalez, and he couldn't help but look at Caterina. That T-shirt. It stretched across her, skimmed her and then fell away like a waterfall, like a river dropping off a cliff, held out from her body in a loose flapping circle that left her belly exposed. Of course he looked. He was a man.

'You'll have to take some of these inside, love. I can't get in the door.'

'No. Wait. There's been a mistake. They're not for me.'

The man squinted down into the pocket of his shirt. He took out a packet of cigarettes with its top ripped off and then a small, white envelope which he handed to her.

'That you?'

Caterina was astonished. It showed in her face.

'No mistake then. There's more, so if you could just get them out of the door, that'd be a help.'

He went off down the stairs again and, when he stopped on the first landing, looked back and said: 'Jesus.' She mistook it for exasperation. Three years later, when things were tight before payday and the florist sacked him after just a little bit of money went missing from the till although he was going to pay it back for sure, when he went off in the van and drove to Punto Del

Rey just to gather his thoughts and the cops found him there
and he got two months in the city jail, he told his cellmates about
the day he met Caterina. Nobody believed him.

Caterina had a way of looking – not that she knew she was
doing it – a kind of angry scowl she wore whenever she met a
man. It was a protective thing, attack being the best form of
defence. It was as if she went about always with her little hands
knotted into fists, ready for a fight, and it showed in her face in
a look that said: 'What do you think you're looking at?' She
knew very well what they were looking at.

But, standing there in the doorway, holding that little envelope
with buckets of flowers all around her and puddles of water between
her toes, the scowl vanished. She looked at the envelope and she
knew who had sent it. She recognized that broad nib, the dark ink.
Caterina put her little finger under the flap of the envelope and tore
it open. Inside there was nothing, or nearly nothing. Just a plain,
white card and 'Chano'. Just one word. Not even 'I write'. Less
than that. One word less and one letter less. No 'love from'. Just a
name. His name. She was delighted. He had not pledged his love
lightly and even that she regarded as a blessing. It meant he might.

Across the landing the door opened and Erica came out. 'Thank
God you're all right,' she said.

'I'm fine. Why shouldn't I be?'

'Haven't you heard about the bomb? It's all over the radio.
Somebody planted a bomb at the university. I thought you were
going in early. I was worried.'

And then she saw the flowers.

'Who sent all these?'

'Who do you think?' Caterina waggled the envelope teasingly
by one corner and fanned herself as if to stave off a swoon.

'No!'

'Yes!'

Erica snatched the card away. Caterina let her. 'Chano! Ooooh, Chano.'

'That's "Mr L.H. Valdez" to you.'

'Did you do it?'

'Do what?'

'Come on! Have you done it?'

'No.'

'He'll want to. For all these flowers he'll expect it.'

'There's more.'

The delivery man was coming, clanking up from the street with four more buckets, and they leaned out over the stairs to watch him. Three years later, in the town jail, he told them about that too and they didn't believe him.

'My God. He'll definitely want to do it now.'

Caterina laughed and said: 'I'd let him.'

Standing there at the top of the stairs the delivery man heard her and he didn't say anything but he thought plenty. He put down the last of his buckets with a gasp, lit a celebratory cigarette and he said: 'You can keep the buckets, they're paid for', but he thought: 'Yeah, I bet you would, but not for me you wouldn't. You wouldn't let me.'

He stood waiting for an awkward moment until he realized they had not even thought to tip him, picked a stray bit of tobacco from the tip of his tongue and staggered back down the stairs. A pale blue trail of smoke rose angrily behind him and grew thinner and angrier until there was nothing left but the smell. That night, when he went home, the wife who had loved him for more than twenty years cooked him steak and took a bath and dried herself and dusted herself in a blizzard of powder and took the ground glass stopper from a bottle of Christmas perfume, as small, as precious as a reliquary, and dabbed herself in secret places and came to bed and loved him. But he didn't tell them that three years later in the town jail. He didn't even remember. All he remembered was meeting Caterina, and nobody believed him.

'Help me with these,' Caterina said and picked up some buckets. 'You'll have to take some. There's far too many for the flat.'

Poor Caterina, she opened that little white envelope and she had no idea that it contained her death warrant. She had read his name without a shudder, not as the name of her executioner but like the name of a lover, as if a man who sent her flowers must be always one and never the other. But, sometimes, that's how life is. Sometimes a tiny dab of glue, moistened on the edge of an envelope, is the only thing that holds together the whole world and everything that's in it. Sometimes life, death, disaster arrive with no more warning than the whispered crunch of a snail shell underfoot. No one notices but the snail.

SEAGULLS ARE UNATTRACTIVE creatures: noisy, garrulous, aggressive, messy, inconsiderate. They are the nasty drunks of the bird world. They come ashore like sailors in every port, walking round with a swagger, hands in pockets, pushing their way through the crowd with their shoulders. They annexe window sills. They claim the chimney pots as *terra nullius*, the property of no one and theirs to colonize. They are white, but they are filthy. They look out on the world with unsympathetic eyes, the eyes of a sociopath, flat, glinting shark eyes. They raid the bins, they scatter rubbish, they mug office girls for their lunches, falling out of the sky with beaks agape, and they splatter everything, cars, buildings, children, washing lines, with long strings of grainy, sticky, stinking shit.

There was a seagull standing on a carved pediment above the door of the Merino and National Banking Company when Ernesto Marrom left work that evening. It pattered about on its pink scaly feet and looked down into the street with its yellow-rimmed eyes, as if taking aim.

But we're getting ahead of ourselves. Go back a few hours to when Mrs Marrom was clawing at the sheets of Mr L.H. Valdez's bed, when her sweat was falling in sizzling drops onto his snow-white, lavender-scented pillows. Then Ernesto Marrom was running his pencil down another column of figures.

Ernesto Marrom understood figures. They sang in his head like the notes of a symphony. Tax rates, tax exemptions, Government bonds, dollar exchange, futures, shorts, offshore accounting, trusts. He could look at an account book and understand it, swim in it and through it like a fish, see how to make it better, richer, see where the holes were, where the money had gone – and who took it.

The banker Marrom was as much of a detective as the policeman Camillo and, like Camillo, he depended on facts for nine tenths of his work. The rest they would both have dismissed as guesswork. It was not guesswork. It was instinct. The jaguar in the jungle does not guess which path the deer will use when she comes to drink. The jaguar knows the things the jaguar knows, the policeman knows the things the policeman knows and the banker knows the things the banker knows even if he can't explain them. Mr Marrom could tell when a stock was overvalued or undervalued, he could tell when the price of coffee would peak, how much the price of beef would fall. If anybody had asked him what made him think that way, he might have had to stop for a little, gather his thoughts and come up with a reason: a string of numbers, the weather conditions these past three months, a shift in the American markets, a twitch in the price of oil. But none of those things was any more than an imaginary justification for what he already knew. Ernesto Marrom had heard it said that a butterfly sipping on an orchid in some faraway clearing could sink mighty ships and send tornadoes battering at the coast of Japan with the tiniest flap of its wings. He believed it. Every morning, when he opened the paper and turned to the stock market report, he saw butterflies and watched the earthquakes that rumbled along the rows of figures when they stamped.

'I know things,' he told himself. 'And I know my wife is having an affair.'

Of course, the rows of figures could not have told Mr Marrom that Maria was unfaithful any more than they had told him that the price of coffee would rise by two centavos that morning, but still the price of coffee went up. There was nothing he could point to. There were no facts. But he knew.

He knew for sure after he called her for the sixth time that afternoon. The telephone jangled on its onyx table in the hallway. It jangled and it jangled but nobody answered. Mr Marrom had often called home in the afternoon and Mrs Marrom had often failed to answer. Sometimes he had called as many as six times in a row and received no reply. But today, far away from his home on the hill, sitting in his comfortable chair with its deep-buttoned green leather, green as a turtle, green as the trees by the river, sitting in his cool and shady office, surrounded by dark wooden panels that dripped with carved fruit, he knew. Perhaps if he had called home only five times that day he would still have been unsure, perhaps the thought would never have occurred to him, but the telephone rang just once too often. He knew and he could not believe he had been such a fool. Mr Marrom, sitting in his dark, cool office inside the Merino and National Banking Company, with the telephone in his hand, listening all alone to a bell ringing far away, knew that somewhere, perhaps very close by, his wife was naked in another man's bed.

Mr Marrom was disturbed to discover that he did not want to murder her. He felt sad and wounded but he did not want to murder her.

After six rings so many things suddenly made sense. How could any woman spend all those afternoons shopping and yet never buy anything?

Mr Marrom began to count the rows of figures in his head, month after month of bank statements, neat piles of cheque-books, every stub meticulously filled out with the date, the amount, the name of the payee. Mr Marrom could recall them all, every bit of paper, every number, debits and credits, the figures rising and falling along the columns in a monthly tide in just the way the taxi driver parked outside his window could recall every score line, every pass, every goal for every FC Atletico match in the past twenty seasons.

There was nothing odd or out of the ordinary about any of it, and that was every bit as strange as a telephone that rang six times. How often had she sat there, on the other side of the silver candlesticks she inherited from Aunt Malvina, how many times had she looked away, darting her eyes down into her wine glass and then up to the ceiling when he asked: 'And what did you do today, my love?'

'Oh, shopping,' she would say, 'just shopping.'

Some shoes or a new dress – 'such a bargain' – and she would always promise to show him later, after dinner. But she never did.

Mr Marrom could not recall the last time he had seen Maria in a new dress and he knew he stood condemned because of it. Why had he never asked to see her in those imagined dresses? Why did he not demand a viewing of all those shoes – 'No, darling, just the shoes. Don't bother wearing anything else. Just the shoes' – why did he not insist on having them lined up like soldiers at attention, each pair with its own smart little box, ready for storage? If only he had demanded an audit. If Maria had been a back-street garage or a pet shop he would have been within his rights. He could have arrived at any time and inspected the books. But she was a wife. He had not cared enough. He had not kept a check on his investments.

'Later,' that was what she said. She would show him 'later'. And now it was too late.

And Mr Marrom knew he had failed in other ways too: things

she had hinted at, things she had asked for, things she had tried to teach him. He had tried to offer compensations: a beautiful house, money, a place in society, and she wanted those too but they were not enough. They were not the things she needed and he knew that. He had always known that. How could he complain now when she had found those things elsewhere?

He picked up the telephone for the seventh time and waited for a moment. He gave her time to put aside her coffee cup, fold her magazine and walk down the corridor, he gave her time to take off her earring, lift the receiver and say 'Hello' in the way she always did and he whispered: 'I am so sorry, Maria. I was not man enough for you. But I am man enough to admit it. There are some things which are simply not in my nature to give. The rest is all yours, my love.' This time he had not even bothered to dial the number. He put the telephone down with a click.

Of course Mr Marrom did not want to kill his wife. He loved his wife. He did not want to be without her and, if he killed her, he would certainly be without her. If he went to jail he would be without her in a horrible place with no one to visit him, and if the police looked at him and saw a wronged husband and a whore of a wife who deserved all she got, if they forgot to investigate too thoroughly or if the bank greased a few palms so the whole thing was forgotten, he would still be without her, alone in a lovely house where the telephone sat silent on its onyx table and the clock ticked.

He would rather not be without her and so he resolved to turn a blind eye. He would know and say nothing and that, he decided, was the real machismo.

If his wife knew he was a cuckold, if his wife's lover knew, if every man in the city had her and laughed at his horns, they would not know of his great courage, his great love. They would not know what he bore, for the sake of his manhood. It was a great and a noble thing, he decided.

And as he finished work for the afternoon, as he straightened his tie in the mirror, as he flicked a finger through the silver hair at his temples, Mr Marrom took some small comfort from that. 'Yes,' he told himself, 'L.H. Valdez would make me the hero of his next book, if he only knew.'

Mr Marrom did not want to kill his wife but he was desperately sad. He stood with his hand on the doorknob for quite a long time, staring at the darkly polished door with its flame-flowered grain. He was in no hurry to leave. He liked his office. It was calm and quiet and secure, so distant, so muffled from the world that he had known nothing of the explosion only a street away until his secretary arrived with his morning coffee and told him.

But everything he loved about his office was sweet to him only because Maria was at home. The heavy furniture oozing its calm silence, the stuttering clock eating his life away, moment by moment, these things were a comfort to him, but at home, without her, they would be a threat and a reminder.

In the office these things were calming, reassuring, they were symbols of his status far above the daily bustle of the banking hall, distant from lowly clerks and customers. At home, without Maria, they would mean only loneliness. The empty chair would scream at him, the clock would hammer in his brain, the silence would shriek until his nerves shredded.

Mr Marrom turned back to his desk, adjusted the blotter to make it straight, checked – again – that all the drawers were locked and then, with the firm step of a man determined to walk to the wall with courage, he opened the door and set out for home, through the dark little corridor, through the banking hall, his heels ringing on the marble floor, nodding his 'good evenings' as he went, through the door that was held open for him by a liveried flunkey, and out onto the street.

And it was then that the seagull, with its yellow-rimmed eyes and its pink scaly feet, pattering on the carved stone ball which forms the dramatic full stop to the gorgeous curlicues and arabesques decorating the façade of the Merino and National Banking Company, dropped the delicious, bloody gobbet it had picked up from Plaza Universidad a short time earlier. The meat fell through the air and landed on the shining toe of Ernesto Marrom's right shoe, bounced and fell down three more steps to the pavement, where it lay for less than a moment until the gull dropped from the roof, snatched it up in its beak and flew off again, choking it down with its throat lopsided and distended like a bursting sack.

Luckily the banker Marrom had no more idea of what had struck his foot than did the seagull, but it offended him anyway; the plump moisture of it, the lavish scarlet, the gull's gorging, the shock of that little blow coming from nowhere. He stooped to wipe his shoe with a handkerchief and pretended to himself that he had not noticed when it came away stained red. Mr Marrom felt his stomach complain. He was tired and sad and now he felt sick too. He needed a brandy – just to settle himself – and he thought of the Phoenix, where he used to go when he was still a student. The Phoenix. He could go there and linger a little, waste a little time, let Maria come home to him. Just to be sure.

Mr Marrom was still in the Phoenix, sitting alone at the corner table, when L.H. Valdez arrived at a little after 7 that evening. His best friend – if only he had a best friend – would have to admit that he was a little drunk, and Mr Valdez, who was very far from being Mr Marrom's best friend, would have agreed.

It was an awkward moment. Mr Valdez had spent almost an hour under the steady beat of the shower, washing the last traces of Maria from his skin, and suddenly it was all for nothing. He had come from his home hoping to find adulation. He had picked up his notebook with its single line of script – 'The scrawny yellow cat crossed the road and crept into the whorehouse' – and he pretended to himself that he was going to the Phoenix to write some more. He would take a double espresso and a brandy and he would sit at the corner table under the big gilt mirror – in exactly the seat where Ernesto Marrom had chosen to sit – and write. Of course there was still a part of his brain which recognized that was rubbish. Mr Valdez had no intention of writing. How could he write? How could he write when Maria had discarded him and he lacked the courage to open the fridge, pick up a bunch of freesias and take them to a woman who might not reject him? Mr Valdez did not want to write. Instead he wanted to be seen writing. He wanted the reassurance that came from admiring glances. He wanted to sit at that table and have people look at him. He wanted to turn his head up from the page and catch someone glancing away quickly. He wanted a huddled conversation on the other side of the room, somebody working up the courage, somebody saying: 'Go on, go on, I dare you! He won't mind,' somebody brave enough to jostle between the tables with a scrap of paper torn from a diary or a smoothed-out napkin, somebody who would say: 'Could I ask? I'm so sorry to trouble you. Only it would be a great honour. Such an honour. I've read all your books,' somebody who would smile and say: 'Oh, thank you. Thank you so much. You don't know what this means.' Somebody who might even try to sneak a glimpse of his notebook and say: 'And is this your new one? Oh, wonderful!', so he could slowly, calmly, with great and gentle discretion, flip the notebook shut, hide it from prying eyes and say something modest and dismissive and self-deprecating.

'Oh, this? Oh, it's just something I'm playing with at the moment. Nothing at all really. No, really, it's nothing.'

That wasn't so much to ask and, in case adulation was in short supply, he had come to the Phoenix, where he was prepared to allow even Dr Cochrane to flap and fuss over him. But, instead of Dr Cochrane, who should he find but Ernesto Marrom, the banker Marrom whose wife had just left his bed for the last time. A man he had wronged, a man who had somehow, inexplicably, beaten him, a man who would never even know it, never have the chance to gloat triumphantly, never shake his head with a pitying look. It was disgusting, infuriating and even, Mr Valdez realized, embarrassing.

Standing at the door he looked away quickly, pretending that Marrom had not already seen him, but it was too late.

'Valdez!' he said. 'Chano! Here. Over here.' He beckoned with his brandy glass. 'Come and sit down. Let me buy you a drink.'

Mr Valdez smiled weakly.

'Come on, I'm buying. Come on.'

Valdez looked round, hoping there might be someone else he could sit beside, some prior engagement he could plead. There was nobody. There was no escape.

'Hello, Ernesto,' he said and pulled a chair out from under the table. They stood there and shook hands like two old friends and, after three large brandies, Mr Marrom was feeling genuinely friendly towards just about everybody. Mr Valdez saw himself in the mirror from the top of his head to where the table cut him off at mid-thigh with his shark-blue suit that fitted like a kiss and a shirt so white that it hurt the eyes. He saw himself and he saw Mr Marrom's back and he saw their hands gripping. He was touching Mr Marrom and with that same hand he had touched Mrs Marrom only hours ago, only that afternoon and on so many other afternoons. With that hand he had wiped his tears away.

'Brandy? You want a brandy? I'm having a brandy.' Marrom

waved his arm around until a waitress noticed and silently mouthed
'Two more' at her.

'Yes, that sounds good.'

'Actually, I've had a couple already. I'm a little ahead of you.
Started early.'

'Celebrating?'

'No. Not really. No.'

'Drowning your sorrows, then?'

Mr Marrom made no reply to that. He sat looking down into
his brandy glass, slowly wiping his finger round the rim until it
began a ghostly, ringing singing. He took his hand away. 'Sorry,'
he said. 'That was rude. Sorry. Oh, look. Here's your drink –
our drinks.'

It was a dozen words, no more than the single sentence in his
notebook, but with that moment of silence and that strange,
mournful note, Mr Valdez suddenly understood everything about
Ernesto Marrom.

'Yes, drowning my sorrows, I suppose.'

'Taken a hammering on the markets?' Mr Valdez was struggling to make bright conversation and he found himself guilty
and embarrassed, even slightly fearful. He was afraid of a scene.
What if Marrom knew? What if that was why he had called him
over? What if this were an ambush? What if Marrom had been
lying in wait, building up his courage as he drank it down and
ready, at last, to spit out his drunken accusations?

'No, nothing like that. No.' Mr Marrom finished one glass of
brandy and moved on to another. 'Life just doesn't turn out like
you expect sometimes.'

'I know. In fact I make my living from life not turning out as
we expect – and so do you.'

'Yes, we do; don't we? But it's meant to be other people's lives.
Turns out I'm the same as everybody else.'

'Oh, we all are,' said Valdez. 'We are all uniquely just like everybody else.'

'You're not.'

'Even I. I have surprised myself these past few days.'

Mr Marrom took a large sip from his glass and closed his eyes as the treacle-sweet fumes burned up through his head. He nodded. 'Even you. Yes, even you. The great Luciano Hernando Valdez. Imagine.'

Now. It was coming now, the screaming and the punch and the accusation and everybody would look and there would be nothing to say, no excuse, no defence to offer and nothing to say except blank, stupid unbelievable denial.

Mr Valdez hurried over his brandy. 'Well, I suppose I should be getting along.'

'Don't be stupid. Oh, forgive me.' Mr Marrom waved his glass again. 'Forgive me. I keep on being rude. I'm sorry. Please don't hurry off. You just got here. Relax. Please forgive me. Please. Stay. I want to talk. Here, is that your new book? Tell me about that. How's that going?'

Mr Valdez laid a hand down on his notebook shielding it. 'Oh, this? Oh, it's just something I'm playing with at the moment. Nothing at all really. No, really, it's nothing.'

'It's not nothing. No, listen, it is not "nothing". What you write changes lives. It changes the whole world. It changes the way people see the world.'

'Oh, rubbish.'

'Listen, it is not rubbish. I know. It's happened to me.'

Mr Valdez was astonished.

'But you're wrong.'

Mr Valdez was astonished again. 'What am I wrong about?'

'You think.' Ernesto took another swig of brandy. 'You think I should kill my wife.'

'No, I don't! I do not!' There was an uncontainable squeak in his voice. 'Why would I think that?'

'I love her, you know.'

'So you should. She's a wonderful woman. Wonderful.'

'She's a whore, Chano!'

Mr Valdez glanced up in the mirror. He was pleased to see that he looked genuinely shocked.

'No, listen, it's true. It's true.'

'I'm sure you're mistaken.'

'She's been having an affair.'

'No.'

'She has.' Marrom finished his brandy in a single fiery gulp and held out his glass. 'Your turn, I think.'

Mr Valdez held up his hand and waved to the waitress in the mirror. He listened.

'My wife is a whore and she's been having an affair but I don't care because I love her and I can't live without her. Strickly. Strictly between ourselves.'

'My God!'

'Yes, that's what I said.'

'How long have you known?'

'Oh,' Marrom looked at his watch, 'Oh, 'bout four hours.'

'My God.'

'My God, indeed. But, look, keep this between ourselves.'

'Of course. I'm sure you're wrong. Have you any idea who . . . ?'

'Nope. No clue. But according to the works of L.H. Valdez – oh, here comes our brandy.' Ernesto let his voice drop until the waitress left. 'According to the works of L.H. Valdez, I'm supposed to find some sort of inner peace by slaughtering her and her lousy stinking boyfriend. Lotsa blood. Lots and lots of lovely blood.'

'No.'

'That's what you would do. That's what a real man would do.'

'That's shit. Those are just shitty stories. It's just stories.'

'Well, I don't want to kill her.'

'No. You mustn't. She loves you. Anybody can see it. She loves you more than you can ever guess.'

'But I might kill him.'

'Yes, that would be allowed.'

'If I ever find out who he is.'

'She loves you, Ernesto. She loves you.'

'That's not the point. The point is I love *her*.'

MR VALDEZ WOKE with a bad case of morning mouth and a head full of angry, buzzing cotton wool. Lying in bed, trying to summon the courage to get up, he was more and more astonished at himself: astonished that he had dared to spend the evening with Ernesto Marrom, soothing his horns, kissing them better, telling him over and over that Maria was not a faithless whore, that she loved him truly and deeply as a good wife should, astonished that he had somehow pulled it off and, most astonishing of all, astonished that he almost believed it himself.

When he slammed the door of the taxi, perhaps a little too heavily for one o'clock in the morning, and waved Ernesto on his way out of the Square of the September Revolution with Orion striding across the sky above the Merino in an icy-blue blaze, he had felt genuinely warm towards him. That manly embrace, the brotherly back-slapping – he had meant it all and, although the brandy fumes had faded, he found he meant it still. That switch was still switched to 'on', the little dripping tap of emotional attachment had turned into a dribble. It was still alarming, but less so, and Mr Valdez allowed these new feelings to wash over him as the addict sinks into the warm, cloud-cushioning waves of the poppy poison.

There was still the sharp, fresh sting of the cut where Maria had been but that would fade. It was already fading. And there was the strong, warm, painful pulse that was Caterina, but that would fade too. He hoped it would fade too and he knew how to start it healing.

Mr Valdez cradled his hands behind his head, squeezed his temples, held his breath and sat up. He was relieved to find he did not want to vomit but he was painfully thirsty. The big blue notebook was lying where he had left it on the bedside table. He picked it up and went to the kitchen.

It was as beautiful as every other room in his house, with its steel and its marble tiles and its dark wood and its huge, double-fronted American refrigerator. Everything was quiet and calm and efficient and clean. Everything was 'right'. And everything was absolutely impersonal. The kitchen of L.H. Valdez was like his sitting room, like his bedroom, like his broad terrace balcony, like his bathroom. Every single room of his house could have come straight from the showroom of the city's most fashionable furniture store. His home was like a catalogue, like a photo shoot, like the glossy pages of a style magazine. It was furnished the way that the magnates of the past had furnished their libraries with 30 metres of green books and 30 metres of red. Someone else chose them. Nobody knew what they said, nobody looked at them again. Mr Valdez had a whole house like that where only the books were real and everything else was for show. If anyone had ever come to the flat – and, apart from Maria Marrom, no one ever did, no friend, no colleague, no student, no wide-eyed, shallow-brained reviewer intent on finding the real L.H. Valdez – but if anyone had ever come to the flat, they would have found almost nothing of him there. There was no conversation piece, nothing to spark a little exchange: 'Oh, that! I must tell you where I picked that up.'

Or: 'Yes, I've always been fond of that. It came from my days in Cairo you know.'

The only photographs he could ever recall in that flat had appeared from behind the skirting boards when first he moved in and began stripping the place back to the plaster.

There were dozens of them, standing upright against the wall, spattered with dust, criss-crossed with spiders' webs and waiting there, side by side, one after the other, hidden, like the frozen frames of a forgotten newsreel, filled with the grey ghosts of chiselled young men who wore the Death's Head on their collars. The last owner, Dr Klement, must have put them there, afraid that they would be discovered but unwilling to be parted from them. Before he threw them away, Mr Valdez had wondered if it gave the old man comfort, when he lay dying, to know his souvenirs were close at hand or if he had been terrified that they would be found.

Mr Valdez had nothing like that. No secrets. Apart from one souvenir of his grandfather, he had made sure that his house was as bare and stripped clean of connection as his soul. That was how he wanted it; clean, functional, fashionable, stylish and, now he realized, cold, empty.

He went to the fridge, groping for orange juice, and found the freesias there, ruined. He had pushed them too far back, beyond the butter, so their petals froze to the back wall, icy and transparent, like the wings of dead, defeated fairies. They tore when he pulled them and they left a green slime of leaf skeletons against the white plastic. Mr Valdez threw them away with a sigh.

Sitting at the table with a carton of orange juice open in front of him, bent freesia stems and damp tissue paper sticking out from the lid of the waste bin beside him, he opened the notebook again and read.

'The scrawny yellow cat crossed the road and crept into the whorehouse.' There must be something else. There must be another line. Something had to follow.

'Wouldn't you rather have sex?'

Something had to follow. There must be another line. There must be something else.

Mr Valdez looked at the page. It stared back at him as blank and cold as an iceberg, one thin line of script in view and, below it, hidden, menacing, fatal, the great mass of unwritten, unseen nothing, page after page of frozen whiteness. But he knew it could be beaten. Line by line he could chip away at it and make a book. He put down his orange juice and went to find his pen.

And while he was doing that, just a little way along Cristobal Avenue, Dr Cochrane was sitting on a bench in the garden of the square outside the Ottavio House, enjoying the morning sunshine. The police were still at work in Plaza Universidad, classes were cancelled, the day was his own and he had chosen to spend it under a tree in the garden.

Just enough sunshine – but not too hot – cool, feathery shadows blowing across the paths, the flowers blazing all around in their well watered beds, the satisfying crunch of gravel beneath his feet – it was perfect.

From where he sat, Dr Cochrane could enjoy the whole street: the neat little children making their way to school, the noise of the traffic on Cristobal Avenue all so pleasantly distant, that dark-skinned girl walking to and fro in front of the second-storey window of the Ottavio House, forgetting – or not caring – that she was as naked as a baby. And, best of all, Dr Cochrane could watch that beautiful young man with his long, brown legs, as he worked on making the garden lovely. Dr Cochrane folded his newspaper and put it down on the bench beside him. He decided it was time to stop pretending to read. It would never be time to stop pretending – not completely – but it was time to stop pretending to read. The paper was full of unpleasant things anyway. It was all about the bombing, it was all about pain and death, full of nasty words and nasty pictures of fearful, anguished people. Dr Cochrane thought it wrong and silly to waste a lovely morning on so much unpleasantness when he could be enjoying the birds and the sunshine and the very long legs and the very short shorts of the gardener.

The young man had his back to him. He was kneeling down, tending to a flower border that ran along the edge of the path. His long black hair hung down over his face, and from time to time he would uncurl a little, straighten his back, tuck his hair behind his ears and go back to work. Dr Cochrane found it a beautiful gesture. There was such grace in it. It was so girlishly simple. Little by little, always on his knees, always with his back turned, the beautiful gardener made his way along the flower border.

Dr Cochrane picked up his newspaper again and turned to the crossword. At 7 Across, where the clue was 'Daily Labours (4)', Dr Cochrane wrote 'KISS'. He looked down the list of clues for four-letter words and he wrote 'KISS' in all of them until no more kisses would fit on the page, and by then the gardener was kneeling at his feet. Dr Cochrane was almost breathless. The gardener stood up. He turned round. He said nothing but he looked Dr Cochrane full in the face and he took off his shirt. He pulled it up over his flat belly, over his smooth chest, up over his head. He stood without saying a word, the crumpled shirt in his hand. His skin was brown and the skin on his arms and in the V of his collar was coffee brown.

Dr Cochrane leaned close to him, so close that he could feel the heat against his face. Dr Cochrane drew in his breath through his nose. He could smell earth and grass and salt and something else. Dr Cochrane held his breath as he would hold a sip of brandy in his mouth for a moment to let it flood him. He was so close to the young man. He was indecently close. He was afraid that one of the mothers pushing her baby in a pram just outside the garden might glance through the iron railings and see them there together. What would she see? There was nothing to see. A respectable university academic sitting on a bench in a public garden and a gardener standing in front of him. That was all. But she would see and understand and know at once. It was stupid and reckless and shaming and irresistibly wonderful and he did not want to stop.

Dr Cochrane leaned on his cane and stood up. There was barely room to do it without touching and then, standing up, he found the bare knees of the gardener brushing against his trousers. Dr Cochrane pressed a folded bill into the young man's hand.

'Thank you,' he said. 'That was exactly right.'

And, when Dr Cochrane was pressing money into the strong hand of a brown young man, Mrs Sophia Antonia de la Santísima Trinidad y Torre Blanco Valdez was looking from her window, down into the courtyard of the building where she lived, watching and waiting for the parcel she had ordered.

She saw the van arrive. She saw the delivery man take a package from the back and when, a moment later, the intercom buzzed she said: 'Yes, of course. Come on up.'

Mrs Sophia Antonia de la Santísima Trinidad y Torre Blanco Valdez walked down the hall of her lovely flat, past the shelf of unread books that greeted every visitor, undoing the cord of her soft, silk dressing gown as she walked, and went to the door.

And, when Mrs Sophia Antonia de la Santísima Trinidad y Torre Blanco Valdez was waiting naked behind the door of her flat, ready to sign for her delivery, Caterina was crossing the busy street outside her flat and hurrying to the telephone box on the corner. She had Chano's card in her purse but she did not look at it. She knew the number off by heart and, when he answered, she said: 'Hello! It's me. It's Caterina.'

He said: 'Hello.' Even in that stale little box, down that thin, tinny wire, it sounded like a warm bath filled with roses.

She said: 'Hello! I've been calling and calling,' and she hated herself for saying that because it sounded like nagging. 'I just wanted to thank you for the flowers.'

He said: 'You are very welcome. I'm glad you like them.'

She said: 'I want to thank you for them. Really thank you. Thank you properly. Can I come round?'

He said: 'I think that would be wonderful.'

When Mr Valdez went back to the kitchen, he found that his glass had left a damp ring of orange juice on the first page of his notebook. He tore it out, crumpled it into a ball and jammed it down beside the broken freesias.

HE SHAVED BEFORE she arrived, stripped the bed and remade it. For a moment Mr Valdez found himself wondering if there might not be something unsavoury about that, but how could there be? There was no question that he would bed Caterina. There could be no doubt that she wanted that too. 'I want to thank you properly': that's what she said. What else could that possibly mean? Whatever it meant, it wasn't: 'I have written you a lovely letter on notepaper with kittens on it and I'd like to hand it in.' No, it meant: 'Wouldn't you rather have sex?'

Mr Valdez knew that this was the culmination of a long seduction. It was not quite as he planned, of course. He had hoped for more of a chase, a token struggle, and he acknowledged there was just a hint of aggression in her call, as if she had been in charge, as if she were the hunter and he the prey. He was unused to that and, already, he felt a tiny pang for the moment of surrender that would not now be his.

'It's her age,' he said to himself. 'She doesn't know how to behave.'

Still, Mr Valdez was ready to be generous and forgiving. Caterina had been his from the moment he decided to have her. He knew that. If it suited her to believe something else, if it made her happy to behave as if she had some choice in the matter, he would go along with that.

He bundled the soiled sheets into the laundry basket and went to choose a suit from his wardrobe. The dark blue would be best, he decided, so soft, so fine, so well cut, and a plain white shirt, enamel links and that tie, so blue it was almost black, with its white polka dots. That went with anything. He was satisfied.

Mr Valdez perfected his knot in the mirror but, standing there preening, tweaking, he felt suddenly foolish. He was dressing to go out when, really, he planned to stay in and undress again very soon. But then what about his shoes? He seemed to have forgotten how to take them off. And those cufflinks. They seemed superfluous. They could be awkward. He pictured himself struggling to take off his shirt as Caterina waited and waited, drumming her fingers on the mattress. And that tie. What was the point of a tie? Or a jacket? Why wear a jacket indoors – in his own house?

It was ridiculous. It was all ridiculous. He was fussing like a girl, like a widow suddenly lifted off the shelf after years, like a divorcee back in the swim again, fretting about which shoes to wear, wondering about what that dress might 'say', worrying over how much leg she ought to put on show. Stupid. Luciano Hernando Valdez was no novice. He was not some schoolgirl looking to throw herself at the local tennis coach in her lunch hour. He was no beginner but, still, he found himself unsettled.

He looked in the mirror. 'It is the *cabeceo*,' he told himself. 'There should be a *cabeceo*.'

Mr Valdez walked back to the kitchen with a sigh, took off his jacket and hung it over the back of the chair.

That would do. She would see it and know that he had a jacket. She could assemble, in her mind's eye, how it should look but without asking why on earth he might be wearing it in his own kitchen. The chair squeaked on the tiles as he pulled it out to sit down. He opened his big, blue notebook again, found his pen and, halfway down the page, halfway across, he began to write.

He wrote: 'The scrawny yellow,' and the doorbell rang.

Mr Valdez closed his notebook and went to the door. His mouth was dry. He composed his face into an expression of wisdom, welcome, interest – but the gilded mirror in the vestibule looked back at him nervously and with fluttering eyes. He took a slow breath, let it out and turned the handle.

'Hello.'

'Hello.'

'Welcome.' He swept his arm into the house, waving her in.

She said nothing, just made a little noise like a stifled giggle and stepped over the threshold.

'A little further,' he said.

'Hmmm?'

'I can't close the door.'

'Oh. Oh, yes.' And that half-choked laugh again.

Outside it was warm but Caterina was wearing a coat that stunned him by its ugliness. It hung about her in a shapeless dome of rough, mud-coloured cloth, like those old horse blankets they wear in the mountain towns with just a hole slashed in the middle to let their heads poke through. Mr Valdez was suddenly reminded of an old book from a long-ago childhood with its alien images of Rumpelstiltskin dancing fiendishly round a fire and odd forest elves who dressed themselves in upturned nutshells.

'You look lovely,' he said.

She smiled and made that noise again. She looked half dazed.

'May I take your coat?'

Mr Valdez was the perfect host but he was beginning to wonder if this might not have been a dreadful mistake. She was an idiot. She could barely even talk. And then she took her coat off and he remembered why he wanted her. The shape of her. It was impossible, unbelievable. The scent of her rising from that awful brown coat. As he hung it in the cupboard by the door it filled him and drove the breath from his lungs. 'My God,' he thought, 'she's young. She smells so young.'

Mr Valdez said: 'Would you like a drink?' as he came out of the cupboard again but Caterina had already left on a tentative exploration and the little vestibule was empty. He followed slowly, listening for the slight suck and squeak of her rubber-soled gym shoes on the tiled floor and then the mysterious cat-silence as she passed across his rich Baluchi rugs.

'You have a lovely house,' she said. Her fingers trailed along shelves as she passed. She looked about herself as if she had just stepped from a glittering silver spacecraft onto an unknown planet.

'Thank you,' he said and stalked her.

'What's this?'

'It's the dining room.'

'It's pretty.'

'Thank you. I never use it.'

'No one comes?'

'No. No one comes.'

'I know,' she said. 'And what's this?'

'My grandfather's sword.'

'He was a hero.'

'He was to me.'

'And this?'

'Some award. Some trophy. I forget. They like to hand out things to dust along with their cheques. It makes the whole thing less sordid.'

'It doesn't say what you won it for.'

'Diligence. Perfect attendance. Biblical knowledge. I don't know. A book. I forget which one. Have it, if you want.'

She looked at him with a fake scowl and said: 'No, thank you. I will wait for one of my own.'

He tried to catch her up, move closer so he could press his face into her hair and bury himself in that smell again, so he could put his hands on her, but she danced away.

'Here's the kitchen,' she said.

'With a big fridge. It usually has champagne in it. Would you like to check?'

'You. You check.' She laughed her quiet, secret, embarrassed laugh again and, while he busied himself with taking down cold glasses from the top shelf and peeling back the foil wrapper and untwisting the wire cage, she danced away again.

'The lounge!' she said.

'Sitting room. It's not a ship.'

'Lovely view. Nice carpet.'

Mr Valdez turned the bottle, not the cork – never the cork – and it came out with a politely whispered belch, like a replete aunt after a good lunch. It was only then that he noticed his notebook was gone.

Caterina was standing at the big window that looks down Cristobal Avenue to the Merino, holding the notebook against her chest, when he arrived with her champagne.

He fought down a flutter of panic and held out the glass. 'Shall I take that?' he said.

'Can I look? I wouldn't look without asking. Can I?'

The flutter came back. 'If I let you look, what will you give me?'

'What do you want?'

'Everything. I want it all.'

'I could just look anyway. I could.'

'That's the price.'

'If I give you everything, can I look?'

'Yes. If you give me everything, you may look, Caterina.'

She opened the notebook. She flicked through its empty pages. 'I think you cheated me.'

'You made your own bargain.'

'So I get "The scrawny yellow" and you get "everything"?' She was pretending to be outraged.

'Three words from the pen of a master – in autograph manuscript too. You can keep them if you like. I'll even sign them, like one of Picasso's napkins. I am paid quite well for my words. It's probably not a bad bargain.'

'Three of your words for my everything? Oh, I think you've done pretty well on the deal.' She danced away from him again and opened the door to the back corridor. 'Pretty well – if I stick to it.'

'I think you'll stick to it.'

'The scrawny yellow what, then? The scrawny yellow Chinaman? The scrawny yellow chicken? What? What?'

'Cat. It's a scrawny yellow cat.'

'And what does he do, this scrawny yellow cat? Where does he go?' She opened another door and said: 'Linen cupboard,' with disappointment.

'He goes into a whorehouse.'

'Just visiting, or does he live there?'

'Why not wait and read the rest of the book?'

'So there's more?'

'Much, much more,' he lied.

Caterina found the last door in the passage. She stood, touching the handle, hesitating like Bluebeard's wife outside the only locked room in the castle.

'This one?' she asked.

'That one.'

'Everything?'

'To the last drop of your blood. To your last breath.'

'All right.'

She turned the handle and went through the door but she

stopped, just inside the room. Mr Valdez stood behind her, a hand on each of her shoulders, holding her, securing her, and he pressed his face into her hair and breathed in her scent.

She laughed again and said: 'Chano', very softly.

'Don't be afraid,' he told her.

'I'm not afraid.'

'Yes, you are. There's no need. Here, come and sit on the bed.' He lay down, his head propped on one arm and she sat beside him, her back to him, two hands jammed down between her clamped thighs.

'Where's your drink?'

'I put it down over there.' She nodded towards his Art Deco dressing table and Mr Valdez saw it and tried hard not to think of the cold damp glass burning a ring into the varnish.

'Take mine,' he said. 'Go on. Just a sip. A tiny sip.'

She unfolded a little and she took the glass.

'Not so terrible,' he said. 'Now a little more.'

She obeyed.

'And again.'

'All gone,' she said and held out the glass to him.

Mr Valdez rolled from the bed and picked up the other glass. He wiped the place where it stood with his plain, white hand-kerchief. There was no mark in the wood. He stood in front of her and handed her the glass.

'Thank you,' she said.

He knelt on the floor at her feet looking up at her. She took another gulp of wine and did not look at him.

'I would like to kiss you now.'

That distant giggle again.

'It's what usually happens. At a time like this. It's usual.'

She tilted her head up a little, her hair falling around her face like a veil. She was biting her lip and he liked that. This suited him. This was the *cabeceo* he had longed for. The chase. The wooing.

'Would you like to be kissed?'

She nodded and offered him her mouth, still damp with champagne, still with a sherbet sparkle lingering on her lips. She tasted fresh and alive and young. God, so young, and she sought him. He felt her hunger. She was electric.

'That was nice,' he said.

'Yes, it was. Let's do that some more.'

He kissed her again but this time when he trailed his fingers over her blouse and touched a button she gripped his hand and pulled it away.

'More kissing first. Kisses.'

'I'll trade you a kiss for every button.'

'No. Wait. Just. Can't we go slowly?'

'Yes,' he kissed her again, this time with the tips of his fingers brushing the knuckles of her fist as she held her blouse shut. 'Yes, we can take our time. There's no hurry. We can take as much time as you want.' He kissed her again. 'But, you did promise me "everything" and, I'm not an expert, but when a beautiful young girl promises "everything" it usually means taking her clothes off.'

'Yes,' she said.

'I'm going to start with your shoes.'

They were like children's shoes, the sort of thing you could see knotted together and strung over the electric cables in grimy back streets, filthy things made of cloth with white rubber on the toes and heels and a white rubber rim gluing them together and flat, woven laces that passed through painted metal eyes. These were not a woman's shoes. Mr Valdez imagined what Maria would have said. She could never have worn such things. She would have been disgraced. There was no heel, for God's sake.

Even when she pruned the roses in her garden, Mrs Marrom wore something with a heel.

When he tugged on the laces, he felt grime on the dusty grey fabric. They came loose, first one and then the other, and he tugged them off. She did not resist. In fact she helped him, offering her feet, holding them up like a little girl getting ready for bath time.

She was wearing socks. He rolled them off and balled them and threw them away with a jokey flourish and a silly, onomatopoeic 'Pop' that was designed to reassure himself as much as it was her. Socks. She might have made more effort.

He rubbed her feet. He trailed his hands over her jeans, up her calves and over her thighs up to the copper button at the top.

'These?' he asked. 'Can I have these?'

She nodded, silently, biting her lip again and raised her hips to help him peel them away. And there she was, long legs bare and wearing that black blouse like an obscenely short miniskirt.

'Now this?' He reached again to her buttons

'No. Soon. Come up on the bed. Kiss me some more.'

So he did. They rolled around there for another hour, playing like teenagers, he in his suit trousers and his shirt and she temptingly, tantalizingly, not quite naked, kissing, tasting, finding each other out until, eagerly, suddenly, all unplanned, that blouse fell open.

She pushed him onto his back and straddled him. 'Here.' she said. 'My cuffs. Undo my cuffs.'

His fingers trembled but he managed it and then she was sitting on him, looking down at him and smiling, dressed in nothing but lace, and he wanted her so much. He reached up to her to touch those astounding breasts. She took his hands and whispered: 'Wait,' and, kissing his fingers, 'Wait,' again.

And then the waiting was over. She was naked with him at

last. Her skin, like silk but without the grain, against his shirt, against his face, in his hands, in his mouth.

She said: 'Everything' and meant it.

Sometimes, if you glance up at the clock at precisely the right moment, time seems to stand still. If the eye falls on the second-hand just at the very instant when it arrives at the next black dash then, somehow, the mechanism seems to freeze. Everything stops just long enough for the mind to notice that the whole world has frozen and there's a tiny moment of exultation and delight at having finally conquered time, at being free to stand outside it for ever, immortal, and there is a cold sliver of glassy terror at the thought of it and then the clock ticks on again. Being with Caterina was like that.

Being with Caterina was like standing on the cliffs above a bay on a bright, clear day, like looking down from afar, seeing the waves hitting the beach in silence, waiting, waiting, waiting until the roar arrives, but by then the waves have gone. Being with Caterina was like that.

Being with Caterina changed everything. Being with Caterina made everything slow, compressed the whole universe into a drop of water, made a single breath fill the sky, made a day and a night and a day into a heartbeat. A whole day and a whole night before they left that bed and a day more before they left the flat.

And even when, in a moment of abandonment, she gripped him tight and called him 'Daddy!' his heart froze for only a second and then he revelled in it.

While he was with Caterina, the Merino congealed into a waxy trickle. The trees in the park wilted. They stood with their branches drooped like disgraced officers on the parade ground, waiting to have their buttons pulled off and their swords snapped.

The whole town filled with heat that soaked into the walls and the pavements and lay there and stank. The dogs howled, the babies cried and, in the prison, the governor opened up the fire hydrants and turned the hoses on the prisoners.

In the cinemas they put huge blocks of ice up on the stage and fanned them with electric fans until they melted away and dripped down into the orchestra pit where the mice lived and the piano stood, furred in dust. Still nobody came.

There was sweat – more than usual – and heat – more than usual. The tango halls smouldered. The smoke of cigars hung there all night and it was still there again the next night. There were fights and the mate of the steamer *Medusa* went out one night on shore leave and didn't come back.

Underneath the Hall of Justice the investigations went on with kicks and punches and flat-handed slaps, teeth knocked out and thumbs tied tight behind the back.

'Ask him again,' said Camillo. 'Keep asking him until he talks.' They all talked. They always talked.

THERE ARE PEOPLE in the *barriada* who live their entire lives immersed in a sea of misery. From the moment they are born until the moment they die — which is usually a mercifully brief parade of moments — they know nothing but suffering and want. Often there is not enough to eat. There is sickness but there is never a doctor. They have nothing, but what they have is enough to attract the wolves. They must do as they are told, obey orders whether they come from the gangster or the policeman and, for the people of the *barriada*, there is very little difference. In the daytime there is no work and nothing to do but sleep. In the night-time the dogs bark and there are gunshots, which are bad, or there is waiting for the gunshots, which is worse.

All summer long the sun beats down on their little tin sheds until the rusty walls glow skin-liftingly hot. The filthy ditches that run past their doors slow to a trickle, clog, solidify and fester so the stink rises up like a fist and the flies come up in angry clouds whenever the children run past.

In winter there is rain and the roofs leak, even on the little shacks where industrious mothers have spent all summer raiding the rubbish dumps and cutting up plastic milk cartons to make shingles. The rain drums on polythene sheets and drips into the tin houses with xylophone plinks. The earth floors turn to mud and the ditches rush with water until a stick or a can or a discarded nappy jams there, gathering more sticks and leaves and mud and half-chewed chicken bones, all knotted and knitted together into a dam. Then the ditches fill and overflow their uncertain banks and the water finds an easier way down the hill, even if that means it must take a house or two along for the company.

But in the middle of all that misery, sometimes the people are happy. Sometimes it is springtime and flowers appear suddenly at the side of a path where nobody ever planted flowers, and for a while they look beautiful.

Maybe one day, somehow, by some miracle, a kid gets his hands on a football and runs with it to a bit of open ground, humped and furrowed like a ploughed field, and plays, hangs in the air like a mosquito and flicks the ball from his toe, straight through the posts. Or a beautiful girl, in that one, brief, summer after she becomes a woman and before she becomes a mother, squeezes herself into a tight yellow T-shirt, bright as sunshine, and walks out into the calle, nose pointing to the sky, titties pointing to the sky, and all the men stand at their doors to watch her pass and blow on their fingers and say 'Aiy'.

Sometimes there would be a lucky ticket in the lottery, sometimes, against the odds, Atletico Club would win, sometimes Santa Ines would hear and prayers were answered, sometimes the electricity stolen from somebody else's cable would stay on.

The people of the *barriada* could wring every tiny drop of happiness out of those things and make them last. That glorious overhead flying kick would fill their conversation for months and, years later, when she was fat and flat-footed, when she was a grandmother and well into her thirties, they would remember the girl in the yellow T-shirt and how beautiful she had been. In the *barriada* they have the gift of happiness. In spite of it all, they expect it.

But Mr Valdez, standing in front of the long mirror that filled the entire wall of his bathroom, did not expect to be happy. Mr Valdez had much, much more modest expectations. He insisted that his mirrors were free of smears, his limestone tiles warm, his towels plump as clouds and as white, his steel taps gleaming, his English shaving brush standing to attention, like one of those silly soldiers sweating under an enormous fur hat outside the Palacio Presidencial, his razor here, his cologne just there. He expected all those things but he did not expect them to make him happy. Even on a day like today when his morning shower was as needle-sharp as he had wished and exactly as warm as he required, when he had shared it with a beautiful girl with impossible breasts in a final, mad outpouring of joy after two mad days of joy, he did not expect to be happy. And yet he was happy.

Now he stood there, holding Caterina, drinking in the smell of her hair, nuzzling that caramel-scented place in the nape of her neck, biting her ears so she squirmed against him and giggled, watching her watching him, and now Mr Valdez felt happy. It astonished him.

That was not the first morning Mr Valdez had made love in the shower but Caterina made it new again.

He stopped himself from wondering if it might have been the first time for her. He would not ask it – not even of himself. It was irrelevant, and not in the way that such things were irrelevant in the Ottavio House.

It was simply not worth considering. Caterina made it not worth considering.

She squirmed away from him again and, when he failed to chase her, she came back, put her arms around his neck and kissed him, standing face to face, belly to belly, unselfconsciously ignoring the mirror for the first time, not performing any longer, not caring how she looked, simply being with him.

'Now stop that,' he said. 'I'm an old man.'

'No, you're not, Chano. Oh no, you're not.' She brushed him with her finger tips and Mr Valdez was amazed to feel his body stir in response.

She kissed him again. 'You are absolutely beautiful. Even this,' another kiss, 'is beautiful.'

'Even what?'

'That mark on your lip.'

'Is there something on my lip?' Mr Valdez went to the mirror and rubbed at his face with a fingertip, as if searching for some stray toothpaste or a blob of dried shaving foam.

She ducked under his arm. 'No, silly. Here.' She kissed him again holding his top lip between her two lips. 'Here. Look,' and, with the very edge of a nail, she traced a horseshoe shape under his nose. 'Even your scar is beautiful. Where did it come from?'

Mr Valdez was watching in the mirror. 'I don't have a scar.'

'Just a tiny one.'

'I don't.'

'Chano, you do. It's hardly noticeable. You needn't be vain about it.'

'But I don't have a scar.'

'Chano!'

'I don't. What are you talking about?'

'Suit yourself.' She was chilly now.

'I don't.'

'Look, the whole world knows that L.H. Valdez has a scar on his lip.'

'I don't.'

'It's in all your pictures. It's on thousands of books – millions – all over the world.'

'Why are you saying this? It's not true.'

'Fine.'

'I don't have a scar. I don't. I'd have remembered. I'd have made up some story, a piranha attack, a jealous husband, saving a busload of orphans from jaguars."

'Fine.'

'I don't have a scar.'

'Chano, I'm getting dressed now.'

He barely heard her. While Caterina was looking for her underwear, moving the bedroom chair, searching under the bed, Mr Valdez was still staring at himself in the mirror. When she was pulling on her jeans, he was rubbing at his lip with a stiff finger. When she was sitting on the wrecked bed and lacing up those silly canvas shoes, he was wiping the mist of his breath from the mirror so he could look at himself again.

She called to him from the door. 'I'm going now.'

He said nothing.

'I said, "I'm going now."' She waited. 'Call me.'

'Yes,' he said. 'Yes, of course.'

'Will you call me? Will you?'

'Of course. I said I would.'

She was standing in that little vestibule – alone. 'Maybe I'll see you at the university.'

In the bathroom the sound of the door slamming made him jump. Mr Valdez walked naked through his empty house and took *The Killings at the Bridge of San Miguel* down from the shelf in his study. He opened the back flap and studied his picture there. There was nothing to see.

It was him – a younger version of him – but there was no scar. Mr Valdez took the book back to the bathroom. He held it up to the mirror, his face side by side with his face. They were the same. There was no scar. He went back to his study. He emptied his shelf and looked at every book in turn, scanning the pictures inside each one, holding them up to the mirror. They were all slightly different, each a year or so apart, all alike. None of them had a scar.

Mr Valdez left his books piled up on the bathroom floor and went to the telephone. It rang for a long time before it was answered and Mr Valdez said: 'Mama, do I have a scar on my lip?'

'YOU HAVE A rare gift for finding useful little bits of happiness.'

'Actually, that's true,' said Caterina. 'I do. But I know how this works. You just tell me something bland but nice, something nobody could disagree with, and I'm expected to say how amazing and insightful it is.'

'Shhh,' said Erica, 'cynics and doubters block the channels with their negative vibrations. I cannot be expected to work if I am surrounded by negative energy.'

Caterina leaned forward across the table and peered down into her own outstretched palm. 'You see, that just adds to my doubts. That's not exactly in tune with the scientific method. Two plus two is always four even if you add them up in front of an audience of unbelievers. Tell me something else.'

She looked down and saw the lines and folds in the pale skin of her palm and they reminded her of that lump of mud on her windowsill at home, drying out to a disappearing of dust, just a million tiny brown specks, all that was left of a ground-down mountain with nothing to show of what it had once been, light enough to blow away, soft enough to melt in the rain, the marks of her father's hand vanishing.

'A new man has come into your life.'

'Well, we both know that.'

Erica held her hand by the fingertips, unfolding it, opening it out on the table like a dissection specimen. Her skin was pale and white and soft when his had been dark and hard-worn with calloused ridges at the joints where reins and hoes and axe handles had rubbed. How gently he had held her.

'Already I can see you have given this man more than he deserves.'

There was a wine glass on the table, with a candle flame reflected in it. With her free hand, she reached out and took a long swallow. 'Is that what you see?'

'It's all there in your hand.'

'Look in the other one.'

'It only works with the left. Always the left.'

'So that's what you see?'

'How can the lines lie?'

Caterina emptied her wine glass. 'You don't expect me to comment on that do you?'

'Of course I do. If you don't tell me, how am I going to know what you've been up to?'

'But it's none of your business what I've been up to.'

'How can you say such a thing? Of course it's my business. My best friend disappears into Bluebeard's Castle and survives to tell the tale – that is top-quality gossip and I am entitled to share.'

'It's private.' Caterina was smiling. She wasn't offended. She hadn't slammed the door completely. But she sounded firm.

'Private? Don't I tell you everything?'

'Erica, you say that as if you had things to tell.'

'All right. I live like a nun. That's not the point. But if you don't tell me . . .'

'What?'

'If you don't tell me, I'll just have to make it up.'

'Make it up then.'

'Mine will be juicier.'

'Oh, I doubt that.'

Erica feigned horror. She clapped a hand over her open mouth. 'You! Well, listen to you. I'm lost for words.' And then, when Caterina said nothing, she said: 'You're really not going to tell me anything, are you?'

Caterina laughed and poured herself some more wine.

Far away on the edge of town, slipping almost silently between rows of white-painted rail fence on his way to the polo ground in his beautiful green car, Mr Valdez would have been delighted with that.

L.H. Valdez made his career on word-of-mouth recommendations. Breathless professors in airless lecture halls talking of things that fashion demanded they should praise and pretend to understand, students in grubby flats, sitting up all night talking of all the books they would never, ever write, and of course the women. There were drawing rooms and coffee shops and boudoirs where L.H. Valdez was discussed in tones of hushed admiration far beyond anything in the literary salons of the capital.

'Between ourselves, in absolute confidence.'

'My dear, I'd die first.'

And, with every whisper, every shared secret, his reputation grew and he became more desired. He was coveted, like the latest, most fashionable handbag, like those essential shoes. There were women who could not hold their heads up in society unless they could say they had spent a night, or two nights or a week of nights with L.H. Valdez, women who would think their lives wasted unless they could sob out their disappointed secrets to a few envious friends. He knew of course. They were blatant. They were flagrant.

'Tell me, wasn't that better than Letitia?' the one after Letitia would say.

'I know you didn't do that with Estella. She wouldn't let you.

She told me,' said the one after that. The mutterings. They spoke of him as he might speak of a polo pony, comparing, rating, like horseflesh, like the conversations he had in the ice-clinking comfort of Madame Ottavio's garden. It was all very discreet of course, all hidden inside the secret world of women, kept away from anxious husbands, but Mr Valdez was sick of it. He went from one to the other, or they passed him round. He could not decide which and he didn't care. But already he did care about Caterina and he cared very much what she said.

When he was making the turn between stone pillars and into the broad, curving gateway of the polo club, far away, in the middle of town, Caterina was saying: 'It's private.'

A beam of sunlight came through the window and struck her where she stood in the kitchen, glass in hand, already, so early in the day, a little drunk, surrounded by gaudy flowers beginning to fade and the faintly fishy smell of old water standing too long in tin buckets.

'It's private.' The sunshine flooded her hair and kissed its way down her impossible, extravagant body, over her thick faded jeans, down to her childish socks. She stood there like a holy statue: the Madonna of the Kitchen, a wine glass in her hand, still warm from the bed of her lover, but a holy thing who understood the holiness of things.

Caterina was no saint and she was certainly not a prude. When Mr Valdez demanded 'everything' she had given it. Everything. She had a country girl's easy, matter-of-fact acceptance of the mechanical joy of it. She had terrified him with her simple, straightforward 'Wouldn't you rather . . . ?' But she understood that, somehow, this was different and sacramental.

The priests would call it 'an outward and visible sign of an inward, invisible grace,' but Caterina never spoke like that.

'It's private,' she said.

And, just as she said that, Mr Valdez took one hand from the bone-white steering wheel of his lovely green car, looked in the driver's mirror and, faintly, gently, he brushed one finger over his lip.

OUTSIDE THE FLAT, down in the shadows at the bottom of the canyon, where the dogs lay panting, where yesterday's newspapers had come to die, where an old man lay on his back on the pavement with piss staining the front of his trousers and a brown bottle rolling from his fingers towards the gutter and making music as it rolled, there, parked between two bins, there was an old blue car.

It was the sort of car that nobody would want to steal. It was dusty. The tyres were bleached and dull grey with tiny splits crackling the sides. There was only one hub-cap left and the plastic steering wheel was worn right through so that a sort of shabby sponge poked out of it. It was an invisible car, a poor man's car, but that car had two large, thick aerials sticking out of the roof and its enormous engine was serviced twice a week in a well-equipped garage at the back of the Central Police Barracks. There was a rough blot of grey plastic putty where the mechanics had repaired a bullet hole in the wing, close to the driver's door, and there was a dent where Commandante Camillo drove the gunman's head into the bonnet with his fist. Nobody bothered to repair that.

Commandante Camillo was sitting in that car amongst curled and blackened banana skins, crushed cans and balls of waxed paper spotted with chilli sauce. The ashtray was full and he had thrown

ANDREW NICOLL · 161

his last two cigar butts on to the floor because his training forbade him to leave the signs of a long watch piled at the pavement edge. All the time that Caterina had been with Mr Valdez, Commandante Camillo had been sitting outside in that car, waiting, thinking, making connections in his head. For two whole days, that girl, that kid, in that house, with Valdez. Dio, what a waste. What a lesson he could teach her, give her the taste of a real man. When she left, he waited a little and pulled out into the traffic without looking, without signalling, finding the gap with the hairs on the back of his hands, driving slowly behind her, speeding up to pass her, waiting for her, watching her come closer in the mirror, watching her walk away reflected in the window of the furniture store across the street, until she got home. He watched her walking. It was incredible.

When Caterina opened the door that led to her stairs, Commandante Camillo breathed out in a hot sigh. He was tired. His suit was soft with sweat. He smelled his own rankness.

On the seat beside him there was a pile of papers in a dusty green folder and, on top of that, the strange journal of a sick, sad boy.

He picked it up and held it against his eyes without opening it. 'Five times I have read this and I don't understand a word of it. What is he to you, Valdez? And the girl – little Miss Luscious Tits? What's her story?'

The Commandante flicked back the cover of the folder with a thick finger. Inside it was exactly the same as it had been all the other times he had read it. There were two sheets of crisp, white paper on top, new, neatly printed. They were dated from the day of the bombing and, under them, another eighty-three pages, frail, brittle, yellow, with words across them in uncertain lines, odd letters out of place, typed in blue-black and purple, soft, leaky unfocused letters made by old typewriter keys striking through worn-out carbon paper. They were nearly forty years old.

Commandante Camillo sighed again. 'My beautiful Sophia Antonia,' he said. 'All this you brought on yourself.'

It's strange that everybody in this story seemed, at that moment, to be sitting on the opposite side of town from somebody who was thinking of them. Caterina, standing in her shower of sunbeams, surrounded by wilting flowers, was thinking of Mr Valdez, gliding slow and stately in his wonderful green car between the paddocks of the polo club.

Mr Valdez turned smoothly into the car park where the long, dusty drive changed to a crackle of fine yellow pebbles that spat under his tyres. He slowed down, stopped. The car park was almost empty and Mr Valdez chose his space with care, sliding his lovely mermaid-green car next to an ancient grey Volvo with a broken tail light. He put his car there the way a jeweller would put a diamond in its silver setting; not to make the metal look dull but to make the diamond sparkle more. His car shone.

In front of him, behind another line of white fence and across a broad lens of lawn as smooth and level as a Persian rug, the polo club glowed with a cool beauty. Mr Valdez ignored it and, instead, he threw his jacket over his shoulder and walked off in the other direction, towards the stables. Mr Valdez liked the stables, the ponies with their soft noses and their hard-spring legs and the warm, clean smell of their flesh and their breath and their dung. But before he reached the horse boxes, he stopped in front of an open set of double doors.

'Hello, De Silva,' he said.

'Oh. Hello.'

De Silva was sitting in a saddle slung over a wooden trestle. He was wearing the suit he wore to university every day and his bald suede shoes were pushed into a pair of stirrups.

He said: 'You don't seem surprised to see me.'

'I spotted your car.'

De Silva said: 'How did you know it was mine?'

'I know about cars. Yours is an old car.'

'I don't think it's as old as yours.'

'Ah, but mine is an antique. Yours is just old.'

De Silva didn't know what to say to that. He made a few idle swings with the polo mallet in his right hand and then he said: 'You must be wondering what I am doing?'

'I can see what you're doing and you're not doing it very well.'

'I'm practising. I'm just learning.'

'Yes. Try to follow through a bit more. Here, try this.' Mr Valdez took a ball from a heap by the wall and bowled it through the thick sawdust on the floor towards De Silva's imaginary horse. He missed.

'I don't suppose you'd believe me if I told you I was doing quite well at this until you arrived.'

'It's always the way and, for all the technique, once you get two or three ponies jammed in together, with the ball in amongst their legs, it's all just a matter of poking about.'

'I don't think I'll ever be good enough to play.'

'Oh, don't say that. I can easily get you a knockabout. We'll get a few of the boys together if you're interested – which you clearly are. What brought this on?'

De Silva handed him the mallet and stepped down from the saddle. 'I don't know. Mid-life crisis I suppose. Polo isn't something we did a lot in the Navy.'

'Hard to get the ponies on the boat.'

'Ship. Submarines are boats.' They walked out of the shed together into the sunshine and, as he put on a pair of sunglasses, De Silva said: 'When I saw you, my heart sank. Thank you for not making fun of me. You always do things so well and you don't suffer fools. I felt sure you would laugh at me. I'm sorry I misjudged you.'

'Don't be sorry. If I'd seen you yesterday or the day before I would have mocked you mercilessly.'

'But?'

'But things change.'

'What things?'

'Just things. People.'

They were almost back at the car park when Mr Valdez said: 'You know that scar on my lip . . .'

And he was not even slightly surprised when De Silva said: 'What about it?'

'Is it really noticeable?'

'Does it bother you? I never gave it a moment's thought. You've had it as long as I've known you. It was always just part of the furniture. I wouldn't worry about it.'

De Silva paused and said: 'Chano, is everything all right?'

'Of course. Why?'

'Well, you forgot to be cruel to me. You're worried about some ancient scar. You tell me that things change. It's not that girl, is it?'

'What girl?'

'Come on. That girl. The kid from Cochrane's maths class. The one from the Phoenix. You know,' he cupped his hands in front of his chest, 'that one.'

'Oh. *That* one.' Mr Valdez lied: 'No, don't you worry about that.'

'And how's the book going?'

Without stopping to think, Mr Valdez found himself telling the truth. 'It's shit. It is total shit. I can't think of a single thing to write. There's no story.'

'How come?'

'I just can't think of what's supposed to happen. There's no story.'

'Come on. There are stories everywhere. Look in the paper. There's a priest who wasn't allowed to take the Mass on Sunday and the bishop sent a message that he was in the asylum after "a complaint". What's his story? There's an old major who saved three of his men from a burning truck. One of those men had a kid and that kid killed the major's son in a car crash.'

'You could have explained that better.'

'I'm not the acclaimed author. Look, I was sitting on that horse and I saw a butterfly. What's his story? Where did he come from, what did he see, what does he think, what are butterfly songs like, do butterflies love or mourn?'

'I'm not a poet – and neither are you.'

'I'm trying to help.'

'Yes, I know. I know. Thanks.' And then it was over and Mr Valdez began to lie again. 'It's just, I've got this character, a fair way into the book, a good way in, and he goes on a journey, arrives at his destination, and . . .'

'And you don't know what happens next.' De Silva unlocked his car and sat down inside. 'Relax. It'll come to you. You've got this far.'

'Yes, it'll come to me.'

De Silva pulled the door shut with the sort of heavy clunk that only comes from the kind of engineering designed to cope with elk-crashes. 'You'll sort it out. How's your mother, by the way?'

'I'm just about to meet her in the club.'

'Be sure to give her my kindest regards.' He turned the wheel and reversed away.

IN JUST THE way that Caterina was standing in her kitchen and thinking of Mr Valdez, Commandante Camillo was sitting in his car and thinking of Mrs Sophia Antonia de la Santísima Trinidad y Torre Blanco Valdez, who was also at the polo club, seated at her favourite table by the window, trying not to fray the lovely napkin in front of her, wondering why her only son would make her take a taxi so far out of town when he could just as easily have picked her up, and dreading the meeting they were about to have.

She was offended and upset and – because Mrs Valdez was always scrupulously fair in these matters, never judging others more harshly than she judged herself, in fact, as she was forced to acknowledge, usually the reverse – she felt completely justified.

And, in just the way that Commandante Camillo was sitting in his car, thinking of Mrs Sophia Antonia de la Santísima Trinidad y Torre Blanco Valdez, she was sitting at her table thinking of him. For nearly forty years she had managed to think of him hardly at all, but now, since Chano had so unthinkingly passed on his regards, he seemed to haunt her.

Things that Mrs Valdez had carefully and deliberately pruned from her memory had now, suddenly, returned in a plague of dark and poisonous blossoms. Camillo was lurking in the shadows of her father's house, washing the Admiral's enormous black car, sweeping the leaves from the drive that curved up to the three marble steps at the front door, kissing her, pressing his mouth into hers and putting his hands on her exactly as she had longed for him to do, but something had changed. He wasn't a boy any more. The Camillo of memory was the same one she saw every day in the newspaper or in TV broadcasts, standing up gigantic and terrifying, surrounded by strong young men with blank and brutal faces just as he had once stood beside the Commandante of Detectives long years ago, just as he had stood outside her house, watching. And now there was this business of the scar.

Mrs Valdez put down her napkin and forced a smile as she saw Chano arrive. She offered her cheek to be kissed.

'Hello, Mama.'

She said: 'Darling.'

'Did you order?'

'No. I was waiting.'

He drew out a chair and sat down and then, after saying nothing for a while when they just looked at each other and examined the cutlery, he said: 'Anyway, I asked you a question.'

Mrs Valdez bristled at that. 'You are very short,' she said.

'I'm sorry.'

'Sometimes you have no manners. I blame myself, of course.'

'Please, Mama.'

Mrs Valdez sighed impatiently. 'What do you want to know?'

'Mama, I have a scar on my lip. I do. Don't I? And yet all my life we have never, ever talked about it.'

The waiter arrived and they ordered coffee and cakes and, sat in a stiff, upright, straight-backed silence while he fussed, pointlessly around the table. When, at last, he left again, Mr Valdez said: 'Why?' very quietly.

'Why? Why have you suddenly become interested? Why now?'

'I don't know. I didn't notice before.'

'You didn't notice?' There was a harsh quality to her voice, like a fork drawn sharply across a china plate, and it made people on the other side of the room look up.

Mrs Valdez looked down into her napkin. She said: 'I have lost count of the times that a perfectly nice morning coffee has been ruined by other people's complaints. The number of times I have put on my gloves to go out to some little gathering, in a friend's house or a pleasant café, expecting a little chatter, perhaps even a tiny acidic pearl of gossip to enjoy, only to find, instead, that it turned into an endless stream of misery! "My feet, my dear. My bunions, my dear. My veins, my dear."

'I would no more discuss my ailments amongst friends than I would, than I would' – she struggled to find something sufficiently outlandish – 'than I would cut my toenails at the table.

'Of course, like a good friend and out of politeness I listen with sympathy, you know I always try to put others first, but it is boring – very boring – and annoying and, most of all, it is unfair. Could there be anything more tedious than other people's illness?

'And out of all of them, out of all those complaining women, none of them, not one of them, would have listened if I wanted to complain about my great trouble; the dreadful, cold gap in my life where my grandchildren should be and, if I should die without seeing my husband's name preserved, which of them would share my shame? It is all too awful to talk about and now you, Chano, you have decided to join in with your strange telephone calls and your "Mama, do I have a scar on my lip?"'

'But I do.'

'Yes.' Mrs Valdez looked up from her napkin at last. 'Yes, you do. What of it? Has it held you back in some way? Has it blighted your life? Do women find you less attractive? Has it damaged your career? Have you been bullied? Has anyone ever even commented on it?'

'No, Mama. That's the point. Nobody has ever mentioned it. You never mentioned it. Children are cruel, they latch on to any tiny difference like a pack of dogs, but nobody ever mentioned it. Not once. Not a word. None of the cousins ever said a word, none of the uncles, none of the aunts. Don't you think that strange?'

'No. Perhaps people are kinder than you know. Anyway, you never mentioned it either.'

'Mama, how could I? I didn't know.'

'You didn't know? How could you not know?'

'That's what I'm asking you.'

She looked at him without understanding.

He said: 'I'm sorry. This is a waste of your time.' And when she still said nothing, he said: 'I don't know who I am, Mama. I don't know myself. We never talk about anything. My father. Who was Daddy? What happened to him? Where did he go? I don't know anything. I don't even recognize my own face. Do you?'

Mrs Valdez fussed with her pastry fork for a moment then she said: 'And you made me take a taxi to get here too.'

'You can get a taxi back,' he said. Mr Valdez stood up to go but she put her hand down on his, her thin hand, with its fragile skin.

'It's hard for me,' she said. 'It's hard for me to remember.'

'I can't remember at all,' he said.

By the time the waiter came, bringing his tray of coffee and cakes, Mr Valdez and his lovely green car were already leaving the car park.

MR VALDEZ LEFT his beautiful car in the basement of his apartment building where it sat, like a sleeping panther, smelling of leather and hot oil and ticking as it cooled. Mr Valdez looked back at it with love, turned and climbed the stairs to the lobby.

On each side of the room there was a broad, red leather sofa and Caterina was sitting on one of them, the one behind the basement door, with her feet flung out in front of her and a big canvas bag on the seat beside her. Mr Valdez didn't even notice her. He walked from the door marked 'Stairs to the Basement' straight to a half wall of pigeon holes, each one sealed with a hinged brass cover, each one numbered with black enamel figures.

Mr Valdez unlocked his box and looked inside and then, with two fingers, like a magician, like a pickpocket, like a man with tweezers picking up broken teeth from a city pavement, he removed a postcard.

It was a postcard exactly like dozens of other postcards he had received before. In the past they had said 'Tomorrow at 2' or 'Tuesday afternoon'. But this one was different. This one said 'I know what a dreadful mistake I made. Dying without you. I am so very sorry. Let me show you how much. Please forgive me. Grant me absolution tomorrow' and it was signed simply 'M'. Mr Valdez read it all in a second and tore the card to confetti.

It was only then, when he lifted his eyes from the wire waste basket at his feet, that he noticed her sitting there, watching him.

'Hello,' she said.

'Hello.' He said only 'Hello' when, before, with his other women, he would have said, 'Darling' or 'My Angel' and he was conscious that he had made the change unselfconsciously. It was natural. The extra parts of him were torn away in front of this girl until only Luciano was left. He was smiling.

'You look happy,' she said.

'I suppose I am. Surprised to see you, too.'

'Sorry, should I go?' She swung her feet under her body as if to stand up. 'I don't want to pester you.'

'No, of course I don't want you to go. Have you been here long?'

'Not long. Half an hour, maybe. Not angry with me?'

'No.'

'Sure?'

'Why should I be angry?'

'Well, we didn't part happily.' She looked down at her ridiculous faded sneakers. 'That business with the scar. I'm sorry. I didn't mean to offend you.'

'I'm not offended. You were right. It's for me to apologize.'

'Silly. Do you want to talk about it?'

'No. Not really.' Mr Valdez was baffled. How could he talk about something he could not see and did not understand? 'Some things can't be fixed by talking. Most things in fact. Actually, the more I think about it, I can't think of a single thing that can be fixed by talking. When you are as old as I am, you will know that too and yet, just a short while ago – earlier this afternoon in fact – I did want to talk.'

'It's not such a mad idea, talking. It cures most things. It can even cure wars.'

'The only thing that can cure a war is excess of pain. When people get sick of the pain, they stop the war.'

'When people get sick of the pain, they talk,' she said.

Mr Valdez took his keys from his pocket. 'Do you want to come up?'

'Again?'

'Yes.'

'Do you want me to?'

'Yes. Do you want to? Again.'

'Yes.'

He took her hand and, in the lift, he kissed her, there, on the palm of her hand.

Caterina said: 'You are very lucky to have a quiet, secret place like this.'

'You mean, like this lift?'

'I meant your lovely flat but, yes, even your lift. Some place where there's nobody watching or listening. Some place where you can be alone or with somebody else. Some place where you can kiss.'

The lift stopped.

'Don't you have such a place?' he said.

'I never did. Not ever. I live in a student flat and, before that, we all lived in the cottage, all of us in the one room.'

'Your mother and father too?'

'There was a curtain.'

'A curtain?' Mr Valdez was amazed. He was amazed at the life this girl had led, amazed that she had so little, astonished that he wanted her so much in his own life.

'Yes, a curtain. We could pull it across at night to split the room up. But we were very young. Anyway, it's not the worst thing in the world to think that your mother and father make love.'

Make love. Her mother and father made love on the other side of the curtain and yet she had asked him if he wanted sex.

'No,' he said. 'Not the worst thing.' He opened the door. 'And is there still only one room in your house?'

'I don't know. I don't think so. Pappi died. I think my brother made another room on the outside of the house. I haven't been home for a while.' She offered her face to be kissed again but he seemed not to notice.

'How did you come here, from that place with your little one-room house? How did you come here? Dr Cochrane says you are one of his best students.'

'I was lucky,' she said. 'And people were kind and I work. I work hard. I know how to work.'

'Yes,' he said. He put his fingers on the buttons of her shirt, his thumb and his first two fingers, ready to press them together and push and turn and open, and he found her fingers there too, brushing against his but this time she was helping him, not fending him off. This time she wanted to be naked with him. This time she wanted to be rid of her clothes.

'Chano,' the word still sounded new and strange in her mouth. 'Chano, I don't do this sort of thing. I don't.'

He took his hand away in alarm. 'But I wasn't the first.' Suddenly the thought horrified him. Before – in the time before Caterina – it would have thrilled him, it would have added extra savour to the conquest, but now it made him feel like a thief. And then, because what he had said sounded like an accusation, he said: 'Was I?'

She flung herself at him. She wrapped her arms around him. She stumbled across her stupid canvas bag so she could be close to him and she pressed her face into his shirt. 'No,' she said, 'you weren't the first. But it feels like the first. There were boys before. You're a man. There were fumbles in the dark but you aren't like them. I'm sorry. I'm being stupid. I'm making more of this than it deserves and I threw myself at you in the first place. And then, when it happened, it was so good, it was all so good and then I left you this morning and I didn't think you'd even call me again and I was ready for that. I told myself I could be grown up about it and then by the afternoon I'm sitting on your doorstep like a lost puppy. It's not your fault. I'm sorry.' She stepped back and started pulling at the buttons of her shirt again, sniffling and saying: 'Come on, come on!'

And now, when he put his hands on hers, it was to stop her and still her. She did not look at him so he took her face between his hands and kissed her, kissed her hair and her forehead, kissed her eyes, kissed her nose, her lips, her chin, kissed her and held her until they both cried. It was the second time Mr Valdez had cried in the past thirty-seven years.

EVERYTHING THAT WAS left of the afternoon they spent together. They sat in the kitchen drinking coffee and talking. She told him about her father and life on the farm, about her village. He told her about his grandfather, the Admiral. She told him why she walked with her arms folded and her eyes downcast like a cloistered nun, avoiding the eyes of men or, sometimes, when it became too much to bear, glaring fire at them and shooting her chin.

When it began to grow dark they moved to the sitting room. Mr Valdez sat on the huge leather sofa with its square cushions and legs of bent chrome pipe and looked down the long vista of Cristobal Avenue, a rising, narrowing V of perspective disappearing into the dusk. Caterina lingered near his desk, trailing fingers over it, brushing it with her hands. Mr Valdez remembered how that felt.

'I don't keep any money in it, you know.'

'I know,' she said.

His notebook was lying there. For a moment he was afraid that she might open it and discover that there was nothing to discover and then he remembered that she already knew. He had bought her with that single line, those few words, which were all that he had in the world.

'Come away from there,' he said. 'Sit here, beside me.'

But she ignored him. 'Be quiet while I idolize profanely,' she said and she turned her back to his and raised her arms over her head, snaking wrist over wrist, twining her fingers and coiling in gorgeous, obscene ripples that shook her whole body as she made obeisance to the desk. She finished by kissing it, like the Bishop, kneeling to kiss the altar. 'This is a holy thing, you know.'

'It's a desk.'

'It's where you write.'

'There's no point drenching me in compliments. I have already willed it to the museum.'

'You can always change your will. You could leave it to me.'

'Already you want me dead!'

She threw herself at him again. 'No, no! Chano, no! Live for ever. Live.' She knocked him over like a puppy and they fell on the sofa together. Nothing happened. There was no kissing. There was something in the way of it. They lay together watching the gathering dark and the traffic moving along the avenue like burning strings of jewels, winking and sparkling on the other side of that vast window. Mr Valdez wondered if he had fallen asleep. He got up, went to the kitchen and made omelettes, came back and they ate. She took off her horrible shoes, drew up her legs and sat on the sofa beside him. They watched TV. Her shoes stank. They went to bed. She asked if she might use his tooth-brush. They undressed in the dark. They lay down together, wrapped in each other, touching the length of their bodies, and they slept. There was no 'Again'. They slept. He woke in the night when her hair brushed against his face, when her new smell filled him. High above the street lamps the city glow was faint at the window and it hummed over her pale skin and there was, again, that shimmering aura of beauty, drawn around every line of her like a protective glow. He could see it clearly, even in the darkness. He put his hand on her, barely touching her, skimming over the curves of her, touching her in disbelief. When she moved, he covered her lightly with the sheets and went back to sleep.

In the morning he woke to the sound of water running in the bathroom. She had left a warm curve, a child's shape, marked in the bed by her woman's body. He let his hand rest there, looking for a memory of her.

When she came back, walking flat-footed across the whispering tiles, she was carrying a plastic folder.

'It was in my bag,' she said. 'I brought it. In case I found the courage.' Her voice sounded tight and dry and faint. She gave a little cough. 'I write, you see.'

'Yes. You told me.'

'Yes.' She climbed into bed. 'I wanted you to read it but now I don't. I want to read it to you instead.' She moved on top of him so he was lying on his belly and she could sit on him, like a grand lady riding her horse through the park on a Sunday morning. He felt her heat in his back, the softness of her thighs down his sides. She stroked his hair and rubbed his back. 'You have nice shoulders,' she said.

'Thank you.'

'I'm going to read to you now and would you, please, not say anything until it's finished.'

'My lips are sealed.'

'I know it's rubbish. I know it's nothing to what you could do but I want to read it to you.'

'I'm sure it won't be rubbish.' Oh, Chano, he thought, you storyteller. How you've changed your tune.

'Shh. Listen.'

This is what she read.

Once upon a time, a long, long time ago (which is the accepted and recognized style for beginning a story such as this and has been since stories were invented), once upon a time there was a hot little hill village set in the middle of some red fields with not much water.

There were thirty families living in that village, including one woman with three clean children who made her living entertaining anybody who passed by along the road and any of the men from the village or the two other villages in that long valley who happened to call. That was nice for the other women in the village, since it gave them someone to look down on and that is always encouraging.

When a man gets so drunk that he falls down in the street, crawls home and slaps his wife, sleeps until noon and then is too ill to go out and look after the animals, it does his woman good to remember that at least she is not the village whore. Life might be bad, but it's not as bad as that, which is a comfort.

Down in the gully at the end of the village, where that woman lived, her three clean little children spent all the morning playing in the stream, building dams and launching stick boats which might, one day, reach the sea.

Then, in the afternoon, when it got too hot to play, they came inside and learned their lessons while their mother washed their clothes and pressed their clothes and combed their hair and told them that they would grow up to be doctors and live rich in the city – which they did. And years later, when the people in the village heard about that and remembered the little children who used to live there, they all agreed that it would be very unpleasant to be ill in the city and find that your doctor was somebody who had clearly spent far too little time contemplating the very great sins that must have been committed to pay for such a fancy education.

Now, if this were a proper story, a story as stories used to be told, we would climb out of the gully and along the street to where the old well sits at the bottom of the hill. We would climb the hill, up the zigzag path, all the way to the beautiful old house at the top, and find the wise old hidalgo who lived there. He would have a handsome son, with flashing eyes and a powerful sword-arm, a prancing stallion black as a woman's hatred – but no wife. And then, after many sighs and much singing, he would get one.

But, as you already know, while things change they never get better, so this is not that kind of a story.

There is no wise old hidalgo and there is no beautiful old house. At the top of the hill there is only an ancient fort, all broken and roofless, with walls of strangely shaped stones, huge boulders shaped into skewed rectangles with flat faces and bevelled edges, all locked together like the teeth of an alligator to stand against the earthquakes. Since the days of the Conquistadores nobody but monkeys has lived there, so we will go back down the hill to the village and the big white house at the end of the street by the well.

It's a nice house, don't you think? Good solid gates painted green and a thick wall all the way round, higher than a man and replastered every year against the rains. Stand on the other side of the street and you can see the tops of three trees waving like slow, green flags. They take a lot of watering, but they give good shade and they make the neighbours envious, which is what counts. Those trees, sucking up bucket after bucket of water and waving their branches over the high wall, are as good as a flashing neon sign that says: 'A man of wealth lives in this house.'

This is the home of Jose Pablo Rodriguez, and when he stands on his roof in the evening, all the fields he can see away off to the south are his, everything in the north is his, everything on every side is his.

Now, it was not always so. In the days of the father of Jose Pablo, there were fields all around the village which belonged to others, but times change. Men die and their little bits of ground are parcelled off among half a dozen sons and some will always want to sell – always. Or there are daughters to be married and dowries to be provided and weddings to be paid for. Sometimes men must borrow. Jose Pablo was always ready to lend – at interest and for the right security. Or there is misfortune. A sick child. A broken leg. The plough standing idle. Sometimes men must sell. Jose Pablo was always ready to buy.

Jose Pablo understood that nothing works harder than money because money never sleeps. Put money to work and it is always working. A man cannot work in the field every minute of the day. It cannot be done. He must rest. He must eat. But he must pay rent every minute of the day. Night and morning, sleeping and waking, the rent is being paid. Jose Pablo understood that. That was why, at last, he owned all the fields.

They had called out to his father in the street, as to one they had known from childhood. They called his father Manolito but him they called 'Señor' because he was lord and mother and father of the whole village and he held it in his hand to crush or caress. Jose Pablo Rodriguez was heaven-born and he walked the street with a heavy tread so that men would notice.

On this morning, when he got up and looked from his roof across the fields – which were all his and his alone – Jose Pablo saw a strange thing. To the south, all the fields were empty. In the north, nobody was at work. To the east and the west, the paths leading out of the village were empty, and this distressed him because he liked to lie late, knowing his money was always hard at work and he expected to look out in the morning and see it working. And then, what was more distressing still, even before he had taken his coffee, he heard the distant tinkle of the brass bell that hung by his gate.

It was a delegation, and that displeased Jose Pablo very much; the whining and the pleading and the childish requests. He was in no mood for it but there they stood, at the big green gate – half the men in the village, and they pushed before them the idiot Julio as the chief of the beggars.

'Oh, Señor Rodriguez, will you not hear the voice of an innocent who has suffered a great wrong?'

Jose Pablo heaved a great sigh and settled himself on the cane chair that sat in the shade under the middle tree of his three great trees. He sat open-legged to give his belly room and he beckoned shortly to the men at the gate.

Four of them came in, the idiot Julio and three of his friends. They stood respectfully just outside the ring of tree shade, examining their feet, or glancing at his.

'Speak,' he said.

Julio said nothing.

'Donkey, speak up. Do you think I have nothing to do all day but watch you standing here, dumb?'

Little by little, with pokes and urgings from the three friends, the story came out, how the pedlar Miguel Ángel, that wicked boy with his hair too long and his smiling eyes and his quick-fingered flute, had passed along the valley and camped up in the old stone fort. And because the pedlar Miguel Ángel is many times cursed and in the pay of devils, the monkeys of the fort had not come at night to attack him and steal from his pack.

Everybody had heard the sweet music of his flute, floating down from the castle walls in the night, and when he moved on up the valley again, the daughter of Julio had a golden comb in her hair.

'This was a month ago, Señor. Also two goats were stolen and the pedlar Miguel Ángel must be caught and punished.'

Then Jose Pablo laughed. 'Two goats! A month ago! A month and only now you have come to complain?' He slapped his hand on his fat thigh. 'I am thinking the pedlar played a good tune with his flute. And where's your daughter now? I heard she walked to the railway station and went to visit a sick aunt in town. Is that right? Maybe she took the goats with her. Miguel Ángel is no thief of goats.'

The old cane chair groaned as Jose Pablo stood up and went back inside his fine house. He was laughing still when he sat down to take his maté and he congratulated himself again on his good fortune. 'The man who can buy jewels for his daughter's dowry need have no fear of a pedlar with a shiny comb.'

It was not many days after that, when a fat moon was hanging in the sky, half behind the hilltop and making the red earth shine blue for miles around, that they heard the music from the fort again.

Jose Pablo stood on his roof, a thick blanket over his shoulders against the dewy night, and followed the tune as it drifted, like silver threads, as weightless as the moonshine up and down the street.

Later, when he was in his bed and the music still played, soft and soothing and far away, he found he had followed it all the way down to sleep, but he never even realized until he woke with a start and remembered, as if in a dream, that a door had banged far off. There was the sound of running in the street, and a little while later, when the fat landlord was asleep again, the music stopped.

The next day, when the men were going out to work, he saw Julio on the path and laughed and called him 'donkey' again. 'I see you have a black eye and a split lip, donkey. Have you been taking flute lessons at the fort? Last night, I heard you. And how many goats have you lost today?' He laughed and laughed but Julio only flung his hoe across his shoulders and walked on to clear his fields.

All that day the men worked the fields, the thin clouds wandered about high up and forgot to shed any rain, the birds flew, the goats clambered over the red hill, the turned earth grew dry and dusty in the furrows and blew away in a fine drizzle like spume from the tops of waves on an ocean which none of them had ever seen or could even imagine. And all that day Jose Pablo sat in his fine house, counting columns in his ledgers and listening to the sound of the fields, where his money was working, and then it was night again. That's how it was in the village. That's how it is in every village everywhere, from the little place at the bottom of the hill under the strange stone fort, to New York.

For the second night in a row, he went to sleep to the sound of the flute calling from the hilltop, and in the morning, when he looked out from the roof and saw Ines, the daughter of his tenant Arsenio, stopping at the well, she had an armful of bangles that were not there the day before.

'Hello there, pretty thing,' he called. 'Has your father counted his goats since last night?'

The girl ran off down the street without an answer but, just a little later on, the men were at his gate to report another theft.

This time Arsenio was at the front of the queue, reluctantly jangling on the brass bell, but before he allowed his tenants into the garden, Jose Pablo called to his daughter, his precious baby girl, his niña, and gave her instructions.

Then: 'Come in, come in,' said Jose Pablo. 'Come here,' and he eased himself down into the creaking cane chair under the shade of the middle of his three great trees. He pointed at each in turn and said: 'In one month the rent falls due, for you. And you. And you. And you. Have you come to tell me that so many goats have been stolen that none of you can pay?'

Arsenio stood with his head bent and his fingers twined together, too ashamed to look up from the dirt. 'Señor,' he said, 'we can pay, but goats are stolen up and down the valley. In village after village it is spoken of, and always after the pedlar Miguel Ángel has passed by. He also should pay.'

'Oh, shut up! And listen to what I have to say. It seems to me that there are just as many goats around the village as ever there were. The pedlar Miguel Ángel has stolen nothing and, who knows, when the time comes, perhaps you will find that he has left a few more little goats in your pen. He knows how to pay his way. All the little she-goats have been paid for from his pack. A bangle here and a hair comb there.'

It was just then that the door of the fine house of Jose Pablo opened and his daughter stepped into the garden, bringing him the tray he had demanded with his coffee and his pile of ledgers.

He pretended not to notice. 'Who could have guessed that so many little she-goats could be bought so cheap? Not like this one, not like my own Dolõres, my diamond – and a diamond who knows her price. This is a proper girl. This is a girl with a pleasing, modest way about her.'

And with a wave of his hand, as if he had been brushing

the dust off his coat, he told them: 'Now get out of here' and he picked up his coffee cup.

They went away, grumbling.

Now, when the pedlar Miguel Ángel went all the way up the valley, he walked through every village and lay where he stopped every night. When he walked north from the village of Jose Pablo it took him two weeks to reach the end of the valley and it took two weeks to come back. And then, after two weeks, when he walked south, it took him two weeks to reach the other end of the valley and it took two weeks to come back. So, every month, when the moon was at its fattest and shining like a lamp over the old stone fort, that was when they would hear the music of his flute floating down from the top of the hill.

That first night, when Miguel Ángel came back, it was so hot that Jose Pablo decided to sleep on his roof.

He let the flute music wash over him like moonbeams until he dozed, but he did not sleep until he heard another door bang and footsteps running lightly away. Then he was content.

But, in the morning when his daughter, his diamond, his Dolōres, his precious niña, climbed up to the roof with his breakfast, he noticed a ribbon of golden taffeta braided through her hair that was not there before and he was disturbed.

That day nobody came to the gate to complain of stolen goats and Jose Pablo grew worried. All day the figures in his ledgers would not add up, his coffee was bitter, the hot wind blew red dust into his eyes and Dolōres gave him a headache with her singing in the garden:

> Enough! now stop
> playing on your flute, dark lover,

> this girl's heart is all aflutter,
> I ask you, please stop playing,
> don't come to my lane all the time
> or, if you come,
> do more than play.
> I am warning you now:
> if you play that flute
> then you must be mine.

Over and over. He slammed his accounts book shut and hurried out the gate to walk his fields, thinking of the rents that would be due tomorrow. Perhaps some would not be able to pay. Perhaps they would have to borrow. Perhaps he could evict them. He felt a little better.

But late at night, he could not sleep. He had eaten too much. The food lay heavy in his belly. He tossed and turned, waiting for the sound of flute music to come from the hilltop, and when it did, it drilled into his head like toothache. And worse than the music was the waiting. He lay for hours waiting for the bang of a door, listening for the sound of running feet, but it never came and then, when the moon was hidden by the broken old fort and the street was dark, Jose Pablo got off his bed and went to the edge of the roof and looked up at the mountain top and yelled: 'In the name of God, be quiet.'

The music stopped.

That was worst of all.

But Jose Pablo lay down on his bed again and went to sleep.

In the morning, when he woke to the sound of the little green parrot chattering in its cage, the landlord Rodriguez went downstairs to collect his ledgers and his ink pot so that he could sit in his garden and mark down the money he was owed.

But, when he went to sit on his cane chair under the shade of the middle tree of his three trees, he found the gates open and his tenants waiting. They were smiling and laughing, nudging one another and talking loudly of goats, but they stopped when Jose Pablo Rodriguez came out of his door and they stood quiet.

There was no sound but the murmur of the wind in the green leaves and the rustle of the golden ribbons that hung from every branch, the tinkle of the bangles that decorated every twig.

Jose Pablo stood and looked for a moment. His old cane chair groaned as he slumped in it and then he looked up and said: 'Friends.'

The men in his garden looked back at him, smiling.

'Friends. You see I have decorated my garden to welcome you because this is a day of celebration.' He gestured up at the ribbons floating from his trees. 'I hope you like it.'

The idiot Julio choked on a snigger. Nobody else said a word.

'Today, friends, I have decided to cancel your rents for this season. This act will be of great benefit to the community and will win me great merit in Heaven.'

They still said nothing.

'But it is principally because of the benefit to the community that I have chosen to do this thing. There is nothing more important than community. We all depend on one another.'

The men in the yard were squatting down now, sitting just as he was.

'And I have become concerned about the recent spate of

goat-thievery. Today there should be no work. Today we will catch the goat thief and, by the witness of the men of this village who alone have lost more than seventy prize animals these past months, we will ensure that he pays the price.'

And that was how the pedlar Miguel Ángel was hanged from a tree not ten miles from the village of Jose Pablo Rodriguez.

As soon as she had untied every ribbon from her father's trees, the girl Dolõres walked to the railway station and never came back.

That was the story she told. When she had finished reading there was a slim pile of pages lying discarded on his shoulders. He felt her fingers brush his skin as she gathered the leaves together and squared them up, tapping them on his back as if he were a classroom desk.

She said: 'Maestro?' and slid off him, lying down on the other side of the bed, her face close to his. He could smell a warm, bready scent on her breath. He sipped it, sucking in the air that, a moment before, had been part of her, deep inside her, mingling with her blood and now was part of him.

'Say something,' she whispered.

He didn't say anything. He just kept looking, his head on one side, propped on the pillow, so close to her he could see himself reflected in her eyes.

'It's rubbish, isn't it? God, I knew I should never have mentioned it. This was a bad mistake.'

He only laughed, very quietly, so as not to break the hush of the tiny cathedral they had built between the pillow and the sheets. 'Now, you must know it's not rubbish. You do know that, don't you?' He brushed a long strand of hair from her lips with a gentle finger. 'You must know it's not rubbish. You've read enough rubbish to know that.'

She closed her eyes in relief: 'You like it.'

'It's a little jewel. Is it true?'

'I hope so.'

'But did it really happen, up in your hills?'

'No. Not that. But stuff like that. There was always a fat man – somebody who liked to throw his weight about, thought he was better than everybody else. Those people need to be taken down a peg. That's what my father thought, anyway.'

'Mine too.'

'And you don't?'

'I don't know what I think. I try not to concern myself with things like that. I've just never thought about it. But I don't think stories are the way to do it. I don't think stories can change the world.'

'Of course stories can change the world,' she said. 'The pen is mightier than the sword.'

He laughed again, but not as he might have done before, not unkindly but because she made him happy. 'You are so . . .' He couldn't find the words.

'Stupid? Naïve?'

'You are so young! Young!'

'I am also right. I'd rather fight with words than blow myself up like that idiot in Plaza Universidad.'

'You are young and beautiful and wonderful and talented.'

'And one day I'm going to write a book *nearly* as good as yours and people will read it and they will nod their heads and they will say: "She's right. We need to fix this."'

Then he kissed her and then there was 'Again' until long after the hour for morning coffee, when the bankers – who rise late – are sitting down slowly at their desks and fashionable ladies are greeting their friends in the street with a brush of the cheek and a soft clash of sunglasses.

They were lying there together, Caterina and Valdez, side by side in the bed, holding hands, with their legs woven and locked together, when the doorbell buzzed.

Mr Valdez untwined his fingers from hers and pushed himself up, untwined his legs from hers and swung his feet to the floor, sat up on the edge of the bed with a sigh, and then, hunched there with his head in his hands, he pushed his fingers through his hair and said: 'Would you answer that, please?'

She said: 'What?'

'Answer the door, please.'

'But, Chano, I haven't any clothes on.'

The doorbell buzzed again.

'The door, please.'

There was something in his voice. She got up and wrapped the sheet around herself but, as she passed, he put out a hand and gripped it where it trailed and pulled.

She stopped. Without turning round she said: 'I will not do this.'

He let go. The sheet sighed over the tiles as she walked away. The doorbell buzzed again and it was still ringing when Caterina opened the door. From far away he heard Maria Marrom say: 'Oh.' He recognized her voice. He recognized the way she said nothing for a moment and the way she said: 'I'm so very sorry to have troubled you. I must have the wrong address,' with that brittle dignity.

A few seconds later Caterina came back. 'She's gone,' she said. She went round the room picking up her clothes and carried them into the bathroom to dress.

The sound of Maria's kitten heels rang through the stairwell, like the ticking of a clock, like nails hammered into a coffin.

'We should see about getting your story published,' he said. 'I could help. If you like.'

She didn't answer.

AT NIGHT, WHEN it was very dark, the light above the door of Dr Cochrane's house came on with a surprised pop. A moment or two later, in the time it took for the lamp to collect a couple of flapping, circling, singeing moths, Dr Cochrane appeared at the top of the outside stair. Dr Cochrane hated the dark. He came down the stairs to the street like the old man he was, leaning forward to find the next step with his cane, pressing down heavily on the broad stone balustrade with the other hand.

Dr Cochrane got into his car, laid his cane on the passenger seat at his side and let out the handbrake. He rolled down the hill, gradually gathering speed, moving almost silently until, just before the bend, he turned the key, started the engine and dropped the clutch. Then he flicked the knob that lit the headlights and drove quickly – but not so quickly as to attract attention – onto the road that took him towards the highway along the side of the Merino. The streets were quiet and there was very little traffic at that time of night. Dr Cochrane drove towards the centre of the city, to the places where it was never quiet and the roar of passing cars never ceased. The road grew into huge humpback hills, rose on gigantic concrete legs. Down below, beautiful houses where merchants and sea captains once lived had run aground on tiny green islands, washed up there in an endless, uncrossable tide of traffic and abandoned until the very poorest found them and rowed out to them in desperate flotillas of supermarket trolleys to huddle inside and pick over the wreck. Down there, behind dirty, broken windows, a light showed here and there. Fires burned on concrete slabs under the throbbing, thundering shelter of highway bridges, dancing shadows leapt, dogs trotted. Men who had once been babies, washed and kissed and nestled in blankets, slept in huts made from folded cardboard boxes, lying on mats of newspaper while overhead, where the sky should be, where the stars were blotted out, the traffic drummed and susurrated with the endless rhythm of the hive.

Dr Cochrane drove on and on until he found himself caught up in a shoal of other cars, a lorry lumbering ahead of him, bouncing and squeaking, shedding gritty dust as it rolled, taxis honking and jostling on either side. He switched lanes, jerking the wheel suddenly to the left, ignoring the blare of horns. He tore across two lanes of traffic, the engine roaring as he surged forward, checked his mirror and swung back across the traffic again, right under the wheels of a sixteen-wheel lorry loaded down with a muddy bulldozer and blazing along its length with a galaxy of twinkling lights. Headlamps flared in his mirror. He pressed his foot to the floor and bounced up the exit ramp that loomed ahead of him, slowing for the curve, checking his mirror again, checking, checking, slowing, turning and following the signs that took him back to the highway, on the other side, back into the stream of traffic, heading the other way.

Dr Cochrane drove for two junctions, switching lanes, always watching in his mirror until he was sure that there was nobody following and then, without indicating, he turned down the slip road that opened in front of him.

The road swung down to a junction where there was a signpost that he could not read because the light above it was broken and hanging loose. Dr Cochrane knew the way. He made another right turn into a little square filled with street lamps. There were stalls selling fried food, shops with newspapers hanging down the front of them like lines of washing where they sold cigarettes and sweets and pulp novels, desperate, envious magazines filled with endlessly repeated images of the telenovela stars and Loteria booths scattered round like lifeboats come to offer rescue.

Dr Cochrane found a place to park down a side street, locked his car and walked back to the square, measuring his way with his cane. He knew the way to the bus stop where the No. 73 would leave from, and when the bus came he threw down his few centavos and sat on the bench seat at the back.

The darkened windows looked back at him blankly. There was nothing to show him where he was, no landmark to guide his journey. He simply sat quietly, saying nothing to anybody, his hands resting on his cane, turning now and then to glance out the big back window and watch for lights following. There were none.

After two stops, nobody else got on. After five stops people started to get off. The bus lurched and stuttered and roared, the gearbox ground. There was a hot smell of diesel oil and Dr Cochrane's seasickness returned horribly. After eleven stops there was no one else left on board except for a tall, thin man in a dirty blue jacket sitting halfway down the bus on the right-hand side. Dr Cochrane had watched him carefully since he joined the bus, when it was crowded and he had been forced to fold himself into a narrow seat over the wheel arch. Now the bus was empty but he had not moved. He sat there with his knees jammed against the polished brass handrail of the seat in front, his head rolling against the window.

Dr Cochrane slid quietly across his bench seat. It changed the angle between him and the tall man and let him use the dark window as a mirror. He could see the tall man's face in the reflection. His eyes were shut and Dr Cochrane did not recognize him.

The bus gave a lurch as it turned a corner and the tall man woke up. He hurried to the front of the bus, swinging from pole to pole.

'I've missed my stop!' he yelled at the driver. 'Let me off here.'

'I can't. I'm not allowed.'

'Chrissake, man. Just open the door at the junction. I'm not going to tell anybody. Up there, look, at the street corner.'

'I'm not allowed. I can't let you off anywhere except at a proper stop. And you are not allowed to talk to me when I'm driving. Stand behind the line.'

'Stand behind the line, pajero! Stand behind the line? Don't talk to you?' The tall man made a theatrical leap to the front of the bus. 'See? I'm crossing the line and this is me talking to you. I'm talking to you right now. So what are you gonna do? You gonna put me off the bus?'

The driver hauled on the wheel as if he were at the helm of a three-master rounding the Horn and stood on the brakes so the whole bus sat down on its springs. The door opened with a wheeze and he said: 'Off!'

The tall man flicked a finger and jumped into the street and the driver leaned out the window yelling after him. 'Cabeza de mierda!' He sat down, growling, and looked in the mirror, right along the length of the bus, at Dr Cochrane. 'Sorry about that,' he said. 'Sorry. Do you want off here?'

Dr Cochrane folded his hands on top of his cane, rested his hands there and tipped his head forward, hiding behind his still-new hat. 'I'm going right to the end,' he said.

'OK.' The driver pressed the lever to close the door and the bus started again with a jolt.

The argument with the tall man was annoying and unsettling.

Bus journeys are supposed to be without incident. A bus driver is an automaton who turns the corner at the same place, changes gear at the same place, opens the door at the same place, brakes at the same place, along the same route at the same time over and over and over every day. He sees the same roads, the same buildings, the same traffic, the same people. There are no bus journeys, there is only one bus journey, indistinguishable from all the other bus journeys, so if a policemen were to come along and flash his badge and push his mirrored sunglasses a little further up his nose and stand on the step of the bus with his hip stuck out and his hand resting on his pistol and ask: 'Have you seen this man?' the driver could only shrug and laugh at his own stupidity and hand the picture back and look at his feet. But not now. Not this time.

Dr Cochrane kept looking down at the worn floor. There was a hatch there, some way for the mechanics at the depot to reach deep into the guts of the machine, outlined in an edge of aluminium with a hinged ring sunk flush into it. Dr Cochrane examined it intently. He trailed his eye along every line, round every angle and every curve, running through equations and formulae in his head, choking down the bile that was rising in him as the bus lurched and swung.

'End of the line!' the driver shouted. The bus slowed, stopped with a high-pitched fart of brakes and a final, shuddering death rattle as the driver killed the engine. The door banged and he jumped down from the cab, stretching his arms over his head, groaning. Dr Cochrane watched him walking with a slow, aching stride, patting his pockets for cigarettes and matches. When he reached the pallid cone of light falling from the street lamp, the damp stain of sweat down his spine stood out in an ugly stripe. The light cut him in half so his feet and his trousers shone and his face was hidden in shadow with just the burning dot of his cigarette to show where his mouth was.

Dr Cochrane stood up and walked as quickly as he could to the front of the bus. He hooked his cane over his arm and swung himself from the dirty pole in the door, down two painful steps and on to the pavement. He hurried the length of the bus, keeping it between himself and the driver, and crossed the street into a narrow passage between two buildings.

He worked his way around, like a hunter moving through the woods when the wind was against him, leaning on his cane, tapping in the dark, discovering broken pavements and tin cans and broken bottles, straining his eyes in the lost light of uncurtained windows, the nebulous grey of unseen TVs that laughed at him as he passed. Slowly he was coming back the way he wanted to go, hidden by the houses, out of sight of the bus driver. He heard the engine start again, the bus shaking itself like an old dog, and he cursed. 'I might just have waited,' he said. And he leaned a little more heavily on his cane until he was sure the bus had gone.

The street was silent. Dr Cochrane limped between two bare and scrubby gardens, back to the bus stop, where he crossed the street and started the long climb up the hill in the dark. He was very afraid. He stopped often, because his leg hurt, because he was out of breath, and when he stopped he listened hard in case there was somebody climbing up the narrow path behind him. Nobody came. He heard dogs barking to each other in the night and the sound of a distant siren but nobody came. Dr Cochrane stood in the darkness, straining his eyes. He concentrated on a gap in the trees where the lights of the houses shone through in a yellow glow, watching. If somebody was following up the path, no matter how quietly, they would pass there. He waited for their shadow. Still nobody came. After a little time he walked on up the hill until he came to a place where bindweed had knotted itself into the links of a broken chain fence and an old FC Atletico shirt had been draped over a post like a flag. With one last fearful look behind, Dr Cochrane picked up the shirt, pushed through the gap and, holding his cane before him like a talisman, went down the hidden path on the other side.

THE GOSPELS SAY: 'You will know the truth and the truth will make you free.' Father Gonzalez knew the truth. Father Gonzalez knew that he was a coward and knowing that did not make him free.

First thing in the morning, in the dark of winter or in bright summer dawns when the sun tiptoed gently over the mountain tops without even waking the everlasting snows and came tobogganing down into the streets of the city, trailing promises of Heaven, Father Gonzalez was afraid. He stood in his robes, surrounded by his brother monks, at the altar the Spanish had built over the rock where the old gods once bathed in blood, and he poured out the blood of his God and he was powerfully afraid.

More than anything else Father Gonzalez was afraid that he would be discovered. Whatever happened, whatever it cost, nobody must ever know. Nobody must know the hold that the Commandante had over him. Nobody must know what he had done for that man. Nobody must know why – but God knew. God already knew and yet, every day, he took God in his own two hands and held Him in his mouth. The terror of it passed, of course. Every morning, when he did not die right there at the altar, when he was not struck down like Ananias, when the lightning bolts did not fall from the sky, the fear passed off, for a little.

He ate his breakfast waiting for the fear to return. He walked to the university knowing that it was waiting for him there.

He sat all day at his desk, St Max Kolbe smiling down at him from the wall beside the window. He was afraid to raise his eyes from the desk and meet that serene smile. The students entering his class read hope, laughter, encouragement in that face but Father Gonzalez looked into those eyes and saw them burning with scorn. He looked away. He looked deep down into the papers on his desk but he was still afraid. He was afraid that the phone might ring. He feared the voice that might be there and what it might demand of him. He feared that the phone would not ring and then the waiting would simply go on.

And at night, when he lay in that little room, as quiet and bare and white as the inside of an egg, lying on the bed whose boards would one day go to make his coffin, the fear raged all around him, curling across the floor and boiling up the walls until, at last, he fell asleep and woke to be afraid again.

Sometimes he was cheated even of that, dreaming that he was already awake and already afraid until the terror of it dragged him back out of sleep and left him to lie there, for the rest of the night, with the dark drumming against his eyeballs. Sometimes he slept until dawn and woke in warmth and comfort to a moment of real peace until he realized that he was not afraid and remembered that he should be. On mornings like that he would pretend to himself that he was still asleep but it never worked, it never worked.

Father Gonzalez was unafraid when the knock came. He was lying on his back somewhere down at the bottom of a deep, velvety pit, so far down that dreams could not disturb him with their fluttering daddy-long-legs feet and the night silence meant only that; silence and not the moment of waiting for a scream.

When Father Gonzalez woke to the knock, he knew there had

been two knocks before it. He remembered how they had reached him, the way the sound of a blossom opening thousands of miles away finds the swallows and warns them it is time to fly towards the spring, the way a throbbing, echoing, trombone note, ringing out in endless depths of a chill black ocean, can find the whale and call him to his wife.

At the first knock, Father Gonzalez stirred. At the second knock he was rising up out of his own warm blackness, faster and faster, accelerating towards awareness like a ping-pong ball released from the bottom of a swimming pool, streaming bubbles as it comes. At the third knock he sat up in bed and his heart gave a little leap of terror and joy because, for a moment, he thought it might be like Christmas morning. He thought, for a moment, that the waiting might be over and the midnight knock might bring with it a bullet and rest.

'What is it?' he said.

'You're needed.' There was a light under the door. 'They need a priest. There's a boy waiting in the vestibule. He knows the way.'

'I'll come,' said Father Gonzalez. Under the door, the shadows of feet moved away.

Father Gonzalez got out of bed and put on the shirt and the trousers he had left draped over his hard wooden chair only a few hours before. He reached into his narrow wardrobe and took down from the shelf his priestly stole of violet silk and a leather case, cylindrical, about as long as his hand, split along its length, hinged and snapped shut with a brass fastening.

He went out into the corridor, walked its length to the stairs, turned out the light behind him and carried on down to the front door where a skinny boy was waiting on one of those uncomfortable wooden chairs that people are made to wait on.

The boy stood up when he saw Father Gonzalez on the stairs.

He was thin and scared and breathless, with huge, deer's eyes and an Atletico shirt that was too big for him and sagged over the shoulders. He said: 'Hello, Father.'

Father Gonzalez said: 'Hello. Try to speak quietly. We shouldn't disturb the others.'

'Sorry.'

'Where are we going?'

'My grandfather's. He is very sick. He's been sick a long time. I think he's going to die.'

'Is that what the doctor says?'

'There is no doctor.'

'Oh.' He ruffled the boy's hair. 'Then you are probably wrong. I bet there's nothing to worry about. I bet he won't die.'

'He says he is. He told me to get you. We have to hurry.'

The boy took him by the elbow and pushed, the way you would push at a reluctant wheelbarrow, urging him on, hurrying him to the door. Father Gonzalez could feel the terror jangling in him like an electric charge. He recognized it. It was familiar to him. He took the boy's hand: 'It'll be all right. I have a car. Show me the way.'

They drove. Sitting in the passenger seat the boy was too small to see through the windscreen. He knelt, leaning forward, with his hands on the dashboard, pointing the way. 'I ran through there,' he said, 'between those shops.'

'I can't drive through there. We'll have to go round.' Father Gonzalez went to the end of the street and turned right but behind the row of shops there was only another alley and no way for the car to go. 'Why did you come that way?'

'There's a stairway down the hill.'

'And where are we going?'

'Up the hill.'

'Up the hill where, son?'

'Up the hill. I don't know the address. It's where we live. I know the way.'

Father Gonzalez took the keys out of the ignition with a sharp twist. 'Then it looks like we walk from here. Come on, show me the stairs.'

The boy scrabbled at the handles and ran from the car heading into the shadows between the buildings before Father Gonzalez even had time to lock the doors. Halfway down the alley he stopped and yelled back: 'We need to hurry. Please. Please!' The only sign of him was a ripple of light shining back from the gutter puddle he had disturbed as he ran. 'Come on!'

'Son, you need to wait. I'm old. I can't go as fast as you. I can't see where I'm going.' Father Gonzalez was going carefully along the alley, one hand on the damp wall, groping his way through the darkness, when the boy came out of the shadows and took his hand.

'I know the way. I'll show you. It's OK. Come on or my granpa's going to Hell.'

Father Gonzalez gripped his little hand until he felt the bones crunch and tugged on his arm. 'Now you stop that! Who's told you that nonsense?'

'He did. My granpa says he's going to Hell unless you come.'

'Your granpa is wrong. Nobody who wants to be friends with God is going to Hell and the very fact that he's calling for me to come proves that he wants to be with God.' How easy it was to say these things and they were easy because he knew them to be true. He believed them. He despised the good and the respectable who dared to put a limit on God's generosity. He fought them, as he would fight the foulest heretic. This little boy, the old man dying somewhere in the dark at the top of the hill, there was a place reserved for both of them in the unfinishable glories of Heaven, but not for him. He knew there was no place for him.

Father Gonzalez was glad of the kindly mask of darkness. 'Now come on," he said. 'Show me the way.'

They found the foot of a cracked and broken concrete staircase and began to climb. Towards the top of its thirty-seven steps – Father Gonzalez counted every one – there was a shattered water-pipe sticking out and the last three steps slumped into the hole it had gouged in the underlying earth. At the very top of the stairs there was another street, with a lamp-post still lit, the last symbol of civic authority, leaning over like the battered flag-pole on a forgotten fortress, but still burning, still hopeful.

After that there was nothing.

Father Gonzalez said: 'Where are you taking me?'

'It's not far now. We just run down here, along this fence.'

'I can't run.'

'We need to hurry. Along this fence then up a little hill and down the other side. Please, Father. Please come. You need to come now.'

'I know where we're going. This is Santa Marta. You should have told me.'

'You wouldn't have come into this *barriada*.'

'But I would. Of course I would. I know the way. I could have come in the car. We could have been there by now. Come on, show me.'

Father Gonzalez slipped and stumbled along the broken mud path. Ahead of him the boy's worn grey track shoes shone white in the darkness and the huge number 7 on the back of his football shirt glowed like a beacon as he trotted ahead. Somewhere off to the right a girl screamed as if she were being murdered – then burst out laughing. The rusted fence ran out. They came into a brief patch of open ground where the path opened out into a dusty delta of tracks like a backwards-pointing arrow where all the tracks out of the *barriada* merged in the path to town.

Then there was grass underfoot and then a jumble of little houses, thrown down anywhere, jammed into every tiny scrap of ground. No streets, just rat runs between the buildings, broad enough to shoulder a way through or as wide as a rope of washing.

These places grew like a tumour. Somebody would flatten a bit of ground, maybe close to the roadside, maybe on some abandoned bit of concrete, and throw up some walls and make a roof and sell the roof so somebody else could start again. And then there were walls to build against and more roofs and more walls until the shacks spread and multiplied, piled on each other like moss on a log, clambering up to the light.

The boy ran ahead. 'We're here,' he said but Father Gonzalez had lost him in the tangled knot of houses. Now he felt the fear rush back. He was hot, breathless, the long muscles down his shins screamed at him and now he was lost in Santa Marta in the middle of the night. How he wished he had taken more time to dress. How he wished he had clipped on his dog collar. It might have been a protection, a passport.

He stood, spinning dizzily in a tiny plaza, no bigger than a tablecloth, where four doll-sized houses nudged each other and greed or hurry or bad planning had left no room to fit a fifth. The bit of ground had become a useful dump and indescribable, unknowable things had been piled there in a foetid pyramid that quaked and trembled under his shoes. Father Gonzalez had no idea how he had found his way into that place and he could not find his way out. A dog began to bark furiously on the other side of a wall. A man swore at it and told it to shut up. His wife joined in: 'Good God, what use is it swearing at the dog, you fat fool?'

Father Gonzalez wanted to yell, wanted to make some noise to bring the boy back to him, but he was afraid of who else might come. And then, where there had been only a dark murmur somewhere in the darkness, something so faint and so normal and so much a part of the velvet night that he hadn't even noticed it, like the sound of a sleeping fire, suddenly there was music and men singing; cracked uncertain voices at first, men embarrassed to sing in front of their mates then, as the tune picked up, stronger, confident.

> We're on the march,
> This road we're treading
> It leads to freedom
> It leads to freedom.
> We're on the march,
> This road we're treading
> It leads to freedom and liberty,
> We'll wave the scarlet banner triumphantly.

'Here!' A skinny hand shot out and grabbed him by the shirt front, bony fingers hooked in above his pounding heart. 'Granpa, we're coming.'

'What's that singing?'

'I don't hear any singing.'

'Yes, you do. You must. Listen.'

'Who brought you up, Father? You don't know much. This is Santa Marta. In Santa Marta you don't hear nothing, you don't see nothing, you don't know nothing. In here.'

The boy ducked down through a curtain of heavy plastic sheets that might have been sliced from fertilizer bags and Father Gonzalez was in a room with an old man dying on the earth floor.

There was light enough to see by. It came from a paraffin lamp, beaten out of used drinks cans, that had been left burning by the old man's head. Father Gonzalez had seen one like it before. There were stalls in the market where they could be bought for 75 centavos – if you had 75 centavos – and the man would shred an old shoelace for a wick at no extra charge.

Father Gonzalez knelt on the floor. The old man's diagnosis was undoubtedly correct: he was dying. He lay under two blankets with the boy's thin blue nylon coat tucked up under his chin. His nostrils seemed to have receded so his nose was hooked and sharp like a hawk. His lips were as pale and grey as the rest of his face and his eyes stood out like boiled eggs under bruised blue lids. Father Gonzalez had seen dying before and he read the unmistakable signs of it again. There was no hope.

The boy stood just at the edge of the lamplight. He said nothing. He was concentrating very hard on trying not to cry.

'Why don't you say the Our Father, son? That might help.'

The boy held his hands in front of his face, like an angel in a picture book, the way he had been taught half a lifetime ago. 'Our Father,' he said. 'Our Father. Our Father. Our Father,' whispered sobs between his teeth.

Father Gonzalez took the stole from his pocket, unrolled it from its rubber band and kissed the gold cross stitched at its midpoint. He looped it round his neck and opened up the little leather case he had brought with him. Inside there was a bottle of oil, specially blessed by the bishop for use in extreme unction. He poured a tiny drop into his hand and wiped it, gently, so gently across the old man's eyes and he said: 'Through this holy unction and His own most tender mercy may the Lord pardon thee whatever sins or faults thou hast committed by sight.'

He circled the old man's ears, brushing them with oil, the way a father washes his baby. 'Through this holy unction and His own most tender mercy may the Lord pardon thee whatever sins or faults thou hast committed by hearing.'

The oil was gone. Father Gonzalez tipped the little bottle into his palms again. He brushed his hands over the old man's keel nose. 'Through this holy unction and His own most tender mercy may the Lord pardon thee whatever sins or faults thou hast committed by smell.'

And down, across his mouth. 'Through this holy unction and His own most tender mercy may the Lord pardon thee whatever sins or faults thou hast committed by taste.'

He held his hands, one after the other, wiping the oil across them back and front. 'Through this holy unction and His own most tender mercy may the Lord pardon thee whatever sins or faults thou hast committed by touch.' The old man was cold. The blood was retreating like a tide, shrinking from the world and taking the life with it.

He shuffled on his knees and folded back the blankets to reach the old man's feet. They were wrapped in filthy socks, stiff and stinking. Father Gonzalez tugged the socks off and the feet inside were black and bony with clawed, yellow toenails.

Jesus Christ did this. Jesus Christ who made the whole world, who made the universe and everything in it, washed the feet of his friends. 'Through this holy unction and His own most tender mercy may the Lord pardon thee whatever sins or faults thou hast committed by walking.'

The old man's skin was so fragile and transparent. Almost imaginary. Just barely holding the life inside, thinning, getting ready to dissolve and let him leak away. There was almost nothing left of him.

Father Gonzalez tipped the oil into his hand once again and reached under the blankets. He was embarrassed and ashamed. Like a doctor. Like a doctor for the soul. Like a doctor. He found the old man's withered penis, like a cold worm in his hand.

'Through this holy unction and His own most tender mercy

may the Lord pardon thee whatever sins or faults thou hast committed by carnal delectation.'

He leaned back on his heels and said. 'That's all there is. I will wait here with you.'

The boy said: 'Our Father. Our Father. Our Father,' and some place outside, a choir of men was singing: 'We're on the march. This road we're treading, it leads to freedom. It leads to freedom and liberty.'

It was like a hymn.

KNOWING HIS PLACE, the old man did his duty and got on with dying quietly and without fuss, unseen and unnoticed just as he had been all his life. There was no final trapped-rabbit shriek, no thrashing about, no fish-eyed, breathless gasping, no watery, lung-filled death rattle, not even the last, drunken snore. He simply died like a candle.

Father Gonzalez was kneeling by the old man's side when it happened. He closed his eyes for a moment's prayer and, when he looked back, the old man was dead. Nothing had so much convinced the priest of the existence of the soul as having seen people on either side of life. He looked down in that instant and knew at once that the old man was no longer asleep or unconscious but dead. There is no way of telling, just by looking, if a clock is broken or simply stopped. You can't look at cars parked by the roadside and know which of them will start with the flick of a key and which has no fuel, which has a flat battery. With people it's different. The old man was empty and scoured out, like a burst football, like an oyster when the pearl fishers are finished with it, nothing left but torn, grey flesh.

The boy had run out of 'Our Father's and lay curled up in an exhausted ball to sleep. Quietly Father Gonzalez tidied the old man up. Symmetry seemed important at times like these. People liked to see order and death can be very jumbled so, before he shook the boy gently by the shoulder, Father Gonzalez straight-ened the crick in the old man's neck, combed his hair and arranged his hands; as if he were on parade and not lying on his back on a mud floor in a shack made of packing crates and old plastic sacks.

'He's gone,' he said. The boy was still young enough to weep without shame. Father Gonzalez held him while he sobbed.

When that had passed – and it passed quickly – Father Gonzalez asked: 'Who lives here with you?'

'Nobody. There's just me and him.'

'What about your mother?'

'She said she was going to town for a job. She brought me here. We didn't see her after that. Granpa said she got a man and he didn't want me around.'

'Don't you have any idea where she is?'

The boy started crying again.

'It's all right, son. It's all right.' But it wasn't all right. Father Gonzalez wanted to explain that there were people who would care for him, a place to stay and food and school and a bed of his own to sleep in, hope and even a cold substitute for love, but the kid drove down with his sharp little elbows and ducked away, out through the sack door and into the last of night, running hard.

Father Gonzalez tried to follow but he was not young. He took some time to get off his knees, and when he groped his way to the door the boy had disappeared into the maze of little sheds and shacks. Walls loomed up in the red dawn, the same red dawn that was breaking over the tall glass towers of the city and kissing the windows of the Merino and National Banking Company, the same dawn that was greying the courtyard of the Ottavio House and redrawing the bottles on the table there. But though dawn came sooner up the hill in Santa Marta, it was like everything else in Santa Marta, a little slower, a little weaker, a little dirtier.

The old priest was just as lost in the dawn as he had been in the middle of the night. He stumbled about from wall to wall, from house to house, slip-sliding in the mud and the half-dark, calling out feebly to a boy whose name he never knew until, on the path back to town, on a bit of sloping grass where two sewage ditches met, he turned a corner and found Dr Cochrane.

It was a ludicrous moment: Dr Cochrane tottering on his cane and the priest with mud on the knees of his black trousers, his elbows, his hands, and his purple stole wrapped round his throat like an aviator's scarf.

Dr Cochrane said: 'Gonzalez!' with an embarrassed squeak in his voice.

And Father Gonzalez said: 'Joaquin.'

'What are you doing here?'

Then Father Gonzalez remembered the singing. He remembered the rebel songs and he remembered what everybody knew: that Dr Cochrane liked the old Colonel. He said: 'I was about to ask you the same thing.'

And, because he could think of no ready lie, because there was no possible reason to explain why he, Dr Joaquin Cochrane, respected reader in mathematics, descendant of the heroic national liberator and cripple, should be there on a greasy path between two stinking ditches in the poorest *barriada* of the city at dawn and also because he looked into the face of Father Gonzalez and read there knowledge and understanding, Dr Cochrane did the only thing he could do. Dr Cochrane leaned heavily on his cane, so heavily that it actually penetrated the soft earth a little and a tiny crater of mud swelled around the rubber ferrule as moon dust blooms around an impacting meteorite, and he knelt there on the path and took off his hat.

He said: 'Bless me, Father, for I have sinned.'

'What?'

'Bless me, Father, for I have sinned.'

'Joaquin, what are you saying?'

'I want to make confession.'

'What?'

'You are a priest. You cannot deny me. You cannot prevent my reconciliation with God.'

'Now? Here? Can't it wait? Let's go back to town. I think I know the way from here. My car is at the bottom of the hill.'

'No, Father, it must be now. I may be close to death. At any moment, I may die unshriven.'

'The Church's view on these matters has changed a great deal. You needn't worry.'

'Father!' There was an angry urgency in his voice.

'Joaquin, you're not even a Catholic.'

'I am a Catholic. I am. I am baptized and confirmed. I am as much a Catholic as the Archbishop himself, as much a Catholic as the Pope.'

'But you do not believe.'

'How do you know that? How do you know what the Archbishop believes or what the Pope believes? You believe and that's all that counts. You believe.'

'Yes, I believe. And you don't know how fervently I pray to be rid of it, this belief of mine.'

'But, if your belief fled,' said Dr Cochrane, 'that would only prove that your prayers had been answered, which must mean that somebody answered them and that, after all, your faith – which had just evaporated – was justified.'

'Are you a mathematician or a philosopher, Joaquin?'

'Please, Father, my knees are not what they were.'

Father Gonzalez wiped his hands on his mud-stained trousers, unfurled the stole from his neck, kissed the embroidered cross there and put it on again. He knelt down on the thin grass beside his friend, two old men side by side, one facing east, squinting into the early sun, one facing west towards the last bruised remnants of night, close enough to catch every whispered confidence but invisible to each other. He said: 'Begin again.'

'Bless me, Father, for I have sinned.'

'May the Lord be in thy heart and on thy lips, that thou, with truth and with humility, mayest confess thy sins, in the name of the Father and of the Son and of the Holy Ghost.'

'I confess to God Almighty, the Blessed Mary Ever-Virgin, to Blessed Michael Archangel, to Blessed John Baptist, to the Holy Apostles Peter and Paul, to all Saints and to thee, Oh Father, that I have excessively sinned in thought, in word, in deed and by omission, through my own fault, through my own fault, through my own, very great fault. I have spent the night in plotting how best to overthrow the state and conspiring in the murder of our national leaders.'

EVERYTHING ABOUT THE sea is perfect. There is no part of the sea you can look at and imagine that it could be improved. It is perfect, but it is never the same. It is different in different places at different times. It is alike in different places at the same time. It is different in the same place from moment to moment and alike, in different places, in the moments in between.

Everything about the sea is perfectly balanced. As it follows the moon around the earth in a great, bulging, expectant teardrop, it grows thin behind. For every crest, there is a trough. For every ocean deep there is a shore as shallow as a ripple. So, Mr Valdez reasoned, there must be some part of the sea where the wind was rushing by like knives and screaming like widows because, there, where he was sitting, looking out from his usual bench in the square beside the Merino, hundreds of miles from the sea but still touching the sea, it was more than still, past still. The air was like glue.

And he knew there must be some place where the rain was falling in torrents, hammering down like angry nails, because there on the Merino the water was rising in clouds, drifting up in a thick jungle vapour to hide the sun. He knew there must be such a place because the sea never lessens, never loses a single drop of water, never gives up a cloud unless it accepts a million raindrops in exchange. So there must have been another place where the sea was wild and mountainous, with great wave crests reaching up to claw at frightened stars, because there, in that place, it was as flat and sticky as syrup in a jar, smooth as a velvet tablecloth in an aunt's parlour and as quiet.

Along the Merino it was chicken-gravy hot so there must be some frozen place with icebergs that scraped the sky. There must be some place where everything was blue as sapphires, blue as cornflowers, blue as ice, blue as eyes, because there, along the Merino, everything was a million different shades of yellow. The hot fog rising from the river was yellow. It rolled in yellow folds towards a hidden yellow sun. The river was yellow. Yellow as a madhouse. Yellow as a villa in France. Yellow as a pot of sunflowers. Yellow as a quarrel or a hair ribbon. Egg yellow. Dog yellow. Daffodil yellow. Certificate yellow. Rust yellow. Rot yellow. Mushroom yellow. Fish-belly yellow. Everything was yellow, except for the black ship tied up under the cranes on the quayside and the flag that hung over the great curving whale-cliff of the stern, as limp and wet as a winter handkerchief.

Something inside the ship belched and a stream of oily bilge water began to spurt from high up on the hull, thin and erratic, like an old man's piss. It splattered into the river and loud drops flew up at the policemen standing there on the dockside and signalling to a shiny-headed Chinaman looking over the stern. They had long boathooks.

The tallest of them said: 'Let down the net.'

The dark head disappeared, the filthy water stopped splashing from the pipe, the whole yellow world was quiet again until an iron clang and stutter from above made the men on the dock look up.

A crane derrick jerked unsteadily out over the side of the ship and a thick net of rope, showing the signs of hard work, began to fall. On the quayside the tall policeman signalled with flicks of his finger. The net fell and sagged and blossomed as it hit the water and Mr Valdez, who found these days that almost nothing interested him, stood up from the bench, where he sat with his notebook clamped shut in his hand and his pen, unused, between his teeth, and walked over to investigate.

One of the policemen put up a hand. 'I wouldn't,' he said. 'This isn't going to be pretty.'

His mates were using their boathooks to poke and drag at something in the water. Mr Valdez looked over the edge of the seawall and saw it was a man, floating face-down, crucified in the water.

'If it's who we think it is, he's been in the water for a while. Not nice.'

'Who do you think it is?'

'Oh, just some sailor who didn't show up for work. They get drunk and fall in. It happens. Now piss off. Sir.'

Mr Valdez retreated a step or two, just enough so as not to appear difficult or disrespectful, but he kept watching as the mechanism on the crane began its clanging and the rope rose and the net lengthened and tightened and drew up out of the water all that was left of a man, curled in a ball like a sleeping baby.

The tall policeman signalled pointlessly at the Chinaman on deck. The crane turned. The net hovered, dripping over the quayside, lowered, spread, opened.

'Help me,' the tall policeman said.

The others came forward.

'Take him under the knees. I'll hold his shoulders.'

They had him. They paused. They shifted the weight. He gurgled. There was a green belch of gas. The tall policeman turned his face away as it broke. They put him down on a canvas sheet and stepped back. The tall policeman arranged him, made him straight, tucked the canvas all around him, folded it underneath.

The others stood apart. One dragged his hands up and down on his trouser legs with a look of disgust.

'May I,' said Mr Valdez, stooping to twitch aside a corner of the canvas.

'Leave it!' the tall man said.

Mr Valdez straightened with dignity. 'Forgive me,' he said, 'but I find this fascinating.'

'It's a dead man, that's all.'

And then, as if it would explain or excuse, Mr Valdez said: 'I am an author.' He actually used that word. 'Author'. Not 'I'm a writer' but 'I am an author,' as if that explained everything, the way that a man could say: 'Let me through, I'm a doctor.'

The policeman stood aside. He had a stomach-calming cigarette to light. He had an ambulance to call and a report to write. It was none of his business if this man wanted to throw up.

But Mr Valdez did not throw up. He flicked back the corner of the canvas and looked at where the face should be and decided it was time to go to the Phoenix for a morning coffee. He walked back across the square and down the little calle and through the fancy doors and down the stairs into the café, where the usual university crowd had already gathered for breakfast.

Sitting in the corner seat, Dr Cochrane flapped his huge newspaper so the air caught it at the crease and helped him fold it into something the size of a bed sheet. He had an announcement to make and he wanted to be seen making it.

'According to this,' he said, 'the face of Christ has appeared in a burrito in Punto del Rey. According to this, the burrito was purchased by a bus driver who was two bites into it when, at the third bite, he noticed the face of Jesus looking back at him from his lunch and so, instead of finishing it, he has put it on display on top of his TV set and people are queuing on the stairs to adore it.' Dr Cochrane gave the newspaper another flap for emphasis and said: 'What do you think of that, Gonzalez?'

The old priest looked up from his coffee, glared at him with a look that was more hurt than angry and said: 'I do not mock the simple faith of simple people.'

'No, but really. A burrito?'

'Why not a burrito?'

'Bread and wine is bad enough, but a burrito!'

'Joaquin, God is not mocked.'

'Yeah, you tell him, Father,' said Costa, as if that settled it.

They nodded their good mornings at Valdez as he pulled up a chair and it was only when his coffee came, only when he took his first sip, when he lifted the bread and the ham to his lips and chewed, that Mr Valdez realized he felt nothing. He had just seen a dead man pulled from the Merino with his face half eaten away and his belly bloated and he felt nothing. He could drink coffee and eat bread and ham and feel nothing. Mr Valdez had no brother and no father, but if he had and he had seen them lying there, he knew he would have felt nothing. He tried to imagine pulling any of his university colleagues from the Merino – Costa, De Silva, Dr Cochrane or Father Gonzalez – and he felt nothing.

The bleakness of that washed over him in a torrent. 'I am an author,' that's what he'd said. 'What a storyteller you are.' That's what he'd said. But how could he be a storyteller when he couldn't feel?

With the second sip of coffee, Mr Valdez looked along his entire shelf of novels and he found, again and again, the same brown dog he once saw in a park, the same couple saying goodbye under the trees he had seen from a passing train. He followed the progress of his various adventures in the pages of his books. This one dreading the end of the week when he must be parted from the woman he wants. Then the consummation. The satisfaction that turns to a glut and the boredom and, finally, the disgust, thousands of different sensations, always producing the same response; ice always cold, fire always hot when, once upon a time, he would have known the difference between the fire of love and the fire of hate. A bright, leaping flame and a slow ember are not the same thing. The meaning is different and once upon a time he could see and feel and understand them differently, write them differently, but it had gone. There was nothing left but a scrawny yellow cat crossing the road and creeping into the whorehouse.

Mr Valdez was terrified. He had once more the sensation of clawing at rocks, kicking up gravel as he scrabbled for a foothold, sliding down a mountain slope where nothing was certain, and then he thought of Caterina. He imagined Caterina pulled from the river and the thought of it almost made him sick. He knew he could not face that nightmare. He knew he could still feel and thanked the God in whom he did not believe for it.

'You OK?' Costa said. 'You look a bit grey.'

'I'm fine,' he said. 'They were pulling a body out of the river as I came in. It upset me more than I realized.'

'You have the tender soul of the artist,' said Dr Cochrane. 'It is the price you must pay for genius.'

Mr Valdez said nothing. It would have been immodest. He dragged flat palms down his face and, as he wiped the sweat from his lip, he was amazed to feel, like a cold wire under his skin, the faint trace of a scar.

BEFORE MR L.H. Valdez left his flat that morning, before he took his usual seat on the bench overlooking the Merino and watched a dead man hauled out of the river, before, as usual, he had written nothing in his notebook, he shaved.

That was something of a moral victory for Mr Valdez. He had come to hate shaving. In the past, when he was much, much younger, perhaps a week before, a shave had been one of the great joys of his life. Mr Valdez enjoyed shaving so much he was almost guilty about it and he was glad that he could do it alone, behind a locked door. Now it made him afraid. Now he left the bathroom door open so that the sound of tango could come stalking in from the radio in the kitchen.

His fear was unlike the fear of Father Gonzalez. Father Gonzalez was afraid because he knew, but Mr Valdez was afraid because he did not know. Every morning he stood in his elegant limestone bathroom, looking out from a reflection of his elegant limestone bathroom, wiry and sand-golden, broad of shoulder, narrow of waist, a triangular outline pointing down into the soft towel knotted around his waist like a warm snowdrift, and he felt a little stab of fear. Every morning Mr Valdez leaned forward across the sink to where Mr Valdez leaned forward across the sink, each examining the other's lip, but every morning it was the same: nothing to see.

The water in the sink was very hot – as hot as he could bear with his soft, writer's hands. Steam rose in clouds but the tile shelf above the basin caught it and condensed it into silver beads or wafted it away, clear of the mirror which never, never misted over. And yet, he could not see.

Mr Valdez had a dark blue wash cloth soaking in the basin. Without putting his hands in the scalding water, flicking with his fingertips as the jaguar claws surprised fish from jungle pools, he caught the cloth, drained it, juggled it hotly from hand to hand, wrung it out and wrapped it across his face. Mr Valdez had the empty taste of steam in his mouth. He tilted his head back. They looked down their noses at one another. The man in the mirror was masked, like a robber, like an executioner. Mr Valdez regarded him with distrust. Mr Valdez regarded him with distrust.

He unwrapped the damp cloth from his face. He took his fine English brush, soaked it in the basin, gave it one, wet-dog flick of the wrist so the water scattered from it and rubbed it on the soap. That daily miracle fascinated him. Like the Feeding of the Five Thousand, when a few loaves and a few fish became a feast for a multitude, the merest touch of soap could be transformed into mountainous clouds of clotted lather by the magical bristles.

He swirled impasto brush strokes of foam across his face. He rinsed his razor in the hot water and he began to shave, cheeks and chin and throat, the edge of his jaw, the upward curve to his ear, the thumb-wide strip of bristle that ran downwards from his mouth, until there was nothing left but his lip. Short careful strokes, with the grain of his beard, backwards to catch any straggling hairs. Short, fearful strokes, taking the soap away, baring the skin until there was nothing left but skin, nothing to see. He looked at himself with relief. He looked at himself and he was still frightened.

There is a gem called alexandrite and it shines with a lustrous green, except at night. At night, when the lamps are lit and there is no sun, alexandrite is red. Some things can't be seen, not because they are not there and not even because they are too small to be noticed, but because we cannot grasp them. Valdez understood that.

Before Mr L.H. Valdez left his flat that morning, before he took his usual seat on the bench overlooking the Merino and watched a dead man hauled out of the river, before, as usual, he had written nothing in his notebook, in a moment of elation after he had reassured himself that, for another morning at least, there was no scar, Mr Valdez wrote a letter.

Still wrapped in his towel, Mr Valdez sat down at his desk. He took from his briefcase a large brown envelope. He opened his wallet and there, beside a fold of pulpy grey paper with the words 'I write' written on it, he found a small green stamp, stuck it on the envelope and wrote the address.

It was the simplest thing in the world.

It was the beginning of the end.

Four days later, only a little later than promised, that same brown envelope arrived in the capital, where it was delivered to the offices of *The Salon*.

Miss Marta Alicia Cantaluppi had been secretary to the editor for only eleven months, but when she opened that envelope and read the great, rolling, spiking signature of L.H. Valdez, she knew enough to take that letter to the boss and, without even knocking, she opened the door of his glass office and walked right in.

SEÑOR JUAN IGNACIO Correa flattered himself that, under his guidance, *The Salon* was recognized as the finest magazine in the country – among serious magazines, of course. Naturally, Rafael Salvade of *The National Review* knew that to be untrue and Fernanda Maria Espinosa had not given up all hope of motherhood and destroyed three marriages – two of them her own – to make *The Reader* the second-best literary journal in the country.

So, when Marta Alicia Cantaluppi burst into his office that morning, Señor Juan Ignacio Correa felt entitled to snort like a horse and slap his pen down on the desk. Even when she held up an apologetic hand and said: 'I know. I'm sorry, but you need to see this,' he was not calmed.

It was only when he read the note she held out in front of her that he began to smile. He took it from her hand and he read it again. He cleared a space on his desk, laid the blue notepaper flat on his blotter and read it again and then, without lifting his eyes from the page, he said: 'Marta, my dear, call Fernanda Maria at *The Reader* and Salvade at *The National Review*. Tell them I have booked the best table in The Grill for dinner tomorrow night and they are invited.'

Poor Correa. Every time Marta Alicia left his office he would look after her and enjoy her magnificent wiggle, but this time he missed his chance. For the rest of that day, as the sun chased the shadows round three sides of his office, Correa sat reading and reading and reading. At six o'clock, when Marta Alicia folded her spectacles into their aluminium case and cleared her desk exactly as she had been taught at college, Correa bid her goodnight with a wagging finger and warned: 'Not a word, mind you. I'll hear of this if it gets out,' and he was so engrossed in his reading that, for the second time that day, he forgot to enjoy her departure.

Before he left the office, Correa took the papers from his desk and locked them in his safe – a safe that had been tested in twenty-four hours of fire and which had survived being dropped from a crane in a plunge of five storeys.

Lying in bed that night, with dots of red and blue dancing on his eyeballs while a night bird in the garden harped on its one-note song like a rusty gate, Juan Ignacio Correa regretted the move to the seventeenth floor of his block. At 2 a.m. he rose from his bed, dressed and drove back to his office and made his way through silent corridors, switching on the lights as he went, waiting at every corner until the shadows had fled.

He drove home with the envelope lying on the passenger seat beside him and when he stopped at traffic lights rocking in the breeze above a deserted junction, he was careful to lock all the doors.

Correa crawled back into bed beside his wife and left the envelope lying on the cabinet at his head, pinned down by the alarm clock. Ten ticking minutes later he reached out, put the envelope under his pillow and slept until morning, when he rang the office and told Marta Alicia he would be late to work.

She was unconcerned. After eleven whole months as secretary to the editor, she knew that it was she, and not Juan Ignacio Correa, who made *The Salon* what it was, and she got on with the business of running the magazine until lunchtime when he finally showed up, carrying a second suit over his shoulder.

Señor Correa had lingered on his way to work. He rose late after his night excursions, breakfasted well and stopped on the way into town at his favourite Turkish barber's, where Mehmet worked his usual miracles, kissing his neck with an open razor, plucking at stray hairs with a taut string, singeing his ears with a candle flame. Señor Correa had the relaxed, replete air of a man who knew that next month's edition was in the bag. He was untroubled. He was unassailable. He walked to the office and spent the rest of the afternoon standing up at a draughtsman's table, designing endless versions of next month's magazine, smiling and taking time to enjoy Marta's wiggle every time she got up from her desk.

Normally, of course, Correa and his staff would keep those designs secret – as secret as the nineteen-year-old hairdresser whom he visited on Wednesday nights – but on that day he was designing his own monument and when, after seven attempts, Correa was satisfied, he took his final version to the big Xerox machine in the corner and ran off two copies.

Correa folded them into envelopes and addressed them: one for each of his guests. Then he put the envelopes into his briefcase, changed his suit and took a taxi to The Grill.

There is some doubt about which is the foremost literary journal in the country. Correa, Fernanda Maria Espinosa at *The Reader* and Salvade at *The National Review* would each have expressed a firm view on that matter and none of them would have agreed, but there could be no debate about The Grill. The Grill was the most fashionable restaurant in the city and it had become so by the childishly simple ruse of being deeply unfashionable for forty years.

Down a narrow street, through an archway that opened off one of the very best squares in the city, The Grill had changed not so much as a lavatory seat since it opened. Not a doorknob, not an ashtray had been altered and so the place went from the very height, the *dernier cri*, of Art Deco luxury to a dusty old relic and back to a charming, bedazzling, authentic antique.

Actors, singers, musicians, soft-spoken businessmen who used to be gangsters, authors, footballers with their garish girlfriends, the beautiful starlets of the telenovelas with beautiful boyfriends – some rather too beautiful, who found themselves gazing longingly at those gorgeous footballers – they all came to The Grill.

Getting any table there was an accomplishment, but only someone like J.I. Correa could call no more than a day in advance and secure the private dining room at the back; much to the horror of the Ambassador of Ireland, who found his little party suddenly bumped. Fernanda Maria simply could not resist.

She regretted it as soon as she took off her coat, and when he arrived, Salvade realized instantly that Correa had summoned them to gloat, but to flee would only have made the old bastard's triumph all the greater. He stood his ground and clamped fingers hard around the stem of his martini glass.

Smiling coldly over the fish course, Fernanda Maria said: 'Now, Juan, darling, why have you asked us here?'

But the editor Correa simply summoned more wine and said: 'My dear, why spoil this lovely meal with shop talk?'

Salvade of *The National Review* stayed silent and sullen and drank more than he should but he cracked between mouthfuls of the tenderest steak. 'Come on,' he said. 'Something's up.'

Correa ignored him with a smile and poured him another enormous glass. He ignored them again over dessert, talking of nothings like the perfect host, revelling in their misery with a well-mannered, sadistic glee.

But Señor Correa faced the dilemma that faces all torturers: that inflicting more agony might mean no more agony can be inflicted. So it was only over coffee, when they crumpled their napkins, when they looked ready to stalk away, that he finally relented.

'Children, children,' he soothed. 'My dear colleagues. Friends.'

They harrumphed. They took a little brandy.

'Have you heard the story of Howard Carter who, in 1922, uncovered the perfect, intact tomb of Tutankhamun?'

'I know he died of something horrible,' said Fernanda Maria. 'The curse of the Pharaohs.'

'I'm sure you are right,' said Correa. 'It was before my time. But I have heard it said that when, at last, he broke into the tomb and pushed a candle into the gap, they asked him what he could see and he said: "Wonderful things."'

Salvade poured himself more brandy. 'Is there a point to this?'

'There is. There is! Imagine then my delight when, like Carter, I opened an envelope and found this.' He reached into the pocket of his jacket and took out a piece of blue notepaper. 'Imagine my disbelief. Imagine how I read and reread these few, brief words over and over again. Imagine, if you can, how happy and how unworthy I counted myself when my little candle exposed this wonderful thing.'

Salvade sniggered into his brandy. 'Tell us again about exposing your unworthy little candle.'

That was too much for Fernanda Maria. Her patience was exhausted and she stretched across the table as if to snatch the letter away. 'Oh, for God's sake, come on! What does it say?'

Correa held up a calming hand, much as Marta Alicia did only the day before. 'My darling, it says this. It says: "Dear Correa, it's been some time since we have spoken and I'm sorry I have had nothing to show you. I am sending you a short story which I hope you will consider for the favour of publication at your usual rate.'

Salvade waved his glass around and said: 'So who's it from?'

'Oh that's the surprise, my friends. That's why I asked you here. Look under your plates.'

'What?'

'Under your plates. Look under your plates.'

'This is ridiculous,' said Fernanda Maria.

'It's pathetic.' But they both looked. They lifted their plates, they found the envelopes that Correa had so carefully prepared, and inside each envelope was a facsimile copy of the front page of *The Salon* with its masthead in that elegant Roman script and, underneath, where the picture should go, where decks of headlines should advertise the more or less interesting articles inside, it said:

'VALDEZ'

Just one word in the biggest, blackest type that would fit on the page.

They looked at him with mouths agape and he gazed back with palms spread wide in triumph.

Salvade said: 'You bastard!'

And Correa, smiling, replied: 'He's back, darlings. Look on my works, ye mighty, and despair.'

THE CAR MOVED under the shadowed trees like a mermaid swimming through waving groves of kelp, dappled by distant sunlight, shining with a metallic marlin-gleam. Last night's rain had dampened down the dust of the track and the car rolled slowly, quietly over the firm earth, leaving a trail of heartbroken music as it passed.

> Go away! I never want to see you more.
> Just let me try to live in peace.
> Don't say that I'm already
> drunk like yesterday.
> The pain and grief of loving you
> hurts more than alcohol can ever do.
> My cup is filled with non-existence
> and in it I will drown despair.
> Go away! The sight of you brings back the hurt.
> Leave me now, now that I can do no more.

Mr Valdez let the car roll to a stop in the shade of the very last tree in the avenue and waited. The steering wheel gleamed as white as bleached bone in his grip. He kept both hands there, holding on tightly because he knew that, if he let go, even to adjust the radio, his finger would fly to his lip. It had become a habit with him, rubbing, tracing, following but never finding the thing he could sense but never see. Time and again he startled himself as if he had suddenly awoken from a trance, touching his lip and wondering how long he had been doing it, catching himself at it as if he had been exposed in something shameful, and then his hand would fly up and he would push his fingers through his hair, as if that were what he'd always intended and the lip-stroking was no more than a moment's diversion on the way. In the great effort to avoid touching his lip, Valdez had taken to rubbing his brow. He had discovered there quite a deep furrow leading in a diagonal flare to the middle of his left eyebrow. It was alone, he noted. There was no mirror image on the right side of his brow and that troubled him until he realized the mark was caused by the way he slept.

There was a fold in his skin where he pressed the left side of his face into the pillow. It was simply another scar, scored into his skin over decades instead of branded there in a momentary assault, visible this time but unnoticed and unremembered, like the other. It was a mark of old age. It was just as terrifying as the other one, the secret one, the unseen one, the one with the unknown meaning.

Mr Valdez looked up to the driver's mirror and tilted his head. There was nothing to see. He was disgusted with himself, like a fat man opening the fridge again. He reached up and flicked the mirror sideways so it showed nothing but a reflection of trees and he stared straight ahead through the windscreen, out across the broad, level parkland at the back of the university campus. He tightened his grip on the steering wheel. He loosened his grip on the steering wheel. He found under his fingers some little crack, some irregularity in the underside of the ivory plastic, and he began to worry at it with his fingernail. Pick. Pick. Pick. As if to smooth it away and make the unseen blemish disappear so every tiny part of his beautiful car could be as beautiful as every other part, seen or unseen, visible or invisible.

The tree above his head was filled with creepers and they in turn were crowded with small white blossoms. Baritone bees moved among them, setting off a tiny avalanche of dusty, spent anthers. Valdez saw them falling on his hands, on the sleeve of his jacket, on the polished leather seat of his car, spotted and gappy, filling in like a persistent snowfall. He knew they must be landing on him too, greying his hair, marking the passage of time like the scattering of dust that finds its way into lost tombs. He kept his hands on the wheel.

And then, across the park, on another path, he saw a straggle of kids, walking along carrying their books and folders, laughing, dodging about, forming and reforming as they walked in line like geese jostling in the sky. Caterina was with them. He spotted her at the back of the line. He recognized her shining hair and the way she walked, flat-footed, in those schoolboy shoes and that coat, that awful, dreadful coat she wore to hide herself in the hope it might dampen the glow of her loveliness and make her unnoticeable. It didn't work. From the other side of the park, she shone amongst all those others who were lovely only because they were young, all beautiful, all exactly as beautiful as each other in exactly the same way, like one of those nineteenth-century oil paintings where the handsome hero stumbles upon a pool of Naiads, each one gorgeous in her loveliness, each the image of the others. And then there was Caterina, who was different and who would never be the same.

She broke off from the group with a wave and began to walk, diagonally, across the grass towards him. As she came Mr Valdez saw, on the path behind her, the quick, shuffling outline of Dr Cochrane following the group of students but watching Caterina, watching where she went until his eye fell on the lovely green car waiting under the trees. Dr Cochrane looked away quickly, pulled his hat down over his eyes and fixed his gaze on the path. There was no other car in the city like that one. Mr Valdez knew he had been recognized and Mr Valdez did not care.

She was coming towards him like a wave of wind across a corn-field, soft and rhythmic and beyond his power to hold or contain, and he didn't care about anything else. He didn't care that Cochrane had spotted them and leapt to conclusions. He didn't care that Cochrane was right. He didn't care who knew. He didn't care that Caterina was too young for him, too innocent, too pure, too gauche, too much a child ever to be the mother of his chil-dren. He didn't care that she would never fit in at the polo club. He didn't care that she would tire of him, that she would still be young when he had grown old and she would betray him with the same enthusiasm that Maria had betrayed the banker Marrom. He didn't care that his plan had not worked, that he had Caterina but still the words did not come. He didn't even care that his seduction had backfired, like a fly trying to woo the fly paper – and succeeding. It didn't matter. None of it mattered. The only thing that mattered was that she was coming across the grass towards him, waving, smiling, curling a twist of hair from her mouth where the wind had blown it, young and real and his if he wanted her and, yes, he wanted her.

Caterina put her hand on the hot handle of the passenger door and Mr Valdez leaned across apologetically to pop the button.

'Forgive me,' he said, 'a lady shouldn't have to open the door.'

'Don't worry about it. I like you even when you forget to be adorably old-fashioned.'

'Good manners are never out of fashion,' he said, 'even if I forget them.' And then he astonished himself by saying: 'I like you too.'

The weight of that hung between them like a thundercloud

waiting to break and, if Caterina had been wiser, if she had been
hard, if she had been two years older, if she had not been Caterina,
she would have made light of it with some silly, belittling comment
like: 'Ah, but I *really* like you' and it would all have been forgotten,
like a scraped knee or a broken vase. Instead, she said: 'Chano,
thank you!' as if he had brought her diamonds, as if he had
drenched her in flowers again, and this time meant it, so now,
when she kissed him and said: 'I like you too. Very much. Very,
very much,' it was like an oath that had been notarized before a
magistrate and could not be denied.

She took her lips from his only slowly and smiled and said:
'Where are we going?'

'I have somewhere special to show you. And I brought a picnic.'
He turned the key and, as they rolled quietly together, all three
of them, Valdez and Caterina and the lovely, mint-green, fish-
green car, he reached up and adjusted the mirror again and then
they were back at the road.

She said something as they drove along but, with the top down,
the wind snatched her words away. He tilted his head and leaned
towards her, inviting her to say it again, and she turned sideways
in her seat and yelled: 'I said,' her words separate and careful and
distinct, 'I said, if there were a public execution in town, would
you go?'

He burst out laughing at that. Through the trees on the other
side of the road the Merino appeared in sunny flashes. He said:
'Hanging or shooting?'

'Could be a guillotining.'

'Or a breaking on the wheel.'

'Look, it doesn't matter how it's done. What I'm asking is,
would you go?'

He wondered if this was a trick question, something that might
be taken as an indication of character, something that demanded

a response and a reaction just as 'I write' had done, something which, like that, might decide his fate. 'No. I would not go. It's a disgusting idea.'

'Oh, I'd go. I'd go in a minute. I'd love to go.'

'Caterina! For God's sake. You'd go to see a man die?'

'No. I don't think that's why people went to such things. Nobody went to see a man die. People die all the time. Dying isn't such a big thing.'

He slowed the car so he could hear what she was saying: 'So why did they go?'

'Not for the dying. That happens every day.'

'For the killing?'

'Yes, maybe for that. No, I think they went to see how they died – everybody dies but this is somebody who knows it's about to happen right now, right there. And there's the whole business of how they take it: do they kick and struggle and fight and resist or do they simply give in and let it happen? Do they hold on to their dignity?'

'Being killed is not very dignified.'

'It all ends the same way. It's not very dignified losing control of your bowels in a hospital bed. But then there's the chance that remaining calm and aloof and contemptuous in the face of death might be seen as childishly weak and obedient – just doing what you were told. If I were dying in a bed, I think I'd want my family around me. I'd want somebody to hold my hand. But, if I were being executed, I'm not so sure. I haven't decided. I can't make up my mind if a friendly face in the crowd would help to give me a bit of backbone or if it would be so sad that it would make me blub. Anyway, I'd go. I'd go for the colour. I'd go for the feeling, to feel it and write it down. Like the way the light is coming through those trees, like the sound of the tyres on the road just now and how hot it is, even when the wind comes rushing along as we drive. Don't you want to feel and write down what you feel?'

He did. More than anything Luciano Hernando Valdez wanted to feel and he wanted to write but there was nothing to write; nothing but the same scrawny yellow cat crossing the same road and nothing to feel in the whole world except for the joy of that girl sitting beside him.

'Yes,' he said.

'Yes? Is that all?'

'Yes.' He smiled at her and, when he should have told her the truth, he nodded like an idiot and said: 'Yes,' again.

'So that's it? "Yes." I'm sitting in this wonderful car, next to this wonderful man, a man who – it's been said – is the foremost novelist of his generation, a respected teacher who even likes me, and all the deep insight I get is "Yes"? Chano, I want to be a writer. Teach me.'

'But "Yes" is all there is to say. I can't teach you to be a writer. You are a writer. You feel and you want to write down what you feel. That's what it's about.'

'And stories.'

'Yes,' he said, 'and stories.'

'You are a wonderful storyteller, you know.' She kissed her fingers and brushed them over his knuckles where he gripped the steering wheel. 'Tell me a story.'

'We're here,' he said. Mr Valdez turned the car off the highway and into a dirty side road which ran between once-white houses where chickens scattered as they passed. Before long, the road turned to dust and he slowed to a crawl and tiny stones popped from beneath the car's taut tyres until they reached the trees where it was shady and the road was damp and gently rutted.

'Are we still here?'

'We are nearly still here.' Almost everything she said made

him smile. The engine stilled and the handbrake gave its rough, creaking laugh.

'Are you sure this is the right place?'

'To tell the truth, no, I'm not.'

There was nothing to see. The road had run out in a narrow strip of grass, grazed short by animals and walled behind by trees and bushes. Mr Valdez got out of the car and took from its tiny and useless boot a picnic basket with a hinged lid. Caterina noticed the price tag was still attached.

'I think it's down here,' he said and he began to push his way between the trees where there was still the ghost of a path. He turned back to see if she was following and, when she held out her hand to him, he took it, edging between the bushes with his shoulder to make a way for her. 'I'm nearly sure this is it.'

A little further on and they found the outline of a wall, like one of those lost cities deep in the jungle that speak of forgotten rituals and blood sacrifice and catastrophe and collapse, places where thousands walked for generations and loved and played and fought and made music and cowered before dark gods and where, now, there are only spiders and cats and sudden stone faces scowling from blank mounds of earth and young men hung with cameras who look up to the sky, to invisible necklaces of satellites strung around the world, and plot their position – in spite of all the proof around them that none of it matters. Mr Valdez followed the path, broad enough for a goat, tripping over tree roots, trying to hold her hand and offer a gallant support until the wall vanished. He was puzzled for a moment until he realized that they had simply reached the corner and there, only a little ahead of them, was a gap which marked the gate.

'I knew this was the place,' he said, as if someone had doubted him and he had been proved right. He kicked away the weeds which had choked the gate, lifted it on its hinges and jerked it open enough to make a space to squeeze through.

'Chano, this is a graveyard.'

'Yes.' He was halfway through the gap in the gates.

'Why have you brought me to a graveyard?'

'You're not frightened, are you? A minute ago you were planning to go to an execution just for the experience.'

'I'm not frightened, but look at it. Do you want us to have our picnic in there?'

Jammed in the gate, one hand in front of him holding the picnic basket, one hand extended behind him, he turned his head away from her and looked into the little cemetery and saw it as it was; lost, unvisited, forgotten and overgrown, not as he had remembered it. The four rows of graves, all lined up to face the east so the rising sun of the dawning day of glory would wake the dead, each outlined with an ankle-high wall of marble, each roofed at the head end with a three-sided covering like a house lacking its last wall, were unkempt and covered in rough tufts of grass. Creepers and ivy were spilling over the outer walls. The gravel paths were almost vanished.

'I'm sorry,' he said. 'Of course you are right. What was I thinking?'

'There might be snakes.'

'Yes, there might be snakes.' He began to squeeze back through the narrow gap in the gates. The iron left a streak of rust grazed into the front of his shirt. 'Would you mind if I left you here just for a moment?' he said. 'There is something I need to do.' He put the picnic basket on the ground, stooped, took something from it and forced his way through the gates again. 'It'll just be a moment. Just over there. I won't be far. I won't leave you.'

Mr Valdez walked a little more slowly than usual, with a heavy tread, careful not to put his foot down where the creepers were knotted together, sticking closely to the last clear places in the path, places where snakes would not linger, making his way to the far wall of the cemetery where a small white mausoleum with blind windows on either side of a bronze door that curled and whipped with *fin de siècle* foliage and marble columns, as plain and elegant as eggshells, was beginning to disappear under a surge of weeds.

He reached up and hauled at a long rope of leaves which had coiled itself over the roof and it came away in a shower of dust and dirt and spiders and shrivelled brown blossoms that fell with a murmur of past summers. He stopped. It was pointless and impossible. If he laboured for days, if he survived the snakes and the spiders and the filthy dust that was already itching its way down his neck and between his shoulders like the loose hairs scattered by a bad haircut, if he cut and dragged and stacked and burned, he could uncover the tomb, but when he left again, in that very moment, with the flick of a hidden green switch, the grass and the vines would begin to grow, climbing back towards the sun and burying everything again. It was as it should be.

Mr Valdez gathered a handful of scattered leaves, wadded them together and scrubbed at a sharply chiselled stone plaque by the door until the dirt that filled the frame and smoothed the script was gone. It took some time. He felt the ache in his arm. He grew hot and breathless and, when he stopped and stood back, because he had to rest, pretending that he was checking his work, he found that Caterina was there, worming her hand into his.

'Torre Blanco,' she said, reading the plaque.

'My mother's family. My grandfather, the Admiral, is buried here.'

'And your grandmother?'

'Yes, I suppose so. I never knew her. He brought me up. You saw his sword.'

'The hero.'

'I always thought so.'

'But not now?'

'Still. Why should I change my mind? The dead don't let us down. They don't alter.' Mr Valdez let go of her hand and picked up the bottle of toffee-coloured rum from where he had left it beside the door of the tomb. 'I brought this for him,' he said. 'A libation for the ancestors.'

'Are you going inside?' She was trying not to sound afraid.

'No. The door is locked. I have no key.' He opened the bottle with twist. 'It will just have to go here, on his doorstep.'

They stood in silence together, holding hands as he emptied the bottle, pouring it over the locks, splashing it across the threshold like an arsonist.

The last of the rum dripped from the upturned bottle. The marble step shone with it, leaving tracks in the dust and dirt as it trickled away. The fumes of hot, burnt sugar rose up and filled the air and perhaps a few drops managed to wash under the locked bronze door, enough to moisten the Admiral's long-dry lips.

Caterina took his hand again. 'If he had been out there,' she nodded to the humble graves that lay open to the sky, 'you could have poured it straight down to him.'

'It doesn't matter. They can't drink. Not even if it pours right into their mouths.' And then, for no reason that he could have explained, he said: 'I'm sorry. This was silly.'

She squeezed his hand. 'Are you ready for that picnic you promised me?'

They walked back to the gate, squeezed through, collected the basket and went from tree to tree, down the goat track to the car.

When they pushed through the last line of bushes, Valdez said: 'I'll take you home.'

She was disappointed. 'What about the picnic?'

'I'm filthy.'

'It doesn't matter. We can clean you up.' She took the handkerchief from the pocket of his jacket – there was always a handkerchief in his pocket and, thank God, he had left his jacket behind in the car.

'Rub your hands together,' she said. 'Keep rubbing. And your fingers. Rub between your fingers. Most of it'll come off.' She stood in front of him, very small and very young, reaching up to brush his face with his own handkerchief. 'It's not so bad,' she said. 'Take off your shirt,' and, when he did, she dusted his shoulders and turned his shirt inside out and shook it and rubbed the collar. 'That'll do. You'll be more comfortable now.' And without waiting to be asked, she sat down on the grass and opened the basket while he did up his buttons.

She found the camera he had brought and it delighted her to think that he had wanted to keep a record of the day.

'Chano! Stand still, let me take your picture. Smile for me.'

But he turned his back to her, his shirt still half buttoned. 'I'm a mess. I'm covered in dirt, my hair's full of cobwebs. You can't take my picture like this.'

'Yes, I can.' The camera clicked.

'Don't. Caterina, don't. Please.' He glanced back at her quickly, over his shoulder, a stupid, coquettish pose, like a model trying too hard to look alluring, checking if it was safe to turn around.

'All right. I'll wait until you're pretty again.'

'But you're pretty now. Give me the camera.'

She handed it to him without complaint, without shifting from the spot where she sat, legs folded under her, on the short grass. 'Ready?' she asked and then she nodded violently so her hair was flung forward over her face and nodded backwards again so it flew around her head in living, moving billows, and she was in the middle of it, smiling, delighted, chin high, eyes defiant.

Click!

And then they ate. It was an ordinary little meal, but they enjoyed it. Sometimes that's all there is. Not everything is important and significant and magical like pouring rum on a dead grandfather's grave. It was just a picnic.

At the end of it, when they were quiet and sitting on the grass together, she said: 'Chano, I lied. I was afraid of the graveyard. My father is in the graveyard and, when we found him, his hands were full of earth and now he's in the earth and the earth is in his mouth and in his eyes. The earth is filling him up. I don't want to be dead. I want to live.'

'And yet you came anyway and held my hand.'

'Yes. I came anyway.'

He stood up and went to the car and, carefully, with the tips of his fingers, he turned the knob that switched on the radio. The radio played tango. The radio always played tango, the way the pocket of his jacket always had a clean handkerchief.

'Come and dance with me,' he said.

'I can't.'

'I'll show you. You can learn.' He held out a hand and raised her up while she rolled her eyes and feigned reluctance.

'How come you can teach me to dance but you can't teach me to write?'

'Because I was taught how to dance but nobody taught me how to write. Now, like this, your hand here, straighten your back, don't look at your feet.'

'Why can't it be happy music? Tango is always sad.'

'It's a different kind of happy. Stop trying. You can't dance in these shoes. We need to get you better shoes – with a heel. Press yourself on me, move with me, forget about dancing and pretend you are in bed.' He pushed his mouth into her hair, close to her ear, and whispered: 'Everything.'

She folded herself into him.

'Everything.'

The music stopped and there was a moment of silence when they hung together without moving and then a flutter of applause and somebody said: 'Bravo, bravo,' in a creaky voice.

They turned and saw an old woman standing at the end of the path, dressed all in black and carrying a hoe across her shoulder. 'Bonito,' she said. 'Bonito. So nice to see a man and his daughter dance like this. Bonito.'

Caterina laughed and, a moment later, so did Valdez.

PRODUCING AN EDITION of *The Salon* is an endeavour that takes months. It takes months because publishers take months to decide their schedules. They take months to tease their authors, like anglers twitching tiny feather flies over the noses of hungry trout, urging, cajoling, pleading, demanding, promising that this book on Napoleon's cigarette cases – above any other book ever published on Napoleon's cigarette cases by this house or any other house – is simply the greatest, the most wonderful, the most important, the most worthy book on Napoleon's cigarette cases ever known. They take months to perfect their trembling, breathless, girlish quivering as they gush and swoon – 'We're all very, very excited about this project, darling, and thrilled and delighted that you've chosen to go with us!' – even if nobody can quite recall the name of the book. They take months because there are covers to be designed and then redesigned and designed again because setting the title page in sans serif type can change the whole feel of the book, you know. They take months because there are lunches to eat, tiny things to be nibbled from sticks, martinis to be sipped. They take months to tantalize wholesalers and bookshops, gently kissing and caressing like the not-quite-sexy-enough girls who never make it on screen but who still play a vital role in those special interest films they show at The Tivoli, whispering over and

over about that special book until the anticipation is too much
to bear. It all takes months. And, months ahead of publication,
Señor Juan Ignacio Correa of *The Salon* must decide which books
will be favoured with a review, he must choose exactly the right
reviewer for exactly the right book, he must commission them
and he must wait. He must wait for months because the reviewing
of important books is an important business. It cannot be hurried.
It takes months. It takes months to let professional jealousy cool
to an icy bitterness. It takes months to sharpen those little shards
of envy into the perfect stiletto, to count the ribs and push. It
takes months to hone the perfect phrase, a phrase that will demon-
strate to the sensitive reader in just a few brief words how much
better that book could have been written if only the reviewer
had written it – if only he had thought of it, if only he had done
the work. That instant flash of caustic insight, the brilliant, biting
epigram shot across the dining table, that moment of spontaneous wit: do you think that sort of thing writes itself? It takes
practice. Practice, practice, practice. Months of practice. It all
takes months and, for the most part, it takes months because
months are allotted to the task.

Just around the corner from the offices of *The Salon* are the
offices of the *Daily Reporter*. The editors of the *Daily Reporter* find
that they do not need months to produce a new edition. Every
night the huge presses run and the building trembles and thousands upon thousands of copies are printed and folded and stacked
and baled and loaded into lorries and taken to the railway station,
and when it's done it's done. The next day the staff of the *Daily
Reporter* come back to work and start again. They make a new
paper every day simply because they have only one day to do it.

Now, instead of his usual months, Señor Juan Ignacio Correa
had only ten days to make a new edition of *The Salon*. Everything
that he had prepared in the last three weeks was worthless the

moment that Miss Marta Alicia Cantaluppi opened the letter. He
had to start again. Of course, it was impossible but, since there
was no choice, he would do it.

Sitting at the desk in his corner office with Marta Alicia, a
notebook balanced on her primly crossed knees, Correa held his
head in his hands and tried to fight off panic as he nursed a fero-
cious hangover. The beautiful ankles of Miss Marta Alicia
Cantaluppi, glimpsed through the cage of his fingers, comforted
him in his hour of distress, but nothing encouraged him so much
as the furious, impotent misery of his rivals. Poor Fernanda Maria.
Poor Salvade. They had been so unhappy and, when they stalked
off and left all that brandy, well it seemed silly not to drink it.
He took another sip of coffee and steeled himself.

'Marta Alicia, remember I told you not to tell anybody about
this?'

'Of course, Señor Correa. I haven't told a soul. Not even my
mother. I will not breathe a word.'

'Yes, but all that's changed. Now we want people to know.'

'I see. Well, won't Señor Salvade and Señora Espinosa talk
about it?'

'Not a chance. Those two? You should've seen their faces. Like
a pair of nuns at a farting contest. No, they're going to keep this
quiet. Who's going to buy their magazines after this? They
wouldn't sell a line of advertising and we're going to sell lots and
lots of lovely advertising.'

Correa picked up from his desk the dummies of the next edition
of *The Salon*. They were lovely things, the best he had ever come
up with. Every month he just got better and better. Last night's
brandy was still rattling through his veins and the pages knocked
together as he held them. He gripped the paper tightly and tore
it in half.

'Right! Let's get on. So now we've got a front page with one word on it and four pages of copy. We need to spin it out. Take notes. Are you writing this down?'

'I'm writing it all down, Mr Correa.'

'Thank God, because when I'm being creative you don't want to miss a thing.'

Marta Alicia looked deep into her notebook. It was very empty. After a moment she made the dreadful mistake of tapping on the blank page with the little pink rubber on the end of her pencil.

'Stop that,' he said.

She was very quiet. So was he.

Marta Alicia tried to be encouraging. 'I liked what you said about spinning it out.'

'Yes. Yes, that's what we have to do.'

'That's very wise.'

'The point is, my dear, we've got a little gem here and I'm the jeweller. So Valdez has been down in his mine, hacking away with his pick. So what? Big deal! He's given us a diamond but it's a muddy, waxy little thing. It's up to me to polish it and show it off with a suitably elegant setting. These—' Señor Correa felt suddenly sick and he had to choke down a mouthful of bile that burned in the back of his throat and then, almost without stopping, in the hopes that Marta Alicia had not noticed, he went on. 'These writers, they think they are the artists. We're the artists. Us. We tell people what's good. We tell people what to like and they like it and they all agree that it's good.'

Señor Correa was looking down at his desk again as if his batteries had suddenly run out.

Miss Cantaluppi found her rubber-tipped pencil almost unbearably attractive. 'I mean, obviously,' she said, 'illustrations are going to take up a lot of space.'

'Yes,' he said. 'Yes. Full-page illustrations.'

'That could double the size of the story.'

'Exactly. That's exactly what I was thinking of.'

'I'm making notes,' she said. 'This is brilliant stuff.'

Nothing much happened.

Miss Marta Alicia Cantaluppi, as well as being extremely effi-cient, was very kind and, as well as having very pretty legs and a rear view as striking as anything you could see from a vaporetto departing from the Grand Canal of Venice, she could make excel-lent coffee. So she offered to make coffee, which was a way of combining kindness and efficiency and her striking rear view all in one.

'Would you like another coffee?' she said.

'That's a good idea,' he said.

She brought coffee and she said: 'I'll leave you to your work. Call me if you need me,' and then, while he worked, Marta Alicia got on with the business of the day.

She looked at the back of the diary on her desk and dug out the number of Dr Alberto Saumarez at the Universidad Real. She rang it and he answered.

Miss Cantaluppi said: 'Dr Saumarez?' with a question mark on the end, as if she had no idea that was his number, as if she had dialled a number at random and she was just as likely to be talking to that little hairdresser she wasn't supposed to know anything about.

'Dr Saumarez? This is Marta Alicia Cantaluppi from the office of Señor Correa at *The Salon*.'

He said something. She laughed a short laugh that ended with a sound like the stem of a champagne glass snapping and said: 'Yeeeeeees.' And then she explained that, since Dr Saumarez was recognized as the foremost critical authority on the works of L.H. Valdez, he was her first choice — Señor Correa's absolutely first choice — to provide the vital critical assessment of a new short story, due to be published in the next issue.

She explained that, naturally, this was a matter of the utmost commercial sensitivity and that, for that reason, Dr Saumarez would have to leave the university and read the story in the offices of *The Salon* and that, since the story was only four pages long, and due to reasons of space, he could have no more than twenty pages for his thoughts.

Yes, Miss Cantaluppi agreed, that was an insult and an outrage, but there was worse to come and, due to pressures of time, Dr Saumarez would have to produce his very valuable reflections within the next week at the latest.

She agreed that it was an impossible deadline and yes, she did know who he was, and she apologized for wasting his time and of course he was right and only a hack could churn something out in that time so perhaps it would be best if, after all, they just forgot all about it and she called Dr Salgado.

'Yes,' she said, '*that* Dr Salgado. Dr Celestina Salgado of the Universidad Catolica.'

Miss Cantaluppi had to admit that she did not know Dr Salgado personally and she might very well be a bitch, but she was willing to write the article and – before she could say more, Dr Saumarez agreed. In fact he insisted. In fact he demanded to write a critique of the new story and he promised to be in the office within the hour.

After that Miss Cantaluppi picked up the internal phone, called the advertising department and told them to cancel every line of space they had sold in next month's issue and sell it again – but this time for 25 per cent more. She called production and told them to add another sixteen pages and then she called advertising again and told them to sell sixteen full-page ads. She told them to call Mont Blanc pens and Louis Vuitton luggage and the Hotel Imperial, anybody and everybody who sold ordinary things like pens and handbags and hotel rooms at unbelievable prices, and offer them an ordinary full-page ad for an unbelievable price.

Miss Cantaluppi was firm in her instructions: 'Tell them we are running a special edition with a new work by L.H. Valdez. Tell them they have until close of business to sign and, above all, tell them it is all in complete confidence and total secrecy. Señor Correa is explicit about that. Tell them all and tell them it's a secret. Got it? Get going.'

She looked to her right. Inside his glass office Correa was staring down at a blank page on his desk, a desk he held on to at either side to stop it from spinning round. Miss Cantaluppi could not have known, but he was considering whether it would be safe to let go of the desk with one hand for just long enough to reach for the metal waste basket by his feet, in case he needed somewhere to be sick. He looked up at her mournfully and she hurried to his room.

She stood on one leg, swinging into the office with her hand on the doorknob. Nothing could have said: 'In a rush. Not stopping,' more clearly.

'I was thinking,' she said, 'all the reviews at the back, they're sort of time-limited, you know. I mean, those books will still be coming out, Valdez or no Valdez.'

'Yes,' he said.

'So we're keeping those?'

'Yes.'

'I thought so.' She gathered the torn pages from his desk. 'I'll get these redone. And I'll see about those illustrations you suggested. In-house, or is there somebody special you want to ask?'

He looked at her like a lost spaniel who's had his ten days in the dog pound and must now go, unclaimed, towards the electric box and he said nothing.

'In-house. That's what I thought. And that critical analysis piece you asked for – to go with the story . . .'

'Analysis.'

'Yes. You do still want it; don't you? I can cancel it if you like.'

'No, of course not. I've made up my mind. It's absolutely essential. It's like I said about setting the diamond. It's essential. We can't just throw this thing at them. We've got to tell them they're getting it, give it to them and then tell them they've had it.'

'Exactly. So that's it. All finished. You've done it again, Señor Correa. I'll get the stuff on your desk for the close of business and all it needs is your editorial. Better make it a killer.'

'It'll have to wait until tomorrow. I'm going home. It must be something I ate. The Grill is not what it was, you know.'

Señor Correa gathered his jacket from the coat stand in the corner of his office and walked to the lift but decided on the stairs instead. They were steadier.

By 2.20 that afternoon, Miss Cantaluppi was taking calls asking if it was true that *The Salon* had a new Valdez and she referred them all to the editor, who was in a meeting. By 2.40 advertising had called to say that all the extra space was sold and it was then that Miss Marta Alicia Cantaluppi knew for sure that, one day, not too far from now, she would be editor of *The Salon*.

Her chance came just six months later when Señor Juan Ignacio Correa passed away suddenly and unexpectedly, seated in the back room of a hairdresser's salon, with his trousers down, his teenage girlfriend kneeling in front of him and his wife standing behind him with a pistol. After a graceful period of mourning the proprietor of *The Salon* gave the job to his nephew.

DRIVING BACK TO town from the lost cemetery, Caterina said: 'It will be summer soon.'

'It's summer now,' he said.

'But in summer the university breaks up.'

'Yes.'

'I'll have to go home.'

He looked at her in surprise. 'Home? You mean to the farm?'

'Yes. Home to the farm.'

'Home to the mountains?'

'Yes, Chano, home to the farm in the mountains.'

The empty rum bottle rolled on the back seat. The burnt caramel scent of it rose up, warm and sharp until it was mixed and mingled in the petrol fumes of passing cars and lost, like rain in the sea.

'Do you have to go?'

'They expect me. My brother. He needs the help.'

'And your mother.'

'Yes. She likes to see me. I like to see her too.'

'But you don't have to go.'

'I do, Chano.'

'You don't.'

'Chano, listen to me. I do. I have to go home.'

Mr Valdez said nothing. He had just worked up the courage to speak when they dipped into the section of highway leading into the tunnel that would take them back to Avenue Cristobal and the roar of the traffic made talking impossible.

Bright, square lights shone from the roof. He looked at her in quick sideways glances, watching the shape of the lights moving, glinting, along the bonnet of the car, flashing on the windscreen, lighting her face, disappearing, as regular as the signals of a lighthouse. She was staring straight ahead, deliberately turning her face from his, and then they were out of the tunnel and sunlight flooded her, so for a moment she vanished in glory.

'Listen,' he said.

'Chano, would you please watch the road?'

'This is important.'

'I have to go.' She reached across to the steering wheel and touched his hand, brushing her fingers over his knuckles as she did before. 'I'll come back. I will come back.' She said it like she would say it to a dog chained to a lamp-post or a child abandoned at school for the first time.

And, like a child, he said: 'I know you'll come back. It's not the coming back that worries me, it's the going away. It's the being away. Caterina, I don't want you to go away. I don't want that.'

Now she was looking at him. There was something in his voice that made her look at him. Just a few hours ago he said: 'I like you,' and now he was ready to admit that he wanted her to stay.

He said: 'Caterina. You will think this odd,' and then he cursed and jerked the car into a gap at the side of the pavement, bumped the wheel off the kerb and parked. He turned to her and said: 'Please don't go. Please stay. Stay with me, if you like. I'm asking you to stay. If it's a matter of money, don't worry about money. I've got money.'

'I can't take your money.'

'Yes, you can. I have plenty of money.'

'For God's sake, listen to yourself. Is that what you think? You think you have lots of money and I have none so you can just pay me to stay here all summer? Or were you going to pay me for one night at a time – or an hour at a time? I can't take your money. A girl can't take a man's money. What would that make me, Chano?'

'Stay with me.'

'Chano!' She turned round and scrabbled furiously with the door catch. Before he could reach her, she was gone. It took him a second or two to throw open the driver's door and he left it hanging open to the traffic as he sprinted round the car to catch her.

He gripped her by the arms and she struggled, but not too much. Just enough to show that she didn't want to get away. 'Stay, Caterina. Please stay with me.'

'No. I won't stay. I won't stay and be your whore.'

'Then stay and be my wife.'

'People are looking.'

'Let them look. I don't care any more.'

'I'll scream.'

'Scream if you want to, just, for God's sake, say "Yes".'

She sagged in his arms. 'Chano, no. I can't marry you. No.'

'Yes, you can. Just say "Yes". Marry me. It'll be fine. I'm an old man. I'll die soon.'

'Stop saying these things.'

He held her tightly, almost holding her up, and she was so small and so lovely and the scent of her hair filled him and made him remember Maria and all those other women in this city, in all the little towns down the length of the river, in the capital. He glanced back at his beautiful car, with the scuff mark of the pavement ground into its white-walled tyres, with its door open to the traffic, with buses shaving past, and he wanted to run to it and slam the door. He thought of the ice in a tall glass and the brilliant, throat-tightening bitterness of the lime juice from Madame Ottavio's table and the girls walking slowly, slowly round the garden, stopping under the trees, climbing the stairs, and he wondered if that was over. Could that be over? And he thought of the scrawny yellow cat, that same cat endlessly crossing the same road, and he wanted it to stop. He wanted to find a way to make it stop and make it right and she was the way.

'I'll stop. I'll stop if you marry me.'

Caterina was crying. She said: 'You don't have to marry me. I'll stay. I won't go. I'll stay and we can keep on like this. I'll do whatever you say. I'll be what you want.'

'Then do what I say. Marry me. Be what I want. Be my wife.'

And then, poor child, she said 'Yes'. There were not many days left until he killed her.

THERE WERE SO many things to talk about but they didn't talk. They went to bed and then, when he brought her champagne, he said: 'You realize you'll have to meet my mother.'

She groaned and covered her face with the pillow.

'There's no point hiding.'

'You'll have to meet mine,' she said, but he couldn't hear her until he took the pillow away. 'You'll have to meet mine.'

'Yes, I will. Soon.' He said that in a way that meant: 'Some day. Never. You should forget about the farm.'

'It's a funny little church up there. I hope we'll be able to fit everybody in.'

Mr Valdez trailed the edge of his chilled glass along the line of her shoulder and he said: 'We'll manage,' in a way that meant: 'We will be married in the cathedral, in front of the Bishop, and my mother would kill you and eat your quivering liver before she allowed you to drag her up the mountain.'

And then he said again: 'Anyway, you'll have to meet my mother,' in a way that meant: 'You will have to be taken out to good shops and clothes will have to be bought for you, women's clothes, not the children's clothes you always wear, not workman's clothes, not student clothes, and, above all, we're going to have to get you some shoes.'

'Yes, I will have to meet your mother. I will have to be examined and questioned and officially approved.'

'You will have to be introduced,' he said, in a way that meant: 'I don't think my mother will approve of you. They won't approve of you at the polo club, they may very well kick me out of the university because of you and literary editors in half the world's newspapers will collapse at their desks, laughing, when they hear but I don't care because I need you and I will marry you anyway.'

Caterina said: 'When I meet your mother, am I likely to face an examination on my virginity? Because I think I may fail.'

'The key to passing any exam is study. And more study.'

'I have to say, in all honesty,' she took another sip of champagne, 'I don't think you have been entirely helpful with my studies. In fact as a virginity tutor, your biggest admirer – and I think that's officially me – would have to say you are rubbish.'

He gave a little nod, a performer acknowledging an appreciative audience. 'It's not an excuse, I know,' he said, 'but, as a teacher, I have to say that I have met pupils who have thrown themselves into their studies with rather more enthusiasm. Looking at your recent exams, I have to wonder if you are really cut out for virginity. On the other hand, if you wanted to transfer to the "Pleasure and Hedonism" course, I could give you a very good reference.'

'I don't want that,' she said.

'What do you want?'

'Do you have an opening on the "Love" course? I would like to love you, Chano, if that's all right.'

'I would like that very much. I would like you to love me until the day I die. I would like you to love me even more than you do now, more every day, and hold my hand at the very last and kiss me to send me on my way.'

'This afternoon you discovered you liked me but now you want me to love you unto death.'

'I said I liked you but you knew what I meant. I want you to love me unto death and I would be honoured if you would let me love you and cover you with kisses and pile you with diamonds and furs, fill your arms with babies, strong sons and beautiful daughters. To love you is a delight and a joy beyond anything I have ever imagined or deserved. But first, you have to meet my mother.'

MR VALDEZ WAS very like the rest of us. Few of us are expert tango dancers, skilled polo players, internationally admired authors and respected scholars. Very few of us have wonderful old cars or enough money in the bank never to have to worry about a thing. But, for the most part, we all believe we are good. We all assume we are more or less decent people, more sinned against than sinning, and if life has not turned out exactly as we planned, if it is a little less than we might have hoped for, if our achievements have not been as great as they might and our disappointments a little greater, if others have been left miserable in our wakes, that is invariably the result of circumstance and never because of any failure of our own, never because of any deliberate act of malice or selfishness. Except for Father Gonzalez, those who believe in Heaven are always sure they will get in.

Mr Valdez was no different. His great ability to see into souls and open them on a page for others to look at, like frogs on a dissecting table, sliced apart and held with pins, did not extend to himself. His adulteries were, literally, past number and, since they could not be counted, that made them trivial and beneath notice. His visits to the Ottavio House, the girls whose names he never knew, whose faces he would never recognize, were no more than business transactions, like buying a suit, like putting petrol in his car. Maria was forgotten, he owed Ernesto nothing, the things he wrote in reviews were simply funny, bright, witty – not cruel, or career-destroying – he was a dutiful son and he was convinced that marrying Caterina would make her happy and enrich her life.

And if anyone had pointed out that he did not ask Caterina to marry him but simply ordered it, demanded it again and again until she agreed, he would have looked at them with puzzlement, since it was obvious that what he wanted was what she wanted too. So, when she said: 'I'll need something to wear if I'm to meet your mother,' he heard what he wanted to hear.

Mr Valdez could write a sentence as elegant as a swan but his sentences were like the swans served before a Renaissance prince: a swan stuffed with a goose, stuffed with a capon, stuffed with a chicken, stuffed with a poussin, stuffed with a partridge, stuffed with a lark, layer after layer, one inside the other, there to be discovered, looking like a swan. When he read the words of others, when he heard the words of others, he expected those layers to be in their words too. Sometimes they were not. There was nothing layered inside Caterina's words – not in the words she spoke. Her stories were her stories but when she said: 'Wouldn't you rather have sex?', when she said: 'I would like to love you, Chano, if that's all right,' when she wrote: 'I write,' that was all there was. The simple truth. No layers. It was absolutely incomprehensible.

After the champagne was finished and they had showered together and he had scrubbed away the dust of the graveyard from his skin and gently washed the smell of his sweat from hers, he took her down in the lift and they went shopping. There was a place along the Avenue which Maria had mentioned and he went there. It was a mistake.

The place was stately, like an ambassadorial anteroom. It smelled of lilies and there were two women – women just like Maria – standing by the back wall, graceful as herons, whispering about something. One of them held up a violent yellow dress and tittered. Caterina was uncomfortable and embarrassed, even a little ashamed, and her unease spread to him, like a spark across a gap. She stood there in her silly cloth shoes – why did she always wear those, when that first day she was wearing heels? – and that coat, that shapeless, brown conical coat, not brown like the browns Maria wore, not honey-yellow, not treacle-black but the colour of rot and mushrooms and compost, and she looked like an intruder. He put his hands on her shoulders and, gently, tugged the thing from her shoulders.

She did not resist. She was stunned into compliance, like a heretic being stripped for execution as the flames are kindling. 'This isn't the place for me,' she said.

'Nonsense. This is exactly the place.' He wasn't listening again. 'It's a bit of a leap, that's all.'

There was a woman approaching across a silent carpet, pallid, bloodless as a vampire, with an impenetrable, unreadable face under a mask of cosmetics, angular, plank-like, a woman with corners, and she was looking at Valdez, not at Caterina. She would not look at Caterina.

'It's too much of a leap. This isn't what I need.'

The woman said: 'How can I help you, sir?'

Even for Valdez, who was used to sipping on a drink in a quiet garden while he explained his requirements and made his selection, that was a brutal epiphany.

He said: 'Why are you talking to me?'

She made no answer. Caterina noticed, although Valdez did not, that the woman's painted eyebrow flickered the way a seismograph does in Paris when a pomegranate falls from its tree in the gardens of the Japanese Emperor.

'Why are you talking to me?' he said again. 'Why are you not talking to this lady?'

Caterina said: 'I think we should try somewhere else.'

But he wouldn't stop. 'Why are you talking to me? Why?'

'Let's just go, Chano.'

'This is a dress shop for women, isn't it? Do I look like a woman?'

Caterina took back her coat.

'Sir.'

'Do I look like the sort of person who wears dresses? Do I look like a pervert? Do you think I'm some *maricon*?'

'I'm going now, Chano.'

His fury spluttered out and embarrassment came in its place. He glared at the woman, refusing to look away from her even when the door clicked quietly into place behind him.

'Besa mi culo, puta.' Mr Valdez fled from the shop to where Caterina was sitting on a park bench across the street.

When he sat down beside her she said: 'I can't be the person who shops there.'

'You make me ashamed.'

'Ashamed? You're ashamed of me?'

'I'm ashamed of myself. Yelling like that. At a woman like that. At a woman.'

'You're embarrassed about behaving badly towards a social inferior.'

'Maybe.'

'No, you are. That's it. You are ashamed about her for the same reason that you were protective of me. She saw all the reasons why I can't be your wife and that made you furious.'

'But you will be my wife.' He took a deep breath. 'Please, be my wife.'

'You are the great L.H. Valdez. I am a girl wearing torn jeans. How can I be your wife?'

'Because we love one another.' Mr Valdez said that and he believed it.

'Yes, we love one another.' She believed it too. 'Do you think that means nobody will notice that I come from a little town in the mountains? All your fancy friends, all those editors and authors and university professors, they won't notice that I'm wearing ripped jeans? They won't care that I've never been to the opera and I'm not clever like them – oh, I'm clever, but not like them – and I never use a fork and knife when I eat a peach? Your mother? She won't notice?'

'My mother won't care. She will love you because I do.'

'You can order that, can you? Simply tell her to love me?'

'Yes. And the rest doesn't matter. I have had enough cleverness to last a lifetime. I have had enough of all the things you are not. Things will be hard for you – much harder than for me. I'm the man with the gorgeous young wife. They will be sick with envy.'

'They will be sick with laughter.'

'I don't care if they laugh at me.'

'But you care if they laugh at me. That woman in the shop, she only ignored me and you went crazy.'

'Nobody will laugh at you.'

'Chano, they will.'

'Yes,' he said, 'they will. Can you bear it?'

In the dress shop, the angular woman drew down the blinds and glided, smooth and silent, putting down one pointed toe, shifting her jagged hips, stepping forward, the thin lozenges of her soles, the vicious needles of her heels, one after another in a single line, marking the thick carpet with her passing as the jaguar marks the moss at the riverside, softly, so it springs back with no sign, walking silently into the shadows.

After a breath, Caterina said: 'I would bear anything for you.'

VALDEZ NEVER CALLED on his mother without an appointment. He could drop in on the Dean, he could meet the editor of *The Nation* for coffee or something a little stronger, and he could probably arrange an interview with Señor Colonel el Presidente if he wanted to, but that would take a phone call and Mrs Sophia Antonia de la Santísima Trinidad y Torre Blanco Valdez ranked a little above Señor Colonel el Presidente and a little below the Pope.

When they met, which was as often as duty demanded, it was never spontaneous and invariably as formal as the tango but without the subtlety of the *cabeceo*. No glances exchanged, no flick of the eyebrow, no opportunity for acceptance or rejection with no offence given, Mrs Valdez insisted on a note or, at the very least, a phone call as an acknowledgement that her time was valuable, that she was in demand, that she might have something else to do. Of course, she never said 'No'. She would die before she refused her son anything, but she liked to be asked.

It had been some time since their last meeting and that ended badly. Time passed, awkwardness deepened, and long afternoons with Caterina in his bed were somehow more attractive than another visit to Mama, another chinking of coffee spoons, another sad, envious report on long-forgotten cousins and their newest brats.

And yet there he was, in the lobby of her apartment block at 10 a.m., pressing the third silver button in a row of silver buttons, the silver button with the Valdez name engraved beside it in ugly Helvetica type. It made an unmusical note.

She said: 'Hello,' recognizably herself but with an electric, robotic aftertaste to the word.

'Hello, Mama. This is Chano.' Nobody else in the world would call her 'Mama'. Of course it was Chano.

She said nothing. She said nothing for so long that he was closing his lips to say: 'Mama?' when she said: 'Hello, darling,' and then: 'This is a lovely surprise.'

'Can I come up?'

There was another electric apostrophe. 'Yes, darling. Of course. Of course.' She pressed the buzzer.

When the lift reached the third floor, when the metallic concertina gate rolled back, when it bounced off its rubber bumpers, squeaked, wafted the scent of watch oil, when he crossed the corridor, when the door opened, it was her feet that terrified him most. It was the middle of the morning. He was shocked to find his mother still not dressed, still wearing a short white nightdress, her dressing gown hanging from her shoulders, her hair loose, but he was terrified by her feet.

It was one of those drowning moments when everything is clear, when nothing can be done. Mr Valdez could not remember another time when he had seen his mother's feet and they frightened him. Her toes were bent, angled, cruelly crabbed from years of elegant shoes. Her toenails had thickened and yellowed and clawed. Her ankles were round and lined and the flesh of her knees had sagged in flabby curtains. Mr Valdez realized that his mother was old.

She clutched at the collar of her dressing gown, pulling the two sides together, hiding herself. 'How lovely to see you,

darling,' she said. 'You should have told me you were bringing
a guest.'

Mr Valdez looked from his mother to Caterina, who stood at
his side, holding his hand, struck dumb by embarrassment. 'Mama,
there is someone I want you to meet. Mama, permit me to present
Caterina . . .'

'Chano, stop!' she said. And then, not unkindly, she told
Caterina: 'My dear, I simply cannot meet anybody in this condi-
tion. Pardon me. Please give me a few moments.'

Mama left, disappearing through a door which, Mr Valdez
realized, must lead to her bedroom.

Caterina sat down on a little round chair under the long shelf
where Mrs Valdez kept her collection of first editions. 'Oh, God,'
she said.

'Oh, God.'

'Chano, this is awful. That poor woman.'

'I'm sorry. I had no idea. It never occurred to me.'

'It never occurred to you that your poor mother might have
no clothes on?'

'I have never seen her like that. Never in my life.'

'Oh, you must have!'

'Never. Not once. Not even as a child. She was always spot-
less. My mother thinks taking her gloves off is reckless infor-
mality.'

Caterina glared at him until she couldn't bear to look at him
any more, then she looked at the floor and said: 'That poor
woman,' then up at the long shelf of books. 'She's obviously very
proud of you,' she said.

'She hasn't read them.'

'How can you know that?' Caterina got out of her chair and
went to take down *The Killings at the Bridge of San Miguel*.

'Don't touch,' he whispered.

'Why not?'

'Best just to leave them alone. She has them all arranged the way she likes them.'

Caterina had the book half off the shelf, tipped backwards by its top edge the way that people who love reading but do not love books do, the way that gets dust jackets torn and bruises the bottom of the spine, but she stopped and put it back obediently. She sat down in her chair again and looked out the window with her chin in her hand. She huffed a sigh. 'We should go.'

'We can't go.'

'This is a disaster. You bring me here to meet your mother, to tell her that you are about to marry some girl she's never heard of, somebody she knows nothing about, and then humiliate her like that.'

'It wasn't intentional. She will understand.'

'And I'm sitting here in these same ripped jeans.'

He said nothing.

'We should go.'

'Stay. It'll be all right.'

Caterina huffed another sigh and she was about to complain again when the door at the back of the room opened a crack and Mrs Valdez said: 'Chano, darling, could I see you for a moment?'

She sounded friendly, bright, at ease but when Mr Valdez knocked – 'Yes, darling, come in' – she spoke in a glacial hiss.

Mrs Valdez was sitting on an embroidered stool, properly dressed, shoes and stockings on, a sober pencil skirt in charcoal grey just below the knee, every hair in place, pearls at throat and ear, make-up so flawless that, if he had not seen her without it, he would not have known it was there.

She glared at him in the mirror of her dressing table. 'How could you?'

'I'm sorry, Mama.'

'How dare you?'

'Dare what? I came to visit my mother. You let me in.'

'Of course I let you in. I am your mother, not a monster. How could a mother turn her son away? And you humiliate me with that young woman. Who is she? And how dare you introduce me? I know about your women, Chano. That's all right, I'm not an innocent, I know what men are and anybody could see why you want her – it's disgustingly, brazenly obvious – but you should have enough respect not to rub my face in it. I do not wish to be introduced to your whores, Chano. Please take her out of my house.'

'You have to meet her.'

'No, Chano, I do not. I am your mother and the mistress in my own home.'

'We are going to be married.'

She looked at him for a long moment, saying nothing. Light bounced from the window into the hinged, three-sided mirror with his mother reflected and half reflected and repeated in it, with the images of the elegant old furniture he remembered from childhood, things from the Admiral's house, things he had not seen since his mother moved to the flat.

Mrs Valdez plucked a tissue from a leather-covered box on the dressing table and another and another, a little stream of cockatoo crests. She folded them into a blunt edge and dabbed gently at her eyes, leaving blackened moth-marks on the paper.

'Is she pregnant?' All in the same piercing hiss.

'No, Mama. But she will be. I promise.'

'What was her name again?'

'Caterina.'

'Good name. Sensible. Religious name. You know she only wants you for your money.'

'She doesn't even want to marry me. She's terrified. She wants to go on as we are. I bullied her into it.'

'Oh, that's the oldest trick in the book! Who are her people?'

'She has no people.'

'I see. She dresses like a beggar.'

'That's why I brought her. It's why we came. There are so many things she needs to learn and you can teach her. You can show her how to dress. Start with that.'

'But she is very young.'

'Mama, it is indelicate to mention a lady's age but I believe you are twenty years older than me.'

'Things have changed a lot since those days.'

'Mama, do you want me to marry a woman my own age or a woman who can give you grandchildren?'

Mrs Valdez stood up, smoothed the wrinkles out of her skirt and offered her cheek to be kissed. 'I am very happy, darling.' They stood there, awkwardly together, saying nothing until she was forced to hint, clear her throat and nod towards the door.

He had only just put his hand on the doorknob when she said: 'I assume you are fucking her.'

Mr Valdez looked at the carpet.

'That will have to stop. Just for now. Just until the wedding.'

'Yes, Mama.' He opened the door.

THE DARK ROOMS under the Palace of Justice were empty again and more or less clean. Policemen took the same fire hoses that they were sometimes forced to train on difficult prisoners and used them to scour down the walls and the hard concrete floors until the blood came off and the smell of terrified incontinence was washed away. The round iron grilles sunk in every floor gurgled with clean water and the grille in Cell 7 trapped a glittering golden tooth.

Upstairs in his office at the very back of the Detectives' Hall Commandante Camillo was on his second cigar of the day and his fifth coffee, and it was beginning to affect his digestion. All through the bomb investigation there had been calls from the capital sometimes three a day, then one a day, then a couple of times a week and now, nothing. There was no reason to be alarmed. Nobody had called to ask why there was no progress on the bombing. Commandante Camillo found that the most disturbing thing of all. There were so many reasons why they might not call for answers. Maybe they already knew. Maybe it was just a little bomb in a little town far away up the Merino. Commandante Camillo saw all the reasons and his mind danced in the gaps between them. Maybe it wasn't important. Maybe they just didn't care, and that was very, very worrying.

Commandante Camillo wanted to find the answer – not that

he cared about the answer. He just wanted to prove that it could be found and that he could find it.

The boy Miralles was mad, the Commandante was sure about that, but not so mad that he couldn't make a bomb and plaster himself all over Plaza Universidad. And he got the bomb from somewhere. Somebody gave him the bomb; either handed the whole thing over and told him which switch to press or gave him the parts and taught him how to screw them together. But there was nothing to show either way. After all the long hours of questioning, nothing. One of the boy's cousins had admitted that he didn't like girls – another one, they were everywhere now – and his Aunt Laura turned in Uncle Arturo for screwing his tax return, but that was it. Five minutes in the cell with their arms up their backs and the whole family was queuing to confess, but that was the best they could come up with. Nobody even mentioned the oppression of the peasants. Nobody mentioned a bomb. Nothing. Nothing to show whether Miralles was a single, independent lunatic with enough cash to fund a spectacular suicide, or part of something bigger, something more interesting, something that would interest even the capital, make them sit up and take notice, make them see the sort of person they were dealing with, someone to be respected, someone to be regarded, not a man to be dismissed and forgotten halfway up the Merino.

On Camillo's desk, beside his brimming ashtray, there was a brown cardboard box, and inside that the diary of Oscar Miralles. Camillo put down his cigar and opened the box. The same book, the same tight, mad scrawl. There wasn't a page of it that he hadn't read a dozen times, straining over the jagged, angry letters until they scratched at his eyes. It was horrible stuff – like being cornered on the street by some stinking madman, but this one you couldn't push aside, this one you couldn't slap down into the gutter. This one sat you down in the padded cell, buttoned up your straitjacket and made you share his nightmare all the way to the last page.

The Commandante tore a sheet of paper from his pad, squeezed it into a tight ball and flung it at the glass in his door. The thud of it made the detectives look up from their desks and one of them, the one whose face he had wiped so tenderly on the day of the bombing, pushed back his chair and came forward.

Camillo waved him in to the room: 'Come on, come on. You don't have to knock – I called you in here.'

The man closed the door and stood with his hands folded in front of himself, as if he had been on parade.

'Oh, for Christ's sake sit down.'

The man obeyed. He said nothing. That was expected of him.

Camillo dropped the diary on the desk in front of him. 'Remember that?'

'I did exactly as you said, boss.'

'And what did you get?'

'Nothing.'

'Why not?'

'I did what you said, boss. I did exactly what you said.'

'Who did you speak to?'

'I spoke to everybody in that book.'

'Everybody?'

'Everybody except the ones you told me to stay away from. Those three.'

'And you got nothing.'

'Boss, they're a bunch of university kids. They dress like revolutionaries and they talk like revolutionaries but their daddies are all accountants. There's nobody mentioned in that diary who gives a stuff about the peasants except . . .'

'Except those three.'

'Well, I don't know that, boss. You wouldn't let me ask them.'

Commandante Camillo took a long drag on his cigar and blew the smoke out towards the roof. He said: 'I like the old man for this. I really, really like him. He makes my palms itchy. He goes way back. He liked the old Colonel – never made any secret of it. At one time liking the old Colonel was the smart thing to do, but it's not smart now. We never got anything on him or he'd have been hanging off a meat hook, but I like him for this. And Valdez goes way back too. He's got bad blood. I knew his father. He looks like he's kept his nose clean but why does he turn up in the diary if he's not connected? And the girl. She's perfect for it.'

'Boss,' the policeman hesitated before he dared to offer a theory of his own, 'you know what I think?' Camillo waved his cigar, signalling permission to speak. 'I think there's nothing to it. Cochrane is in the book because he was Bomb Boy's teacher, the girl's in the book because she was in the same class and Bomb Boy fancied her and Valdez is in the book because he muscled in. That's all. It's a love triangle. The kid blew himself up to impress a girl. He was showing off.'

After what Father Gonzalez had told him, Camillo knew that might be true but he chose not to acknowledge it. 'You mean: "You may have gone off with the international best-selling author while I was trying to get my hands in your knickers but, look at me, darling, I can magically transform myself into soup," that kinda thing?'

The policeman shrugged. 'It's a theory,' he said. 'It makes as much sense as anything else. And he wasn't planning on blowing himself up. Maybe he was trying to kill her or Valdez.'

'Those three, where were they when the bomb went off?'

'Boss, I don't know. You told me not to ask.'

Camillo said nothing.

'Do you want me to ask, boss? I can go and find them right now.'

'No. Forget it. I'll do it. I need to do it.'

'You getting heat from upstairs?'

'Son, there's nobody anywhere in this building can give me heat.' He paused to draw on his cigar again. He paused a little longer to let that sound important.

'Higher up than that?'

'I've got nothing to say.'

Do you see what a beautiful lie that was? Do you see how a frightened man who feared that he was unimportant, a man who feared he was being ignored, by saying nothing at all, just by rolling his tongue around his cigar for a few moments, made himself important?

'I've got nothing to say to you but I have a few words to say to Mr L.H. Valdez and I know exactly where to find him.'

NATURALLY, WHEN MAMA issued her ridiculous order, Mr Valdez had no intention of obeying. He agreed at once, of course, but only to make her shut up, only to make the moment pass. To hear such a word in his mother's mouth! Mothers never forget that they have seen their sons naked, suckled them, wiped their shitty arses clean. Mothers refuse to relinquish that degree of intimacy. They think it gives them licence to say anything, but Mr Valdez, like all sons and in spite of the irrefutable evidence of his own existence, preferred not to acknowledge that his mother had ever had sex and the idea that she had taken pleasure in it, even once and no matter how long ago, was simply too much to contemplate. He banished the idea of eagerness from his mind. Mrs Sophia Antonia de la Santísima Trinidad y Torre Blanco Valdez was not Maria Marrom. Mrs Sophia Antonia de la Santísima Trinidad y Torre Blanco Valdez could not possibly have behaved as Caterina had behaved only a few hours earlier. Mrs Sophia Antonia de la Santísima Trinidad y Torre Blanco Valdez was not capable of that kind of famished need. That was what he chose to believe and, in exchange, he expected her to believe the same of him, so when she said: 'I assume you are fucking her,' Mr Valdez looked at the carpet and agreed only because it would make that nightmarish moment of confrontation end.

And yet afterwards, after he had gone through that door, after he had begun again and introduced Caterina to his mother and his mother to Caterina, in that order, respectful of their status, pretending that they had not already met a few moments earlier when his mother had been as good as naked, it had come back to him. Not when Mama extended her hand and smiled with a smile like a bacon slicer, not when she turned a cheek as cold as the steppe and waited . . . to be kissed, not when she said: 'My dear, I'm thrilled,' as she would have done if the cleaning woman had just tipped over an entire cabinet of her best china, not amidst the endless sharp chinking of coffee spoons, not when she pleaded, as a sergeant-major would plead: 'Darling, say you will,' for the chance to take Caterina shopping, demolish her and rebuild her in kitten heels, not even when she said: 'I'm so glad you came. It's been a joy to meet you. I think this is the happiest day of my life,' and the door closed and the lock snapped shut with a noise like a coup de grâce, no, even then he had no intention of obeying.

And when Caterina asked: 'Did I pass?' and he kissed her as a reward, when they spent the remains of the day together, wandering the art gallery, drinking coffee, walking under the trees that taunt the prison, and all through dinner and then when he took her home, not to her flat but to his, where now she had a toothbrush of her own, taken from a plastic packet of three in the bathroom cabinet and left out, brazenly, beside his, above the sink in the gorgeous limestone bathroom, Mr Valdez had every intention of defying his mother.

But then nothing happened. He went for a shower and she didn't come with him and nothing happened. He lay down between crisp sheets of Egyptian cotton and nothing happened. Caterina walked through the bedroom, smiling, scattering clothing behind her and nothing happened. He lay listening to the water running and he thought hard about where it was running but nothing happened and she came back, wrapped in a thick, white towel, her skin dewed and sparkling and nothing happened. She stood at the side of the bed and let the towel drop away and nothing happened. She threw back the sheet and nothing happened, lifted one knee, moved her leg, tipped forward, shifted her weight, moved from the floor to the mattress where she lay beside him, folded her skin against his, covered him with her leg, brushed him with her hair, kissed his shoulder, dragged fingertips down his chest and nothing happened. Nothing.

She kept kissing him. She nuzzled him. She made a noise in her throat.

He said: 'It's been a long day.'

'It ended better than I would ever have imagined,' and she kissed him again, slowly, right under his ear.

He didn't move. 'You must be exhausted.'

She was still kissing him. She stopped. 'Yes,' she said. 'It has been a long day. I'm very tired.'

'Let's wait until tomorrow. I don't mind.'

She rolled away from him. He felt the curve of her back against his as she curled into a ball on the other side of the bed and he sighed. Mr Valdez measured the passage of time in her breaths. He reached backwards, finding her skin with his fingers, but she inched away from him. It was just a tiny movement but he read disgust in it.

'I'm really tired,' she said, but he knew she was only being kind, she was excusing his failure, and naturally he blamed his mother; his mother who was old and dry, his mother whose knees sagged, his mother with her crabbed, bent toes, with her cold bed, empty these forty years, his mother, with her thin, chicken skin, his mother who had choked down her bitter snobbery only because it was the price of a grandchild, his mother who had shrivelled him with her stupid curse.

Before long, Caterina went to sleep. He recognized the softness of her breath and that whistle in her nose. Mr Valdez did not go to sleep. The night weighed heavily on his eyes. He was too ashamed to sleep and his shame translated itself into anger.

When Mr Valdez got up, Caterina never even stirred. When he sat down at his desk, naked, and lit the lamp with its green shade and picked up his pen and opened his notebook where there were still only those same dozen words, neither of them heard, at that very moment, far away in the distant capital, a plane taking off loaded with mail.

He wanted to write. He looked down at the page. 'The scrawny yellow cat crossed the road and crept into the whorehouse.' That was all there was. He sat with his pen at the very end of the line until the ink began to pool out of it and soak its way down through three sheets of paper.

Two miles up in the sky, hundreds of miles away, lights twinkled, drawing closer.

Mr Valdez tore pages from the front of his notebook and wrote again: 'The scrawny yellow cat crossed the road and crept into the whorehouse,' and then he astonished himself by adding: 'where it hoped the beautiful Angela would scratch his belly'.

Mr Valdez stared at the page in amazement. After weeks of nothing, here were ten new words. The words were coming back. There was a beautiful girl lying naked and untouched in his bed and yet he smiled.

Looking down from his cockpit in the dark and lonely sky, the pilot looked at the Merino glittering in the moonlight and nudged the nose of his aircraft down towards a distant runway he could not see. Dials glowed. Needles twitched. The electric voices of people he would never meet gabbled in his ears. Far behind him the sleeping dogs in little mining towns heard the murmur of his engines and whined in their sleep. Babies, who had heard him pass every night of their lives, heard him pass again and did not notice. Down in the jungle, round-eyed monkeys looked up at the roaring lights in the sky and clung more closely to their mothers. The plane flew on and on, until the jungle thinned and turned into fields, on again until the fields sprouted houses that grew as thick as grass and taller than trees and then, with a final low circle over the *barriada* of Santa Marta, it landed at the city airport in the hour before dawn.

The plane taxied close to a long line of low, white buildings, blazing with lights, and trucks with 'Servicio Postal' painted along the sides came out to greet it. By the time they arrived, the pilot had operated the machinery that opens the hold and men in white overalls started unloading sacks of mail. When the first birds were starting to sing, when Father Gonzalez was standing at his altar, afraid again and cold, as Madame Ottavio closed her front door and gathered up the empty bottles from her garden, sacks of mail started arriving at the central sorting office. One of them contained a thick white envelope addressed to Mr Valdez and stamped with the letterhead of *The Salon*.

Caterina was still asleep.

THREE HOURS LATER, when Mr Valdez went into the kitchen to make coffee, Caterina woke up. She was awake when he came into the bedroom and took his blue-black cotton dressing gown from the hook behind the bathroom door but she kept her eyes closed and lay still, sprawled across the bed with her hair tumbled around her face like a cloud and an annoying village-idiot trail of spittle tickling its way from the corner of her mouth. She could not decide if it would be more suggestive of sleep to let it roll its way into the crumpled pillow or to snap her jaws and lick her chops like a labrador. She chose to do nothing.

Mr Valdez did not notice. He was not watching her. He wanted only to get across the room, cover himself and go without waking her. There was more to it than a new-found modesty imposed by his mother. There was more to it than the echo of his failure from the night before. Mr Valdez planned to serve her coffee and eggs and rolls from the stock he kept in the freezer and Mr Valdez was an aesthete with a fear of the ridiculous. He knew he could not arrive, naked, carrying a tray.

He went back to the kitchen. He clattered about. His espresso machine hissed and bubbled and, after a decent interval, she took that as a cue to rise.

Caterina had her own toothbrush now, but she had no dressing gown. She came into the kitchen with her hair scraped back off

her face, wearing a nearly-white T-shirt and yesterday's underwear. She looked like a goddess and she smiled at him and kissed
him but there was something missing, a chilly gap that had not
been there the night before, like the space where a tooth used to
be, and teeth do not grow back.

'This is nice,' she said. 'Thank you.'

'I was going to bring it to you. Sleep well?'

'Not really. I missed you.'

He looked at her disbelievingly over his coffee cup.

'I did. Really. I'm like an old woman. I'm getting used to you.'

'I had hoped to keep the magic alive for just a little longer.
Say until we get married.'

'You don't understand,' she said and she was right. Mr Valdez
had no idea of the way she loved him then. He told himself that
he loved her, he knew he loved her because she had made the warm
blood flow again into that amputated stump where once, long ago,
he had been connected to the world, but he loved her with a reason-
able love, because she was young and beautiful, because she gave
him sex, because she held out to him the prospect of children,
sons, companionship in old age, the possibility that he might not
die alone in this flat and lie undiscovered until neighbours whom
he did not know complained of the smell on the landing.

Like the rest of us Mr Valdez was unable to conceive of a
world where he might not exist, where that lamp would go on
burning, where those trees would go on growing, where rivers
would flow, cities grow up and turn to dust again, where stars
would roll endlessly across the empty sky and all without him.
But it was the measure of his love that there was a part of his
mind where it was possible to imagine a world without Caterina
in it. Even without her, he would survive. His life would be less
lovely, it might not be sweetened with children to brighten his
old age, but life would go on. He knew it.

But for Caterina it was very different. She was an aficionada, obsessed with the stories he had written, an orphan wandering the world and searching for a place to shelter. Caterina was crippled too, but not like Valdez. He gloried in his cold, dead scar, but Caterina had spent years looking for the missing part of herself, the part that died clutching at a handful of mud in a mountain field, and she counted herself as blessed that he had noticed her. He had no friends and any one of the small circle which gathered round Valdez, his university colleagues, Maria Marrom, even his own mother would, if they were honest, have to admit that Caterina was worth ten of him but she would not have believed it. She wanted to give the rest of her life to making him happy because she believed that would make her happy. She wanted his children because it would be an honour to bear his children and she wanted to sleep in his bed because she could not sleep without him. It was a mad love. She was besotted with him.

And yet, there at the table he could say something stupid and cynical like that, something about how the magic had gone. It was astonishing. More astonishing yet, she bore it.

'Anyway,' she said. 'You were up very early. What have you been doing?'

'I wrote.' He sounded proud of himself and he said it with a smile of accomplishment.

'You wrote? Oh God, that's fabulous.' She was so sincere, so enthusiastic, that she almost sounded mocking. 'I haven't written anything for ages. Not for days. What did you write? Tell me. I want to know all about it.'

'It's not done yet. I don't like to – not before it's ready. I'm very superstitious that way.'

'Please.'

'Maybe. Maybe later.' As if he had been responding to some outlandish request from a fractious child.

'Well, what did you write?'

'Lots.'

'Lots?'

'Lots and lots. It was like a dam bursting. It just came pouring out.'

'Oh God, I love that. When it happens to me.' She was suddenly modest, as if what she wrote and how she wrote it was not fit to be mentioned in his company. 'I love that,' she whispered.

'I feel like I've turned a corner. You know?'

'Yes, when it takes on a life of its own.'

'Yes,' he said, 'like taking dictation.' Oh, what a storyteller he was. All that excitement for less than a dozen words. In bald percentage terms, of course, his output of the night before had been prodigious, but that was all it was: less than a dozen words. The other half of that sentence came spurting from the end of his pen and the beautiful Angela suddenly appeared on the page and then nothing. Nothing again. Nothing in the bedroom and nothing at the desk. It was as if somebody had opened the door of a prison and then slammed it again. It was like the profound silence that rushes back after an echo, like the darkness that comes after a lightning flash, something even less than there was before.

Mr Valdez had sat there for hours fighting that full stop, trying to find a way past its blockade, until, sick with fright and close to tears, he decided to make breakfast and now breakfast was over and another day loomed and that blank page would scream at him again.

'Are you going to the university today?' he asked.

'Yes. Dr Cochrane on transcendental numbers.'

'Too good to miss.'

'A mathematical roller-coaster ride. Are you going?'

'Later. I should have a shave.'

'And I need to get some fresh clothes. Maybe I should keep

some here.' She left a big question mark hanging on the end of that sentence.

He said: 'Do you want a lift?'

'No. It's OK. I'd like to walk.' She carried her coffee cup to the sink and rinsed it, standing there, flat-footed, her underwear sagging unbecomingly behind her, a spot with a greenish white head boiling up on her shoulder and still that glow of beauty fizzing and sparkling all around her, the way that rainbows hang over waterfalls. 'Better hurry,' she said.

'Yes. I'll come down with you.' He left his cup on the table and followed her to the bedroom where he pulled on a sweater and a pair of cotton trousers, enough to be decent when he went with her to the street.

The lift took a long time to come and there seemed to be nothing to say as they waited. Standing there, he felt her finger against the palm of his hand and he gripped it instinctively, as a baby does, but only for a moment and then he dropped it again. It was as if, despite everything, despite even their decision to marry, he remained afraid that they might be seen together.

'We should have taken the stairs,' she said.

'But, if we go now, the lift will arrive.' Mr Valdez said that the way that everybody says it, as if all the moments they had wasted from life's pitiably small store of moments, tiny shavings of time which they could have spent dancing or kissing or eating peaches or reading a book or writing a book, had actually been well used in waiting for a lift but would be rendered meaningless, would be needlessly squandered and wasted, if they stopped waiting and did something else instead.

She looked up at him. He glanced down and caught her doing it and looked away again, watching the doors doing nothing. The lift arrived. They got in it and closed the doors. Downstairs the postman had already come. He had already pushed open the big

bronze doors into the lobby, taken a bundle of letters from his
sack and, standing in front of the wall of named and numbered
metal boxes, delivered each one as his oath demanded. The large
white envelope which had flown from the capital, the one stamped
with the letterhead of *The Salon* and the printed plea 'DO NOT
BEND', he folded double and jammed into the box marked 'L.H.
Valdez', and by the time the lift arrived at the lobby, the doors
to Cristobal Avenue were closing softly behind him.

Mr Valdez said: 'I have been thinking.'

'Yes.'

'I didn't get you a ring. You should have a ring.'

For Caterina the thought of it was almost as wonderful as the
thing itself, and her hand flew to her mouth.

'Perhaps, after classes, we could go and choose something.'

She only said: 'Oh Chano!' and then, because the lobby was
empty and they were alone, he kissed her.

GETTING A LETTER, a real letter, not an advertisement in disguise or a bill or a bank statement, is one of the best and nicest things that can happen to anybody. When Mr Valdez was only a little boy, a faraway uncle sent him a letter, and in the envelope there was a red cardboard box, printed with the image of a cat, and inside the box there was a piece of soap shaped like a cat and the soap grew fur when it was used. It was wonderful and miraculous for a few days and then it ceased to look like a cat and became instead merely strange, like something festering, something forgotten at the bottom of the fruit bowl.

And then, when he was much older, there were letters from publishers – rejections first of all, but even they had a certain bitter tang, like a good cocktail, and he learned to savour it. Rejections were part of the learning process, in the tango hall, in the bedroom and in literature. He harboured no grudges.

But before long, letters started to arrive from magazine editors who agreed to publish his stories and then from publishers who begged to publish them, letters from critics, letters from fans. He enjoyed them all but the ones he liked best were the ones that came from people who had once turned him down. He lay in his bed at night, holding them up to the lamp, sliding one sheet of paper over the other so the edges lined up, so the letterheads and the typed addresses matched exactly, so they were precisely the same apart from where one said 'No' and the other said 'Please'. He remembered the deliciousness of it, long after he learned to take it for granted. There was no gambler's thrill any more for L.H. Valdez, no excitement and anticipation over the unknown outcome. He wrote a story, he sent a story, the story was published. That was how it was or, at any rate, that was how it had been. That was how it had been when he was still writing stories. That was how it was.

All the same, when Mr Valdez went to the wall of named and numbered metal boxes where he and his neighbours received their mail and he found that huge white envelope with those two words '*The Salon*' printed along the top left edge in ink so thick that it stood out under his thumb, he felt a thrill of delight and a little fatherly pride.

He knew what was in the envelope: a modest little cheque, a kindly effusive letter from the editor Correa and a couple of copies of the magazine with Caterina's story tucked in somewhere near the back, between a dull interview with a first-time novelist and the start of the paperback reviews. And it made him happy that he was able to do that for her, that he had that much influence. It made him happy because he knew she would be happy. It made him happy because he remembered how proud and delighted he had been the day he first saw his work in print and now he had made that happen for her, he had opened a door for her, which was nice because the next time it would be easier. Next time she could say: 'And I have been published in *The Salon*,' and she would be taken seriously. Mr Valdez was glad that he had given her career a little push. He had set her on the road to being a writer although, obviously, she would have to set all that aside for motherhood, but only for a few years, perhaps ten, maybe fifteen depending on when the babies came and how many they were, and he was delighted to do it. Best of all, he was glad that she had not done it alone and part of her success, whatever it was, would always be his. She would be in his debt. She would be grateful. She would have to be grateful.

Mr Valdez was so excited when he saw the letter that he almost tore it open right there in the lobby. But he didn't. He gathered it up with his other letters, with that day's copy of *The Nation* and with all the other brown rubbish that lay in the brass box, and he rode up in the lift, planning how he would take his ironing board from the kitchen cupboard and smooth out the cruel folds in the magazine, make it new again before he presented it to her.

And, inside his flat, that was exactly what he did. He went into his kitchen and, standing over the table, he sliced the envelope open with a cheese knife – because it was the first that came to hand – and he pulled out those two copies of *The Salon*.

Mr Valdez was not a nice man. He was not *simpático*. There was nobody in the whole of the city who would have gone to the wall for him. But his worst enemy – and there were several who would gladly have claimed that title – would surely have felt for him in that moment.

The back page of the magazine was ordinary enough, just a full-page colour ad for American Express, but when he turned it over in his hand, Mr Valdez could make no sense of it. He stood staring at the front page, not understanding it, unable to comprehend what he was seeing. The words were there, he could see them, they were going into his eyes, but it was as if they were jammed there without penetrating his brain. There, under the usual headline, exactly as Juan Ignacio Correa had imagined, was the single word 'VALDEZ!' embellished with an extravagant exclamation mark which Miss Cantaluppi had confected at the last moment.

It made no sense. He could not understand. And then he understood. He flicked through page after page of glossy advertise-

ments, searching for the index, as his panic rose, pretending to
himself that this could not possibly be true. But it was true. It
was written all over Correa's gushing editorial, announcing to
the world the birth of a new short story by L.H. Valdez. And
there was more, over twenty pages of critique and assessment,
expert opinion from somebody he had never heard of, explaining
'his' story and what it meant and its themes, its 'mythic tropes,
memes and dream symbols', and setting out exactly where it fitted
in the canon of L.H. Valdez stories, from his first, green efforts
to this mature, accomplished masterpiece, the crowning achievement of a master storyteller.

Mr Valdez dropped the magazines on the table with an enraged
roar and tore the big white envelope open, hunting for something else, some explanation for this lunacy. He found it. A letter
from Correa – oh how Marta Alicia Cantaluppi had thrilled to
type it, carrying the final draft to the editor's desk before her like
a monstrance in the saint's day procession – and he had addressed
it in his own hand.

It said: 'My dear Valdez, I can never thank you enough for
choosing *The Salon* to publish your latest story.'

'But I didn't, you fool. I didn't!'

'The whole world of literature has been holding its breath and
waiting for a word from you, waiting and wondering as the weeks
turned to months and the months to years . . .'

'Oh, for Christ's sake!'

'. . . with no word from our foremost writer and, now, the
waiting has ended in this triumph. With "The Pedlar Miguel
Ángel" you have truly opened a new "chapter" . . .'

'Jesus!'

'. . . in the history of the national literature and . . .'

There was another page and a half of that unctuous drivel until
it ended with:

'You asked to be recompensed for your work at our usual rates. I need hardly explain that such a thing is simply unthinkable. There can be no usual reward for such exceptional writing and no reward, however exceptional, can ever be adequate. Therefore, I trust you will accept the enclosed cheque, not as payment for something which it is beyond my power to purchase but in recognition of an art which belongs already to the whole world.'

Correa's huge signature took up the whole of the bottom half of the page in a swirl of violet ink, and stapled to the back there was a stiff, yellow cashier's cheque which offered to pay to the account of Mr L.H. Valdez the sum of 250,000 coronas.

Mr Valdez tugged it free and held it up to the window. 'Well,' he said. 'That should soften the blow.'

PLAZA UNIVERSIDAD HAD recovered like any other burns victim. Everything was back in place, everything was much as before and there was nothing to show for what the madman Miralles had done except for the newness of it. New railings had been set in amongst the old. Cranes came in the night and brought new concrete planters to replace the ones with chunks blown out of them. Municipal gardeners brought new plants in thin wooden crates, and in a few days they grew back just as they had been, but there was an uncomfortable freshness about the place. New paving slabs marked the spot where Miralles had stood, there were new steps in the staircase leading up to the university gates and there were other places where the stone and the concrete had been washed and scoured so it stood out perfect and pale, like tight, pink new skin emerging from under a scab. People looked away politely without mentioning it, as they would from any disfigurement, and pretended there was nothing to notice, but when they came down the steps into the square they avoided the new slabs and walked on the old, dusty ones instead, as if what was not there on the bright, white concrete might touch them somehow, might stick to their shoes and taint them.

Caterina was just like all the rest, and when Mr Valdez arrived in the square he saw her coming down the steps, hugging the left-hand side, away from the leper-white treads on the right.

For the first time since he met her downstairs in the Phoenix she was dressed as a girl. No more torn jeans, nor workman's jacket. She wore a skirt – still of denim but a skirt all the same – and a white blouse with her hair tied back in a severe and formal pony tail and, Mr Valdez noticed, she had dumped the stupid playground sneakers and she wore instead a pair of simple black pumps. It was a gift to him, a putting away of childish things. She had dressed nicely for him so they could go together and choose a ring, the way she would have covered her head in her little mountain church, because it was appropriate, because it was the thing to do.

When she saw him across the flower beds she gave a little skip and almost broke into a run, but she held back, smiled secretly at him because she knew he had seen through her new persona, said 'goodbye' to the girl beside her and came to him quickly through the crowd.

'Hello,' she said. 'This is nice,' and she stood in front of him, holding her face up to be kissed.

He failed to kiss her. He had kissed her often, of course, but for enjoyment, to savour the taste of her and not like this, in a show of gentle, easy affection, not in public with people looking on.

'Hello.' He offered his arm, and if she was disappointed she did not show it and they walked out of the square together, side by side.

'Surprised?' he asked.

'Chano, everything is a surprise these days.'

'You look nice.'

'Surprised?'

'No.'

'Yes, you are.'

'I always thought you looked nice.'

'Yes, but not with clothes on.'

'Even with clothes on. Especially with clothes on.'

Long weeks before, on that first day in the Phoenix, she gave him that tiny piece of paper with two tiny words written on it: 'I write.' His life story. Her death sentence. Now it was in his wallet, still there, still treasured, not forgotten but not read, like the books on his mother's shelf, valuable for what they represented but not for what they were. He remembered how it had burned and glowed on the day he got it and now there was another bit of paper that threatened to ignite in his suit pocket: that cheque from Correa, smouldering there, fizzing like a running fuse and ready to explode.

'Aren't you going to ask me about my day?' she said.

'I'm sorry. I'm not used to this new mode of domestic conversation.' He heaved a deep breath and tried to sound bright and interested. 'So tell me,' he said. 'How was your day?'

'It was lovely, thank you. Wonderful, actually. I worked very hard at pretending to listen to Dr Cochrane's lecture but I spent most of the day thinking about you and that was very nice and I wasted a little more time thinking about, oh, silly things like diamonds and that was quite nice too. And I had a coffee with Erica.'

'Who's Erica?'

She looked at him in surprise. 'We really don't know anything about each other, do we?'

'Yes, we do.'

'No, we don't. I feel like I know you because I've read your books. Every one of them, over and over. Dr Cochrane calls me an aficionada.'

'Yes, I know.'

'But it's worse than that, Chano, I'm a fan. You've been talking to me since I was a child – in your books – and, God help me, I've talked back to you. You don't know what that's like. You don't know what it means.' She laid her hand on his chest, on the thin, silver-grey suit fabric over his beating heart. 'This wonderful man, who wrote such words, who knew so much about life and about people and the world, this man who told me such wonderful stories and, suddenly,' but her voice dropped to a whisper and a truck rumbled past and she turned her face down to the pavement.

'And suddenly?' he asked. 'Suddenly what? I couldn't hear you.'

'Forget it. It's OK.'

'No. Please. Tell me.'

She looked him, drilling into him with her gaze, and said: 'Suddenly, after all this, suddenly I feel him, this wonderful man, suddenly I feel him moving inside me.'

The shock of it must have shown in his face.

'You can't imagine what that means, Chano. You're not a fan. I love you insanely, but we barely know each other.'

'It doesn't matter,' he said. 'It's enough. We can do this.'

'Do we dare?'

'I can dare anything. If you're brave enough, I am brave enough.'

'Oh, I am brave,' she said, which was true. Valdez was a liar and a coward but she was brave. 'I am brave and I will dare anything and then there will be time enough for you to learn that Erica is the girl I share a flat with.'

'I knew that,' he said, which was another lie.

'Of course you did. Of course.'

'So you had coffee with . . . ?'

'With Erica! Erica! Erica!'

'I knew that.'

'Yes. I listened to Dr Cochrane talking about transcendental numbers, I thought lovely, filthy thoughts about you and I had coffee with Erica. That was my day.'

'And what did you talk about?'

'Oh, this and that. A little of this and a bit more of that.'

'Did you, for example, mention the fact that you and I are about to be married?'

Caterina smiled a secretive smile and she said: 'I wanted to. It was like an itch I couldn't scratch, but I decided not to. I still can't believe it. I can hardly believe you want me.'

'Oh, I want you.'

'Yes, but that way – enough to marry me.'

'But did you tell her?'

'No. I said that, didn't I? Would you mind if I had? Chano, you sound like some horrible man trying to lure little girls into his car and making sure that nobody knows where they are. Why shouldn't I tell? Is it a secret?'

'I just asked.'

'Who have you told?'

'Nobody. My mother. Obviously.'

'And nobody else?'

'No.'

'Nobody at the university?'

'No.'

'Not Dr Cochrane?'

'No.'

'What about those other teachers I used to see you with?'

'No. Not them either.'

'You're not exactly enthusiastic, are you?'

'I'm not like you. I have no Erica.'

That made her a little afraid. It made her wonder if that was what their married life would be like: not parties and drinks and a houseful of eager students sitting at his feet, not a kitchen table packed with poets and authors, arguing all night, drinking wine, passing the coffee pot round, but something much less, both of them locked away together, alone in that flat until the sex ran out. She pretended not to have thought of it and, instead, she said: 'Well, I haven't told anybody either. It's so astounding that I can't quite believe it myself, so how could anybody else believe it? I'm going to wait until I've got that ring on my finger. It'll be all right to speak of it then, won't it?'

'Of course,' he said.

'Chano, do you love me?'

He said it again: 'Of course,' and then, because he realized how disappointing that sounded, because he remembered her stupid shoes and the way her hair fell across the pillow, because of the smell of her in the night, because she could still feel joy, because she would never be able to dance the tango, because of the day that the bomb went off and how he had feared for her, because it all came back to him so sharp and bitter-sweet and in spite of a tiny pang of adulterous guilt when he thought of his beautiful car, he said: 'I love you more than I have ever loved anybody or anything.'

THEY HAD WALKED together almost all the way back to the river, towards Paseo Santa Maria where, down the hill to the left, all the smartest jewellers of the city had congregated together for generations. There is somewhere like it in every city in the world, some little quarter where the very best shops of one kind or another are found and the shops which are not found there are, obviously, not of the best. It is a badge of pride to buy one's jewellery from the arcades of the Paseo Santa Maria. For the jewellers it is a badge of pride to occupy premises there and a matter of honour to pay the inflated rents which, after all, are reflected in the prices that customers of quality are honoured to pay. Commerce and snobbery meet in a happy symbiosis.

But down the hill and a little to the right, away from the jewellers, there was a quiet square where lovely old houses, a little down at heel, stood around a well kept garden with iron railings surrounding shaded flower beds and neat gravel paths. Mr Valdez knew that garden well. It was the garden outside the Ottavio House and, God alone knows why, he decided that the garden outside the Ottavio House was the place to take Caterina.

After he said: 'I love you more than I have ever loved anybody or anything,' which was true, at least in part, he said: 'There's something I need to tell you. We should talk.'

'There's something I need to tell you.' What could it possibly be? What could he possibly need to say after saying: 'I love you more than I have ever loved anybody or anything'?

'We need to talk.' And that signalled urgency, panic, emergency, yet he held off.

'Let's go down here,' he said and he led her towards the back gate of the garden where there would be quiet and seclusion and a place to sit and, although she could see it, with its railings and its flowers, it seemed a long way off.

'There? The gardens? Chano, what is it? Look, if you've changed your mind, you only have to say. Just say it. I told you we can go on as we are. It wasn't my idea. I won't hold you to it.'

'I haven't changed my mind. Can we just stop for a minute and sit down quietly?'

'Sit down. Oh God, what's wrong? Chano, tell me.'

'There's nothing wrong. I just want to talk to you. There's something I want to tell you and I don't want to say it walking along the street.'

'Are you in trouble?'

'No. Can you just come with me?'

It was only a few steps to the garden gate, just a few more to the dark green iron bench under the pepper trees, but it took for ever, walking in silence because there was something important to be said – but not yet – so that meant nothing could be said. By the time they sat down together, he was sorry he had ever begun this.

Caterina sat beside him, twisting her body towards his, one leg crossed over the other, like one of those old-fashioned equestrienne portraits of a grand señora riding side-saddle over her husband's estates.

He looked at her and said nothing, pushing his fingers through his hair.

'Just say it, Chano.'

But still he could not find the words. At the other end of the long gravel path through the garden, at the side closest to the Ottavio House, a place she did not know was there, a place she had never even heard of, the iron gate squeaked open and he saw Dr Cochrane come in and take a seat close to where the gardener was pruning some overhanging branches, his hat tilted down, his cane in his hand, his newspaper folded, the crossword puzzle ready to be filled with kisses.

'Do you remember that story you read to me?'

She looked relieved. 'You don't like it? You hate it. Is that all? Oh, thank God. That doesn't matter. Well, it matters, of course, but I'll get better. I know it's rubbish but I will try to get better.'

'It's not rubbish. It's very far from rubbish. In fact, I liked it so much that I sent it to a friend of mine.'

'Oh God.' She looked mortified. 'Who?'

'Oh, you don't know him. He lives in the capital. His name is Correa and he runs a little magazine.'

'Which little magazine?'

'Oh, a little magazine called *The Salon*.'

She clapped both hands to her mouth and squealed like a twelve-year-old.

'And Correa agrees with me that it's a very good story. So good that he has decided to publish it.'

She did not move. She sat very still with her hands peaked over her nose like a pilot's oxygen mask. Mr Valdez saw that her eyes were brimming with tears.

'There's nothing to cry about,' he said, and he gave her his handkerchief – the white one from his trouser pocket, not the blue one from the breast pocket of his suit. 'But there's something else I have to explain to you.'

Caterina was smiling now and dabbing at her eyes and laughing.

'First, I want to give you this.' He opened his wallet and took out Correa's cheque. 'It's your payment for the story.'

He held it out to her between two fingers, still folded shut, and she took it from him the way bomb-disposal men pick up tiny bits of machinery, opened it, read it and read it again.

'That can't be right,' she said.

'No, believe me, it's right.'

'This is a cheque for quarter of a million!'

'Yes, it is.'

'I could buy a car with that. I could pay my rent for years to come.'

'Buy whatever you want with it. Put it in the bank, save it up for a rainy day. Do whatever you want except, please, don't use it to travel – I want you near me – and don't waste it on rent. You can live with me.'

'Chano, this is amazing. Thank you. Oh, thank you.'

'Wait. Didn't your mother tell you, "There's no misfortune that doesn't come with good"? Well then, you are about to find out that there is no good that doesn't come with misfortune.'

She looked at him blankly.

'Caterina, I am so very sorry but there's been an awful mistake. I wanted to help. I wanted to help you. I sent your story to *The Salon* and – I can't think how this happened – somehow or other Correa got it into his head that I wrote it. He decided that it was my story.'

She was suddenly sad. 'Oh,' she said. 'That's why they paid so much.' She was making an effort to be brave about it, like a schoolboy whipped by the teacher who refuses to let his classmates see his tears. 'Well, it was nice while it lasted. You never miss what you've never had.' She held out the cheque. 'You'll just have to give it back to him. Do you think he might print the story anyway? I mean, he'd pay a lot less, obviously. I wouldn't care if he paid nothing at all, if it comes to that.'

He looked at her for a moment, willing her to understand, hoping that she might guess. 'No. It's not like that. The fact is, he has printed it. Your story is leading the new edition of *The Salon*.'

She still didn't understand.

'Caterina, your story is leading *The Salon* but it has my name on it.'

She looked at him. She looked at her feet. She looked back at him. 'But what does that mean?'

'It means just what it says. Correa printed your story with my name on it.'

'Well, we'll just have to tell him he's made a mistake. We can sort it out.'

'It's too late for that. It's out. It's printed. It's in the shops, on the news-stands, in the libraries, in university common rooms.'

'That doesn't matter.'

'It does matter. Look, you have to understand. You need to see the magazine. I should have brought it. Your story is the front page. Nothing else. Just your story. In fact, just my name, advertising your story. The editorial is all about your story and nothing else. They hired somebody to illustrate it. Page after page of pictures. And they gave up half the magazine to literary critique about how important your story is.'

She started to cry.

'They can't go back on that. How can they admit they know nothing, they can't tell the difference between you and me? If you had dared to send them that story they probably wouldn't even have read it and now look at it – the whole magazine!'

And then she shouted at him: 'That's not the point!'

At the other end of the garden Dr Cochrane looked up from his newspaper.

Valdez put his hand on hers: 'So, tell me the point.'

'Christ, Chano, don't act stupid. You know the point.'

'You want the credit for writing your story.'

'Obviously!'

Dr Cochrane turned round on his bench and looked down the gravel path. If he recognized them, he made no sign.

'Caterina, you wanted people to read your story and people are reading your story, more people than you could ever have imagined, reading it and talking about it and thinking about it.'

'Thinking about *your* story, talking about *your* story.'

Dr Cochrane turned and shaded his eyes with his hand as he peered at them, disapprovingly.

'I can't believe this,' she said. 'I just can't believe it. How could this happen? It's just not possible for anybody to be so stupid. Nobody could have done this by accident.'

'Surely you don't think I did it on purpose. You can't think I stole the credit. Look, I gave you the money.'

'The money means nothing to you.'

'Oh, and it means nothing to you either. The only thing you care about is the glory.'

'Screw you, Chano. Screw you.'

'Listen to me. Listen. It doesn't matter. You think it matters but it doesn't matter. Nothing matters less. Money matters. Of course it matters and I've given you the money and, I promise you, you will never have to be poor again, but taking the credit doesn't matter. The work matters. Your story is your story. It is the same story no matter whose name is on it. It means the same, no matter what those academic idiots say.'

'You have the money and you have the glory and you tell me that nothing could matter less. All these things that everybody else has and I don't have, none of them matter – not if you've got them. A house and clothes and education and money and glory, all pointless fripperies and worthless nonsense. Try living without them, Chano.'

'You have all those things. The only thing you don't have is the glory. Not yet. Caterina, there are martyrs shot in cellars every day. They still count as martyrs. Even if nobody ever knows. Just grow up, will you?'

Caterina held up her left hand in a fist and made a spidering motion with her fingers, gathering up the paper of the cheque into a ball. She flung it in his face and it hit him with all the force of a dandelion, with the sting of vitriol. Their eyes locked for a second, pain and fury and fury and pain, and then she got up from the bench and hurried down the path, away from him, away from the gate where they had come in, away from the jewellers of Paseo Santa Maria and towards Dr Cochrane. He stood up as she approached and tipped his hat. Valdez saw them talk for a moment and then they left together, Dr Cochrane holding the gate open for her as they walked out into the square.

Mr Valdez did not see and they did not notice that, just across the street, a shabby car with two thick aerials sticking out of the roof and a mark on the wing where a bullet hole had been filled in was parked right outside Madame Ottavio's house. Commandante Camillo was inside it, watching.

THEY SAT THERE, Mr Valdez on the bench under the pepper trees, Commandante Camillo in his car, neither of them knowing that the other was there.

After a time there was a clang of tools from the far side of the garden. Mr Valdez saw the gardener, long brown legs and tiny shorts, pushing his wheelbarrow to a wooden lock-up that hid itself in the middle of a stand of dusty bushes. A little later he emerged again and came crunching down the path and out the gate. He looked like a man who had been cheated out of a fistful of notes but he remembered to shut the gate behind himself when he left. It squeaked on its hinges and a bird up in the high branches took up the note and repeated it until, after half a dozen see-saw screeches, it grew bored with the game and flew down to the ground, where it kicked about among the dead leaves under the trees.

Mr Valdez stood up. He looked under the bench for Correa's cheque, found it, picked it up and sat down again, unfolding it and smoothing it out on his thigh with the heel of his hand.

He was very annoyed. It infuriated him that he had been stung by so empty a gesture. It could hardly have been more theatrical if she had torn the cheque up and scattered it round the garden, but that would have been just as meaningless since the cheque was his, not hers.

'She knows damn well I'd just have asked for a replacement,' he said. Mr Valdez imagined what it would be like to take the cheque to the banker Marrom. New editions of *The Salon* would be on sale soon. Everybody would be talking about it and that cheque – such a conspicuously large cheque – with the name of the magazine written right across it, well, it would be noticed. Marrom would notice it. He would probably make some remark on it, something encouraging and complimentary, and Mr Valdez thought how nice it would be, after so long, to be noticed and complimented. Not that he had any intention of keeping the money, of course, it was Caterina's money, but she could never use it unless it first cleared his accounts. Of course he wouldn't keep it. He was doing her a favour. Mr Valdez wondered if, perhaps, Maria might be at the bank, but only for a moment. It was a silly idea.

He folded the cheque along its original creases and put it away in his wallet. He waited for Caterina to see sense and come back. The little black bird down among the dead leaves screeched its rusty-gate note again and flew off. Two streets away the traffic throbbed with the sound of a distant beach, softened, grew fainter, quietened. Mr Valdez began to wonder what to do.

Out on the street, at the other side of the garden, Commandante Camillo was sitting in his car, watching Dr Cochrane and Caterina. It was her sudden quick movement that drew his eye, like a bird rising from cover, a signal of alarm and fright that made him turn to her. She came hurrying along the path and straight at the old man Cochrane. Commandante Camillo was disgusted. Why pick a public garden for a meeting? It was amateurish.

Cochrane stood up and tipped his hat – he even kissed her hand, the old goat. But, if a bit of old-fashioned charm was the way into those pretty knickers, it was worth it.

Camillo turned the handle that wound down the car window and a sprinkle of bird song came in, like bright beads falling from a broken necklace.

The girl was upset. Guilty conscience, probably. God, how often had he seen that moment when they got to the very edge and one more push was enough? Just the gentle reassurance that they would feel so much better if only they told the truth and then the tears would come and all the rest with it. Camillo could read it in her face. She was ready to crack. She knew they wouldn't get away with it.

Cochrane opened the gate and stood aside with a little bow. Quite the caballero. Still, good luck to him if it got results.

Outside the garden Cochrane offered her his arm and they walked together on the other side of the narrow street, back towards the university.

Camillo read his newspaper, not holding it up like a mask – that would be idiotic, a flag waved to draw attention to himself – but folded, the way a man folds his newspaper when he's waiting. Commandante Camillo knew there is nothing more interesting than somebody who is interested, nothing more noticeable than somebody noticing. When the girl and the old man came down the street, he ignored them. When they walked past his car, he was bored by them. They didn't even see him.

Camillo looked at his paper. For three slow, shuffling, limping steps, Cochrane passed the open window. He said: 'After so long' and he said 'revolution' and a lot of other words that were just noise. He was being soothing and reassuring. It didn't take much to fill in the gaps. 'After so long we've got away with it. After so long these stupid cops are never going to track us down.'

It made Camillo long for the old days. Back then that would have been enough. Back then, taking the piss like that could have got you shot right there on the street. And why not? He fired his pistol-folded fingers at their backs. Pop, pop. Pop, pop. Simple. Two each. One to knock them down, one in the head. Quick and easy and then all it took was a phone call to the clean-up squad. Nothing to see, nothing to worry about. But not now. Things had changed. Now there was 'due process' and 'international standards' and all that crap.

No, it was still the same. Nothing had changed. There were weak and stupid people who thought they didn't need any rules, who thought they could decide for themselves and drag the whole country to Hell with them, and there were strong people, ready to show them how wrong they were. Camillo was one of those and he was glad of it and there were plenty of others who should be glad too – glad and grateful that they could sleep in their beds at night because of men like him. But they were not grateful and that was why he hated them.

Dr Cochrane was one of the weak ones, one of the foolish ones who thought they could manage alone, without a strong leader to show them the way, who thought that singing songs could change things, fragile people who, if they lacked the strength to smash the system, had the courage to stand in front of it and let it crush them. But he was not a bomber. Dr Cochrane had too much love for that, so when he saw Caterina hurrying towards him and obviously in distress, his only instinct was to help.

At first, when she disturbed him, he had been resentful. But then, when she came down the little gravel path, sniffing, crying, making a great show of her dignity, when he recognized her and knew her for one of his own, he put that aside and went to her with kindness, lifting his hat before he spoke to her because that was what one did.

'Caterina. My dear, can I help you?'

She was embarrassed. She had seen him there almost as soon as she fled from Valdez but there was no avoiding him without turning back the way she had come and the thought of that was unbearable. She said: 'Hello, Dr Cochrane. Thank you. I'm fine.' But, when he looked at her with those sad old eyes, something broke in her and the tears came and, in a few moments the whole story came with them.

'Let's walk,' he said. He opened the iron gate that led out to the street and stood aside to let her pass, offering her his arm. Caterina noticed the handsome young gardener working in the flower beds. He glared at her as he gathered his long black hair into a pony tail and fixed it with a rubber band.

'I shouldn't have told you,' she said. 'We were going to announce it later.'

'Everybody knows.'

'What do you mean?'

'Everybody knows. Everybody at the university.'

'They know we are to be married?'

He looked at her in surprise and noticed for the first time that she was actually a little taller than he was. 'Married? No, nobody knew that. But everybody knows that you and he are,' he hesitated, 'together.'

'Oh,' she said. 'Together. Everybody knows that.'

'Don't let it worry you, my dear. Nobody takes any notice of that sort of thing these days.'

Caterina said nothing. She did not say that she took 'that sort of thing' very seriously indeed. 'I threw myself at him,' she said. 'Almost as soon as we met I begged him to take me to bed and he refused. He was a perfect gentleman. You mustn't blame him.'

'And now you are to be married.'

'We were until a few minutes ago, at least. We were on our way to pick the ring.'

Dr Cochrane stopped at the edge of the pavement and pointed back into the garden with a swing of his cane. 'I'm sure he's still there. I'm sure he's simply waiting for you to come to your senses and run back to him. Go on. Run back to him and tell him what a silly, headstrong fool you've been. Blame your youth. Better yet, let him blame your youth and don't disagree. You'll have that ring on your finger within the hour.'

'You say that as if it's a bad thing.'

'There's something you should know.' Dr Cochrane waited but she said nothing.

'My dear, you should know he is not a nice man.'

'He is a wonderful man.'

'Yes, wonderful, but not nice. There is no 'Cochrane's Theorem' but the books of L.H. Valdez will last. He will leave that much behind – more than almost anybody else – but some others less wonderful will be remembered with love. He won't.'

'He will. I love him.'

'I believe you. Now.'

'I won't stop. I know my own mind. I'm not a child.'

'Yes, you are.'

'I am older than I look.'

'I know,' said Dr Cochrane. 'I see it in your eyes.'

Walking with Dr Cochrane took a long time. He went so slowly, with his limp and his cane, and now he was strolling, taking his time to make his point. The street narrowed. The pavement narrowed.

'I am afraid of his mother.'

'Sophia.'

'You know her?'

'It was many years ago. He knows nothing of it.'

'She hates me.'

'She is frightened. You have to understand how hard her life has been – and lonely. She has struggled to keep things as they are and, after so long,' they passed a shabby blue car on the other side of the street, 'after so long, having you come into her life must be like a kind of revolution. My advice to you is to be kind and patient. If you are determined to go ahead with this marriage, it will never work without her. Not without Mama. Not if I know Chano. Not if I know Sophia.'

'You are wise and kind,' she said.

'I am merely old. Let me buy you dinner.'

A long time after they had walked down the street together, when the noise of the faraway traffic had grown too faint to notice and shadows thickened under the pepper trees and crept out to fill the garden, when the sky went like velvet and two stars came out, Mr Valdez, who felt sad and angry and very lonely and a little afraid, heard a woman laughing and the sound of ice in a glass. He stood up from the bench and walked towards the square and the Ottavio House. The quickest way was straight through the garden.

WHEN MR VALDEZ went into the Ottavio House he was a little afraid. He had not hurried from the garden. Instead he sat there, waiting for Caterina to return, until the wait itself became the reason for staying.

He waited on the bench, alone, with the cheque in his wallet folded over next to Caterina's note, until he saw the first star in the sky. Mr Valdez was no astronomer. He could barely have found The Scorpion even if the light of the city had not washed the whole sky with orange, but the Admiral had taught him enough to know that first light was Venus and not a star at all. It betrayed itself with its steady beam, reflecting back the endless light of the sun just as the moon does, while stars, real stars, gigantic burning suns made tiny by distance, would flicker and dance.

When Venus appeared Mr Valdez decided that he had waited for long enough but, because he was afraid, he did not go. Caterina deserved one more chance to admit what a fool she had been. He could afford to be generous. He was the grown-up here. He resolved to stay a little longer – until the second star came out. It arrived remarkably quickly. It was the proof that Caterina would not return.

Mr Valdez stood up and walked down the gravel path, the same gravel path she had walked down, the very same little stones underfoot, in the same direction, past the bench where Dr Cochrane had sat, out of the same iron gate and out into the little square.

The double doors of the Ottavio House were flung open. Standing with one hand on that gate Mr Valdez could hear the twitter of women's conversation, laughter, soft music. He found he had developed a powerful thirst and only the bitter-green spring-sharp tang of limes would take it away. His green fairy was calling to him. He had not tasted her kisses for weeks but he was afraid to go in. She was waiting but he was too afraid to rush to her.

Mr Valdez was afraid that Caterina had left him. He was afraid that she would not marry him. He was afraid that wounded pride and disappointment would make her withdraw her love. He was afraid that he would end his days like the old Nazi, Dr Klement, with no one to mourn him. He was afraid he would live his life like his mother, with no one to love him for forty years, going down to death with nobody to bear his name, without even duty to give his existence some meaning, and stepping inside Madame Ottavio's house might make those things happen.

He was afraid that they might not happen. He was afraid that his life would sink into ordinariness and nappies and conversations about Erica and curtains and colour swatches and drains and domestic certainty, and stepping into Madame Ottavio's house might make sure that those things did not happen. He was afraid. But it was only a drink and, perhaps, a chance to see some old friends in a sort of club. That was all. Nothing more.

Mr Valdez took his hand from the iron gatepost and he allowed himself to touch his lip, finding that raised question-mark outline there, stroking it until he decided what to do.

'The scrawny yellow cat crossed the road and crept into the whorehouse,' he said. He decided what to do.

Sitting in his car in the shadows, Commandante Camillo could hardly believe his luck. He watched Valdez crossing the street, watched him step out of the shadows of the garden, into the bright light of the open doorway and inside the house. He waited for a moment, threw his newspaper down on the passenger seat and got out of the car.

THERE WAS NO stench of sulphur when Commandante Camillo entered the courtyard garden, no rolling thunderclap to announce his arrival, no crashing chords or Grand Guignol effects like the final scenes of *Don Giovanni*. Nothing. He was simply a man in a crumpled suit, shambling towards retirement, less sure of his place in the world than he felt he deserved. Angry. Nature had forgotten to fit him with any of her usual warning signs. The wasps flash yellow and black to advertise their venom, the viper has her zigzag of diamonds, the shark his sickle fin, but Commandante Camillo was as ordinary as a mushroom. Only experience could mark him out from the rest as a killer.

But for some reason, when he arrived in the garden a cold breeze came up from the river and over the wall to greet him, just for a moment, so the flames in the lamps knelt to acknowledge him, like penitents before the altar. Mr Valdez saw it happen and he seemed to know instinctively what it meant. In that moment he felt every flame in Hell dip too, as if in salute to one they were ready to welcome. When he turned and found Camillo standing there he was not even slightly surprised.

Quickly Mr Valdez turned round again. He concentrated on measuring out the ice and the lime and the gin. He knew it wouldn't save him.

'Hello, Valdez.'

He did not look up from the ice bucket. 'Good evening.'

'Could you make me a brandy and ginger?'

'I'm sure one of the girls would make a far better job of it.'

'Yes, but I'd still like you to do it. It would be a nice, friendly thing to do. I'll be sitting over there.' He nodded into the shadows.

Mr Valdez did not feel friendly. He didn't feel like doing the nice, friendly thing, performing that simple service that a whore might have done. He felt afraid – properly afraid – and threatened and intimidated and belittled, exactly as Camillo had intended. There was nothing to make him pour that brandy. Camillo was not holding a gun at his head – not literally – and for a moment Mr Valdez considered not pouring the drink. There was no need. He could simply walk away, find his own chair, sit at his own table and then what – sit and glare across the garden at Camillo, defy him? What if he came over? What if he insisted? What if he stood there and demanded, ordered, with his jacket flung back and the butt of his pistol on show? So what if he did? Camillo couldn't just gun him down. Not there. No, not there, but he could, later, somewhere else. He could. Mr Valdez poured the drink, dutifully, and took it to the table.

'Your drink, sir,' he said.

'Thank you.' Camillo emptied almost half the glass in a single swallow. It was a tall glass. He put it down on the table with a lip-smacking sigh. 'I've wanted to have a word with you for some time.'

Mr Valdez had no idea how to respond to that. There was a tightness in the back of his throat.

The policeman said: 'I'm a bit worried about the company you keep.'

'I'm touched by your concern.'

'Don't be smart. Please. Some of us are looking out for your best interests.'

'Then, in the interests of not being smart, I'd better say nothing.'
Mr Valdez leaned back in his chair, the way Camillo had done
before, legs flung out in front of him, feigning relaxation. He
held his long green glass gripped in one hand, resting on his
stomach, and with his left hand he worried at his upper lip.

Commandante Camillo said: 'What do you know about Dr
Joaquin Cochrane?'

'Nothing. That's the truth. He works at the university, teaches
maths. That's all.'

'I never like it when people tell me that they are telling the
truth. It makes me suspicious. What else?'

'He walks with a stick.'

'What did I tell you about being smart?'

'That's all I know.'

'Where does he live?'

'You don't know that?'

'Of course we know that. We know everything, Valdez. We
always know everything. I want to know what you know.'

'I have no idea where Cochrane lives.'

'What about his girlfriend?'

'If Cochrane has a girlfriend, I don't know her.'

'Yes, you do. She's your girlfriend too.'

Mr Valdez stopped rubbing his lip and took a big drink.

'You didn't know? Oh, that was something you didn't know.
Not so smart now.'

Mr Valdez put his glass down. 'Which girlfriend?'

'You know which girlfriend. The little one with the big tits.
Caterina. We've been watching her for a while. Since before she
spent the night at your place. They met up earlier tonight, her
and Cochrane, in the gardens right outside here, and they went
off together arm in arm. You didn't know that either.'

Mr Valdez was suddenly hopeful. The lime juice had tightened and dried in his throat and he was bitterly afraid but there was hope because there was something that Camillo did not know. Camillo did not know that Caterina had been with him in the garden. Valdez saw and understood: she left him, she met Cochrane and Camillo saw them together. He said: 'She's not my girlfriend.'

'No, you've got that right. You thought she was, but she's Cochrane's girlfriend – and she's up to those pretty tits in trouble, so if you're wise, you'll tell me what you know.'

'She's a student. She's interested in writing. She came to my house because I agreed to help her. That's all. I was coaching her.'

'That's a new word for it.'

'She is one of Dr Cochrane's students, that's all.'

'She's a terrorist. He's been a political agitator all his life and he's got her dragged into it. I'm going to have them and, if you don't want to go down with them, you'd better start telling me lots of interesting things – things that will make me more interested in them than I am in you.'

Somehow Mr Valdez found the courage to look the policeman in the face. He remembered what Caterina had said about going to her execution, about being brave right up until the very last. He knew what he was going to say before he said it but not why he said it. Even in that moment he was unsure if he wanted to stand in the way between Caterina and Camillo, protect her with his own flesh, or if he hoped that by daring to act like a character from a novel by L.H. Valdez, he might save himself. He said: 'Camillo, I'm going to tell you the truth now. I'm going to tell you something I wouldn't admit to another soul. You frighten me. You and people like you, you frighten me. But I don't care what you do, I'm not going to hand anybody over to you. Not the girl, not Cochrane, nobody.'

Mr Valdez was an artist and he knew, as soon as he had said

it, how pathetic that sounded. He saw from Camillo's face that he knew it too.

'You would give me anybody. You'd give up anything. You'd do anything I said.' Camillo swallowed the last of his brandy. 'I bet you'd even get me another drink if I told you to.'

'You don't know what you're talking about.' In spite of himself, Mr Valdez found he was touching his lip again.

'I know a lot more than you think, Chano, son. I even know how you got that.'

Valdez snatched his hand away from his face. 'Unless you're going to arrest me, I've had enough of this.' He stood up from the chair.

'That's it. Run away home to Mama. I've got man's business to be about.'

All around the garden, the lamps flared again.

A CHILD OF six years old knows that he has lived a lifetime of experience, knows that he understands the world and all its works and that there is nothing more to learn about the ways of men. A boy of fifteen knows as much and a man of twenty-one and a father of fifty. Sometimes it is necessary to live to a great age, sometimes even for more than one lifetime, before we find out how little we know, how much there is to learn and how infinitely surprising are all our fellow travellers.

To understand is to forgive, as the proverb says, and those who have suffered most have most to forgive, and who suffers more than men like Dr Joaquin Cochrane?

There could hardly be a man more unlike L.H. Valdez. Dr Cochrane, short, shuffling, stiff-legged, Valdez, even if he was feeling his age, still an athlete.

Valdez a man of words, Cochrane who played with numbers. Valdez commanding attention, demanding to be noticed, revelling in adulation, insisting on it as his right, Dr Cochrane keeping to the shadows, hugging the skirting boards of life.

Valdez believing in nothing, boasting of his uncaring uncertainties, Dr Cochrane nursing his passionate, secret zealotry.

Valdez squandering himself endlessly, lovelessly, until when love came late it was a stranger and it frightened him. Cochrane always alone but always ready to love, like a filled lamp waiting for the match.

Valdez a ladies' man, very definitely a ladies' man, and Cochrane not, Cochrane most definitely not, and yet, because life is infinitely surprising, it was Cochrane who sat across the table from Caterina, restlessly turning the salt cellar.

They sat there in that little restaurant for almost four hours, and long before that time was up, Dr Cochrane decided that he liked this young girl.

They spoke of her village in the mountains and how small it is, how far away from everything, how clear is the air. She told him that she missed the stars and the long, bright smear of the Milky Way cutting across the sky but it comforted her to think that, when she saw the moon, the same moon was shining on her mother.

Dr Cochrane spoke of his ancestor the Admiral, but it was all new to Caterina and she could listen without forcing interest – for a while at least.

They spoke of food and books – especially the books of L.H. Valdez – and, most of all, they spoke of love. Love in general and her love in particular.

He said: 'I blame myself. I am your teacher. I should have stepped in. I could have prevented this.'

'But this is what I want. *He* is what I want.'

'My dear, I believe you. Truly I do. Valdez is a great catch and, forgive me, there are many women – many, many women – who have tried to do what you have done. Believe me, making L.H. Valdez care is no mean accomplishment. I have tried for years. I have loved him for so long, you see, but he pays no attention to an old man like me.'

Caterina looked down at the tablecloth, suddenly embarrassed. She could think of nothing to say beyond: 'I am sorry.'

Dr Cochrane laughed. 'Am I so obvious? All these years I thought I was hiding myself.' He put his hand on hers. 'No, child, not like that. Not that way. As a father. No, that's not right either. As an uncle perhaps. A secret uncle.' He smiled. 'Or a fairy godmother!'

Caterina smiled too. She felt he had given her permission, as if he would understand that she was laughing at what he said and not at what he was. Dr Cochrane made her feel at ease in a way that Valdez somehow never did. With Valdez there was always the feeling of sharing a cage with a tiger. It was exciting but it was uncertain and it's hard to love a tiger.

'Men like me,' he said, 'men such as I am, we find ourselves disapproved of.'

'I understand.'

'But Chano's father was kind to me.' Dr Cochrane was afraid he had given the wrong impression. 'Oh, not in that way, you understand, but he was good to me. Kind. A good friend.'

'What happened to him?'

'Nobody knows,' he said, which was almost true. 'In those days people simply disappeared. They still do, of course, but for different reasons. Or the same reasons. I suppose nothing really changes except the people who do the disappearing, and they are always more or less the same. Anyway, the point is that he was a good, brave man. He made Chano what he is.'

'But he wasn't there,' said Caterina. 'How could he?'

'Tell me about your father.'

'He's dead too.'

'And how did that change your life?'

Caterina nodded. She understood and she knew that he was right.

'Child, things which are not there can shape us just as much as those that are. A man who loses his eyes is not the same thing

as a man born blind. They see the world very differently.' Dr
Cochrane poured himself more wine. 'You are so young,' he said.
'How often have you fallen in love?'

'Until now, never.'

'And how often after this?'

'Never!' She was shocked.

'Can you be so sure? Just like poor Sophia, denying herself for
so many years. What a waste.'

'And you,' she asked, not too unkindly, 'how often have you
loved, Dr Cochrane?'

'Child, I fall in love almost every day. And I have my heart
broken every other day. But I don't mind. That's the price on
the ticket of admission to life. That's the price poor Chano Valdez
has decided not to pay.'

'Until now,' she said.

'Until now,' he agreed politely. 'But I am glad to pay it. I
would pay it twice over and pay it gladly for the *cabeceo* alone,
even if I never got another dance.'

Dr Cochrane talked. Dr Cochrane was good at talking. He
ordered brandy and that helped with the talking.

Outside the restaurant the darkness deepened. Shadows filled
the streets and thickened and crept up the walls and the orange
street lamps blotted out the light of the friendly stars and only
made the darkness blacker. Caterina felt it.

Dr Cochrane talked and she smiled at him, pretending to listen,
looking over his shoulder, across the street, listening instead to
the stories she could hear muttering along the pavements in ways
that Valdez was deaf to, ways he had long ago forgotten. She
looked through the dark, down an alley to where, three streets
away, a young man was stealing morphine from an ambulance
to help his father die. And, up on the hill, she saw a beautiful
woman leave her beautiful house in her beautiful car, watched

her drive all the way to town where she parked, tossed the keys to an old man selling newspapers on the street corner and simply walked away.

'I blame myself. I blame myself. Maybe, if Sophia had responded differently. Maybe if she had been hard and brutal – as hard as she pretends to be – if she had forgotten him instead of raising monuments to him, maybe if she had married again, but she knew I saw. My fault. All my fault.'

Dr Cochrane stopped talking for a moment, gulped wetly and said: 'I feel sick. Time to go home.'

CATERINA AND DR Cochrane left the restaurant as they had arrived, arm in arm. When they met in the garden and he bowed and doffed his hat and offered his arm, that had been a gesture of old-fashioned courtliness. Now Dr Cochrane linked his arm through hers for support and he leaned on her a little too heavily. His leg was painful and that last brandy had made his cane unsteady and his voice loud.

'I am not myself a Freemason,' he said.

'Shhh, there's no need to shout.'

'No. You are quite right. Thousand apologies.' He began again, just as loud as before. 'I am not myself a Freemason but I belong to a sort of Freemasonry.'

'Is it a secret association?'

'In this ignorant, backward, nasty little country, yes, it has to be a secret,' he confided noisily.

'Then don't you think you should try to keep it quiet?'

Somehow, almost in the middle of his last, long anecdote, Dr Cochrane had become suddenly very drunk. His walk was uncertain and his stagger transmitted itself to Caterina. More than once she had to stop and steady herself to keep from bouncing along the wall.

'Absolutely!' Dr Cochrane held his finger to his lips in a gesture of silence. 'I can keep a secret.' He tugged on her arm and hissed:

'That is why the *cabeceo* is so important. Important to men. Men like me, you understand. You do understand? You understand what I'm saying.'

'Yes, I understand.' Caterina really had no wish to discuss it. She did not condemn, but she saw no reason to go on and on.

'We need the *cabeceo*,' he said. 'We need it to identify one another. We need it for signalling to one another. We need it for asking and agreeing. Secretly. That flash of the eyes,' he gave a ridiculous, moon-faced look, 'so subtle, almost unnoticed, but it is seen and recognized and understood. It is enough.' And then he said: 'Freemasonry' again and: 'I can keep a secret.'

'Can we talk about something else?' she said. They were arriving at a street corner and she was looking for a gap in the traffic which would be wide enough to cross the road in safety while dragging a drunken cripple.

'Some of the happiest nights of my life have been spent in tango halls, you know. Special tango halls. No ladies.'

Caterina half dragged, half carried him across the street, looking for a taxi rank where she could abandon him in good conscience. But she wanted to take her time. There was something she needed to know.

'Why did you say you blame yourself?' she asked, casually.

'Blame myself for what, child?'

'You said you blamed yourself for the way things turned out. With Chano and his mother. "I was there," that's what you said.'

'Oh,' he said. 'That. Did I say that?' and he swallowed a belch, daintily. 'I think I may be a little drunk, you know.'

'I know.'

'But I can keep a secret. I have been keeping secrets for more than forty years.'

They arrived at the taxi rank and Caterina knew she had missed her chance. They would make their farewells, Dr Cochrane would get into his taxi and wake up in his own bed in the morning with his sore head and his secret, still safe, inside it.

She gave him a little peck and said: 'Well, goodbye then. I'll leave you here. Thank you for looking after me.'

But Dr Cochrane took her hand and gripped it. 'Do you love him?' he said.

'Of course!'

'But do you *love* him? Do you love him hotter than Hell and longer?'

'I said it, didn't I?'

'Say it again. Do you love him?'

'Yes! I love him.'

'And when they come for you and do vile things to you — things that can't be spoken — when they do things to you that no woman should ever have to bear, when they leave you ugly and don't kill you, what will you say then?'

Caterina tried to twist her hand away. 'Stop saying these things!'

'What will you say then, child?'

'I will still love him.'

Dr Cochrane let go of her hand. 'Then get in the taxi with me. If you really want to know.'

THE CAB WAS closed and hot. Dr Cochrane told the driver his address and sat back in the seat, burrowing into the corner with his hat down. He might have been asleep, but for the hand he kept slipped through the worn leather strap that hung down from above the door. It was a clear signal that he did not wish to say more, and for the second time that evening Caterina found herself forced into silence, waiting for something momentous to be said.

The headlights cut through the hot night. The windows misted up and Caterina had no idea where they were going but the taxi driver knew the way, following some mental map the way the eels come swarming out of their nests in the far Sargasso Sea to sniff their way back to the same rivers year after year.

Lights loomed up against the glass, the neon signs of bars and shops streamed past, and then they were on the highway, cars and lorries jostling by on every side, flat, harsh signs screaming overhead and off again, down the broad curve of an exit ramp to a set of traffic lights, across a junction, left, left and into a quiet side street on a hill.

'You've gone past it,' Dr Cochrane shouted. 'Here! Stop here!'

Not trusting his handbrake, the driver swung the wheel sharply so the taxi came to a halt across the width of the street, defying the hill.

Dr Cochrane was not a nimble man and drink had made him clumsy. The cab was listing on the hill like a sinking liner. Even if he could have reached the passenger door on his, the uphill side, he could never have opened it. Instead he scrambled to the door on the downhill side, urging Caterina, 'Forgive me child. No, I can manage, thank you. I'm fine,' ahead of him, getting tangled in her legs and stumbling out on to the pavement.

Caterina waited quietly while he paid the driver and then they walked off together, still side by side but not, now, arm in arm, down the hill a little to Dr Cochrane's gate. Caterina did not know where to go, she did not know what to expect. Walking slowly beside Dr Cochrane she was paying too much attention to her new surroundings to notice the car, with two detectives inside it, parked four doors down the hill.

'I can see why men find you attractive,' Dr Cochrane said.

She hesitated. 'Some men do.'

'Chano Valdez does.'

'It would seem so.'

'And the boys at university?'

'Some, I suppose.'

'You never . . . ?'

'No.'

'Never?'

'No.' She didn't even bother to insist.

'We're here,' Dr Cochrane said. He stood at the bottom of the stairs and drew out his house key from his pocket on the end of a long silver chain. 'Please go up. I don't want to keep you waiting.'

He took a long time to come up the stairs, shifting his cane to the other hand so he could grip the banister rail and then his painful, limping climb, a step at a time, stopping at every tread, rocking his weight on his hips, climbing again.

'Come in,' he said, although it took half a dozen attempts to get the key in the lock. 'Come in and let me offer you a refreshment.'

'Perhaps a coffee,' she said. Caterina was growing impatient. She had come only for the sake of his story, after all, not for his coffee.

'Would you, niña? I don't think I could,' and he collapsed into a fat green chair with his leg thrown out in front of him like a dead log. He was still wearing his hat.

Caterina found the kitchen, found the coffee, boiled the kettle and returned a few minutes later with everything on a tray.

Dr Cochrane thanked her. 'I think I am beginning to sober up,' he said and made a fish face. 'I can feel my lips again and that is always a good sign.'

Caterina waited until he had taken a sip before saying: 'You were going to tell me something – do you remember?'

'Was I?'

'Something important.'

He made no reply.

'About Chano and his mother. You were there. Remember? You were there.'

Dr Cochrane put his cup back in his saucer and looked at her angrily. 'Yes, I remember.'

'Have you changed your mind?'

'Have you changed yours?'

'No.'

'You love him? Fiercer than death? Knowing it could kill you. Or me.'

She nodded at him across the shadowed room. He saw the glow of the street lamps shining in her hair as it moved.

'Am I still drunk enough to tell you this? Once you know a thing, child, you can't unknow it, you understand that? You can't unknow it!'

She nodded again.

'Oh God.' Dr Cochrane dragged his hand down his face. 'You need to know this,' he said. And then, with a deep sigh, he began to speak. 'It was more than forty years ago. A long, long time ago. When I was young. Valdez was my friend. He felt as I did. He believed as I did. He wanted to find a better way. He was a wealthy man from one of the best families in town, generations of them, piling their money up – a lawyer, and he wanted to use his money and the law to help the poor, help make the world a better place. Just a little better. Nobody wanted to listen. He made enemies. He got noticed. That was a bad thing.

'I warned him. I begged him to stop. He didn't listen. Soon they were watching him. Other people vanished – people we knew – just disappeared, and they were getting closer and closer. They wanted to frighten him. There was a policeman outside the house all the time.

'Valdez and Sophia used to get into their car and drive. I don't know where they went, I don't know what they said, but in the car they thought they were safe. Nobody listening. Nobody watching. They were wrong. There was always somebody watching. They used to come out of the house with little Chano in his pyjamas wrapped in a blanket. They used to carry him away into the night and drive. I only watched. I was his friend and I only watched. It was what I could do. Look at me. I am small and lame. What else could I do? I stood in the street and I watched the policemen watching. I thought I was helping, do you understand?'

'You did what you could,' she said.

'I wish. I wish to God I'd never bothered. I wish to God. I don't know what I thought I was going to do. I had some mad idea that I might step in if they came for him, fight them, die with him at least. Anything. And then it came to the last night.

We had talked about it, he and I. I don't know what he told her. I don't know what he told Sophia.

'They got in the car with Chano in the back and they drove off. I saw them come out of the house together, Sophia carrying the boy, and she laid him on the back seat, still asleep, and she closed the door and they drove off together. The police had stopped following them – at first they used to follow just so they would know they could not escape, but they stopped that. Once they knew that he always came back, once they knew that he didn't stop and he didn't meet anybody, they let him drive around as much as he liked, the way little boys do with bees on a thread, just for the fun of it. Go in that cupboard, niña, find me some brandy.'

Dr Cochrane held out a trembling coffee cup and Caterina poured. He drank and held the cup out again.

'I stood there like an idiot in the bushes, watching and waiting. I never knew if the policemen knew that I was there or not. They might have been playing with me too. I don't know. Eventually I had to pee. I was standing there, with my, with my hands full when the car came back. Valdez was gone. Sophia was driving. And Chano was sitting beside her in the front seat, the top of his head barely showing through the window – as if that was ever going to fool anybody. The moment she pulled into the drive the policeman knew what had happened. He ran across the street. He was crazy. He was screaming. He hit Sophia. I was standing there, pissing in a bush, and he hit Sophia. Can you imagine anything more ridiculous? Fumbling round in the dark, trying to do my trousers up while my friend's wife was getting beaten up across the street. Pathetic.

'But little Chano wasn't pathetic. He was a tiger. He came out of the car to defend her. And I just stood there. Long after I'd finished what I was doing, when I had no excuse for doing nothing,

I stood there in the bushes. That little boy went to his mother and I did nothing.

'The policeman was standing over Sophia with his gun out when Chano came and kicked him in the legs and then he swung round, with his gun in his hand, this huge, black lump of metal, just swung round and smashed that little kid in the face. Hit him right in the mouth. Chano flew backwards and landed in the street.

'That was too much even for a coward like me. The kid – my friend's son – was lying on his back on the pavement with blood spurting from his mouth and I took my cane in my hand and I pushed out from behind my dark little bush and went to help with all the haste of a terrified snail. Sophia was lying on the ground and the policeman was standing over that little boy with his gun pointed down at him and the hammer cocked and I was halfway across the street and each of us was about half a second away from a bullet when Sophia sat up and screamed: "For Christ's sake, Camillo, don't do it. He's your son!" And then both of them looked up and saw me.'

Caterina sat in the dark and said nothing.

'Yes,' said Dr Cochrane. 'That was exactly how I felt too. And now you are like me; you cannot unknow it.'

'But that doesn't mean it was true. She was desperate. She only said it. She wanted to save her son.'

'Of course, child. Of course you are right, but she could not have said such a thing unless she thought Camillo would believe her. There must have been something at the root of it and even that would not have been so bad. Very few of us manage to cling to your high moral standards. A discreet little indiscretion is not so very terrible.'

'What happened then?' Caterina said.

'Camillo looked up from the boy and looked at me. I was

standing there in the middle of the street, in the middle of all that screaming and shouting, with all those houses round about where nobody came to the door and nobody opened their curtains, where everybody sat inside staring hard at their televisions and reading their papers and noticing nothing, and I stood there waiting to be shot. But instead, the policeman put his gun away and ran. I think in those days he still had a soul, something in him that could be touched. He ran past me and got in his car and drove off and then I went to help Sophia. Naturally she never forgave me.

'She sat there in the kitchen of her house, holding little Chano while he screamed and soaked blood into her blouse. Blood. Blood everywhere. I waited with her until the doctor came and stitched the boy's lip together again. When he was finished she ordered me from her door and told me never to return. She expected to hear from her husband. She didn't want me around to remind anybody of what she had said – not that I would have done. But Valdez disappeared. She never heard of him again. It was then, I suppose she began to build his shrine and entomb herself inside it like a penitential sacrifice.

'That's what you have to know about the man who will be your husband. He is damaged goods, child. Locked up for years in a mausoleum dedicated to the glory of a father he never knew with a mother like that. It's not his fault he has no love left. We must love him all the harder.'

WHEN MR VALDEZ left the Ottavio House he walked home alone all the way back to his flat and he complimented himself that not once did he stop and check who was walking behind. Through the dark little side streets where the sound of his heels on the pavement echoed back from the houses on either side, along Cristobal Avenue, where the cars cruised by, jammed in tight together, one after another, where the pavements were crowded, where he was jostled, where he imagined the touch of the pickpocket or the pistol in his ribs, by an effort of will he never once glanced behind him. He closed his door and turned the key in the lock and relief swept over him as it does over a drowning sailor who manages to throw his arms around some floating piece of timber, as if it would save him, as if it could defy the waves and the gales, as if a few planks of wood and a brass bolt could stand up to a bullet or a boot or the crushing weight of a search warrant.

He had not pleaded. He had not wept or whimpered or cried out or visibly trembled. He had kept control of his bladder and his dignity. He had that much to be pleased about. But Mr Valdez was bitterly afraid. In the garden he had been afraid that Caterina might leave him and afraid that he might turn into a husband. In the Ottavio House he was afraid of Camillo, afraid of what Camillo might say and do, afraid of what Camillo might do to

Caterina unless he spoke up for her, afraid of what might happen
to him because he dared to speak up, afraid every step of the way
home, and he was sick of it. The warm pulse of life was throbbing painfully in the stump Caterina had somehow kissed back
into life and he wanted it to stop. He wanted to go back to a
time before, when he was cut off from life and other people, but
it was too late for that. He had tasted of the fruit of the Tree of
Knowledge and he knew that he was naked. There was no way
back to the time when he did not know.

Foolishly he thought of dragging furniture through the house
and piling it against the door – as if it would do anything but
add a few moments of miserable terror to his ordeal. It was pointless. He knew it was pointless. If Camillo wanted it he could
simply make him vanish like a rabbit in a magic act, like his father.

And then, for a moment, the fear subsided again. He thought of
Caterina. He had defied Camillo for her sake. He had refused to
betray her. He knew she must be warned. But he did not warn her.

To warn Caterina, he would have to leave the flat again, go
out in the dark again, walk down the avenue again, down that
grubby side street to a place he had never visited but which Camillo
knew all about, a place where, even now, Camillo might be waiting
to catch him, and that wouldn't help Caterina.

'That wouldn't help her at all,' he told himself. 'It will have
to wait until morning. If she's not in the Phoenix I can find a
way to bump into her or get Cochrane to pass on a note. Get
that business with the cheque sorted out and tell her. Safer. Far
better to wait.'

That was how he excused himself. Dr Cochrane, who called
himself a coward, would have been ashamed to say such things
even to himself, but suddenly Mr Valdez wanted to be safer. Safer
seemed the thing to be. Safer was the thing to do.

He poured himself a lot of brandy in a tumbler and he was

surprised to notice that, as he drank it, his hand did not tremble. He was surprised to notice that he had noticed.

Mr Valdez took off his shoes, clumsily, with the toe of one against the heel of another in a way that would ruin the leather, and he walked through the flat to stand at the big window that looked down the avenue with its long strings of moving lights.

It looked like civilization. To the untrained eye it looked as if the jungle had been cleared, the snakes forced out of their holes, the jaguars chased away with smoke and drums, but Mr Valdez knew that what had come in their place was something far, far worse, far more vicious and something that did not fear to walk out in the light.

And then Mr Valdez did something he had not done since he was a boy. His hand found the hilt of his grandfather's sword. He tugged it from the brass scabbard and it came out quietly through the collar of sheepskin, still oiled to protect against the faraway ocean it had not tasted for decades. It spoke to him of ancestry and blood, pride and honour, and he moved with it across the room, holding it, moving it, presenting it just as he had been taught to do, and he heard his grandfather saying: 'Keep the tip up' and 'Bring the leg back' and 'That's the way, boy. Never give a sword to a man who can't dance.'

Mr Valdez could dance. In his silent flat he heard the Tango of Death and he moved on the balls of his feet, like a cat with one long, vicious claw.

> I have no friends
> I have no lovers
> I have no country
> Nor religion
> I have only bitterness in my soul
> And sickness in my heart.

A tawny cat who ended up where he had begun, crossing the road and going into the whorehouse only so he could come out again, over and over and over, stalking the flat until he finished, with the tip of his sword poised against the fabric of a cushion on his beautiful leather couch, pricking it but not piercing it and wondering if the warm thumbprint of flesh between Camillo's collar bones would feel that way.

He was sweating. He was hot. Mr Valdez drank some more brandy and went to bed. He took the sword with him. When he lay down alone in a bed that smelled of Caterina, on a pillow that smelled of Caterina, the weight of it comforted him.

WITH DR COCHRANE asleep in his chair, Caterina got up to go. She took the coffee cup from his fingers and left it, sticky with brandy, on the shelf by the window. She looked down into the street. She had no idea where she was, no idea how to reach home, but she knew she had to find Chano and kiss him and make things right.

She shut the door quietly and went down the darkened stairs and out into the street. The policemen had already gone. They had seen enough.

Caterina stood at the edge of the pavement, deciding which way to go and she chose 'downhill'. It was the way she had come and it was what her father had taught her to do. If she got lost in the mountains, Pappi told her, go down. The rain goes down and the rain would turn into a stream and the stream to a river and where there were rivers there were always people and they would bring her back to him.

People were easier to find in the city. In the city they grew as thick as weeds, they filled the houses and clogged the streets, they swarmed like ants but they lived lonely lives — far lonelier than the most solitary mountain shepherd. He might walk into town once a month to get drunk or buy a pair of trousers but people would know his name. His neighbours would know all about him though he lived two valleys away and if, one fiesta day, he failed to appear they would come looking.

But not here. Not in the city. Here men slept out in alleys wrapped in stinking blankets, old people stood stooped in the streets with their hands out and nobody said: 'Mama, here is bread,' or 'Come in and share this bit of soup with us.' They walked past. They drove past and nobody saw a thing and she was becoming like them. After two years in the city she knew her way from her flat to the university, she knew Erica and she loved Chano, but there was no one else and now she was lost.

Caterina walked down the hill to the junction and turned right but it brought her closer to the highway. She could hear the roar of it hidden behind the houses like a waterfall lost in trees. The cars scorched the sky with their lights as they passed and the lamps along the roadside towered on their concrete stalks in an endless scream of light. Caterina turned back. She wanted a river but this one was too big to cross, too fast-flowing. She went back up the hill and walked through endless side streets, looking long into the night at every junction until she spotted the bright jungle of shop signs because there, she knew, there would be a bus stop and although she was lost the bus driver would know the way.

The timetable screwed to the lamp-post was nothing more than a hopeful lie, and when the bus arrived at last it couldn't take her back to Cristobal Avenue. She had to change. It took a long time to get across the city but that didn't matter. It gave her time to think of the things she wanted to do for Chano, the special gifts she would bring him, the things – apart from herself – that she would lay at his feet, the ways she would reach out to him and reassure him, remake him and rebuild him, the things she would do to show him that he was loved. He could be saved – damaged goods or not. What did that matter? Damaged goods? Everybody was damaged goods. Dr Cochrane had made her admit that, even if he could not see it in himself. Chano could be saved and Caterina knew she was the one who could do it. She was right, of course. Caterina could have saved him – if he had wanted to be saved.

A long time ago the priest in that little mountain church told a story about a nasty old woman who was sent to Hell and left to starve. She wept and she prayed until, at last, God took pity and sent down a mouldy carrot on a string, and the nasty old woman grabbed the carrot and held on to it as God hauled her up out of the pit. When they saw her rising, all the other poor souls down there tried to cling on but, instead of helping them, the nasty old woman struggled and kicked and fought until the string broke and they all fell back down, taking the carrot with them. Caterina had forgotten that story and she would have done well to remember it.

The bus stopped with a shudder and she got down. Even at that hour Cristobal Avenue was choked with traffic. She had to go to the next corner to cross, hurrying through a break in the traffic and walking back down the avenue to the brown little side street where she lived.

Caterina walked quietly – as quietly as the grown-up shoes she had worn to buy her engagement ring would allow – towards the flat, a little fearful of the shadows, her feet sliding on the dusty, dirty, crunching stairs. She turned the key silently in the lock, careful not to wake Erica – who, anyway was not there – moving quickly through the darkened flat to her bedside, where she picked up a fat folder and left again, back out to the night and the streets, which were frightening, and to Chano, which was far, far worse than she knew.

WHILE CATERINA WAS walking the whole length of the avenue from where she lived, down amongst the second-hand dealers and the motorbike repair shops and the angry little bars, all the way to the other end, where Chano lived, amongst the smart restaurants with their glass tables outside on the terrace and the banks and the department stores, where you could look up at night into lighted rooms and see moulded ceilings and believe that you could hear the notes of a piano drifting over the traffic noise, he was locked inside his flat, pretending that he was not hiding.

While she pushed her way through the late-night crowds, that fat grey folder held across her chest like armour to deflect a sword thrust or a glance, making her way to him, brave, unstoppable, driven by love the way that the tides are driven by the moon, he was inside, being afraid and making excuses for why he could not go to her.

And when she walked down the dark curve of the ramp that led from the street down into the garage beneath his block and through the petrol-smelling parking bays and up the stairs, avoiding the front desk and the all-night porter waiting there, when she climbed up alone and kept climbing although the echoes chased her and there were shadows at every landing, when she came to his door and knocked, gently at first, and then louder, he lay in bed, holding a sword.

He still had the sword with him when he went to the door, slowly, fearfully, peering round the corner as if he had been waiting for it to disappear in a storm of splinters and bullet holes. The tip of the sword dragged over the tiled floor, singing, behind him and he said: 'Who is it?' in an angry whisper.

'Chano, it's me.'

He hurried forward and stood behind the door and looked through the spyglass. 'Are you alone?'

'Of course I'm alone. What's wrong?'

He hesitated. She was standing there in the corridor in bright light and, although she was so short, he could see it was her, he knew it was her and yet he hesitated and stood, shifting from foot to foot, turning his head, squinting with each eye, checking along the walls behind her and on the pale carpet at her feet, looking for an unfamiliar shadow that might betray a hidden watcher, flat against the wall. That was what Camillo had done to him. It only took a second or two but she noticed.

'Chano, aren't you going to let me in?'

'Just a moment.'

The sword was ridiculous. He knew it was ridiculous. He opened the narrow cupboard in the vestibule, the place where he had hung her coat that first night, and laid it there along the floor, corner to corner so it would fit. Even that took time.

'Chano!' A worried hiss from the other side of the door.

'A moment.' He undid the chain and turned the key in the lock. She heard him and she was pushing at the door before he had a chance to open it, although he did open it but by no more than a crack, just enough to let her slip through before he shut it again, quickly, and put the chain back on and locked it again.

'What's wrong?'

'Nothing.'

'I thought you might not let me in.'

'Why?'

'We quarrelled. Don't tell me you've forgotten?'

'You had every right to be upset.'

'I was rude and unkind and I accused you of things.'

'It's all right. You were disappointed. You are so young.'

And then Caterina was satisfied. She had done what Dr Cochrane had suggested. 'Let him blame your youth and don't disagree.'

'Kiss me,' she said.

He did.

'Still love me?'

'Of course.'

But he didn't say it. Only 'Of course,' not 'Of course I still love you.'

'What's wrong?' she said.

'Nothing.'

'Something's wrong.'

'A bad dream, that's all. It was just a bad dream. A nightmare. I got a fright.' That was half the truth again. He was frightened. He had suffered a nightmare. But he had not been asleep.

'Tell me. Then it won't come back.'

'It never goes away,' he said. 'It's always been there. All my life it's hung over me.'

Caterina brushed her hand gently over his face and – he did not imagine it – let the tip of her finger rest for a moment too long on his lip. 'I can kiss it all better,' she said. 'I promise.' She walked ahead of him into the sitting room where the scabbard of his grandfather's sword lay empty and abandoned on the sofa. He found it suddenly embarrassing but Caterina seemed not to notice.

She walked to the window and looked at the lights of the avenue. 'I was down there a minute ago. Way along there. You see the world differently from up here. Maybe it is different.'

'It's just because you are further away from it. It's the same world. It's the height, that's all.'

'No, Chano. This isn't high. The mountains, they were high, but I felt like I lived in the same world then. It's not the height that separates you from the street. It's the money.'

'Are we going to argue about money again? I'm too tired. Come to bed.'

'No. We're not going to argue about money – or anything else. Not ever again. If I had all the money in the world, I'd give it to you to make you happy. Everything I have, I want you to have but I don't have anything so I want to give you this.'

He was standing there in the clothes he had lain down in, exhausted from the effort of trying to sleep and the pain of finding himself so afraid, and she was close to him, holding out her scuffed grey folder to him as if it had been all the gifts of the Magi.

'What is it?'

'It's everything. That's what you asked for, isn't it? Everything. All I have in the world except for a couple of pairs of jeans and a jacket and some shoes you don't like. It's my book.'

'Your book?' he said.

'Yes. I've been writing a book and I have nothing more precious to offer you. It's for you. I will write your name on the front in a deeply respectful dedication and with love. With all my love.'

'Your book?' He said it again, as if she had no right to write a book, as if nobody had the right except him, as if the very idea of 'book' was his copyright, the sole property of L.H. Valdez, and if he chose not to exercise those rights for a time, perhaps for years, perhaps for ever, then that was his business and it certainly did not mean that Caterina, this girl, was permitted to write a book. 'You wrote a book.'

'Yes, Chano. I wrote a book. Now come to bed.'

'What's it about?'

'It's just a story. Come to bed.'

'I will. Yes. You go. I'll be there in a moment. You go.'

'All right,' she said, 'but hurry. We have making up to do.'

Chano stood at the window, holding her great gift, that worn, grey folder, by his side, watching the lights of the avenue until he was sure she had gone. He took Caterina's book to his desk and turned on the lamp but, before he sat down, Mr L.H. Valdez crept through his own house like a thief, back to the front door on silent feet. He opened the cupboard. He picked up his grandfather's sword. When he sat down at the desk again, he laid it across his knees. Then he opened the folder and he began to read.

He was almost sure he hated her.

BEFORE TOO MANY hours had passed, he knew. He read Caterina's book, her great gift to him, and the fury mounted in his chest. She lay in bed, waiting or sleeping or pretending to sleep, and he sat at the desk he had already willed away as his memorial, a cone of yellow light falling on the pile of pages, hating her.

It was an ordinary little story. Ordinary enough. A tale of a young man with his eyes on his aunt's money. But he spent it before he got it. He promised it to one of the foremost artists of the day in exchange for a painting – but not a painting on canvas. It was tattooed on his own skin, a dazzling cascade of lions and angels and orchids, wrapping him in glory. Then the aunt died and she didn't leave him her money. Then the artist died and his widow wanted to be paid and, when the young man couldn't pay, she auctioned off his skin.

For another 200 pages the decorated boy fled from one scalpel-wielding art-lover after another, running, hiding, falling in love, rising in value, being sold on, becoming more valuable every time.

It was ordinary. It was the sort of story a beginner would write. A silly, contrived thing, but it was beautiful and brilliant and not like anything he had ever read before, packed with people he would remember for ever doing things and saying things he would remember for ever in places he would remember for ever. It was beauty and laughter and love, page after page of beauty and laughter and love, and he hated her for it.

Hadn't he offered her everything? Hadn't he taken this little girl from the country and offered her his bed and his name and access to a world she had never imagined, clothes and cars, good food and good wine and the chance to be the mother of his sons? And all she had to do in exchange – all she had to do – was love him and unlock the thing he had lost.

But she had failed, and far from opening the way for him to write, she had decided to write something of her own. And, worse than that, something new and fresh and original and young, everything that he was not, rubbing his face in his own failure, throwing salt in the wounds, laughing at him, feasting on what was his and making it her own like a vampire. It was vile and unforgivable and he hated her for it.

Dawn was still two hours away when Mr Valdez closed the folder and switched out the light. He left the sword propped against his chair and went to bed and to Caterina. He hated Caterina and that was why he wanted her. He didn't want to make love to her, he didn't even want to have sex with her, he wanted to inflict himself on her, like a fire, like a terrible earthquake that sweeps away mountainsides and forests and pastures and leaves nothing but bare rock, barren for generations.

She cheated him of even that. She should have been lying there bathed in moonlight like the milk-skinned heroine of some grand, Romantic oil painting, high artistic pornography masquerading as mythology, like Danae or Leda, like Andromeda chained to a rock and writhing at the monster's approach. Instead she lay on her side like a little girl, open-mouthed, her hair falling about her in wanton mounds, every part of her a gorgeous ogee curve and a sprinkling of fairy lights coming up from the street in orange and red and white and green falling on her like angel kisses and that mouth, those lips, her amazing, impossible breasts, her candy-pink nipples and, over it all, that same pale, electric glow of beauty hovering over every inch of her, coiling like a Leyden jar full of cobras.

Seeing her, he changed his mind. Mr Valdez slid into his bed, trying not to wake her, but she stirred and reached out to him.

'Where have you been? I waited. I must have fallen asleep. What time is it?'

'It's the middle of the night. Go back to sleep.' He lay down on his side with his back to her but she folded her body to his and reached over him, touching him, planting little kisses on his neck and his ears, dragging her fingertips over his chest, murmuring to him, touching him, urging him.

But he ignored her, clutching the sheets to his chin like a virgin, lying there cold as a marble figure on a tomb, stiff, but not everywhere.

'Good night, Chano,' she said. 'I love you very, very much.' She gave up and rolled away from him.

Mr Valdez lay for a long time, listening to the sound of the avenue, the wave-sighs of the traffic, an occasional siren drawing closer, passing, moving further away, and he knew that Caterina was beside him, feigning sleep, making up stories about where the siren was going, about corrupt policemen or heroic policemen, about young girls dying in the back of an ambulance, their last drop of blood pooling on the floor, about their gangster lovers, about the people they would leave behind, filling in all the dark gaps, spinning stories out on a long thread, knitting them together. He tried to do that. He lay in the dark, chasing stories the way the insomniac chases sleep, and none came. She had taken them all away. His stories were all gone and now the sex was gone too. The two things he could do really well and she had destroyed them both. He had swallowed her whole, thinking that she was medicine, and she had been poison all along.

So many realizations piled up in front of him. All the ways she had led him on, from the day she said: 'Wouldn't you rather . . . ?' Dear God, how could he have been so stupid? How could he have fallen for that? Throwing herself at him and then dancing backwards. The way she had let him cheat her into his bed for the price of a line in his notebook. The way she had forced him into demanding that she married him. The way she had made him make her do it. All that innocent reluctance.

Before he went to sleep Mr Valdez decided that he would be done with her. In the morning he would tell her it was over – not in the kind-as-possible, matter-of-fact way he had told his other women to go. There could be no question of taking the blame on himself, no 'Darling, it's not you, it's me' excuses. No, this would have to be short and brutal and he would make it clear that it was, undoubtedly, her fault. He would lay out for her all the ways that he had seen through her. He would tell her that there was no way back after her display in the garden. He would not be accused like that. It was an insufferable insult from a mere child and it was not to be borne. No, Mama had been right with the very first words she said: 'You know she only wants you for your money.' Mama was right. Mama was always right, damn it, and yet he had defended her, spoken up for her. Obvious. Stupid.

In the morning, he would be done with her. In fact, it should be now. He sat up and turned to her, but the bed was empty and the room was full of light.

CATERINA WAS SITTING at his desk with that sword at her side like an allegorical figure when Mr Valdez arrived in the room. It made a strange picture, both of them naked and straight from bed, Mr Valdez unshaven and sticky-mouthed and Caterina sitting in that chair, spilling sumptuously over the seat, just a little, her hair pulled back and tied with a rubber band she had stolen from the desk, and a cutlass resting, just so, by the leg of her chair. She would not have looked out of place if she had been cast in bronze and left on the lawns of the Academia Maritimo – which was still accepting students, despite the lack of a coast – as the embodiment of naval education.

She didn't hear him come in. She thought he was asleep.

'What are you doing?' he said.

Caterina made a quick motion of her hand and he saw her shoulders tense. 'Chano, you frightened me.' She turned round to him with a forced smile.

'What are you doing?'

'Nothing.' A stupid childish thing to say, and it only annoyed him and confirmed all the things he had already decided.

'Caterina, I asked what you are doing.'

'You are very rude to me, sometimes, Chano.'

'There was nothing rude about it. I asked you perfectly politely what you were doing and, for some reason you refuse to tell me.

I think you're the one who is being rude. You are being rude to me now just as you were yesterday when you accused me of stealing your story.'

'I apologized for that already, didn't I? Chano, don't lecture me. Don't talk to me like I was one of your classes. Do you want me to apologize again, is that it? I will happily begin every day with another apology if that's what it takes to make you happy. All I want is to make you happy.'

Mr Valdez had already decided that she would never enjoy that particular privilege. There would be no 'beginning every day'. Not with Caterina. And yet he did not tell her. He hung back from throwing that in her face, in spite of the chilly pleasure it would have given him.

Instead he said: 'Spare me. Just tell me the truth. Just tell me what you were doing!' and, as he was saying it, he walked from the door to the desk, and again she made a quick, fluttering movement, but this time to move her hands away from the desk, to let him see that there was nothing to see.

'Happy now? Nothing. I was just reading my book.'

'Haven't you read it already?'

'Yes. Have you?'

He didn't say anything. He had read it of course and he had fallen in love with it and that was why he hated her, but he was in no mood to admit that. With the tip of his finger Mr Valdez pushed the worn grey folder a little aside.

'I'd better get dressed,' she said. 'Kiss?'

He kissed her quickly and suspiciously and, when he did not kiss her more, she got up from the chair and went away.

Mr Valdez did not go with her. It seemed to him that getting dressed together was an act of intimacy just as much as getting undressed together, and somehow the time for that had passed.

Anyway, he was afraid. Just as afraid as he had been in the

garden with Camillo. When he nudged Caterina's folder aside he had noticed beneath it the cover of his own notebook, and he knew at once what it was that she had been hiding.

He flicked open the cover. He read: 'The scrawny yellow cat crossed the road and crept into the whorehouse where it hoped the beautiful Angela would scratch his belly,' and he remembered all the pathetic lies he had told her, how he had sat up all night writing when he had left her alone in his bed, without touching her, how it was like a dam bursting. How the words had come pouring out of him. And there they were. This was the reason he had sat alone at his desk when he could have been with her.

He had bought her for 'The scrawny yellow' and the promise of a cat to come and now, after all that time, there were just – Mr Valdez put his finger on the page and began to count – just nineteen words more. And it was then, after he had finished counting, with his finger still on the paper, that Mr Valdez noticed a single hair lying on the page, a long, shining thread that was definitely not his own. She had seen this. She knew.

'Time to go,' she said. She was dressed and standing close beside him again and she saw the page open in front of him.

Without looking up from the notebook, Mr Valdez said: 'I read your book. It was very good. Did you read mine?'

Caterina reached out and put her hand on his shoulder.

'Did you read it?' he said again.

She was desperately afraid. Long weeks ago Erica had said that a night with L.H. Valdez was like a night in Bluebeard's Castle, but the point of that story wasn't the castle – it was the secret room filled with blood. As soon as Caterina read that line, she understood everything, she knew everything. She knew there was no more. She had looked inside Chano's secret room and she wanted to scream.

'Yes, I read it.'

He picked up that single hair from the page and held it, pinched between two fingers, in front of her face. 'At least you did not lie,' he said.

'I have never lied to you. And I never will and I'm telling you the truth now.' He was still holding that hair out to her like an accusation. She reached up and pushed his hand away. 'This is the truth, Chano. It will get better. I've been stuck for weeks sometimes. This will get better. I'll come back here tonight and we will make love again and you will write again. It will get better. I promise. It will get better if you let me love you.'

'Just go,' he said.

'I'll go. But I'm coming back. I will be back tonight and I will love you.'

'Forgive me if I don't escort you to the door. I seem to be completely naked.'

'That as it should be with lovers,' she said. 'We should always be completely naked with one another and, anyway, it suits you.' She kissed him, just once, lightly on the chest, letting her hand rest there briefly. When he made no reply she left. 'I'll be back tonight,' she said and he heard the door click shut.

Mr Valdez sat at his desk for a few moments, looking down at Caterina's novel and at his own, listening to the sound of his empty flat and the noise of the dust falling every day for the next forty years.

When he was certain that she was gone, he got up to check. Mr Valdez walked to the door and found it locked. He checked behind the coats hanging in the dark, he looked in every room, opened every cupboard to prove to himself that the house was empty, and then he came back to his desk and picked up the telephone and dialled.

After a time he said: 'Hello? Commandante Camillo? This is Valdez. That girl you told me about yesterday.'

Camillo said: 'The girl you said you would never give up.'

Valdez said: 'She was here last night.'

'Don't lie to me. She was with Cochrane.'

'Maybe she was with Cochrane first, I don't know, but she came here after that. Your spies might not be as good as you think.'

'I'll look into that. Why are you telling me this?'

'Because she confessed everything. She told me about the bomb plot.'

'And Cochrane too?'

Mr Valdez hesitated. 'Yes, Dr Cochrane too. It's all exactly as you said. I felt it my duty to report it. I am a patriot.'

'Oh, we never doubted that.'

'So, will you arrest her?'

Camillo hung up.

Mr Valdez went to his wardrobe to select a suit. He had a large cheque to pay in at the bank.

MR VALDEZ WAS not a monster. When Caterina did not return that evening, although he sat in his chrome and leather sofa until after midnight waiting for her, he felt it sorely. He went to his desk and switched on the lamp. There, at the back, amongst the pigeon holes stuffed with stamps and bills and fan mail from stupid school girls and still stupider professors, he found her photograph – the one he took of her that day at the graveyard, with her wild hair flying and her chin stuck out proudly and that look in her eyes that said: 'I see you. I know you. We understand each other, you and I.' She was alone in the picture, but Mr Valdez knew he was in it too, with her. He had taken the photograph. He was holding the camera. He was part of the scene. Perhaps, if he looked closely, he might see himself reflected in those eyes, like the artist who paints himself reflected in a mirror, right at the centre of the picture. 'See? You think this is your picture, a picture about you. No. It's my picture.' He read again from her novel. That comforted him. It made him feel that she was still close. It was an admission that she would not come back. He cried himself to sleep.

And when Dr Cochrane failed to appear for his lectures, when he was absent from the common room, when his chair stood empty in the Phoenix and Father Gonzalez nearly went mad with grief, everyone could see that Valdez was as badly affected as any of them.

Something dark and cold had reached into their little circle and snatched one of them away in the night. It was an affront to them all as men. They knew they should hit back. If they knew where to land the blow. If they dared. Instead they raged and feared and wondered who might be next and whether it might be themselves and they knew that nobody would help.

Father Gonzalez tried. He went to the police station and reported Cochrane missing. Nobody paid any attention. He went back every day for a week and filled out forms. He prayed constantly. He offered masses and, at last, he went back to the police and accused them. He hired a lawyer and asked the others to help with the bill. Valdez was more than generous.

Little by little Mr Valdez recovered from his loss until, at last, he felt strong enough to pay a visit to the Ottavio House.

It was a wonderful evening. Even then, six weeks on, people were still talking about his fantastic story in *The Salon*. 'Thank you,' he said, sipping on a second, bright gimlet. 'Actually, I've just finished a novel. It's with my publishers now. If I say so myself, it's quite an original idea – but I won't say more. I don't want to spoil it for you.'

He was happy. The evening was warm. The stars hung in the sky like a contessa's necklace and even when that dark-skinned girl with the lisp hung around his neck and said: 'I have written something I'd like to show you,' it did not dent his mood.

He gave her arse a squeeze and said: 'Oh, you have no idea how much I want you to show me. Put it under your pillow, my love. Show me later.'

He was happy. And then the lamps around the garden flickered in the breeze and Camillo sat down in the chair at his side.

'It's been a while,' the policeman said and he tilted his glass. 'I wanted to thank you for all your help with that unpleasant matter. I have to tell you that people in the capital are very grateful. Your patriotic assistance has been noted. Are you well?'

'Very well,' said Valdez.

'And your mother?'

'She thrives. We see each other almost every day.'

'You are a good son. You know, I don't mind admitting I had my concerns about you, but I was misguided. You come from good stock.'

And then the policeman began to tell a story. He told how two of his closest and most trusted colleagues had gone to see old Dr Cochrane early in the morning. How the old man was drunk and argumentative and reeking of brandy. How he tried to start a fight. They had to arrest him. They had no choice. And the girl, but then, sadly, they had both attempted to escape from the facility where they were being questioned and, well, these things only end up one way. Nobody escapes. Nobody ever escapes.

'Did they talk?'

'No, they didn't talk. And, forgive me, but we asked them about you. They had nothing to say. They didn't talk. Strange that she should confess everything to you but not to us.'

'It's not so strange,' Valdez said. 'She unburdened her conscience to me. The stakes were rather higher with you.' He was pleased to see that his gift for making up stories had returned.

'Maybe so. But they didn't talk. And then, at the end, on the night they escaped, she said a strange thing.'

Mr Valdez made no comment. He remembered sitting in the square by the Merino, wishing more than anything that Dr Cochrane would not speak, trying so hard not to give the slightest sign of interest, but still the words came.

'On the night they,' Camillo paused to sip from his glass, 'escaped she said to him that she was glad he was there. She said it made her brave. She was crazy for him. You did well to get away from that one. She was carrying his child, you know.'

Valdez said: 'How do you know that?' with a squeak in his voice. But he already knew the answer and he did not want to hear it.

'Oh, interrogation. Sometimes it can get,' another sip, 'a little vigorous.'

That was a terrible moment. Mr Valdez found it preyed on his mind for weeks and there were nightmares. Night after night he was awakened by the sound of a baby crying. When he switched on the light there was no baby there. His son was not there. The grandchild he had promised was not there. He ordered a new bed and a new mattress and he covered it with new sheets, straight from the packet so there could be nothing of Caterina there, no scent of her, not a single hair, no flake of skin, but that night the baby still screamed.

He switched on the light. The crying stopped. He switched on the light by the door and the one in the hall and in the sitting room. He lit the lamp on his desk and he found again the picture of Caterina. Mr Valdez took the picture in two hands so his thumbs met in the middle, ready to grip and twist and rip. But he hesitated. She looked exactly the same. There was no sign to show that she was dead. Nothing had changed. She was the same. She would stay like that, always.

Mr Valdez found his grandfather's sword and took it from the scabbard and then, so gently, so carefully, he stood close to the wall and pressed the point of the blade down against the top of the skirting board. The edge of the wallpaper parted. The wood began to move. It bowed out from the wall by the thickness of a sword blade. Mr Valdez knelt down and dropped Caterina's picture into the gap. He went to the table in the dining room and picked up three petals which had fallen from the vase there. He put them with the picture. He put the sword in its scabbard and pushed the skirting board back into place. After that, life got a little better.

Gradually things went back to normal. The baby stopped crying. Mr Valdez slept through the night in his new bed. Perhaps once a week and then sometimes twice a week, there was space in his diary for a visit from Maria Marrom.

One day, not long after his meeting with Camillo, Mr Valdez got up and went to the bathroom and decided, after looking in the mirror, that it was time to grow a moustache. Maria liked it very much.

His new novel was published and the critics went wild. Everybody agreed that *The Hidden Landscapes of Alfonso Borrero* was unlike anything he had ever written before, so new, so fresh, so vital – almost a new direction completely.

In fact that book was such a success that Mrs Sophia Antonia de la Santísima Trinidad y Torre Blanco Valdez felt she should read it for herself, and she enjoyed it so much that she decided to read all the others on her shelves, starting with the very first.

Just about the time that she sat down with *The Mad Dog of San Clemente*, an old man was walking unsteadily down the gangplank of the Merino ferry, carrying a birthday cake. He had come to look for his friend.

ACKNOWLEDGEMENTS

My thanks are due to my cousin, Jane Holligan, for her invaluable assistance with Latin American customs and vocabulary.

The lyrics of *La Soledad* are by Carlos Gardel and those of *Tango De Le Muerte* are by José Agustín Ferreyra. The (rather free) translations are my own.